nobody dick in
Dreamtime

ƒRANK QUESTING

D0654961

Fourth Estate · London

First published in Great Britain in 1989 by
Fourth Estate Limited
Classic House
113 Westbourne Grove
London W2 4UP.

Copyright © 1989 by Frank Questing

British Library Cataloguing in Publication Data
Questing, Frank
    Nobody Dick in Dreamtime
    I. Title
    823'.914 [F]

    ISBN 0-947795-34-0

All rights reserved. No part of this publication may be reproduced,
transmitted or stored in a retrieval system, in any form or by any
means, without prior permission in writing from Fourth Estate Limited.

"Story of Frankie Lee" (Bob Dylan) © Warner Chappell Music Ltd

"Once in a Lifetime" (Talking Heads) © Warner Chappell Music Ltd

Extracts from both songs reproduced by permission of Warner Chappell Music Ltd

Typeset in Garamond by York House Typographics, London
Printed and bound in Great Britain by Richard Clay Ltd, Bungay, Suffolk

TO ELECT-RON

1

I had always thought gravity was only a conditioned concept hammered by evolution into our DNA to prevent us from falling. Here on the edge of the Nullarbor, Western Australia, I was walking on blue. Blue reflected in the impossible whiteness of this salt-glazed desert, so alone in all this arid radiance, the daemons of my thoughts all I had for company.

I was wrong, for I was not the sole possessor of this vastness. I shared it with another, at first only the barest smidgeon on the merging of sky and plain and then, as the blip grew into something comprising shape and form, I recognised an ancient Holden, a model of car as peculiar as any marsupial.

Responding to the magnet I keep concealed in my thumb, this relic of fifties Oz, an amalgam of various wrecks, ground to a halt, spewing a stinging spray of gravel a bare few feet from my unprotected knees.

With the vagueness of delirium I resolved, as I stumbled forwards, to change out of my kilt at the first opportunity . . . Such an impractical garment for this desert terrain.

Window glass, smeared and grimy, blurry underneath its Pickwickian Christmas card coating of white dust; the driver leaning over to unsnib the lock, stuffing something bulky underneath the passenger seat; then the door groaning open to reveal a white face, bloodshot wide-angled eyes, a crooked, broken-toothed grin. No introduction necessary: anywhere, any place, the Furry Freak Brother . . . And myself, yea, just another Scotsman on walkabout.

Tucking my tartan about my knees and gratefully accepting the sag of the torn leather seat, I slumped back, blissfully closing my eyes as the car took to the road . . . A wounded camel escaping a rodeo of circus sadists . . . A motor

1

launch surging against a choppy sea, the tang of salt . . . burning rubber . . . oil . . . and . . .

Sitting bolt upright, I asked him abruptly, 'You wouldn't happen to have a smoke on you? Something real? Right now I think I'd offer up my soul in exchange for one little joint.'

Scratching his light beard, the nail long and yellowing, Furry Freak Brother seemed to be weighing me up for a nark; then as he stretched the elastic moment to breaking point, he chuckled, a covert smile breaking free from under the sparse thatch, and drawled, 'Reach under your seat, cobber, and ewe'll find a baag 'rapt in an owld bit of sack. Paypers and maytches inside. Carefwul ewe down't spill it. Beyst goddamn weed in Awz-traylia . . . Jest dreven one thouswand K's tew geyt et from a Chinah-man.'

So, Nirvana was a Chinaman's creation. I guess I'll believe in about anything, just so long as it gets me there.

Whining voices from the speaker beside my ear, a familiar rhythm. Talking Heads, I guessed, my favourite band, though I couldn't recall having heard the song before.

> You may find yourself
> In another part of the World,
> And You may find yourself
> Behind the wheel of a large automobile.
> And you may ask yourself, Well how did I get here?

No doubt prompted by the words of the song, Furry Freak eyed me a screwball gaze. 'Lesten, myte,' he said, 'we-ell how did ewe come tew be hitchin' owt 'ere, in all this fuckin' desert? A Scotchman een a kilt . . .' He slowly shook his head, 'I mean, part of my brain still thinks I'm fuckin' hallucinatin' ewe.'

Sighing I looked out of the window: blue of the salt now tinged with red dirt, road signs, what was left of them, triangulated jumping kangaroos peppered with gunshot. Passing Furry Freak the joint I asked him then, 'Are you sure you really want to know, it's a long story, and once I get started . . .' I let the sentence hang meaningfully.

A grinning Bugs Bunny gone to seed, Furry Freak slowly expelled the smoke between the gaps of his nicotine-stained teeth. His voice squeezed out like pressed garlic. 'Why not, cobber, passes the time dun'it, we ain't goin' nowhere fast, an' besides thies owld bweuty's engine loikes to overheat, so we got to take it re-al slow.'

Automatically reaching into the bag once more, I asked him, 'You don't mind if I roll another one do you, mate, a big one this time?'

'Sure', he drawled, 'It grows, it grows.'

I noticed then my hands were shaking. The story was welling up inside me and I had to spit it out . . .

> And you ask yourself,
> What is that beautiful house?
> Who is this beautiful wife?
> And you may ask yourself,
> Where does that highway go to?
> And you may ask yourself,
> Am I right, am I wrong?
>
> And you may say to yourself,
> My God what have I done?
>
> Into the blue again, after the money's gone . . .

2

I created a small stir somewhere over Papua New Guinea. I had just changed into my kilt, sporran, and all. I was not seeking to attract attention, merely fulfilling an oath sworn on the road and observing fealty to my ancient clan.

There was another reason. I couldn't make up my mind whether I should declare my case of bikinis – all I had by way of collateral bar a few dollars – at the next set of customs. If I did I would have to pay a large tax. But who would suspect a Scotsman in highland dress of smuggling a load of glittery bikinis, hot from Bali, all three hundred of them in neat little draw-string baggies? I decided to choose the smuggler's option.

The puffy white clouds parted and I found I was looking down onto the out-out-way-back. Strange, like viewing a red planet from a spaceship. Mars? It all looked as though a dirty red giant had taken a bath, then pulled several plugs out. As it spiralled counter-clockwise, the great tide left salty nebula swirls in dusty red.

I don't know if you've ever seen Australia from above, mate, but it's like some bloody Plain of the Nazca down there. Quite discernible from the occasional fencing are myriad faint straight lines, sometimes tracking for hundreds of miles. I wondered, looking down on it all. Perhaps the pre-Aboriginal settlers of this land were millions of Eric Von Daniken clones, toiling midgets leaving mysteries for future books.

It was a bit of a comedown, landing.

Sydney, ten a.m., December 31st, is overcast, drizzling. I though it never

4

rained here. Insult is added to injury by the first Australians I see – two officials who walk the entire length of the plane spraying all of the passengers with some insect-killer loaded with DDT. Do Frenchies always need delousing? I felt like shouting, 'I'm all right! I'm a Scotsman. You don't need to spray me.' I didn't think the Frenchies would appreciate it, so I waited humbly in line to get off the plane.

Sydney airport is a meat market. Six lanes of queuing cattle waiting to be dissected at six customs desks. Spreadeagled possessions on rubber-covered tables. Never in all of my travelling life had I seen any customs to compare with these.

Better to make a clean breast of it and declare all of the bikinis rather than see them impounded; and so, feeling like Mary with her little lamb, actually a little piggy-bag on wheels, I stepped bravely to the fore, deciding that if the duty was too high, I'd abandon them.

My stony-faced Australian customs officer stared blankly as I started my pre-rehearsed speech. Hoping I was the image of a kilted playboy, I held up a piece of paper marked with illegible scribblings, and gabbled, 'Here's a list of the contents of this small bag and a receipt showing you how much I paid for the contents – three hundred bikinis.' I observed that I had made a slip, said 'contents' twice, but I thought, that will screw up his head, shrugged and continued.

'I have to admit that I plan to sell half of the contents, but the rest of the other half of the contents are intended as gifts. You know, and I recommend this method, it works every time.' I reached into the bag and pulled out a loose bikini, dangling it before his eyes by its silken strap. 'The trick is to insist they try them on.' I brayed like a camel, winking at him.

The deadpan customs officer neither blinked nor lifted his gaze from mine. From the way he shifted his feet I deduced he had a bad case of haemorrhoids. Pointing over my shoulder he said in a gravelly voice, 'My mate over there wants to know, what does a Scotsman wear under his kilt?'

I leaned forward until my face was only an inch from his ruddy pockmarked nose, and rasped in a whisky-drinking voice, 'Baaallss.' My long one-syllable response was measured. Perhaps I could have said, 'A ball and chain, just like any other man,' but the magic of the kilt, Hogmanay and all things Scottish was just the job.

The customs man drew himself up to his full height, jerked his thumb towards the black rubber doors, condoms to the great outside. 'I don't want to know about your fucking bikinis, just carry on mate.'

First jet-slag stop: a hostel, garret no. 23. As I opened the door I was confronted by a large TV screen, a video playing of one of the bands I'd worked with so long ago. Pop stars, who needs them? Yeah I'd heard this song before. 'I promised me a sex change . . . Love between your dirty sheets will change me into you.' So the toiling headbangers had made it to number one here too, bunch-a-midget-creeps. What had I ever seen in them?

I threw the door wide. Loud English accents, four young men, each of them clutching onto a tube of Foster's lager like it was the last can in the world, an argument raging. The subject: cricket.

I stopped in my tracks, saying weakly, 'Sorry chaps, I've got the wrong room.' I slammed the door behind me. Fuck this shit.

I descended the stairs, bruised my knuckles raising dust from the cluttered reception desk.

A loud voice came booming through the wet-look opaque-glass office door. The silhouette turned out to be a profusely-swearing bald pus-ball. It leaned around the corner of the door, repeating again, 'Wha'd'y'want?' Gusts of stale garlic assailed me.

Yes, German extraction, and no duelling scars – must be low caste. Fuck him too.

I demanded, 'Have you got any lockers? I want to leave my bags in a secure place.'

The pus-ball foamed. 'Wha'd'y'expect for five dollars and ninety-five cents? Fort Fucking Knox? This is a genuine dive, mate. You get one sagging bed, two sheets, and a lot of company. What's the problem? Room not to your liking? Shit, everyone else comes in with a rucksack, not one of these bloody executive briefcases on wheels. Now, what can I do to help you?' He leaned forward, trying to smile.

I left. I couldn't even stand to argue with this mountain of bile. Probably just another average Australian. Millions of them out there, in the fucking hostel or out on the street, what's the difference? I headed for the railway station and the left luggage office. As I looked at the Turkish-Cypriot baggage handler who handed over my receipt, he began to turn into a Doberman Pinscher, a slavering one, too. No, it was not my demented imagination.

What was it those first Dutch discoverers had called this continent? Van Daemons Land. Yea, truly I had descended, my long fall broken at last. Landed on my feet, I had, in the terrestrial hell. Nothing could have prepared me for this jangling ugliness, this crude crowd bustle. I didn't even feel this was really Australia. It seemed so much like England and the States all jumbled up. Over there a red mailbox, beside it a Morris Minor sandwiched between two big fast cars, behind it a hamburger joint.

I needed to see something that was genuinely of this land. I needed to feel a connection. And so I set off in pursuit of beauty.

New South Wales Art Gallery: I am searching for their permanent Aboriginal exhibit through a hotch-potch of western art – Matisse, Cézanne, Jackson Blowjob, Desperate Dan à la Lichstenstein, nineteenth-century visions of Highland cows transported along with stags, castles, kilted Scotsmen, Landseer *et al*, to Tasmania. Yes, there is a picture of this Tasmaniacal vision in some ghastly room of this gallery. There are nymphs, satyrs, bounding kangaroos and centaurs frolicking amid Grecian temples. Corridors and corridors of the bloody stuff, until I want to scream and retch.

I took a few wrong turnings in the labyrinth but finally, after an aching age, I discovered the sub-sub-basement. In a room adjacent to an exhibition of art college student photographs, I found the displays of Aboriginal art.

Jesus, I thought. Poor black bastard nigger coons, relegated to the base of this Antipodean shit-pile, over-lorded by the white establishment of European and American artists.

This is the professor talking: 'Recent evidence has been unearthed that suggests that the Aborigines have been in Australia for forty thousand years. Some hot-headed researcher has even suggested seventy thousand years. These discoveries are still being howled down by the establishment of the Australian universities. Many of them still uphold and expound "the woman, the dog, and the log" theory. Let me give you a brief summary.

'A pregnant woman, Big Black Bess, was swept off to sea while holding a female dog by the scruff of the neck, which was also pregnant. Somehow they slithered onto a log, which drifted many thousands of miles to Australia. The woman and her male child founded the race of Abos. The dog and her young founded the species of Dingos.

'Both the dogs and the humans degenerated through inbreeding, which explains the inability of Aborigines to construct boats. What other explanation could there possibly be for the Aborigines' presence in this land so far away from everything else? And after all, didn't the white Australian need one hell of a good excuse to salve his conscience as he hunted the Aborigines, shooting them down like wild pigs in Tasmania?

'A new theory has emerged in recent years to counter the legend of the dog, the log and the woman. Cranium consultants have discovered that the skull of the Aborigine is a mix between that of Peking Man and Java Man. The Aborigine of today is similar to our ancestors of Neolithic times, perhaps the most valuable genetic storehouse walking the planet today, the living atavistic record of our uncoded past. Could it be that if we learned to understand the mind of the Aborigine, discover the meaning of dreamtime, we might find the key to understanding ourselves?'

3

I should have known, even sensed it, but I had no premonition . . . A letter was waiting at Sydney Main Post Office, a malevolent hand reaching out from twelve thousand miles away. Two enclosures – both from my daharling wife.

Ragna-Rock Castle,
Butty-howe,
Leven

Frankie,

The castle has not sold, the deal fell through, and don't ever think of coming back. Our joint accounts have been closed. I enclose the Circle of Gold chain letter, your best hope for the future.

Wishing you well,
Annioff.

PS. Don't EVER write, or call.

In a daze, I ripped open the envelope entitled 'Circle of Gold'. My eyes scanned the false print quick as a ferret. A chain letter – you know the kind. You pass it on to two people, sending money up the line. And then you wait a long, long time. Warnings were attached of the terrible misfortunes that would befall anyone who broke the chain.

I laughed bitterly. How characteristic of her to issue a curse without even putting pen to paper. Lady Macbeth has got nothing on that bitch. She didn't even have to wash her hands. Pontius Pilate could have learned a trick or two from her. Jesus Hieronymous Bosch. Suffering father of all those millions of little dickheads out there. Me included.

The sheets of paper trembling in my hands felt heavier than lead. Her pinioning malice was a drop-kick in the balls. Thwarted rage gripped my ribs in a cheese-press. Christ, and I should have been walking into a cheque for fifty grand, the first instalment of what was so rightfully mine. I didn't even have the cash to buy a ticket out of this godforsaken land. I'd been going to start my new life, and now I was fucked.

I could hear her tinkling cocktail-party laugh. She'd gotten what she'd always wanted, total control of our property, and there was nothing I could do. After all, wasn't I on Mars, and home a long long way away? Some home. A blighted chalice of ruin. But of one thing I was sure. I'd never return. Women? I'd never trust one of those Jezebel spawn ever again.

I was shocked, a Humpty-Dumpty man, the cracks appearing on my forehead – one sharp tap and I'd fall apart . . . The teeming throng of this city pressed in on me. I needed to lose myself in this continent.

I was jolted from my reverie by whistles and catcalls from workmen on the scaffolding across the street. Looking down I realised what had attracted their attention: checked socks, white-blanched hairy knees, and of course the tartan of my ancient clan. I couldn't go around looking like this.

My gesture of derision, the old familiar raised forearm followed by a tapping of the left hand on the elbow, was greeted by a chorus of more jeers and catcalls. Maintaining my dignity, I turned stiffly and marched on. Then, as I reached the corner, I bent down and showed the barbarians what a real Scotsman wears under his kilt. Feeling somewhat better I walked in the direction of the railway station. Fucking shitheads, the pox on them all.

I took one hell of a long look at my reflection in the railway station toilet. My face leered back at me. A corner of my mouth drooped. I pushed it up with a finger. It dropped again, rubbery and dead as if I'd just spent an afternoon with the Mad Dentist. I was sure of one thing, I needed surgery. I'd never seen anything so ugly. I hadn't shaved in a week. My eyes were decaying cabbages, the pupils black spots of blight. My skin was stretched drum-tight over cheek and jaw, the accumulated poisons of stress, rage and thwarted revenge etching livid streaks into my face. Fuck it, what did I care. I made the pretence of washing, splashed water over my face, changed out of my kilt, deciding then to leave it with the rest of my possessions at the left luggage office.

The view of the Sydney suburbs out of the train window did nothing to raise my spirits. Endless bungalowville sprawled like a ghastly one-storey diarrhoea. No confines in Australia to hold these slopping cities in – someone once told me that Sydney is almost a hundred miles across. I was seeing it now – squares, bloody squares, each house surrounded by a quarter-acre plot. Plastic swimming pools in back yards. Artificial lawns. I had not travelled so far to see this.

I hitched a ride in a dung-coloured Beetle. I judged the driver to be a little over twenty and he was clean-shaven apart from the blonde fuzz of his crew-cut hair. His most obvious feature was the typically Aussie cotton-wool-stuffed crotch of his Bermuda shorts.

I guessed this to be Mr Normal Australia. It turned out he was a policeman. Does this make him normal? I should say so.

I told him I wanted a ride to Melbourne.

There was a long moment as he looked me up and down, then he said tersely, 'Get in, can't say I'll take you all the way, but I'll take you some.'

He drove the vehicle as if it was an aged perambulator, hunched over the steering wheel, his inadequate cranium almost touching the windscreen, marbles glued to the road. In order to get a better view of his face, I squirmed forward in my seat.

He corrected me tartly, his acid voice somehow reminding me of my old school's vice captain. 'It is forbidden by law not to wear a seatbelt. In other words, BELT UP!'

To make conversation I ventured, 'What are your views on crime and law enforcement in Australia.'

His reply was instant. 'The sad fact is, in this country the police force is seriously short of manpower, the wages are too low. Too many bloody socialists around if you ask me, mate.'

I wondered if he'd incurred permanent damage through constant exposure to constricting shorts, his asinine voice was pitched so high.

'Politicians give lip-service to the need to combat the growing crime-wave, but many of them are in the pay of mobsters. The judiciary ain't too clean neither. A lot of scandal has been swept under the carpet these past few years.'

I mumbled, 'I'm truly, um, shocked to hear it,' as he continued his tirade. Obviously I'd hit on the motherlode of all his resentments.

'The bleeding wages aren't too good neither,' he repeated. 'I'm twenty-three – *twenty-three*!' His knuckles whitened on the steering wheel, his puckering mouth reminding me of a rodent. 'Forced to live with my parents because I can't afford to buy a house. But the bloody Dagos, Vietnamese, bloody boat-people, Wops and Poms waltz into our country, and that's not all. Social

Security' – he thumped the steering wheel emphatically – 'a fucking permanent meal-ticket for the rest of their lives. Yeah, fucking politicians. Bleeding hearts. Intellectuals. Do-gooders. This country's going to the dog.'

SHUT UP SHUT UP SHUT UP. This Son of Sam sounded like something slimy spawned by an editorial in one of Murdoch's better rags. I turned my head to get some relief, just in time to note the passing of the bungalows. Up ahead a three-lane road, a motorway by Australian standards, beckoned. Rolling hills, dusty in shade. Wide open country. The occasional house surrounded by eucalyptus trees. Heat-haze. The land dry, seco. Up above, the skies – canned blue, straight out of a tin. Poured by the hand of the Master Architect. No nuclear radiation here – clean.

Hands shaking I reached into my breast pocket. God, if ever I needed tar to coat my lungs it was now. A brand new soft-pack – I ripped open the cellophane, tapping the pack theatrically. For once the damn trick worked and two cigarettes popped up, twin smoke-stacks thrusting for air. I waved the packet close to his face, saying, 'Care for a duty-free, mate?' while I searched the dashboard for the cigarette lighter.

Every filament and muscle of my companion's body stiffened. His pink finger stabbed violently towards the red-lettered sign prominent on the dash bearing the legend of that famous black New Orleans Jazz trombonist NOSMO KING. I was confused, so I replied blankly, 'Oh . . . Uh . . . Yeah . . . Nosmo King. Didn't he once play with the Duke?'

For the first time he took his eyes from the road. Washed out blue pinheads scrutinised me closely. He said caustically, 'I hope you're not one of these bloody Poms trying to sneak into our country.'

Blinking at this effrontery, I replied starchly, 'No I certainly am not one of these "bloody Poms" as you so aptly call them. I am a Jock. A true Scot of the blood. The name's McVicar. I come from a long line of them. And we all feel much the same way as you do about the bloody English. As for being an immigrant, I'm sorry, but I like my country far too much. I'm just a tourist with a big zipper . . . Uh, I mean, just a tourist on walkabout, mate.' Tapping the two cigarettes back into the pack, I pushed the packet into my breast pocket with a flourish, ripping it audibly.

A hint of a smile curled around his bloodless lips. 'Hmm. Ahuh. . .' He nodded, and then with a sudden awkward movement crossed his right arm over his left, offering me his hand. 'Well, that's all right then, mate. Welcome to Oz!'

Suppressing a groan, I gripped the dangling sweaty kipper, experimentally rubbing his second knuckle with my thumb to test if he was a Mason. He did not seem to register the signal. Maybe he was suspicious.

The sudden cacophony of air horns alerted us. Out of the emptiness loomed a giant chromium-plated truck. My companion, quick to react, swerved the car to one side.

'Bloody hell!' His tinny squeak was almost drowned out by the massive din of the juggernaut. 'I broke the first bloody rule of the road.'

'And what was that?' I shouted.

'Never take your bloody eyes off it, that's what, mate.'

At that moment I would have welcomed death, especially if there was only oblivion on the other side. Fucking women, God save me from their predatory molestations. I winced as I remembered what an effort that hard-on had been the last time I got laid in Bali. How long had it been? God! That was a necrophiliac fuck.

'What was that, mate?' he said.

I looked up in surprise, realising I must have talked aloud. I replied quickly: 'Oh, I think it was indigestion. Don't worry. It's not infectious. I'm still suffering from jet-lag.'

I went on rapidly smearing the grease of small talk over my tracks. 'Before that little interlude I was becoming quite enthralled by your views, ah . . . on immigration. Do you take an active interest in politics? Let me ask you the big question. What would you do if you were the prime minister of this land?' Grinning hugely, I pretended to hold up a microphone.

The cop's jaw jutted like a brick knocked out of place on Mount Rushmore, his eyes widening. 'I'd build a bloody wall all round Australia. That's the first bloody thing I'd do.' A viperous wriggling erupted in the basket of his face, spittle flecking his mouth, head bobbing like a dingo in a stormy sea.

'Yeah, a bloody wall, to keep out all the immigrants and imports.'

His voice rising in volume and tone, he was squirming in his seat, sweat shadowing his crotch.

'What do we need from the rest of the world?' he raged, his face reddening. 'You can all go and hang as far as I'm concerned! Let me give you an example. Take these Vietnamese, the so-called boat-people. All of them communists. Too bloody left-wing for the reds in Vietnam, that's why they were slung out. And what does our country do? Welcomes them with open arms. Talk about a red carpet, it's soaked with good Australian blood. Our soldiers fought in two world wars to prevent this from happening.

'Do you know the reason for the current crime wave in our cities is the arrival of the bloody boat-people. We can't penetrate their organisation, no one in the force can speak their lingo.' He threw his hand up in disgust. 'And why should we?'

'Yes, why indeed?' I said, suppressing a yawn.

12

'And then there's the bloody Poms. They take the biscuit. They take the fucking can. Bloody agitators. Socialist wolves in sheep's clothing. Behind every strike. Nothing's too good for them, all of them welfare experts, they get every type of benefit going.'

He jabbed at his chest, taking his eyes off the road once again. I prayed the next truck wouldn't miss. Perhaps if I nudged his arm at the right moment we could both go together. Now there's a thought, my last service for the biosphere, two less of us to fuck it up . . .

'And look at me,' he glared, 'born and bred an Australian, and I'm forced to stay with my parents while our bloody government gives these bloody immigrants houses, jobs, loans to start up businesses that only employ more Wops, Poms and Dagos.'

I shook my head sympathetically 'Sounds bad, mate, really bad. Do you ever see an end to all this?'

'What? For the country or me personally?' he snapped.

'Oh, yourself of course. Tell me about your family for instance.'

The policeman paused a moment, rubbing at the freckles on his smudge of a nose. 'It's my uncle's funeral I'm going to. He was thirty years a preacher in the Dutch Reform Church. In a couple of years, when I pass my exams, I'll become a lay-preacher. One day I'm going to raise a family. Two girls and two boys. Yeah, and when they're grown up, I'll buy them all a house. Not like my parents.'

'Oh,' I smiled. 'Have you got any woman in mind to get married to? Tell me,' I waggled my eyebrows, 'is there a fair damsel waiting in the wings?'

'As a matter of fact, no. I'm going to buy the house first, then I'll get the wife. Yeah, and when I get married, it'll be for keeps.'

I chuckled. 'Throw away the key, eh? That's what to do with them. Even then they're too much trouble.'

He went on: 'Yep, I'm one of these people who believes that the woman's only place is THE HOME. That's how God planned it, and that's what's gone wrong with the world ever since – mothers out working. A woman's job is to bring children into this world, and to bring them up to be decent, loyal citizens.'

'Take them to church as soon as they can toddle, stop the rot before it starts. Sounds like you're a very reasonable sort of guy,' I said, waving my hand airily.

We passed a garage. By the exit sign a lone hitch-hiker optimistically raised a thumb. The policeman swerved into the opposite lane, at the same time twisting his neck to gaze over his shoulder. 'I didn't like the look of that one. You've got to watch yourself on the roads. A lot of people go missing every year.'

'What?' I sat up, allowing a tone of worry to enter my voice. 'I thought Australia was a safe country for travelling.'

'Listen, mate,' the policeman shot back, 'you'd better be bloody careful. There's killers stalk the roads. They even hunt in packs. Especially up north in Queensland. Lots of people don't like hippies and some take the law into their own hands.'

I said hotly, 'I hope you don't mistake me for a hippy.'

'Ha.' I got the first laugh of the trip. 'Listen, mate, if I thought you were one, it wouldn't be a lift I was giving you.'

Well, there you have it, straight from the Enforcer's mouth. A policeman said I wasn't a hippy. Next best thing to a signed and sealed certificate.

My bloody mate dropped me somewhere at the bloody edge of bloody suburbia in bloody Melbourne beside a bloody railway station. Clear black night: no moon, sky encrusted with diamante stars. They're not real in Australia. Check out the Australian flag, it's got seven seven-pointed stars on it.

My bloody mate waited to see if I was in time to make the last train. My declared destination was the house of a mate I'd met in distant Bali so, with an enquiry in mind, I approached a spectral being striding back and forth in front of the empty station. The crunching of gravel under my feet alerted him. He stopped in his tracks, swaying gently as if a gossamer-wind rocked him on the balls of his feet. He asked in a tremulous tea-strained voice, 'You waiting on a train to the centre, mate?'

I nodded, rendered speechless by the strangeness of this apparition.

'The mail train comes in twenty minutes, mate. Goes all the way to the centre.'

'Great!' I exclaimed. Cupping my hands I shouted back to the cop hanging out of the window of his car. 'I'm all right, mate! There'll be a train here in twenty minutes. Thanks for the ride.'

The cop acknowledged my cries with a wave of his hand and as he pulled out from the curve, I added, 'Hey man, and don't forget to keep a clean nose for the plainclothes at the funeral.'

As I watched the vestal-virgin tail-lights winking a bloody goodbye, a hole was knocked in the floor of my mood. The spectre was still dancing. It was then I realised he was totally, tropically mad. Hoping I was wrong, I addressed him in a strict voice, 'Are you sure there is a train in twenty minutes?'

His dancing became a furious tattoo. 'There IS a train in twenty minutes. It goes ALL the way to the centre. There IS a train, there IS a train. Chookady-choo, chookady-choo, and it goes under tunnels, goes under tunnels, ALL the way to the centre!'

Oh my God. I just gawped, my jaw slack. Then I was alerted by a noise from somewhere over my shoulder. I turned around.

A disembodied voice wafted out from the cavernous bowels of a bus shelter, crying out plaintively. 'Hey whoever you are. Don't listen to him. He's a crazy. Now if you'll all be quiet, maybe I'll be able to get some sleep.'

I rapidly crossed black tarmacadam, stepping over a long slat of streetlight to peer into the gloom of the shelter. I could just make out a lumpy turnip shape protruding from bunched blankets. A radio crackled nearby and through the static came the distant voice of an announcer on the World Service: *And now, an everyday story of country folk, The Archers . . . Da di dum dee dum di doo, da di dum di do da, da di do di dum di do, dum di diddly do da, dum di diddly dum di diddly dum di diddly do da . . .*

I couldn't help it, I shouted at the sprawled thing, 'For God's sake man, what are you doing lying out here? Don't you have a home?'

'Oh yes sir, oh yes mate, I got a house, I got a home, I got a wife, I got a grasscutter. I got babies, mate. I got seven babies. I got a job, I got a job, and that's why I'm here, so I can get some sleep and catch the five-thirty mail train in the morning. I work all day, and I got to suffer this chattering idiot beside me, every night, every night. Now listen, I'm trying to get some sleep here and you can take my word for it, matey, there ain't no train. Not till five-thirty. Now will you both shut up.'

The spectre loomed over my shoulder, hanging like an upturned iceberg, spinning on the balls of his heels. He would have done any dervish troop proud. In many countries he would have been pronounced as holy and infused with the spirit of God, but here in Australia he was an outcast living in the gutter. He chanted, as a mantra, 'Oh yes there is, oh yes there IS, oh yes there IS a train.'

The turnip jerked up, throwing the blankets aside and cutting 'The Archers' off just as Walter Gabriel was about to enter the back door of Mrs P's thatched cottage. As the radio clattered to the ground, he shouted, 'You're all fucking mad! Just SHUT UP SHUT UP SHUT UP! I'm trying to get some sleep.'

Then, somewhere over across the square by some boarded-up shops, a telephone began to ring. Welcoming this distraction I ran from the station and discovered the phone booth under a headless street-lamp. It was a wrong number, but I chatted the caller up, told her my tales of the traveller, and what do you know? This night-owl promised to call a cab for me, which was just as well. I had no change. I felt just like a circus dog who's jumped through a hoop, or a Swiss yodeler mouthing spaghetti. I know I'll get out of this one – at least that's what I told myself. There's always another hoop waiting.

The taxi came, I leapt for it, and not a moment too soon for the spectre was hot on my heels. Instantly I snibbed the door. Very irate now, he thumped impotently on the paintwork, his breath steaming, sliding lips reminding me of slugs on a greenhouse window. He yelled, 'I get to ride in taxis! I get to ride in taxis! I get to ride in taxis!'

I shouted back, 'Well, you're not fucking getting in this one, mate.' I turned to the driver, 'Get me out of here.' He needed no encouragement. I was thrown back in my seat as he gunned the accelerator.

'Where to?' he shouted, as we took off.

'Kangaroo Grounds, mate,' I called back. 'The address I've got here says Upper Dangalong. Know it?'

'Yup.'

4

My purse groaned audibly as I peeled forty bucks from my wad and handed it to the driver. It was just beginning to sink in: the news from home. I could feel the noose tightening. Two hundred dollars and a bag of bikinis is a slender passport in a new land. The notes were hardly out of my hand when the driver pushed the car into gear and shot down through the tall overhanging eucalyptus trees, turning onto the main road a hundred yards distant.

Where was I? In front of me a shack. A shabby-white paint-peeling patched thing propped up by a porch and a veranda. Had it not been for the light leaking out of a back window of this crate I would have presumed this was a derelict orange crate with no inhabitants.

Slatted wooden boards creaked loudly as I stepped onto the porch. From somewhere nearby came the clanking of a chain and a strange reedy mewing. I discovered later this was the sound of Horace, the pet sheep. I had a sudden feeling of trepidation, as I took the head of the kangaroo-knocker and thunked it down on the metal plate.

A shout from inside, 'Who the fuck's that, at this hour. Maybeline! Go see who it is!' The command was imperious.

Slow shuffling steps in the hall, and then yellow light spilled out as the door swung slowly back on rusty hinges.

I liked the face of the woman who stood before me. Long black hair gathered up by a spotted neckerchief, in the style English working-class women used to adopt in days of yore. I liked that, so I smiled, and then she smiled.

I ventured hesitantly, 'You don't know me, I'm Frankie, a friend of Sheila's.

17

You know, Sheila Hardknob? I met him in Bali, he invited me to come and stay.'

For a moment Maybeline held a look of blank puzzlement on her face. And then she seemed to click 'memory' into her recognition.

'Ow yeah, Sheila, yeah. Ow, 'e's out at 'is girlfriend, Porridge's 'ouse.'

'Jeez,' I said as I followed her down the darkened hall, almost tripping over the rucked carpet, 'you've certainly got some strange names around here.'

'Ow, that gows with the territory.'

'By the way, what is your name?' I asked.

She stopped and turned, her gypsy face strangely attractive, eyes now bright and shiny. It was as if I knew her from some place. Something about that voice. She smiled as she said, 'Maybeline. I 'opes you don't think that's a strange name.'

'Definitely not,' I replied gallantly. 'I think it's a very lovely name.'

Something in her step. A lilt or a tilt or a jaunty something. Then I knew. She reminded me of my wife.

Opening the door at the end of the sloping hall, she bounced into the room. My sinking spirit dropped a couple more notches and my eyes filled with tears, as the inhabitants of this cave swirled into my vision through the smoky atmosphere: two bearded, seedy-looking men, both on the turn from adolescence to old age.

Maybeline announced, 'Ere, Big Licks, look wot the night blew in. This 'ere is Frankie, 'e's a friend of Sheila's.' She turned to me, leaving a gap through which I could see the man of the house scowling at me. She said, 'Frankie, I'd like to introduce my 'usband, BL, and 'is bruvver OD, which stands for Owpen Door.'

Ignoring for the moment OD lying comatose on one of the three sagging couches behind a pyramid of empty stubbies, I studied BL closely. This Australian version of Attila the Hun greeted my entrance into the smoke-dark room with a loud guffaw, throwing back his head but at the same time holding me with narrow, flint-stone eyes.

'Who the fuck are you?' he yelled, banging his drink down so hard frothing beer spilled on the floor, then falling back into a lolling position in the big chair. Waving big hands in the air, he shrieked in a mock-British accent, 'Not another Pommie baastaard! Chroist, the grass isn't growin' over the last one yet.'

I didn't like this at all. I didn't like Australia and, particularly, I didn't like him. The sight of this drunken sod, his head a leering pumpkin, made me want to strike out. I felt sticky red stuff pounding in my temples. Jutting my jaw forward, I growled, showing fangs and bulging my eyes menacingly. 'Listen, mate, I'm a Jock. A true Scot of the blood. Aren't you getting yourself mixed up? We don't like Poms any more than you do.'

Attila extended a fat and dirty hand, 'All right, all right.' He waved towards a sagging couch. 'So have a fuckin' beer, mate. So tike a fuckin' pew, Jocky. We're 'aving a little rage here. That's 'strylian for party.'

Keeping my distance as I accepted the proffered stubby and leaning forward at an angle to avoid the possible drop-kick, I renounced tension, as an act of will, and gratefully accepted the couch's sag, taking in my companions with little shifty glimpses.

The Hun was now staring morosely into the empty fireplace half-filled with cigarette butts, empty beer-cans, detritus. Flaming red hair suggested a mean temper.

OD more than merited his name, whatever it meant. He lay splayed out on the sofa, legs hooked over the armrest, hobnail soles facing my way. At the other end of the couch, all the blood had drained into the cistern of his head, giving his face a marbled look.

A curious geometry about this room – for one thing, the three couches: I had one all to myself and OD was definitely occupying the whole of his. Mine, presumably designated the visitors' pew, was furthest from the fireplace and angled towards the door that I imagined led out into the back yard.

Maybeline's small sofa abutted against BL's leatherette swivel armchair. Just by looking at it I could tell that it and its contents were part of the Hun's personal and private domain, the inner keep of the castle.

A television was upended on the floor beside the back door, the screen stove in. It lay where it had landed, I guessed from the way the glass was splintered around it. The walls of the room, as the outside of this crate, were constructed from overlapping boards. I concluded that only people so mad as Australians would construct a house this way. Through inkblot cracks in the boards the occasional highlight of a star glittered. All around night, and this shack in the middle of nowhere. Poste Restante Mars . . .

My attention returned to the Hun and Maybeline. What was it, I wondered, that kept them together? The reins were almost visible. *I bet he puts on the spurs when he gets in the saddle*. Maybeline looked downcast, embarrassed even, as if she sensed my very thought. I moved uncomfortably on the sagging couch, scratching myself. This heat was unbearable.

My movement alerted the Hun. Two fingers loomed, resembling huge, soggy penises as they swam into my heat-crazed vision, the fat, ugly, flaccid things vee'd on a veritable Roman candle of a joint which spluttered and stank of burning leaves.

Out of politeness I accepted this offering, choking on the first toke as the rush of grass, tobacco and noxious smoke hit the back of my throat. The shaking of my hand causing embers to fall and attach to my clothing. I stood up flailing. I could hardly bear it, the barbarity of Australia and all things Australian. They couldn't even roll proper joints. I bewailed the cruel God that had brought me to this land.

Another can of Tooey's, and another can of bloody Tooey's. Then the Tooey's ran out and I was passed a can of XXXX. My head began to pound with the savage drums of the local Tonton Macoute. Refusing the next can the Hun thrust my way, I said, 'No thanks, mate, I've had enough. If it's no bother to anyone I'll just crash out on this sofa. I've travelled a long way to get here, half way round the bleeding world.'

In one sinuous movement the Hun hoisted himself up in his chair, a cobra rising from a straw basket. Taking one smooth step towards me, he intoned slowly, spitting venom into every syllable, 'Listen carefully, mate, and think yourself lucky to be gettin' advance warnin'. Out 'ere in the bush, we keep by nasty surprises, speshly for foreigners who can't take good 'strylian beer.'

To give myself something to occupy myself while I thought out my next move, I jumped to my feet and dusted off the dirty covers of the sofa behind me. Then, looking the Hun straight in the eye, I allowed a lean and hungry smile to play across my face before I said, 'Just try anything you like, mate, and while you make up your mind what you're going to do, I'll crash out here on the sofa. OK matey?'

Maybeline flapped across the room to stand between us, curiously reminding me of a hen taking a dust-bath. She turned first to the Hun and then to me, saying, 'Ow no, BL. 'Ow could you? 'E's sow tired, can't you see? 'E's been travelling a long way.' And, 'Frankie, it's just BL's sense of 'umour. Down't pay 'im no attention. You can sleep tonoite in Sheila's room. It'll be less noisy in there.'

The sagging bed in the dark closet was no more comfortable than the sagging couch in the sitting room. As I lay down, a gremlin Shostakovitch played a symphony on the springs. Bing! Ding! Bwoi-o-oo-wing!

The images of the posters on the walls and the ceilings swam around my head like a kaleidoscope. Heavy metal memorabilia. Big blondes on motorbikes. My bearded friend Sheila had an eye for the ladies.

Suddenly the door swung open and the Hun bumped off the door post as he lurched in. In one hand was a stubby, in the other a large joint.

I waved a hand as my head spun. Suddenly there were two, or three, or four, five, six images of the Hun, revolving on a cartwheel. I saw their six mouths open, and then I heard them say, 'Look mate, down't get us wronggg. We were only jokinggg.'

I shook my head in an effort to clear my brain, thinking, poor bastards, I guess being born an Aussie is like having a club foot. You're always putting it in it.

With effort, I pretended a yawn. 'BL, don't worry about it. I've just got to get some shut-eye. See you in the morning, mate. Ta ever so for the bed.'

The Hun had one endearing quality – he was predictable. If you half-inched around, scrupulously making sure that he noticed you were avoiding 'his territory', keeping your hands off 'his woman', and not sitting in 'his chair', and if you did not flinch when he talked about sticking Abos into holes, then he liked to have you around. Anybody in the house automatically became part of his court, an essential adjunct to his position in life of local gangster chief.

This watering hole was the favourite port of call for the ne'er-do-wells of the surrounding badlands because the Hun was a dealer and a fence, trading in anything that was stolen, or illegal. You might think that such an occupation would be short-lived, but the Hun had been at it, and from this address, for years. He kept an ace up his sleeve – friends in high places. At one time he had been employed by ASIO (Australia Secret Intelligence Organization) His job? To hunt out terrorists in Malaysia. For his services he had been awarded *carte blanche* to deal in whatever he pleased on his home turf, without any interference by der local Polizei. In the unlikely event of a raid, the Hun would be forewarned several hours in advance by his old friends.

In the week that I waited for Sheila to reappear, I noted much of the Hun's time was taken up by mysterious journeys. He would return towing a trailer stowed with plunder behind the truck. Once he showed up with a motor launch. It was gone the next day.

I made an enquiry about the possibilities of investing in some low-quality weed, strictly for resale. When the Hun asked how much cash I had on hand, I shrugged my shoulders, replying 'I've got other collateral.'

'What like?' he grunted.

'Quite apart from my many abilities and talents, I am the proud possessor of two hundred and ninety-nine bikinis, and each one of them wrapped up in a neat little draw-string baggy. Just the thing for the ladies.'

'Bikinis?' The Hun threw back his head with laughter, waving open palms at the ceiling. At that moment a small black spider fell, dangling a line of thread, right onto the centre of his palm. Quicker than thought, he clenched his fist, crushing the poor bug and yelled, 'Maybeline! Why the fuck don't you clean this place? What do you do all day while I'm out? Moaning cunt!' He turned back to me, smiling. 'Now what's this latest line in patter, Jock?'

'Well, BL, I was going to suggest you take some bikinis as collateral for the grass. I could sell it and come back with the cash, then buy some more grass as well, mate.'

'Sucking fuck, mate.' BL spat with derision on the floor. 'Who do you know man? You don't know nobody man. And as for your idea of selling bikinis, the place is bloody flooded with that Balinese shit. You want grass? Get me the cash, all right, Jocky? That's it.'

I drew myself up defiantly. 'Listen BL, laugh if you like, but when I'm travelling, moving about the planet, I meet lots of people. There's loads of punters out there who don't know where to buy grass, and you can charge them what you fuckin' like, mate. Yeah,' I snorted, furling out my nostrils like a horse, 'and don't knock the bikinis mate. Maybeline loved the one I gave her.' I held my hand over my mouth. 'Oh Christ,' I exclaimed, 'I wasn't supposed to tell you that.'

The Hun exploded, storming out the room, slamming the hardboard door behind him. Bugs of all description rained from the ceiling.

'Fucking floozy! Where are you, you cunt!' Screams and the sound of pots falling. Then more doors slammed, as he stomped the boards back to the sitting room, the entire house reverberating to the sounds of his rage. He threw open the door, following his finger which had turned into a heat-seeking missile, targeted on my forehead. It stopped just an inch away, quivering slightly. His eyes bulged, and a thin flecking of nicotine-yellow foam clung to the corners of his mouth. He spat out his words very slowly, dry-ice coals, each one steaming visibly in the air.

'Listen to me, mate, you leave my fucking woman alone, otherwise you're dead meat, do you hear me! Don't you fucking lay one finger on her, or pollute her with one more of your fucking ideas. Fucking Pommie shithead!'

I shouted back. 'I'm not a fucking Pommie, and I didn't lay any of my fucking fingers on her. So there, mate. Will you get that in your head. I just wanted to make her a present, I had nothing else to give her. Alrighty?!'

The Hun nodded his head slowly, 'Yeah, well, get it straight, mate. One more move in her direction, and you're a goner. Got it?'

'Loud and clear,' I replied firmly. The only way to treat offensive yobbos.

The Hun held my eye, 'Over and out mate, over and out.' He spun on his heel and once more exited the room, this time striding for the front door. He shouted as he slammed it. 'I'll be back, and you'd better have my supper ready. Cunt!'

Later on, Maybeline provided me with a lifeline. Together we organised a tupperware-style bikini-party, and I the sole male on hand. Yes, I have cast an eye over the shapely forms of flesh supposed to be viewed only by their handlers' ogling eyes, and survived. There was the occasional comment such as 'Ow Gaud, they're sow scratchy.' Or, 'Are you sure it isn't just a little bit bowld? Me teets're fawling out.'

Well wha'd'ya expect if you must try on a pair of postage stamps? But I never said that, for there is one thing certain, 'to reveal all is to loose the sale' – that's what my Jewish shrewish Granny once told me, 'And keep your hands in your pockets, boy! It fair drives me mad to see you fidgetin' like that.' Obviously the shrivelled old crone had forgotten, there are other things to play with in little boys' pockets.

I'd lean back in my chair, cupping my jaw in a thinking man's palm. The other hand would be deep in my trouser pocket. 'Hmmmmmmm, that colour goes better with your flaming auburn hair.' Or I'd say, 'Yes, yes, yes it's good, that's very good.' And if I sensed the sale was slipping away, I'd say authoritively, 'Yes, but I have one that's just you, I've got it at the bottom of the bag. It's purple. Don't tell any of the others. It's the only one.'

Maybeline insisted we keep this party a secret, as if I needed to be told. The Hun never found out. Just as well. We managed to tidy up all the evidence before he returned from his treasure hunting.

Enter Sheila the Knob, my ginger-bearded friend who looked like an orangutan. Definitely not cotton wool stuffing those bulging jeans. You could tell by the way it throbbed and vibrated.

Once he confided, when we were on Bali, he had a terrible problem. He said, 'Listen mate, don't laugh. The doctors told me it could happen to anyone. You see, it's periodic. I mean it comes and it goes, but . . .' he hesitated, his eyes searching mine for evidence of future betrayal, 'you see, I get hard-ons that last for weeks at a time, and there's nothing I can do about it. There's only temporary relief in having a fuck. I mean, seriously man, I have to go on a special diet when it comes on, otherwise my whole body would become wasted. I've got to take lots of steroids. It's unbelievable.'

'How did this come about?' I enquired sympathetically, like a counsellor.

'Well, it all started when I got gang-banged by a group of women in the criminally insane ward of the mental hospital where I work. It was a long weekend, we were low on staff. I got locked in, and nobody knew. They stole my keys. First they took off all my clothes, strapped me down to a rubber table, and put a wig on my head. Then they took it in turns to jump up and down on me, while one of them kept me firm by clenching her fist on my dick. Forty of them. They all had several goes. It was unbelievable. The Industrial Injuries Compensation Board said they'd never heard a case like it. Then their report was leaked, and that's when everybody started called me Sheila Hardknob, it's stuck to me ever since.' Sheila took a deep shuddering breath, and sighed, mournfully.

He paused for a long moment before continuing. 'The psychiatrist explained it was a psychosomatic condition. They suggested I should act out my fantasies. So now the only way I can get rid of the hard-on is to wear a long blonde wig and a dress, then gradually it subsides.'

I shook my head incredulously. 'You poor bastard, I've never heard anything like it. You poor bastard. Tell me, is it good? When I think about it, it doesn't sound too bad. Listen mate, you could make a fortune in a Hamburg brothel.'

'Ow Christ, I'm disappointed,' said Sheila. 'I thought at least you would have had a different reaction. All my friends say things like that, but God, you don't know what it's like. For one thing man, it's painful, and it's endangering my health. The doctors said I've got to wear a special corset when I get these attacks.' He broke down and I held him while he sobbed. Just the confessions of another traveller one night on Bali in a tropical hotel.

Sheila said it was all right if I slept in his room. It was a good excuse for him to stay away. He was looking for a new place, a shack of his own, as he put it. He confessed that he couldn't stand living with the Hun. And he couldn't stand the way he treated Maybeline.

Well, that just suited me fine, because I wanted to wait around for this damn grass. I had seven hundred dollars now. Just enough to buy a pound. The Hun said it could be here any day. Some pals of his were bringing a load from Mount Gambia in South Australia, just over the state line.

I occupied much of my time – while the Hun was away – by giving art lessons and encouragement to the apple of Maybeline's eye, Claude Duvalier Jr, CD for short, her four-year-old son from a former relationship.

When BL returned one day Maybeline was standing over the table cluttered with paper, scissors and glue, courtesy of the Occupational Therapy Dept of the Victoria Mental Institute, and Sheila. Maybeline was admiring CD's first completed artwork, a large collage of a tower, an angry-faced king poking his head out of the topmost window. All the apples from the trees surrounding the tower had fallen to the ground. In the sky, dark clouds hung like bats.

She took it over to BL, cracking open a beer from the fridge. he scowled, stepping back for a second as if it was radioactive, and then he reached forward, grabbing it from her.

'What's this pissy little thing?' he demanded.

Out of the corner of my eye I saw the expression of expectant hope drop from the face of little CD, perched on the high stool and leaning his elbows on the table.

BL glared at Maybeline accusingly. 'Has that bloody Jock been filling your head with poofy ideas?' He looked down at CD and smiled. CD smiled back. Then the Hun very slowly and very deliberately tore the painting in half. Then he threw back his head and laughed, both hands holding his sides.

'Ow Gawd, BL, did you 'ave to do that?' Maybeline cried, tears flooding her eyes.

I left them going at it hammer and tongs. I needed space. I had to get away. As I rounded the house, I tripped over the chain that tethered Horace. 'Fucking shit-head,' I shouted. 'Fucking creep,' and kicked the poor little bugger.

Stricken by an attack of conscience, I patted him and attempted to stuff his mouth with a handful of leaves, and then I noticed: no teeth, poor bastard. He baa'd at me miserably. What a fate. Poor pathetic thing, eking out a miserable existence. Sheila kept Horace handy in case of a particularly bad attack. perhaps the Hun and Sheila did it together at different ends.

Then I started wondering, how did he get the name Horace? I wondered what it was really like for Sheila when he penetrated Horace. I wondered if it was better. I wondered if the whole of Australia was full of people like these. I supposed I was going to find out.

I jumped over the rickety fence and struck out for open pasture. The sun was sliding down into the bucket of the horizon. Strange bird sounds in my ears. I was startled when half a dozen rocks turned into kangaroos and started bounding for the distance, just like so many giant bunnies.

5

I ran from the house of the Hun, as if all the furies of hell were snapping behind me. I was ragged. My head ringing from all the abuse the Hun poured over his kept woman. But, all things considered, I hadn't done so bad. At least I had achieved one thing in the two weeks of subterranean existence: I had converted some damned bikinis into a little over a pound of lousy grass. No mean trick, I'd say. I rubbed my hands with glee, anticipating all those punters, 'out there'. 'Hey man, this is the best grass from South East Asia man, I brought it all the way!'

A bagatelle of rides, and I'd reached the state border. State border? I couldn't see it. Just rolling, dust-brown hills and the odd cluster of buildings near a water-hole. Here and there, clumps of sad, spindly eucalyptus trees. Scattered terrestrial cirrhus clouds. Wandering packs of puffy white merino sheep. Baa bloody baa bloody baa baa. Australia, ya big mother. Waving her dummy tit in my face.

I was about ready to sprawl flat-face forward when a big souped-up jalopy with smoking heavy-tread tires ploughed dust a foot or so from my bag. The back door was flung open and I simply flopped on to a seat that immediately seamed itself to me, sticky flesh of my legs on hot vinyl. I looked down just in time. My balls were rolling out from behind the high cleft of my shorts. In near panic I grabbed the large road map beside me on the seat and laid it over my knees. I looked up, saying to the likelier looking of the two girls, 'Hey, either of you got any materials? I'd like to roll you both a big joint.'

The blonde brunette with the smudgy red lips addressed her mate, 'Wha'-d'y'know? I had an intuition we should pick him up.' Holding up her hand she spoke in a stage whisper, 'Debra here doesn't like men, so be warned . . .' She flickered a smile at her companion, almost nervously.

Debra snarled and chucked the cigarette papers onto my lap.

'Good shot,' I said.

She did not reply, merely concentrating on the twisting snake of a road, driving truck style – an elbow resting out of the window, one hand on the wheel, the brim of her brown leather cap pulled down over her eyes, a dead roll-up clenched in her teeth.

Making conversation, I ventured, 'Are you both gay by any chance?'

Debra breathed in sharply, and the blonde-brunette nodded towards her, saying, 'Oh, what a perceptive diddy man this one is.'

I went on regardless. 'I'm a bit inclined that way myself. I think everybody is. At least I can only speak as a man. Maybe it's only the effects of this climate. Recently I have begun to have doubts as to my preferences. Tell me, do all Australian men stuff cotton wool into their pants, or are they all built that way, or maybe they're just always pleased to see each other?'

The girle with the blonde-brunette hair laughed. 'Oh no, didn't you know, little Aussie boys are all made of puppy-dawg tails? Floppy, droopy, dangly puppy-dawg tails, and their heads are full of mince.'

She was warming to me. I could feel it over the heat. Resting an elbow on the seat-back, she leaned over twisting and pouting, long eyelashes flapping. 'It's mostly a case of what's available. Australia is like a big supermarket with lots of cheap offers. But we welcome the occasional passing stranger with open arms and flapping gussets! Wha'd'y'say about that?' She grinned cheesily.

Debra whipped around and whacked her companion sharply on the shoulder.

I laughed disarmingly. 'Don't worry about me. I never come between a couple. Why don't we have another joint and change the subject. I wonder if you know of a really cheap hotel in Adelaide. Or do you know anyone who wants to buy some Indonesian grass.'

'Oh,' Debra exclaimed, 'Is that the good stuff? Or are you saving that for later?'

I smiled and resumed rolling, playing with the four skins on my knees.

We arrived at the rusty shack that was these two girls' dream of an idyll in the hills as day turned to night. A view out through the trees over the world: Adelaide, a necklace of fireflies, stretching out on the great plain fringing the gulf of St Vincent; the sea, a slate discus; the lights of a few boats between the city and the horizon bleeding into night.

The stars up above, the mirror of the city, or was it the other way around? In the constellations I could read the spreading of suburbia as if the blight was leaping on the galaxies. Suddenly I was alerted by a mote of light zig-zagging across the sky. Way off in the distance, a beam cast a pool of light across water. I wondered, is that from a lighthouse?

Damn mosquitoes! I slapped my face. Sticky blood in my palm. My blood, for God's sake! Another landed on my lip. It flew up and danced around my descending fingers, then resumed its munching, gobbets of my flesh. I ran for the door, a frame stretched with mosquito netting hanging at a crazy angle, and slammed it behind me. It fell off its hinges, but it didn't matter, the room was already abuzz with squadrons of miniature von Richtofens.

Sleep that night was impossible, even if it had not been for those damned mosquies. The heat was a mind-fuck, and there were sounds I cannot describe coming from behind the closed door of the girls' bedroom. Or perhaps they kept a wild pig in there? I wound myself in a wet shroud, in a passable imitation of a mummified pharoah, and did my best not to go stark staring raving mad.

Debra was up early. She seemed pleased when I asked for a lift with her into town, explaining that I had to travel on.

I noticed on the long drive that the road sides were peppered with signs warning the traveller of the danger of starting fires. Billboards proclaimed this was National Fire Safety Week.

Debra screamed as I flicked my cigarette out the window, 'For Christ's sake, don't do that. You could've started a bush fire back there.' She shook her head in disapproval. 'A forest fire in these parts is very scary. It's part of the natural cycle of the eucalyptus tree. A bush fire works in two ways. It can whip through at the treetops, burning off the leaves, or it stays down below, burning off the undergrowth. It runs faster than any animal, even faster than a car. Eucalyptus trees are incredible, mate. Thousands of varieties. Some have seeds that will only sprout after the earth has been baked by a bush fire. The fires actually help the trees grow, stripping off the undergrowth and providing nitrogen and carbon compounds for the soil.' She jabbed a finger at one of her barely visible tits. 'I should know. I'm a bleeding biology teacher. Sometimes,' she continued, 'the heat gets so much the trees explode like bombs.'

'Does anyone ever survive a bush fire?'

She nodded, 'Yeah, if you've got enough warning to dig a hole in the ground. Otherwise, mate, you ain't got a bleeding chance.'

I discovered, as I took a rest in a street-side cafe after Debra had dropped me off, that I'd left my large diary in the rusty shack, I'd been writing up some accounts of my travels.

My first reaction was to shrug and tell myself, 'I'll go back in a couple of days.' But then another voice seemed to issue from within my head. It said: *You must return immediately, otherwise the book it will be lost.*

I was astonished. I'd never experienced anything like this. A voice had actually spoken inside my cranium. A strict, no-monkey-business, no-messing voice demanding instant obedience. I breathed very slowly. There had to be something important about this. A part of my spirit had spoken.

The digital read-out on the nearby brick tower, rising above a shimmering of city blocks that merged into the heat-haze, was flashing between 11.00 a.m. and 42°C. The newspaper heading covering the face of the man at the next table predicted 'KILLER HEAT' for today. Tell me something new. Damn voices in my head. But I've spent a lifetime following signs. I'd even come to Australia because I'd had a dream about it.

And so, obedient to this genie within my head but complaining bitterly, I started on the journey, wading through this sticky heat towards the Horseshoe Hills above Adelaide.

Outwith this, the most English of Australian cities. The timetable informed me that the next bus up the long hill was in three hours time, but I conjectured that if I walked fast enough I might just catch the return bus in a couple of hours. I remembered there was a stop very near the lesbians' poky little hole.

The heat was unbearable, and every time a truck passed I was deluged in swirling devil whirlpools, stinging my flesh wherever the sweat poured from it. But I made it. I got my book. And the return bus drive was a cool, swish glide. I savoured the air-conditioning like a birthday treat.

I had an address. It seemed like a month but in fact it was only thirty-six hours ago that I'd been standing in the entrance to the Hun's drive when a Jaguar XJ6 had pulled up – my first ride on the way to Adelaide.

The dame at the wheel rolled down a smoked-glass window, gave me a long, searching look and then said, 'No funny business, mate, jump in. I'm going to Benayeo near Bringalbert, a couple of little places just before the state border. I'll let you off at Neuarpurr where there's a truckstop. You might only have to wait a couple of days for a lift.'

It wasn't long before I was playing with my four skins, my passport in this land. A joint of grass and I'm the most popular person in the party. The lady had said, 'You're travelling to Adelaide, right? Well, if you get any more of this stuff, pop in and see me. I might buy some of the hedge-clippings off you. You don't have to tell me how good it is and all that shit. I know it's rubbish, but I might buy some anyway.'

When I arrived at her charming period cottage in a terraced row, she quickly put me in my place by opening the door and then, when I stepped forward, half-closing it to bar my way. She stood in the small gap, a delicate cork sealing an equally delicate bottle. Her voice came over large as the gap was small, and harsh to go with it.

'You're just here to sell me some grass, right?'

I had been well prepared by the lesbian finishing school in the Andean peaks of the Horseshoe Hills. And so I replied in a snap-happy voice, 'That's exactly right, Ma'am. This visit is purely business. I'm not going to thrust my loathsome body onto you' – I hesitated before adding archly – 'if that's what you mean?'

'Fine,' she said, deigning a snarl of a smile. 'You can come in then. I won't have to give you the boot.' She led me through a poorly-lit hallway into a sitting room strewn with piles of books and papers, and cluttered with artefacts from other lands and ages past. Dark, heavily-varnished paintings of naked men obfuscated themselves on the walls. Some had been slashed. I began to wonder, was she the spider and I the fly? A framed square of vellum caught my eye. I strode up to it – a page of text from some ancient Hebraic scroll.

'If you're interested,' she said, 'that's a page from a Gnostic gospel. The true story of Mary and mother worship, suppressed by the Judaic-Christian patriarchy. And they've been dominating the world ever since.' Suddenly she was as rigid as a plank – a plank that oozed hostility like suppurating black tar.

'I've had it up to here with fucking men! Do you hear me?' Her talons clawed the air, castrating a memory.

I had seated myself on a couch. I was placing the four skins together.

'Well,' I asked her, in a voice designed to lead her out of this Kali death-dance performance on the Baluchistan rug centre-floor, 'who was he then, this lucky man? Someone special?'

'Too true, mate. Too bloody true. You only see him on bloody television every night. That is, ever since this fucking election was called. He's only the next future incumbent of the Pine Lodge in Canberra, the next big-wig to govern us all. And when he takes office – which he will, by the way – he'll be like a bloody hawk amongst the cockatoos. Oooooohhhhgggrrr, that bastard! He dresses up in the white wool of a socialist, but inside he's black as pitch. He's got the luck of the devil.'

I looked up, the big unlit joint clenched jauntily in my teeth. I drawled, 'Sounds like a right motherfucker.'

'He is,' she replied, her jaw moving up and down as a seamstress's needle, stitching up this memory. 'And I should bleeding know. I lived with the bastard off and on for seven years.' Smiling she showed perfect white teeth, a thin pointed tongue slashing at crimson lips, Persian harlot's eyes narrowing with bitter laughter.

'You know what I'm going to do, mate?' she declared, cocking her hand on a Venus hip.

I blinked and asked, 'What?' passing her the fat prick of a joint.

She took a deep toke. 'I'm going to send him a congratulatory telegram when he takes office saying, 'Sucker, bet your dick's three feet long!' And I will demand the ambassadorship to Tibet and leave this stinking rotten country forever. You see,' she laughed razor blades, 'it's just a joke we used to have when we were lovers, about his little prongy. Have you ever watched how he moves his hands up and down and side to side when he's on the soap-box? When he does that, it's actually a form of frustrated masturbation. You see, that sonofabitch gets a hard-on whenever he speaks in front of a crowd. You can observe the same phenomenon in packs of baboons. I once read in a scientific paper that the top male baboon always gets a hard-on when he's dominating the rest of the pack! A hard penis is an ape domination gesture. Some things never change!'

She stood in the middle of the Baluchistan rug breathing deeply, but despite her efforts to control her rage, the tendons of her neck stood out so taut I could have reached out and plucked the Moonlight Sonata on them.

After a moment she continued, her rage nailed below decks: 'In the old days, when I used to accompany that dickhead to every rally, as we drove in the car I would nudge him in the ribs and say, "Bet your cock's a foot long already, ya bastard." And he would reply, "Betchya life." Then he'd take my hand, and show me. Bleeding bastard's got a cock like a mule, and a head that's just one big bloated louse on his shoulders. OOOOhhhgggrrr, men! I hate them. I was a stepping stone on his road to the top. Oh, he used to hold up his two fingers and cross them and say, "Pat, you and me are just like this. We'll be together forever and a day." I haven't had a lover since. Seven long years. But you know, I'm better off. I don't need men any more. I've gotten rid of them out of my life, and THANK GOD!'

Changing her tone, she commanded me with a cast of her hand. 'Now, why don't we take a beer from the fridge and go out and enjoy the last of the day in the garden. You never know, it might be a bit cooler outside. Bloody Australia. The beer. The flies. The men. The heat. I bloody hate it!' She clenched at her brow with a clawing whitened hand.

We'd just emerged onto the patio when suddenly the sky turned a dreadful colour, like ground-up burnt umber from a Manichean painter's palette, the light through the bamboo slats turning the room behind us to tiger stripes.

'What's that!' I cried out in genuine alarm.

31

'Oh, that.' She laughed contemptuously. 'That just means the dreaded bush fires have finally struck. Thank God. Finally something real is actually happening to all those turgid lives out there. Should shake 'em up a bit. What do you think?'

Later I discovered that seventeen people died in those Adelaide hills. They called it the Ash Wednesday Massacre. I wondered about that cigarette butt I'd thrown out the window. Oh well, I'm just a man. Correction, I'm just a human. I guess I don't really give a shit. How can I give a shit? If I did give a shit – where would I put my head? In the oven? There's no gas round here . . .

6

Remember the lesbians? Connections, connections – that's what you need if you want to get on when you're getting around. The gay world grapevine lead me to Melbourne and the house of Renaldo Monte-Video, the Panamanian theatre and film director famed – if not exactly around the world then certainly in Australia – for his keynote movie, 'Stepping around the Gum Tree'.

As Renaldo explained: 'One night, after an excruciatingly invigorating workout with a young and able seaman from Liverpool, I get the most fantastic of ideas. All my most incredible inspirations come after exercisings, as I relax in the steam room at the club . . .'

Renaldo turned away to light a long, gold-ringed menthol cigarette, exhaling the smoke almost instantly. 'You will understand,' he continued, 'I am sure, when I say I have always been adoring small children, and my love for them is pure. But of all these little ones my favourites have always been those innocents that society in its ignorance has labelled the Mongols.'

Renaldo breathed in massively, a hand flat across the palm trees of his yellow South Sea Islands shirt, his chest swelling to Jayne Mansfield proportions. 'Yes, I have always known they were the closest to God, so much love they have in their hearts.'

He went on tritely: 'It came to me then, I would create for them a play with the biggest budget, the best theatre, the most gorgeous costumes, top professionals – in fact, the whole of the works.' Renaldo squeezed my shoulder with pudgy fingers heavy with rings, overlong nails making a deep impression.

'And so, cap in my hand, actually a towel I seem to remember, I go straight to the top, to the Minister of Arts. One thing you must learn, Frankie, there is no door that stays closed when you are gay, always there are connections. This man is so simpatico. Originally he is granting me but ten minutes of his time. The interview runs into hours. I bring photographs. How do you say it' – Renaldo stroked my shoulder, furtively – 'comprising photographs?'

'Compromising photographs?' I suggested.

'Yes, yes, Frankie, that is the word.' Renaldo pouted. 'They are photographs of my whole career.' He pointed to the silver-framed picture of a Virgin Mary amid a vast display of exotic flora. 'Look at this face. Isn't she angelic?' Renaldo reached over to press the frame into my hand. Absently I noticed his palm was damp with perspiration.

'Wait a minute. Wait a minute.' More than astonished I exclaimed, 'Hey! Renaldo, it's you!'

He turned his head away, raising his chin on the stalks of his fingers. 'Dah-arling, don't you think my profile looks like Bette Davis or maybe Za-Za Gabor? I've never been able to make up my mind. With make-up, I can transform myself into the most gorgeous of creatures. I know I am beautiful.' He stroked his raven locks, then frowned suddenly. 'Even though I'm not looking my best at the moment. My flatmate Rex gives me so, so many problems. Poor darling, he's been through the wars recently.'

Tongue in cheek, I declared, 'Renaldo, to my eyes, you resemble a great noble eagle, even more magnificent than the eagles the Romans carried on their battle standards when they set off to war.' Even then I wasn't far off the mark, I'd rarely seen a nose more hooked.

Fluttering mascara'd lashes at a hummingbird's rate, Renaldo crossed his hands over his chest; then sinking back into the sofa, he imitated a swooning Solomon. 'Frankie! You have just paid me the most wonderful compliment I am receiving in my whole life.'

Suddenly he sat up, casting off his gay torpor, rubbing his hands vigorously. 'For that, we open a bottle of the very best tequila. We drink it all tonight. And you must tell me all about yourself. I want to know everything, dah-arling!' Renaldo moved a hand to my knee.

I stood up. Too quickly. 'Where do I find the drinks?' I asked, swaying slightly as I recovered from the sudden attack of dizziness.

Renaldo flapped a hand. 'Oh, there, darling, in the antique Sheraton corner cupboard. How do you like the furnishings? I have a flair for design, don't you think?'

I swivelled on the balls of my heels, drinking, no, scuba diving, into the three hundred and sixty-five degrees of it: wide bay windows faced out onto St Kilda beach (all those skinny-dippers) and just visible through all that awful eternity, the silver-twisted tips of Antarctic mountain ranges. I wondered if an iceberg was headed this way. Outside the window a seagull, wobbling on an up-draught, hung for a long moment staring Micawberishly into the room. I continued my turn, gulping down a cocktail of dizzy colours – hand-printed silk curtains, rivulets of cream, the brightest turquoise, the most brilliant of reds, criss-crossed by slashes of Sargasso green; and behind all this billowing, a stern discipline imposed by the heavy oak skirting framing the room. In the centre of the parquet floor a Persian carpet floated on the high-gloss lacquer: silk, maybe one hundred knots to the square inch. Automatically I appraised its value: five grand at any auction. The mantel of the large grey marble fireplace was frothing, nay cascading with theatrical mementoes, frilly clusters of high-kicking dolls, signed photos of gilded frames, dangling good-luck pendants. To my eye, this room, this shrine, resembled an over-the-top Catholic grotto. There, in a tarnished frame, was another Virgin Mary – no photo-trickery this time but a real medieval icon – praying before a candle; on each side were small, framed collages: Renaldo holding up the leaning Tower of Pisa with one hand; Renaldo dressed in archbishop's vestments leaning out from behind a curtain to kiss an ass, the head of a donkey turning round to show the beaming face of the Polish Pope in place of its own. I wondered if Renaldo was into de-frocked priests, buggering choirboys and Black Masses.

Reaching full circle, I broke my pirouette, stepping forwards to throw open big French windows. The terrace outside was a-riot with African violets, cascading spider plants, begonias, yellow-headed irises. Emerging out of this lush vegetation and set on a marble plinth were two life-size bronze statues of nude male ice-skaters, arm in arm. Many vigorous hands had left a patina on the raised and comely buttocks of the youths.

My head full to the bursting with this kaleidoscopic melange, I said, 'From my heart, Renaldo, it is all so beautiful. I think I could find peace in this room.'

Renaldo's whinny was that of a gazelle on heat. 'My dear boy, you will, and I make a promise, you are welcome to stay just as long as you like. But Frankie, before you sit down can you please remember to get that bottle of tequila and the Babycham glasses. I save them only for the most special of occasions . . . And be a dah-arling, bring also the sliced lemon and the salt.'

I passed Renaldo his glass. He patted the soft cushion of the sofa at his side. I sat down, leaning slightly away.

His voice reminded me of sticky hot-cross buns squashed under jackboots at a Conservative Party jamboree and oozing peanut butter. 'I was telling you about the play. Yes? And how we get the budget. In fact, I show you.'

Renaldo knelt down. 'You see, I get on my knees before the Minister like this.' Renaldo grabbed my legs and deposited his head on my lap like an over-

35

anxious spaniel. 'And then I finish him off saying, "I do not ask for my sake, but for the good of your very soul!"'

Renaldo stood up and, resuming his seat, pushed in close. 'Do you know what he replies to me?'

I shook my head dumbly.

Renaldo's eyes rolled. 'He tears at his hair and eyes, saying to me, "Tell me one thing or I go starkers mad. Why in God's name must you put on this play, *and* with Mongol children? Still I do not understand."'

Renaldo's grin slowly became a fox supping from a long, thin wooden spoon. 'I answer him with difficulty because my mouth it is so full at the time. "It is a mystery! And even to myself, why I must do this, but maybe by doing it, I discover the reason. This is how it is with all the great artists."'

I chuckled, 'Renaldo, he must have been very confused.'

Renaldo shrugged, looking to either side like a paraplegic who'd misplaced his arms. 'You know how it is with these bureaucrats, none of them understand life as do you and I. We are both heroes.' Renaldo raised his glass to salute me.

After a heroic pause for mutual reflection, Renaldo snorted, tossing back his mane of shiny black ringlets, 'Do you remember "Seven Brides for Seven Brothers?" First movie I ever see.' His puffy cheeks dimpled with pride. 'Always I am the odd one in the family. My father, you know, makes a fortune importing the first sewing machines into Panama, but then we lose every peso in the revolution. A great tragedee, but we soon recover. Our blood it is strong. My brothers each keep to the family tradition, all of them growing up to be tailors, marrying enormous fat Indian women from the hills who beat them up at weekends and give them babies, lots of babies.' Renaldo gestured with his hands like a contestant at a Guess-the-Baby's-Weight stall and sighed. 'You know, it is a very rough town, Panama City, like a Turkish bath but without the fun. In the open-air theatres you hardly can see the screen for the shadows of mosquitoes. I knew it is not for me, and I have to strike out. I arrive in Australia ten years ago, not one cent in any of my pockets. Three months later I am starring, and directing my first play. I even write it! But oh my God, Australians are so dumb, and even though I am always looking, I never yet meet an intelligent one!'

'But Renaldo,' I pleaded, 'you haven't told me, what happened with the play?'

Leaning over, flapping a hand down on mine from a hinged wrist . . patent nails, painted the deepest shade of crimson . . . Involuntarily, I shivered.

Sitting back, Renaldo coughed theatrically. 'Dah-arling, you would simply have adored it. Of all my successes that was the most fabulous. Never in my brothers' lives do they do such good work. The materials, the brocades, the set,

36

all are superb. The play you know, we are basing on the Merchant of Venice. Canals all with water, lighted from below, gondolas and mermaids. The Doges' Palace, a reproduction of an Egyptian temple, and the Doge himself, a mechanical skeleton in rusty armour bound to a throne, and all the time we have him vibrating, trying to break free of his golden ropes.'

Renaldo smiled beatifically. 'On the table at his side, the whole performance, a heart gushes blood, and at the end of the play the blood is deep at the bottom of the stage, so we must put the Mongols on stilts, suspending them with wires and running them around like trams. Fantastico!

'But out of everything, the most amazing of all happens back stage. One day in the Wardrobe Mistress's workshop I hear noises from a big basket of clothes. When I lift the lid I am discovering our leading boy making the most beaut-i-ful love with our leading girl. Such is their passion, they have no eyes except for each other. I realise that very in-stant, I am witnessing a true miracle, for all these children are segrated by sex in institutions. The whole of their short lives they are forbidden to know love. This is a terrible crime. Sometimes I cannot sleep at night for thinking about the tragedee of it . . .

'I realise then that God in his wisdom is appointing me for their protector. This love must go on. It doesn't matter the boy is eleven and the girl nine. And all through the months of the production we follow their affair on camera. Half the budget of the play is to make a documentary. The story of their love becomes the film . . .'

Renaldo beamed. 'After all the successes of the play, the premiere for the movie becomes the event of the season. We are absolutely besieged for invitations.'

Renaldo rolled up his eyes. 'Three thousand people in the auditorium, the Prime Minister, all the most famous and rich. The women, of course, they are the best, so beautifully dressed.' Renaldo frowned. 'But the men. Pah! So dull, and conforming, like undertakers, in horrible penguin suits. My brothers leave adhesive business labels on each one of the seats. They make a good business, and leave for home very happy, they know their wives do not beat them when they see all the money they bring to them.'

Renaldo stroked his hair, pouting victoriously. 'Nevair in the whole life of Australia has there been a sensation like this! The first five minutes is not even up, and half the audience is walking out. Ten people are injured in the crush, and before even twenty-four hours is up, the Minister of Arts is resigned. I feel sorry for him, always there has to be a victim.'

Renaldo sighed, then brightened. 'The whole country then, it is split up to the middle. I of course am banned from working for ever in New South Wales. It is the least I expect. If you had heard me speaking at all the marches and demonstrations you would have been proud. I am glorious. Then the film wins a prize at Cannes Film Festival, and I am invited here to Melbourne, and they give me the charge of the Opera House, and the authorities here who do not like the Sydney government they find for me this lovely house . . .'

Renaldo's tale was interrupted by the front door slamming. A basket of exotic foods topped by a large bunch of chrysanthemums emerged in the doorway, supported by bronze, athletic legs. A voice erupted excitedly from behind the smothering display. 'Oh Renaldo, I've had such a wonderful day, the sessions went extraordinarily well. Max promised he'd use the photograph on the next cover. But that's not all,' he continued. 'I met the most beautiful, beautiful boy, and I fell quite madly head over heels in love with him.'

The voice stopped short, breathless. Two arms settled the basket on the low coffee-table. Two accusing eyes looked at me. 'And who is this?'

I rose from my seat. 'Just what the north wind blew in. All the way from Scotland. Pleased to meet you. I'm Frankie.'

'Such a tantalising name, don't you think Rex?' Giggling, Renaldo collapsed back onto the sofa.

Rex smiled, hands on hips. 'Well you both sit there while I go fix some Panamanian coffee. And I hope you're staying, Frankie. I've got boeuf a la Jekyll and Hyde on the menu tonight.'

'Just so long as I don't have to go into the pot,' I murmured.

My sleep that night, on the sitting-room sofa, was undisturbed. I awoke in the early afternoon to the sounds of a key scratching in the front door – Rex returning early from his photographic session.

I lazed in the kitchen, enjoying all Rex's cosseting as he fussed over me, ridiculous in his frilly apron, treating me to garnished little nonsenses and endless cups of coffee, till my head was quite in a spin.

Leaning back in my chair and viewing Rex's almost androgynous face, I was struck by a feeling I'd seen him before some place. I guessed he was a reluctant forty-plus. A porcelain tracery of spreading hairline cracks suggested yawning crevasses deep inside. And then I realised I must have seen him more than a hundred times before, and in what poses! Uniformed in blue and gold, cool and debonair behind the wheel of a yacht, superbly disdainful, gazing past the teeming lines of commuters ascending and descending the escalators on the Bakerloo Line; sultry in silks, hiding behind a Rudolf Valentino smile and staring back at me as I numbly thumbed through magazines in dusty waiting rooms; yes, and attired in the sharpest of sharp Italian suits, a nymph on each arm, masterful and commanding against the backdrop of the Taj Mahal or the twin towers of the World Trade Centre.

But the image that popped out of my memory banks was of Rex standing beside a nine-foot-high bottle of malt whisky, all rigged out in Harris tweeds, a shotgun cocked in the crook of his arm, one brogued foot planted atop the neck of a twelve-pointed stag; a gamekeeper standing behind at a respectful distance, holding aloft a brace of grouse, the keen wind ruffling his red curly hair; in the background a swollen peat-brown river, a fat salmon leaping for a fly, the gloaming hills fading away forever in a leaching sunset.

Rex, the man with the one face that fits all, had spent half his life as an international model. But now, in this the twilight of his career, desperation leapt from sad whirlpool eyes. Here was a man in a male-strom sea flailing for anything to clutch onto. That log wasn't going to be me.

During my reverie I had been gazing fixedly down the long telescope that was the hall, and for a moment seemed to see myself from above as if I'd split in two and left my reflection hunched over the table, the round of his moonface framed by cupping hands.

I was jolted back to the table as the front door was thrown violently open, then glided mysteriously to a halt just a half-inch away from the doorstop. First one bronzed leg kicked into view, then another. Brown scissors clicking in mid-air, and out of a blur a small, bronze-coloured, grinning man with startling, glittery slit-eyes slithered into view. Glued to his forehead was a bandana sprouting feathers, plumes and . . . steam? May he'd just stepped out of a Turkish bath, and it was swirling around him yet.

I've got to be serious now. I *am* being serious. I'm only trying to describe the perilous state of mind I'd slipped into the moment the door was slung open and those feet did that nifty scissors kick. It seemed I'd deviated into another reality. I was wobbling, as if I was stood on the edge of a bottomless crevasse.

The slithery male took the hall in giant strides that belied his tiny stature, which was about five-foot two. But nothing puny about him. Here was a miniature Adonis scaled down to perfection, the same sharp edge about him as a Grecian statue.

'Huh?' I exclaimed in astonishment at his appearance: red satin hip-hugging boxer shorts; a yellow string vest festooned with fish-hooks; a fierce, noble face, as if cast in a furnace; a jaw broad and square as an architectural theorum; lips rolled back like a stage curtain to reveal a double row of snow-capped mountain ranges filed flat to perfection. I took him to be a Mongol pirate dropped out of one of Renaldo's more bizarre productions.

As he advanced our eyes lunched on each other's gazes. It was one of the most extraordinary feelings I've ever experienced in my life.

Without looking up from the sink Rex said, 'Did someone come in?' He half-turned, soap suds up to his elbows. 'Oh my God,' he muttered, advancing a step, hands out in front of him. 'Lobo.'

Lobo gestured in my direction. 'Is this the Scottisman you are telling me about this morning?'

Rex seemed to collapse inwardly before he replied. 'Oh yes, uh, Lobo this is Frankie. I'm sure you'll both get on like a house on fire.' He turned, resuming once more his position over the sink, a few degrees more hunched now.

For a long moment Lobo stood motionless, surveying me intently, one perfectly-manicured finger stroking his upper lip. A nail-clipper of a voice reminding me of a German U-boat captain in an old movie: 'Yes, you are the one.'

I was startled. 'What was that you said?'

Lobo raised his Japanese paint-brush eyebrows, shrugged. 'Oh, nothing in particular. It is just that I am having a voice that sometimes is telling me things. It is telling me I meet you here, today.'

I was unsettled by this, but saved from the necessity of replying by a dart from Rex, arcing across the room. 'Oh, Lobo's got all the superhuman qualities you know. He's a psychic, telepathic, an athletic, not to mention all that gleaming musculature.' He laughed bitterly. 'And it's all because he comes form the highest country in the world, Tibet, where all the people survive to be over a hundred years old. They live naked in caves at twenty-thousand feet, performing incredible feats of mind over matter.'

Ignoring Rex, I asked, 'Lobo, tell me. How'd you get your name? Surely it's not Tibetan.'

Lobo sat down and, reaching into his hip-pocket, pulled out a gold cigarette case and flipped it open. I noticed it was inscribed with the initials JHB.

'You like to smoke?' he said curtly.

'Yeah,' I drawled, picking nervously at the meticulously arranged row of cigarettes. Quixotically selecting the third from the left, I tried to lift it in langorous style, but only succeeded in dropping it into the small pool of coffee I'd spilled as Lobo bounded into the room. Lobo's eyes seemed to flicker disapproval. Ridiculously, I felt a sudden hot uprush of shame.

Lobo shouted over my shoulder, 'Hey, Rex! Please to throw me a dishcloth. There is coffee puddles, grains of sugar, they are scattered everywhere, and now a dirty wet cigarette too.'

'Oh my God!' Rex shouted. 'Has Frankie made a mess again. Renaldo and I have been trying to teach him the rudiments of civilised living but I'm afraid it's a losing battle. He's so stubborn.'

After Lobo had sponged the otherwise clean table down from end to end, then dried and polished it with a towel, he resumed his position on the chair opposite me. He leaned over, the open case in his outstretched hand. 'You care for a cigarette?' This time I managed to retrieve one without mishap. He selected another.

As Lobo pulled out a gold lighter, I noticed the same initials, JHB, on the lighter and on the cigarette I held in my hand.

Lobo smiled. 'You asked me about my name a moment ago.'

'Yeah,' I nodded brightly. 'I'd like to know.'

'Well . . .' Lobo took a deep draw, and smiled. 'You like Greek cigarettes?'

'Is that what JHB means?' I asked.

Lobo laughed briefly, 'No. You want to know about my name or not?'

I nodded.

He continued after a pause. 'I get my name in Arizona desert. I am jogging across Death Valley with a friend. He gives it to me after I am spying the coyotes hiding behind rock-es, I call to them and for a time they run beside us. They are liking us for the company, you know.' Lobo showed his teeth. 'My name it is meaning wolf in Spanish. I can tell you that with the exception of this man, all the Gringos I am meeting in America are stupids and asleep.' Lobo delivered this last remark deadpan.

'Really, Lobo? Surely not all of them.'

'Yesss,' Lobo hissed, the tip of his tongue like the head of a protruding little snake. 'All of them, full, to the brim with the dirt of their unclean lives. This I know.' Lobo flicked his cigarette into the empty, wiped and still wet ashtray before him.

I was confused by this statement, and so I said, 'You seem to have a firm grasp of the facts. Tell me, have you done a lot of travelling?'

'You ask one question, and I ask one question. OK? Now, I ask you the same question.'

'What?' I replied, even more confused.

Lobo frowned, eyebrows clashing Samurai swords. 'You know. You say it yourself. Have you been making travels much. Tell me something. I am making many enquiries.'

'Ah,' I said, 'um, oh, well, uh, I've been to a lot of places. Morocco, Algeria, Iran, Egypt, the overland trail through Afghanistan to Pakistan. India, south-east Asia generally. Oh, and I almost forgot. Egypt.

Lobo leaned forwards, 'Tell me something about that country. I am very interested in pyramid-es. We have a few in Tibet, you know.'

'Yes, pyramids,' I repeated as I sat back in my chair, wondering what I could say on the subject. I knew nothing about pyramids. Wriggling, I reached for the bag of grass deep in my pocket, then gummed cigarette papers together. I took care to manufacture a most deadly joint, selecting flower tips scattered through the mixture that was otherwise third-rate leaf-mould. I toasted the tip of the completed bomb on the flame, and with a flourish, as if conferring a signal honour, which I was, passed it over.

Lobo sat back in his seat, took a deep drag, and closed his eyes tight shut, assuming the stillness of a block of stone. His meditation was interrupted by a cupboard door slamming shut. Rex, tearing off his apron, shouted, 'I'm going to get some peace and quiet on the beach.' As he passed Lobo's side he stopped in his tracks, regarding him almost menacingly. His mouth twisted sourly. 'And I'll see you at the party. Otherwise, I'm going to be extremely upset.'

One of Lobo's eyes blinked open, coolly regarding the white flannel shorts as they hoisted Rex's frumpy buttocks up the corridor.

As the front door closed, Lobo said, 'You know, I am so glad he is leaving. I do not trust this Renaldo and Rex. Do not you realise? The both of them are like the trolls of the old tales, whose only plan is to entrap the passing traveller. You like to stay with trolls?'

I waved my hand, indicating the terrain. 'Oh, I don't know Lobo. I think they're pretty OK as trolls go, I mean, they're inordinately hospitable and I've got an idea that I might get a job with Renaldo on his next film.'

Lobo's lip curled contemptuously. 'I tell you, Frankie, you are the mountain with the cloud on his head. You do not see the land below. These trolls, they are not even men. They are the ants who would climb into your pant-es.' Lobo smiled, his voice softening. 'Listen, I have a car who is a bird that flies. I can show you the whole of Australia. My voice has told to look for you here and I know the why. You have a brain. Even though you are not yet knowing how to use it. I can help free the power that is inside you. Think about what I am just saying.'

Lobo stood up, his face deadpan once more. 'Tonight I promised Rex I will go with him to a boring party. I do not want to, but I give my word, so I will go. Tomorrow we leave this place.'

And without another word, Lobo strode out of the room.

Distantly over the rainforest hiss of the shower came the sounds of Lobo's happy singing.

Renaldo returned. Out of sorts, exaggeration being the better part of valour, I complained of a splitting headache. Renaldo suggested I might recover if I rested on his bed.

I was half-dozing when Rex flounced in, throwing wide the glass-panelled double-doors.

'Come along now Frankie, I don't believe all this about a headache, it will soon disappear.' Stooping over me, he breathed, 'I've got the most beautiful girl in Melbourne lined up for you. You'll absolutely swoon when you see her. She's an old friend, I know the type of men she fancies and I don't need a tape measure to know you'll definitely fit the bill.'

'Oh my God,' I moaned, wondering if my fly was open, rolling over on the lilac satin sheets. 'You'll have to go on without me,' I said, making my voice as mournful as I could, 'I feel terrible. Give my regards to the girl.'

Like Goldilocks in the house of the three bears, I did not mean to fall asleep. I knew that Renaldo's bed was dangerous territory. But it was so comfortable. I dreamed I was chased by a huge hyena, across an endless plain overhung with leaden clouds . . .

I was awaken by a fox snickering in a nearby bush – unmistakably Lobo with someone in the sitting room. Scratchings, snufflings, then a ginormous smacking kiss.

A girl's voice sharp through the thin walls: 'No, Lobo. Just cuddle.' And more loudly now, 'Hey, push off! I've got herpes.'

Lobo crooned, 'What is this herpes? Explain you please?'

Inaudible mutterings from the girl, then Lobo's voice boomed, 'This herpes it cannot touch me. I tell you, I am clean. It will be the water off the back of a duck. Listen, my darrleeng. I am only lying on top of you. I promise not to do anything.'

Bang crash as the door was thrown open: Rex and Renaldo. Rex's voice twanged like a broken violin string. 'I tell you, they're here in the front room. He's here with her. And I thought she was my friend, the bitch! As for Lobo . . .'

Renaldo's soothing voice interrupted. 'Now now, dear, I'll make you a nice cup of Milo and tuck you into bed. You're much better off without him. He's only a tease.'

Rex replied, 'It's not fair. I have no fun in my life.'

'Come, dear.' The sounds of Renaldo's reassuring hushes and Rex's perplexed expostulations receded down the hall. Once more I fell into a doze.

I was rudely awakened by Renaldo's hot hand on my naked thigh. I did not know how I'd lost my trousers. The last I'd seen of them the zipper was pulled up tight. I groaned, pretending a fevered dream. Next, Renaldo's hot breath steaming up my ear, 'Frankie,' he crooned, 'it's me, Renaldo.'

I sat bolt upright, pulling the sheets tight. 'Renaldo,' I exclaimed. 'What are you doing?'

Renaldo made a sad clown's face. He brushed a non-existent tear aside. His voice was crumbly as plaster of Paris. 'I was just hoping against hope. There's no harm in that, is there, dear boy? I had thought you were an oasis in the desert. But now, I know you're not one of us. I'll leave you to get some sleep.'

Leaning forward he planted a rosebud kiss on my forehead, squeezed my shoulder comfortingly. He closed the door quietly behind him. Then I heard the sounds of his timorous knocking on Rex's bedroom door, followed by the tremulous answer, 'Is that you Renaldo? Oh, come in dear, I need you.'

7

My dreams that night were of a highway stretching to eternity. A burning salt-dust road turned crystal by a sun cruel and unforgiving. Only emptiness around. In one hand an empty water bottle. Useless. I cast it away. With the other I was hauling a piggy-bag on wheels, as if the bikinis it contained were the last things on earth. The stubble sprouting on my chin encrusted with white from drinking at the saline pools which the road occasionally skirted. Overhead, a couple of black birds circling in silence. Sand gritting my eyes.

Prising open the lids, rubbing the sandpiper droppings from them, hard, surgical light incising my retinas. My head aching, as if it had been replaced by a hollow anvil, blood pounding inside with the force of a mighty blacksmith's hammer. Pulling the pillow over my ears, shrinking back into the territory of bedclothes.

A fearful piercing whistling noise. The room swimming into focus. Lobo is seated on the edge of the bed, a tuneful expression on his face, lips puckered like a Polo mint.

I had awoken into a reality I had no business belonging to. Nor was there any refuge in sleep. I was a castaway on a treasureless island, three thousand leagues from the Moluccan shore.

'Lobo,' I croaked. 'Do you have to make that dreadful noise?'

'Frankie, I thought you would be so pleas-ed to have this cockatoo on your nest, but instead I am finding you frowning in this way. The sun it is up, and yet you lie here. Are all Scottismen like this?'

'Wha-at? Cut it out, mate,' I groaned. 'I can't stand cheerful people in the morning.'

Lobo sprang to his toes and, selecting a stretch of beige tufted carpeting between the bed and wardrobe, threw himself into a handstand and viewed me for a moment through upside-down slit-eyes. He shouted, 'Frankie! So good it is to be a-li-ve!' Then, with the speed of a circus monkey, he flipped to his feet and regarded me with a mock-serious expression.

Attempting to gain some ascendancy on the day, and especially this grinning Tibetan ape, I demanded, 'Lobo, are you always like this in the morning? How long since you got up?'

Lobo rubbed his hands together vigorously. 'I have no need of sleep. Too boring it is. I sit here for one hour watching, wondering when you will wake. You sleep like a slug, and the fat pig in his bed does not snore so bad. Never I hear the like. Frankie, what you are needing is fresh air, sunshine. Do you want to live under a stone the whole of the life.'

I attempted a laugh at this apt description of how I felt. The laugh turned into a cough. Phlegm filled my mouth.

Lobo looked concerned. 'My gosh! And you are not well. You need to clean the whole body, the inside and out.'

'Cut it out,' I said firmly, rolling over and reaching for my trousers which I'd spotted crumpled beside the bed.

Lobo's mouth flickered disapproval as he pulled a thread of cotton from the sleeve of his one-piece light blue jogging suit. Turning his attention downwards, he dipped his fingertips into the gold of a long shaft of sunlight and began closely inspecting his nails.

'Well?' he said, as if to no one in particular. 'Have you made up your mind?'

'What mind? I don't have one. This morning I'm a zombie eggplant, I don't even recognise myself.'

Lobo laughed. 'Do you want to see the whole of Australia with me?'

I sat up, ruffling my feathers. 'I can't make up my brain. I have this overpowering need to make money. Everything I've got is tied up in grass and bikinis. I'd love to come travelling with you, but . . .' I shrugged. 'I've got the chance of a steady clientele here.'

Lobo spoke, more to the ceiling than to me. 'Frankie, you worry too much. We were destin-ed to meet, you and I. You are not even recognising yourself, but I know who you are. You need my help. You are not well. But after a few days on the road, I promise, you will be a new man.

'Listen.' He sat down beside me. 'You think to stay here for selling, huh? Well, I say this, these people are not helping you for nothing. If they take your money it is for the best, for otherwise they take your soul.'

He waggled a finger, 'The best place for selling grass in Australia, it is King's Cross, Sydney. You get the double the price, no problem. All the club-es I am knowing. Many people. There, I sell it all, and ask for nothing in return. I am not like you. I have no time for worrying about money. But' – he stood up briskly – 'you must give to me your answer, and now, for I am not staying in such a place any longer. I tell you it is because these peoples,' Lobo looked around, 'they are so sick, you are not well. They infect you, and if I were not a friend I would leave you to stew in their dirty juices.'

I sighed. 'Yeah, all right Lobo, you've got a deal, but only on one condition. You must positively guarantee to help me sell my dope. It's a matter of personal survival.'

Lobo proceeded to make a strange bird sound. It went something like this: *Doo-doo-doo-de-looo-de-looo-doot*, and involved a complicated motion between tongue and palate. All this while he was pirouetting around the room like a speeded up Scottish highland dancer.

'Frankie, I am so happy. We will be hunters together, companions of the road. We will have no need for women, and stupid things like this.' Dismissively he waved his hand toward the clutter of vibrators, creams and dildos on Renaldo's glass-topped dressing table.

Sucking in my breath, and holding it, I wondered: have I just made a cataclysmic mistake.'

Too groggy from sleep to bother about washing, I stumbled into the kitchen to find Rex piling clothes into a large straw Ali-Baba basket. As he looked up I noticed for the first time the metronomic twitch of his upper lip. Perhaps he'd developed it since I'd come to stay.

'Frankie, strangely early to see you . . .'

Casting a glance at Lobo, safely out of earshot as he closely examined his face in the hall mirror, I told Rex: 'I didn't have much choice in the matter. Our K-9 companion can be quite forceful.' I grinned as if re-tracking a happy memory. 'He's so full of rude health, don't you think?'

Rex arched an eyebrow, his nasal sneer adding a scaffolding of malice to his voice. 'If that's the way you like it. I suppose there's no accounting for taste.'

'Well buggers can't be choosers, dear chap,' I said imitating his bitchy high camp. 'Actually the darling boy is giving me a lift to Sydney. We're off this morning.' Not caring what he thought any more, I began to pick my nose. My headache had begun to subside. 'and what are you doing Rex?'

Rex leaned on the laundry and the creaking basket sagged under his weight. 'Oh, I've decided to clear out my wardrobe. D'you know how many jackets I've got? Forty-five. *Forty-five*. Each one a marker-point in my career, and each one the tombstone of a star I thought would never set. Finally it's dawned on me, all I've got to come is the trash-bucket at the end of the rainbow. It's bloody reality setting in.' He shook his head bitterly.

Jumping a track, he jerked up and began waving his hands in the air, 'And look at all these poor people caught in the bush fires. Whoosh! Suddenly your house goes up in a sheet of flames, and is just burned away. Everything gone.'

As if to remind himself of his corporality, Rex pressed his hands to his sides, moving them up and down. 'I have finally realised through that disaster that even though I'm at this terrible place in my life, there's some people even less fortunate than I. So I've decided to give my whole wardrobe to the poor victims.'

'What are you going to turn into, Mahatma Gandhi? Run around in a bath towel? No, seriously' – I pushed my palms out forestall his reply – 'I think it's highly commendable. Listen Rex, you should give me a bagful. I'll make a point of finding some victims on our way north. There were a lot of fires on the state border. You know what aid agencies are like, they'll keep such fine clothes for themselves!'

Rex massaged his brow. 'Oh well then, if you solemnly promise, I'll make you up a bundle.'

'I promise,' I said, rapidly criss-crossing my heart with a finger, then reaching for the blue blazer I fancied. This Pommie-Jock needed a new outfit.

The door to Rex's bedroom opened and Renaldo wobbled uncertainly into view, shuffling in fluffy purple slippers, dripping with the gardenias patterning his silk kimono, groaning and flapping his hands. 'Coffee, coffee. I am *so* worn out.' An old spaniel caught up in an overheated hair-dryer couldn't have looked more frizzled.

'Oh goddamnit!' Rex snapped, throwing down the shirt he'd been folding. 'I suppose I'll have to get it.' Reaching up, he selected the big cup labelled 'All Good Boys Deserve Fudge' and filled it from the jug on the stove.

'Anything else?' he demanded sarcastically, pushing it over.

Renaldo turned his face away saying, 'I need sugar. I can't face the world without sugar!' And then hanging his head to avoid Rex's glare he cajoled, 'Put in three, no put in four lumps . . . dear.'

Rex, furious, bruised the lino and his heel. 'I WILL NOT. Only three days into your diet and your nerve goes. You should be ashamed of yourself. Look at that paunch.' He prodded the bulge then, switching the attack, pointed to Renaldo's frizzled head. 'And look, grey hairs already. Next they'll be carrying you out in a wheelbarrow. Really, I don't know why I live here. It's such a bloody circus. And I thought we'd agreed it was strictly nice boys only. And you pick up such riff-raff.' He folded his arms, staring at me icily. 'And I've had quite enough of YOU!'

Renaldo banged his cup down, slopping coffee on the red-tiled breakfast bar.

'And I've had enough of *you*!' His voice broke into a ghastly falsetto. 'You're such a nag, Rex. Frankie's my guest, and he can stay as long as he likes.'

Rex piped in joyfully, 'Oh but Renaldo, didn't you know? Frankie's leaving today. And I pray he never, *never* comes back.'

Renaldo implored me, palms supplicating: 'Frankie, what is this?' Above the puckering eyebrows, a multitude of limbo-ing worms.

'You know how it is Renaldo. I've got to go. Lobo's offered me a lift up to Sydney, so . . . I've got to go.' I laughed nervously, suddenly embarrassed.

As Renaldo slumped down over the breakfast bar, Rex reached over to wipe the spilled coffee around his cup. Renaldo jerked up, slapped the hand away, yelling, 'Really Rex! Leave me alone. You're always fussing. God, I can't stand you sometimes.'

Rex stiffened. 'Well I can't stand you either. We're supposed to be sharing this house and it's always your friends who come around. I never get any peace, and I'm expected to clear up all their messes. And yours too. Oooohhhhrrr!' He started vibrating like a clockwork dildo.

I felt an insistent tug at my elbow. Leaning his head towards the door, Lobo murmured, 'Are you ready to go? Now?'

'Just a moment.' I turned. Rex's eyes were a clown's bouncing on springs. Hesitantly I ventured, 'Uh . . . Er . . . Rex?'

'What is it?'

'You were going to give me a bundle for the bush-fire victims. Remember?'

Rex grabbed a black plastic bag filled with clothes, thrust it into my arms. He pointed to the door. 'Take it and GO! My whole life has started falling apart since *you* came.'

Renaldo began screaming in a high C. 'DON'T DARE TO TALK TO MY FRIENDS LIKE THAT!'

I left them at it, going hammer and tongs.

Returning to the sitting room in search of my things, I almost tripped over the girl trussed up in a quilt on the floor. Long coiling locks spilled over patchwork silk. The hand that flicked back the curls was aristocratic to the point of being skeletal. Her ivory cheeks were stained with comic mascara runs, the eyes distrustful. But what briefly fazed me was that double-visioned lipstick-smeared mouth, as if she wasn't tuned in quite right. Tossing her head back she addressed me haughtily, as if I were a galley slave and this her galley. 'Where is Lobo? I want to see him now!'

I smiled crookedly. 'Oh, don't worry, he'll be coming. He's busy at the moment.' I reached over her – 'Excuse me, dear, there's a bag of mine in the corner behind your head' – to grab the handles of my bag. I tried to swing it wide but a corner caught the quilt, ripped it back to reveal a bony shoulder and a small, pointed, freckled breast. Attempting to pass myself off as a gentleman, I averted my gaze towards the marble fireplace.

She exploded, the spear of her astringent wrath leaping for my ear. 'Ain't you seen a bleedin' tit before? Gawd almighty, bluddy men.' She levelled a finger. 'Just you tell that jackass Lobo to come here at once. I need to see him.'

'OK, OK. I'll tell him.' I retreated backwards, smiling and keeping a firm grip on the piggy-bag and all my worldly wealth.

'Haven't you got a cigarette?' she shouted. 'I'm going to go out of my mind if I don't get a cigarette.'

'All right, all right.' I waved around the doorpost, 'I'll see you get one. Back in a minute. Don't move.'

I almost bumped into Lobo, still preening himself in front of the gilded mirror. Shrill voices streamed from the kitchen. Lobo indicated the contretemps with the merest incline of his head. 'You hear how it is with these people? Lift the lid on their stinking lives and all you see is the sheeet.'

I jerked my thumb over my shoulder. 'And what about her?' She wants a cigarette.'

Lobo's lips curled. 'She needs a penis more than a cigarette. All these women want to be men. She is trash. I care nothing for her any more. And now, are you ready?' He raised an eyebrow. 'I am so sick for this waiting. Here, I will help you.' He eased the black plastic bag from my grasp. 'Ahhh,' he breathed, examining the collar of a folded shirt, 'silk . . . And Christian Dior. Oh, this it is very nice.' He grinned foxily. 'I think maybe we work well together, Frankie.'

'Lobo, before we go I've got to say goodbye to Renaldo and Rex.'

'You want to say bye-byes to peoples like this? For why?' He shook his head in bewilderment. 'Listen to them.'

Rex was shouting, 'You fucking tart. I didn't suck his dick. You're just upset because you wanted to suck his dick.'

Lobo continued icily, 'You want to take a bath in dirty words such as these? No, I do not think so. Not even you. And now,' he growled, 'you want to stay? You stay.'

I did not say a word as I followed him out. The door snicked behind me. No rat ever felt dirtier deserting a sewer for the main stream.

Beaconsfield Parade – the wide, busy road stretched before us, cars parked nose to tail by the low wall of the esplanade, high tide slapping the deck.

Lobo led me to the corner of the block and, laying a hand on my arm, pointed to a gleaming white pick-up parked under a lamp-post on the side-street.

'There it is,' he breathed, 'my Baby.'

I trailed my fingers along the taut black rubber tarpaulin covering the open back. Not a scratch on the lustrous deep-waxed paintwork. This baby was a late-model homegrown Ford Falcon Ute pick-up.

Inside the cab – showroom condition, not a trace of occupation. Seated in the driver's seat, Lobo had begun swishing at the dashboard with a feather duster. He looked up, a huge grin stealing his face. 'What do you think? She is a beautiful. No?'

He suddenly lunged forwards and pushed his hand at me. Disconcerted, I gripped just the fingers, not the palm. The handshake was angled, crooked. Lobo's eyes narrowed to impossible slits. Looking me up and down, he said, 'Always there is much to tell from the handshake. You notice? Mine it is above yours. This it is not good.' Letting my hand go, he raised a finger. 'I will say this, and listen well for I do not repeat myself. One day you will take my hand and we will meet as equals. This I know.' Lobo tapped his head twice and smiled briefly, like a glimpse of the sun through a crack in a dark cloud.

We had been travelling for perhaps five minutes through city streets, when Lobo, who had seemed to be settling in for the long journey ahead, made another disconcerting manoeuvre, drawing up sharply in front of a grey concrete two-storey house.

'Why are we stopping now?'

Lobo frowned. 'I have some things to pick up. And I must to say bye-byes to my friend. He will be sad it is you and not he I choose to travel with. I have been staying some weeks with him, and I think in that time I help him, and he changes much for the better. Come, I wish for you to meet with him.'

Lobo, a three-steps-in-one-leap man, had already entered the building. The front door was glossy brown, the hall painted in two shades of the same colour – cream and shit. There was no furniture, and the carpet, predictably brown, had hessian backing showing through in places. Daylight filtered through sackcloth curtains. Pushing open a thin hardboard door I stepped into another café-au-lait room. All the walls were covered in lumpy woodchip paper; the plaster bulged.

Lobo was talking to a giant buttoning his shirt over a T-shirt. The lower part of his uncovered, protruding stomach was of the palest white and scaled with black hairs. But I'm hovering on the edge of a subject. This man-beast's absurd, top-heavy, muscled bulk withered down to pipe-cleaner ankles. In his clinging black fishnet tights he seemed positively medieval, as if these were undergarments for a suit of armour.

The only furnishings were a sturdy black high-backed wooden chair with a dog-chain and a collar hanging from the top bar of the back, one square table and, in a corner, expensive-looking photographic equipment – lights, tripods and cameras.

Lobo waved me into the circle. 'Frankie, I want you to meet my friend Jesus Terre-Blanche.'

Anticipating a crusher, I winced as he took my hand in his huge palm, but the grip was strangely flaccid. Remembering the recent homily on handshakes, I puzzled over what category this one fitted into and, more to the point, what was that smell, only partly covered up by the stink of antiseptic?

Uh . . . And then it came back to me, the smell of a brothel I once visited in Paris: semen and carbolic. Yup, I'd clocked it. This was a male bordello, probably specialising in S & M, and where Lobo had no doubt starred in those photo-sessions.

Lobo interrupted my cogitations. 'Frankie, I am wanting to talk to Jesus on my own. Please to take to our car my bag which is by the door.'

I was only too glad to escape. After a few minutes Lobo emerged onto the top step, followed by the mighty Jesus. They embraced. The giant seemed unbearably distraught. Above their heads, on the glass panel over the door was a faded gilt inscription: *Gethsemane*. Lobo kissed Jesus on both cheeks.

Melbourne was a long way back and the fuel gauge dipping into the red when I suggested I'd pay for the first lot of petrol.

Lobo nodded curtly. 'If it makes you happy to get the petrol, you get the petrol. We are approaching a garage here.'

I replied bravely, 'We might as well get everything straight from the start, huh? If I get the first lot and we fill the tank, you can get the next lot, and we can go on like that.'

Lobo appeared bored. He gazed out the window. 'OK Frankie.'

I wasn't prepared for the total I read on the pump. Thirty-seven dollars! Drawing forty bucks from my moneybelt, I passed the notes out to Lobo, who'd been locking the petrol cap. Settling back in my seat, I removed the uncomfortable money-belt to count my wad as Lobo walked to the garage shop.

Two hundred and three dollars in crumpled notes. Smoothing them out, I counted again. One-hundred and ninety three. What was wrong with my brain? Ever since I'd gotten up this morning I'd been like a punch-drunk somnambulist. I decided, out of pure laziness, I'd been right the first time.

Surreptitiously I tucked the belt under the rubber matting beneath my seat, concealing the bulge with my bag of grass.

'Hey!' Lobo bounced up and down in his seat like a deprived child on a trip to Blackpool. 'Frankie, I am so pleasing. I feel for the driving. It is so good to have the road up ahead. You not mind if we do not stop till night-time. You roll the joints and put on the sounds. The cassettes are in the glove compartment in front of you, as well as the map. I have cigarette papers.'

We're on the road to nowhere moaned the raucous voice of the singer as Lobo keyed the ignition.

We'd been travelling for hours it seemed, through scantily-populated, rolling-pasture country. The odd herd of black-and-white cows in a big wide field reminded me of the English countryside; but when I thought about it, this was as thin margarine compared to the fat of the English land.

Thumbing towards a farming complex in the distance surrounded by a cluster of spindly trees all the same height, I remarked, 'Not much evidence of bush fires around here, huh?'

'You want to see bush fires?'

'Not particularly,' I laughed. 'But I promised Rex I'd hand out some clothes. I've got it on my conscience.'

Puzzled, Lobo played a frown. 'You worry too much for these peoples. Do not you know they are making money from the insurance. Next year they buy a bigger house, and no wurries.'

'You've got a point, Lobo. With all those gardening tools in the back we could make ourselves some real readies. We've just got to find a stricken area. The companies will be writing out blank cheques. If we got it organised we could get other people to do the work.'

Lobo nodded sagely. 'This is true. In Sydney one time I am needing for money, so the first house I am finding with the garden a mess, I knock on the door. The lady she is most pleas-ed to see me. It is not a hard work. Just take a pile of leaves from one place to another. I love to make the world tidy. At night I sneak plants from the parks. After two days the garden is much more nice. But I do not feel for this work any more. Frankie, I have so much to show you.'

As he indicated the vast panorama beyond the horizon, Lobo was struck by a beam of the setting sun. His skin shone like burnished bronze, his teeth a blizzard in his wide square mouth, his pupils dark as beetles' wings, his voice a razor chopping words out on a spotless mirror.

8

My gnawing stomach was a Davy Jones's locker full of rats scuttling. No manna in sight, just the uncluttered emptiness of Australian night. A string of broken pearls had scattered into the constellations of Scorpio and the Southern Cross. I couldn't recall having seen a single car for hours. I rolled another joint to forget the hunger pains. We shared it in silence, the veil of smoke as dense as a fog-bank between us.

Lobo brought the car to a sudden and unexpected halt – just stopped dead on the straight two-lane road, so dark with overhanging trees. He was half out of the cab before I could react. 'Where the hell are you going?'

Lobo said grimly, 'I am not going to any hell. I am going to make pee-pee!' He pointed to his eyes, mockingly. 'Always watch for the bad fellow, sneaking.' The door snicked shut and that was it, he was gone, disappeared, like this was a Hitchcock film set and someone had pulled the switch.

Blinking, I attempted to focus red-rimmed eyes. Not a sign of his blue jogging suit anywhere, only rumours of vegetation, gathering cloaks of inky turbulence. Reaching over I turned on the cassette. Nothing happened. Damn it. Lobo had taken the keys.

Slow time passed on a slow boat to China. We hit a typhoon near Tasmania, almost capsized on a reef near Bangkok. Three thousand leagues, then we were taken by pirates in the Bay of Molucca, preferring to scuttle the ship rather than see it falling into their hands.

Jumping out of dreamtime, I sat bolt upright, rigid with annoyance. Lobo had been gone for at least half-an-hour.

A grey shape swam out of the darkness about twenty feet distant, a wolf on oiled castors, gliding in to view. Hanging from his arm was a wickerwork basket topped by a red and white checked cloth, neatly tucked in around the rim.

Lobo opened the door. 'Now you get out Frankie, we must make ready for the meal. Here. Take these.' He passed over a knife and fork rolled in a red serviette.

Bereft of speech, I watched incredulously as Lobo flourished the cloth across the seats and then, as a conjuror dipping into his hat, lifted two shiny dinner plates from the basket, laid them side by side on the cloth and, for his next trick, produced a frosted bottle of German white wine and suggestively tucked it upright in the space between our seats. Stretching over, he pressed the corkscrew into my palm. 'You can open bottles, I am hoping?'

Resuming the task in hand, he began efficiently filling up the plates from containers in the basket: a chicken breast, and a leg each, then potato salad and a dollop of coleslaw; a couple of celery sticks, black olives, itsy-bitsy pastry cakes stuffed with cod roe. My mouth watered as he unrolled the bomb from its spiral silver sheath – a loaf of steaming garlic bread, fresh from the oven.

In utter disbelief, I punched a hole in the silence. 'Lobo . . . Jeez, it's unbelievable, I mean, where the fuck did you get all this?'

A cloud of the darkest fury tracked his brow. 'Frankie,' he growled. 'At this moment, it is shame I am feeling for you. Do not you realise when a person swears it is the same as the droppings of dogs falling out of the mouth?' He seemed to be having problems with his breathing. 'I would not say this if I was not your friend.'

My jaw hung slack. 'Lobo . . . I'm sorry, I didn't mean to offend you. Try to understand – I'm shocked. Can you explain, please, how you managed to get all this stuff? I was worried. God! It seemed like you'd been gone for hours. I mean, did you run all the way back to Melbourne to get a carry-out, or what? It's only that I'd like to know.'

Lobo rolled his eyes. 'I am finding a house, I go in. It is a nice house . . .'

'Ahrrm . . .' I coughed. 'Lobo, could you start from the beginning. What is this house? And where did you find it.'

'I am making pee-pee, when my Voice it is speaking to me: *Walk a while from the car.*' Lobo shrugged. 'Always I listen for my Voice. It is nice just to stroll, is it not?' He smiled disarmingly. 'After maybe ten minutes I am seeing the light and my hand it is finding the gate, my Voice it speaks to me then: *Follow the path, the door of the house it is open. What are you needing you find inside.* It is a big house. Peoples talking upstairs. In the kitchen, all this nice food laid out.'

'And you took it?'

'Of course.' Lobo's eyebrows registered blank amazement that I should even ask. 'It is waiting for us. So for why not? You know, I am making a phone-call to a friend. For maybe ten minutes we are chatting. Then I am finding this basket. I like to make everything nice. You like this cloth?'

I exploded, 'Fucking hell, Lobo! That's . . . that's stealing!'

Lobo barked: 'I should not be having to tell you again, clean the filthy muck from your mouth. I think maybe these people they are lucky. They leave their door unlock-ed. Another fellow he takes everything. I am not a-greedy. I only take what we need. And all the way back I am thinking to myself of the look on your face when you see this, and how you clap me on the back and say, "Hey, Lobo, we have a party." But instead you complain in this way. You tell me I am stealing?' He shook his head slowly. 'No, I do not think so. But I do know it is a favour I am giving these peoples. From now on they are the more careful. Really Frankie' – he frowned in puzzlement – 'I am not understanding you.'

I did not say anything in reply. In a way, I agreed with Lobo. I did not understand myself either, and I knew there was no way I was not going to partake of this feast spread out so temptingly before me.

It was then that a voice spoke, seemingly from within my head. *Listen to everything this man tells you. Do not reject any of what he says or does.* I wondered if I'd been infected by the plague. Was I cohabiting my cranium with another personality? Who had spoken?

I did not realise how hungry I was. The food was unbelievably good. I couldn't get enough of it into my mouth at one time. I felt infantile, orally fixated.

Lobo had wrapped his chicken leg in a serviette and was holding it delicately between thumb and forefinger. Swallowing daintily, he regarded me severely. 'You know, I am thinking to myself, my friend Frankie, he never has a mother to have manners so bad. Tell me, do you live in caves in Scottisland? From the way you behave it seems so.' He curled his lip derisively.

Deliberately wiping my mouth with the back of my sleeve, I stared back at him. Taking a slug of wine from the bottle, I noticed the sudsy rim of half-processed proteins I'd deposited last time.

Lobo's slit-eyes hardened to bullet peas. He pointed. 'Look! You are a Godsent gift to Chinese laundrymen. I am serious you know. Even though I make a joke. Do not laugh.'

I viewed him evenly. 'Lobo, don't even contemplate trying to change me, it's a waste of time. I've got seven sisters, three grannies, and more aunts than a warren full of bunnies, and I haven't even mentioned my wife. She's the equal of ten of them, if nagging were the measure. By Christ, how she used to moan. Bonemeal I'd be now if I hadn't been made of sterner stuff . . . ' I took another bite. 'And one more thing. Don't go slagging off Scotland, mate.' I jabbed at him with the chicken leg. 'You're Tibetan, right?'

Lobo nodded, the grin emptying all expression from his face.

'I've heard that in Tibet, when the winter winds come, the "peoples" sew themselves into their clothes for six months, and of course they never wash. You have a saying, do you not? "Two fleas make a summer."'

Lobo frowned angrily. 'Where do you hear this rubbish? Peoples write many lies about my country. I do not believe it.'

Casting the bone over my shoulder and out the window, I leaned over. 'Pass me another drumstick.'

Lobo shook his head. 'There are none left. If you are yet hungry, it is because you gulp so. I chew my food forty times.'

An iron band seemed to be tightening around my head. An iron band *was* tightening around my head. Bastard. I could feel it, with my fingers. Christ, if this was round two of a contest between Tripitaka and Monkey, this time it was Tripitaka with the iron hat on. It occurred to me my fingers might be greasy. What the fu— what the heck do I care . . .

'If I'm still hungry, it might just be because I'm bigger than you. Look' – I leaned over, pulling at my belt buckle – 'I'm losing weight!'

'Frankie, I not want to look into your trousers.' Lobo turned away. 'You know, all this time I am thinking to myself, the whole fault it is not all on you for behaving the way you do. Always the parents they must take some blame. Now, I will tell you why your ears they are so fill-ed up with the dirt. It is because of all the dirty words you are speaking. But I do not worry. My Voice it is telling me, in time you learn, and meanwhile, you are good for prak-tik-ing my patience.' Lobo grinned, 'You see, always I am looking on the bright side of the house.'

Jesus, Mother of God have mercy on me.

I waved my hand deliriously, as if this was a valid technique for casting off devils. 'Can't we talk about something else apart from this dirt. For instance, how come a Tibetan has a bloody German accent?'

Lobo snapped, 'I do not speak with a "bloody" German accent. Now, if you are ready, we clean up, and please to make an effort.'

One by one he placed all the empty containers into the basket, gathering the corners of the checkered cloth, making sure nothing spilled. Smiling amiably, I flicked the crumbs from my seat onto the floor.

'Is this how peoples live in Scottisland?' Lobo roared, truly angry now. 'My gosh! You must be cleaning up your mess immediately. This it is a small house and the both of us have to live in it.' Reaching behind his seat he brought out a tiny pink dustpan and brush set. 'Take this. I do not drive until the floor it is spick and spam!'

'OK, OK, anything to keep you happy.' Bending reluctantly to the task I was careful to keep my butt turned away. 'When are we going to get some shut-eye? Don't you ever get tired?'

Lobo's glare was a rod of Prussian steel. 'Frankie, I do all the driving and I am not in the least bit tiring. So what is it is wrong with you? All you must do is roll the joints. Hey, Frankie, do not you think this straw-work is so nice?'

Jesus, what was he on about now?

Finishing my brushing, I looked up. Lobo stood in the headlights, holding the basket in the beam.

'You see how the people make this? Out of sticks in the field. They are smart. No? One day maybe it comes in handy for making disguise.' He sat it down on the ground, pulled out the checked cloth. 'Look, if I wrap this around my stomach' – he lifted the basket again – 'and carry this on my arm like so, I only need a walking stick and I am the fox who is playing grandmother in Little Red Riding Hood? You know this story?'

He must have seen the incredulous look on my face. No? This it is not the picture? He lifted a finger. 'Wait one minute, I show you.'

Turning his back, he marched to the side of the road and, shaking the basket vigorously, emptied out all the rubbish onto the grass.

'Now I wear the basket on my head, like this, and the cloth around my shoulders like so. It is better. No?'

I stepped forwards, appalled. 'Good God, Lobo, you can't go chucking crap about like that. It makes a mess for everyone.'

Listen to me,' Lobo growled. 'Everyone, they do not care for me, so why should I care for them? I like to keep the Baby clean. Is there anything wrong in that. These peoples in Australia, they care nothing for their country, so why should I?'

He removed the basket from his head. 'I keep this. It is good for putting my sunglasses in. I have a collek-ton. Is this the correct way to say the word?'

Lobo had walked to the rear of the Baby and was tucking the basket under the tarpaulin. He continued, filling in my silence like a crossword puzzle. 'Frankie, listen, we make a deal. You help me to speak the good English, and I help you to clean yourself. I try to be patient. But I must tell you, I know it will be difficult.'

Back behind the steering-wheel, Lobo was drumming his fingers impatiently. 'Are you ready? In one hour and a half we find a town call-ed Wagga. If you are still tiring you can rest before we reorganise.'

The glow of Wagga was a torch-beam beckoning. As we approached the outskirts, I noticed the needle of the petrol gauge hovering over the red. I piped up, 'Well, looks like this town is just in time. Your turn to get the petrol. I'll keep a look-out for an all-night garage.'

Lobo looked contemptuously. 'I do not need you to look. I know a place which is always open, every day and every night of the whole year.'

I sat back, prepared to be surprised.

Wagga was Anytown, Anywhere, Australia: squat bungalows dipping and rising with the undulating terrain beneath; wide suburban streets scattered with cars and fringed with overhanging trees; the occasional street-light casting an orange pool. It must have been late, for apart from a few leaves drifting from the tree canopy above nothing stirred.

Lobo brought the car to a purring halt in a patch of darkness, the street-light across the road casting his features in bronze. He commanded me like a Caesar: 'Frankie, do not move from the car' — the raised finger — 'and no sleepings on the job. Always there are sneaky fellows.'

'Uh, yeah, I know.'

The only sneaky fellow I could see was my lupine friend, circling to the back of the Baby. I heard the popping of the toggles that held the tightly-stretched tarpaulin. In the wing-mirror I saw him reach inside and place a pair of chunky-soled running shoes and a camouflaged army-style jacket on the deck. Swiftly he changed his shoes. Then, as he slipped his arms into the jacket, I noticed the lining was divided by many thin pockets, each snugly encompassing a variety of tools. It was then that the fluttering snowflakes of my doubts became bouncing tennis balls.

More tinkering in the guts of the bird: hey presto, a couple of khaki-green petrol cans — and I almost missed the last trick, as he conjured a two-metre length of hose out of the very sack of night, inducing it to coil into the palm of his hand.

My chest tightened. So this is how Lobo gets petrol? I sighed. Well, I suppose it's his concern, his crap. I guess I'll have to put up with the nagging dingo, until we've sold all the grass and the rest of the bikinis in Sydney. Then I'll take off like a fucking fudge-driven rocket. That soothed me for a while, watching my rocket's vapour-trail glimmering out into the night. Scratching a trail to . . . wherever. Another dead planet. Shit. Try the red shift.

About half-an-hour later, Lobo returned. No, he didn't return — I don't wish to imply there was anything normal about his reappearance. He floated down, along with the snowflakes and tennis balls, an ethereal being descending from a cloud above. In each hand was a five-gallon petrol can. Now he was tap dancing by my window like a slit-eyed Fred Astaire.

'Frankie, Frankie,' he crooned, 'I am finding two beaut-i-ful full-up cars around the corner.' Lobo put the cans down. 'You know, I think all Australians sleep with the mouths open like the sheeps. Nothing here that interests me. We drive on. In Bathurst you rest.'

I leaned out the window. Lobo had stopped dancing. He raised his hand, Indian fashion. 'If you are going to offer to help, I do not need it. I fill the tank. We have another two hundred miles in these cans. You roll a big joint of grass and make it a pure one. I do not like the way you mix tobacco with it. It gives me a headache.'

9

Passing over the pure grass spliff, I asked, 'Lobo, why don't you tell me about your family in Tibet. And, ah . . . How the heck do you speak with a German accent?'

'One question at a time.' Lobo raised a pinkie, inhaling deeply, the double emissions escaping his clenched teeth to conjoin in a dragon's weave. 'I am twenty-six years old, but already I think my life it is the three to the one of yours. Hey, you know, this grass it is good, and the better for no tobacco, I feel myself getting ston-ed.'

'Lobo,' I growled, 'you don't start a story by a evading the subject.'

Rolling down his window, he flicked the ash into the slipstream. 'OK. You want to know? It is because you are my friend I tell you, but you must promise to tell no other. My Tibetan name is Djorji. It is meaning, "Little Sunrise". When I am three years old, the Chinese invade my country. My parents they flee, along with many other peoples from our village.'

I interjected. 'The word is "people", Lobo.'

Lobo showed me a mouthful of gleaming teeth. 'Thank you Frankie, and now, may I continue?'

Nodding dutifully, I assented, concealing my smile with difficulty.

Lobo continued in a matter-of-fact voice: 'It is a high pass over the Him-al-yas where the soldiers they are ambushing us . . . ' He paused to pass back the joint. 'My parents, the other peoples, the yaks, goats, all the animals, are shot. The Chinese spare my sister and myself, for the reason they are fearing much the spirits of the mountains, so they leave us for a sacrifice to the wind and snow. My sister she chooses to die, and soon she is dead.'

'How so?' I said, croaking on the smoke.

Registering puzzlement with raised eyebrows, Lobo shrugged. 'It is because she decides it.' Lobo tapped his chest. 'For me, I am choosing to live. I do not know how long it is I wander, but maybe it is for weeks. For eating I am digging under the snow, finding worms and bugs, even the earth. Many times I am sick. And then comes the part I am not recalling. Another escaping party find me. All night around the fire they are hearing the Yeti roaring, and then as the light is coming, it is I who walk into the circle. The spirits of the mountains, they do not want me to die.

'Then for a time there is a camp in India, and one day the nice nurses are tying a label round my neck with a red cross on it and putting me in the stomach of a big bird. When I wake up, the peoples they are all white in the face . . .'

Lobo frowned. 'Do not snigger, this it is how I remember it. Of course the bird it is the plane of the Red Cross, and this place I am waking up, where all the peoples are white, it is Switzerland. This I am finding out later.'

'I remember very well the first time I am meeting with my new parent-es, and the tears I am crying, but then my Voice it speaks to me, *This it is now your life, and you must take it.*'

Lobo smiled, almost wistfully. 'My new parent-es are calling me Peter, from my father, and Justice, after my new family's name.' His face brightened. 'Frankie, I am wishing at this moment I could show you my family's house. It is in a small town below the Matterhorn. From the outside it is black timber, white plaster. Inside the rooms are all lining with wood, the most old house in the town. And so very beaut-i-ful.'

'What? So beautiful?' I said, passing back the half-smoked spliff.

Toking deeply, Lobo continued, one hand – absentmindedly? I doubted it – reaching out to pick some invisible grain of dirt from the instrument panel. 'Always I am a-lucky. It is a good mother I find. Never you are seeing a home so clean and tidy, always she is polishing, polishing. Even the cuckoo in the clock, every day his nose gets a rub. Such a lucky fellow. A Scottisman finds it a problem if he wears the famous kilt, the floors they shine so. Never a speck of dust anywhere.'

Lobo leaned over holding the joint up for grabs.

Silently thanking God I did not have such a mother, I carefully tipped the ash into the ashtray.

Lobo's knuckles showed white on the steering-wheel. 'Look a-here, you dirty fellow, how many times must I tell you, do not make messes in my car.' He pointed. 'Dirt in there it makes the car to smell.'

Another tightening of the iron band around my temples. 'Good God, Lobo, there's no need to go flying off the handle. That's why they put ashtrays in cars, for the fucking ash.'

More lectures on the dirt that comes out of mouths of Scottismen, and the dirt that should go out the window.

I sighed, wondering at which University of Life they might run courses for dealing with such recalcitrants. Meditatively, I sucked on the last of the joint, then tossed it into the slipstream.

The roach, selecting a boomerang flightpath, showered me with ash and touched down somewhere behind my seat.

Guiltily I turned to Lobo, spreading my hands wide as if to say it wasn't really me who was responsible.

Lobo shouted harshly, 'Why always are you making such messes?'

Twisting around in my seat I located the roach. This time I made sure it did not return. 'I'm sorry, Lobo. Now, could you please resume your story.'

Lobo pursed his lips. 'You are good for listening, and for that I will go on. You are not tiring?'

'No,' I lied, amazed at such solicitude. 'I'm feeling much brighter now.'

Lobo's lips rolled back, revealing his showroom of perfect teeth. 'You know, my father he is a dentist. The best in the whole of Switzerland. I think maybe even he could repair teeth as rotten as yours. Also he is a Jungian dream-analyst. People fly from all over Europe, get their teeth to be fixed and their minds to be read.'

I laughed. 'And pockets emptied, no doubt.'

Laying his eyebrows low, Lobo glared, his pause registering intense displeasure.

'When I am a boy, always you know I am trying hard to please peoples, but many times they are finding fault, not with what I do, but for other reasons. I have problems in understanding this. The first day I go to school, I am truly shocking, I do not know there are peoples such as this in Switzerland. My parents never make me feel different, but these children they call me names like zip-eyes. This is because I am half-closing to see them the better. The first time I walk home alone, the bad ones throw stones at me. Once twenty of them cover me in mud.'

Lobo scowled. 'Yes, they say in Switzerland such things do not happen. There are no racialists, and they are so clean. But I know better. The dirt they hide inside – every one of them! Even my own father he tries to cheat me when we go into business. The Swiss they are so boring and predictable. Everyone of them with no imagination and minds full of holes as the cheeses.'

Lobo made a fist. 'So one day I say to myself: From this moment on, I trick the white peoples. They think it is because they are clever they rule the world, but I know the better. It is because they are the most greedy. Always taking what they do not need. This is not something to be proud of. And I tell you this. I have not yet met many who are even smart.'

Lobo looked me up and down. 'But it is different with you, Frankie. My Voice is telling me, your brain is not just a lump of stone. You have a Voice, too. And if you clean up the lump between your ears, we can divide the world between us, you and I. We make the black to play against the white.'

I blinked, trying to focus on his dimpled cheeks which had gone all fuzzy — such malfunctioning no doubt due to the dirt clogging my lump of porridge.

'You know, when I am living in Manila —'

Christ what's he on about now?

Lobo droned on — 'I study the yellow peoples. So fast they are. The way they count with the abacus. As quick as calculators. But for me it is difficult to trick them as you can. They are not understanding the white man. You and I should leave Australia, travel this world together.' Lobo, with a cast of his palm, indicated out there everywhere.

'Yeah, yeah, after we've sold the grass maybe. But just this once, please Lobo, will you stick to the story? Come on, tell me more about your life in Switzerland.'

Lobo shrugged. 'As you like. When I am five years, I am top of my class in skiing. And on my seventh birthday they are making me the youngest ever member of the mountain-rescue team. You see already, even at this age, I am, how you say it, a progeedy?'

'The word is prodigy, Lobo.'

'Prog-idy, thank you Frankie.' He smiled. 'As you see, always I learn fast. Many times I am rescuing, peoples, animals, goats, sheeps, even dogs. One time a party of psychologists from the University in Berlin. While they are doing primal therapy they get lost on Mont Blanc. Because of their screaming an avalanche it comes. I dig a few of them up, but I decide to leave the leader to find his own way out. I shout down the hole I make to him. "You must to face this on your own. I do not want to spoil your trip."'

Lobo nodded sagely. 'You know, Frankie, it is very strange if a mountain of snow it catches you. It happens to me now three times. When it catches you, first you must kick off the skis and rotate, in this way you make for yourself a sack of air. When the snow it stops moving, you do not know which way it is up or down. But for me it is this simple, I just wait, enjoying the whiteness. There is no sound in there, it is not cold, more like being in the heart of something. I hear my Voice more clear. It talks to me, tells me many things, then it says: *This way it is up, now you must go.* And so I go. Life is only difficult if you make it so. Everyone has a Voice, this I know. Mine is not buried like the others, I listen to it, I always have, I always will.'

As Lobo talked, one hand on the wheel, the other chopping the air, his voice became a lazy buzz-saw of flies, cutting a trail through the drift of his life, the images fleeting and gleaming. Betrayed by a woman – a child she had of his blood but not of his heart – he left the thing, sex not specified, with its carping mother a week after its birth. Lobo's repeated sneer showed disappointment with kith, kin and foe alike. He mentioned the dreamy last words of a junky in a blood-spattered room. 'Nothing really matters, man, it's all the same in the end.'

In his late teens it had been fast cars and the playboy life, trips to Iran in stolen Mercedes, return legs with suitcases loaded with hash, concealment provided by a thin covering of banknotes – all the insurance he needed. The customs men averted their eyes when they saw the notes, the life-blood of the Swiss economy. I saw Lobo's friends and accomplices as an army of cardboard soldiers brushed up for parade: some good and some not so good.

Lobo's motto for dealing with wrong-doers who had crossed him? Discover what they love the most, and make that the target for punishment. In the case of one fellow, it was his brand new Maserati. This man owed Lobo some seven hundred dollars. As Lobo said, 'Seven hundred dollars is nothing, but it is the principal that is the point.'

Lobo knew that his lying accomplice loved his Maserati more than his wife, child and family put together – indeed, he loved it more than life itself. So after much thought, Lobo 'borrowed' a ready-mix cement lorry. He filled the car, engine and boot compartment included, with cement, leaving not a trace on the gleaming paintwork.

He avoided conscription into the Swiss Army by frothing at the mouth and screaming, 'I VANT TO DESTROY GERMANS!'

Finally, from his Alpine closet Lobo brought out the most treasured memento of all: a photograph of Heidi, his step-sister, forever lost in the avalanche of his psyche.

And so Lobo left the land of cowbells, boring minds and clockwork time. He set sail first for Nepal, and from thence on to Tibet, travelling incognito over the mountain passes. He was welcomed as a homecoming prince – the glamour boy, the dharma bum from the lands of the West.

Lobo continued: 'And it is there I find my teacher. The most remarkable man ever I am meeting. He lives in a cave at the top of a mountain, where all year round there is snow. Although it is so cold this man has no need for cloth-es. He tells me the cloth it is to save the visitors from embarrassment. I stay with him for six months, and I learn much. One time he tells me if he wishes it, he can burn the whole world clean.' Lobo shrugged. 'But he does not care to. He teaches me the two most important things in life: breathing and keeping clean. But even now I am not nearly perfect. Much there is for me to learn. When first I am meeting this man, you may not believe this, I am almost as dirty as you. We all of us have to be making a start somewhere. If you learn to live correctly, in time you will gain so much power you have no need to eat or sleep.' Lobo jabbed his chest. 'Look at me, Frankie, I have to work to become what I am.'

'Uh huh. You've already adequately established that point. But could you explain, please, what happened after you left Tibet?'

Taking a quick puff, I passed over the newly-rolled joint.

Lobo inhaled deeply. 'As I am telling you, I am a champion skier. Have you ever been at the end of a ski-jump, Frankie?' He shook his head. 'I think not. To take off from over one hundred feet up it is a big danger. Once I am paid two thousand dollars for doing a ski-jump in the nude for a ladies magazine. I also make them insure my legs for one million dollars. I tell you, these people, they pay two thousand dollars, and then they think with the money they buy your life.'

'But Lobo,' I said, 'what happened when you left Tibet?'

'Many offers of jobs I am getting. But I choose the one with the irrational agency.'

'Lobo,' I ventured, leaning over to pluck the joint from his fingers, 'I think what you mean is, you took a job with an *international* agency.'

Lobo smiled. 'Thank you, Frankie, for improving my English. I say it again. I take a post with an international agency for teaching skiing all over the world. You know, to the sons and daughters of the rich. They send me to many places. And so, because I like to travel, for a time I am happy. I live in Colorado, the Andes, Argentina, in New Zealand, the Pyrenees, and the Beetle Mountains in Japan. Then for my last job they send me to the Blue Mountains here in Australia . . .'

10

Tired as I was and despite Lobo's hypnotic whinings, I did not fall asleep. All of it part of the dreamtime parade: awake, asleep, what was the difference? Even the dawn when it came creeping was just another curtain rolling back on night. The white slit of the horizon was a crack under a coffin lid. It seemed like I was called in by the ramparts of this citadel I'd built to seal out the memories.

Lobo's harsh voice came over to me, a hangman's noose whipping me upright.

Frankie, always you are dreaming. Wake up! Are you going to roll for me a joint? Soon we are approaching Bathurst and then you get all the sleep you want.'

Yeah, fucking shit-head, Superman Adonis. Lobo bloody Bonypart. Bloody champion ski-jumper. Bloody bare-faced lying yogi cheat.

I looked outside. The sky bled blue, thin and bloodless, bleached acid. My guts twisted. Jesus. I thought of my wife and her thin, screwed-up face, and my past enveloped me in a spitting cobra's cowl. The revenge of Lot's wife, her shadow engulfing even the future I was fleeing to. There was no escape. Wasn't this journey just another version of the same nagging hell? There is no future, only this endless dreamtime.

The Baby crested a rocky ridge in time to catch the first shards of the morning sun. Below us, stretching to the curving limits of the planet's bowl, lay a dusty plain. In the middle distance, the only definable feature, sprawled the hazy confines of a town. It seemed to me like a broken-backed army in full retreat, frozen into immobility by the cruel eye that gazes over the terrible vastness of Australia's barren heart. This was no ordinary sun, no ordinary smelter belting out the heat, for skulking in every shortening shadow, fractured by my insomnia into a million shifty glimpses, I spied the Reaper, busy about his scythe, his long whetstone tongue slicking over every blade.

We were passing fields, or what passed for fields, and their inmates – listless cattle garnering dust, each leathery A-frame a Belsen rib-cage of hunger and thirst. A billboard declared: BATHURST – 365 DAYS WITHOUT RAIN. A diagram displayed the previous records. It hadn't been this dry since the great drought of 1877.

'Hey Lobo, it says Bathurst is an old goldrush town. This was the Australian Klondyke. I guess these are the descendants.'

I waved to the drab bungalows dreamily drifting by on tickertape. Lawns dehydrating into carpet squares, brown and curling at the edges – signs on telephone poles warned of heavy fines for the use of sprinklers and hoses. Everything shoddy, insubstantial, worn out. A cardboard town packed up and ready to go. For whom does the bell toll? Dead Dog City.

Lobo chose a deserted garage forecourt for the next item on the agenda, and, while he conducted a major reorganisation of the stores, I hitched a ride out the only way I knew how. Only too soon I was awakened by a familiar voice. He wanted to clean out the cab.

'Again?'

That's what I said. We argued some.

Furious war broke out when he 'discover-ed' a particle of food behind my seat. I had the hump anyway, but this was almost the crisp that broke the camel's back.

Half-an-hour staring at nothing in the gloomy cool of the garage rest-room, slouched on the toilet seat. Then I washed, shaved, combed the tangles out of my hair. Sometimes I had to do it. I returned to face the tyrant.

Unbelievably, Lobo complimented my appearance. A warm glow immediately suffused me, like I'd been implanted with an electric coil. The pleasure I felt at his approbation seemed to make all his nagging worthwhile . . . Maybe I was sick, a masochist. After all, hadn't he reminded me of my wife?

I judged it was about eleven. The forecourt smelled of burning rubber. The greasy attendant behind the even greasier window hadn't noticed we'd been parked for hours out front, or perhaps he didn't care. Lobo's rage, like a hurricane, had played itself out. He seemed satiated after his early morning meal of my head, and whistled as we drove through the listless, barely-beating heart of the town. Just off the main street, a curving ramp rose to a one-storey car-park. We pulled up facing a low concrete wall overlooking the 'MEGA-MART' on the other side of the road.

Lobo laid his hand flat on black vinyl. 'You know, it is not for nothing this car it is call-ed for an eagle . . .'

'You mean, this car is called after a falcon.'

Lobo gestured his indifference. 'Your words do not change my point. The Baby it is a bird, and we are hunters, you and I.'

A lazy finger picked out figures in the street. 'Do not you see how it is with the peoples down below. Watch how they move, see how every one is asleep. 'Frankie' – he beamed – 'I want you to imagine this is your first day at school. And now I show you how we take from peoples such as these . . .'

I chuckled heartily. 'I thought you were coming to that. How you choose to live is your own business, but I'll have nothing to do with ripping off.'

Lobo grimaced, disgusted. 'You think I steal. I am not a thief. I do not believe it is stealing to take from such peoples.'

'Taking without paying is criminal behaviour. You can't convince me of anything else.'

'Frankie,' Lobo sneered, 'it is not reasons you are giving for why you believe this, all you do is repeat the same thing, using different words. Do you not realise this country it is stolen from the Aborig-in-es? These peoples –'

'The word is *people* Lobo, not peoples,' I interjected, doing my best to annoy him.

Lobo smiled beatifically. 'OK, peoples. Tell me, Frankie, how can you steal something that is already stolen?'

'You tell me.' I was too tired to argue any more.

Lobo narrowed his eyes, continuing in a softer tone. 'It seems, Frankie, I have to start at the very beginning, as you do not have a clear thinking on this subject. The starting point it is, everything you can lay your hands on in places such as these supermarkets, it is already stolen.'

I raised my eyebrows. Even Lobo could not prove that.

Lobo again gestured towards the shoppers below. 'Where do these peoples live?'

In houses mostly . . . I guess.'

'Exactly correct. And what are these houses made from?'

'Wood, stone, metal, sand for bricks, I suppose.'

'Correct again, and the wood it is stolen from the forests, the metal dug out from the earth, our mother –'

'Come off it, Lobo, that's stretching a point somewhat.'

'I do not think so.' Lobo scowled. 'You cannot to stretch a point, and even if you do, it does not remain a point. I start again. Everything it is alive in some way. We stand on the earth, it is our mother and we must respect her, if we ourselves are to be respected. We must also be respecting the things that come out of the mother. These peoples who are the trolls, the slaves, it is they that dig up the precious things of the mother, the gold and the mineral-es. In this way they rape her, they and their masters. But what happens to the plunder, huh? I tell you. They make trash things that fall apart. You buy something, you throw it in the bucket the next week. Is this a way to live? This is not what I call respect. Everything I keep I look after and protect. If I have something I do not want any more or cannot use, I leave it for the next fellow who comes along. I take only from peoples who do not look after what they have. In this way I help them.

'You talk of criminal behaviour. Think to yourself about the first wars, when peoples fight by hand. If I take a man's life, I have to live with what I do. But after a while it comes the bow, the rifle, bombs, and with each change the other person's face is more far away. Now the aircraft they fly so high the city looks like a dot, and the bombs are so big, you press the button, whoosh, one million peoples they are gone, the whites of their eyes you do not see, it is easy to sleep at night. For the politician, the big businessman, it is the same, for his crime it is written across the sky in words so huge the letters you cannot see. He does not have a care for whose lives it is he destroys. One night as he returns home to his little wife, he sees drunk men fighting on the corner. What does he do? He phones to the police and you are knowing what? It is the drunks they are taking to court, and not him. So, please be telling me, what is this criminal behaviour? Really, I am wishing to know.'

I looked away, wondering how much more I could take of this rubbish.

Foreshortened in the mirror, Lobo's face had become a chastising pumpernickel. 'Do you listen? Do you realise I try to teach you the way to live as my guru he teaches me. You work hard not to understand. For why?'

I whipped around. 'Your Tibetan guru! Pull the other one, you made all this up. Admit it. You can't convince me, Lobo. I know stealing is wrong!'

Lobo scowled, furious now. 'What is this wrong? I do not know this word.' Inhaling sharply, he gritted his teeth, playing the air out slowly through his nostrils. 'I start at the beginning, always you know, I am being so very patient –'

'Oh, ho ho ho,' I roared, tossing back my head.

'Frankie! For once in your life will you be serious at the right time. Here you are many thousands of miles from your home. Try to imagine it, you are a-hungry. Go to any one of these peoples, or these shops below, and say "I need to eat, I am hungry," and what do they do? I tell you, they laugh in your face, or maybe even call the police. They tell you must have the money. But show them a pile of the stupid not-es of paper, and like magic they become all smiles. The snake you can trust more. I tell you, whatever money you still have will soon be gone if you spend it in places such as these.'

Lobo pointed across the road. 'In supermarkets the more fancy the package, the less it is inside. Everything on the shelv-es to tempt. Women's bodies, colours, penis packets, smells, music and lies to hypnotise. Such places are like the fly papers my mother she hangs when the weather grows hot. The money these poor sheeps exchange for this trash is dust of their lives, measur-ed in days and months and years. And the whole of the life it is the same . . . Each one a candle with no flame. No light, no life. It is as simple as that.' Lobo snapped the side of one hand into his cupping palm as a guillotine striking through to the block.

'You must ask yourself then, who it is who are the thieves? The person who only takes what he needs to live in this world, or the owners of these supermarkets and factories and the slaves that sell the time that is not theirs to sell. I tell you, it is these peoples who are the thieves. But the worst thing of all is that they trick you to believe in their system. In this way they steal your mind and freedom. Now, to help you to understand, I tell you how I get this cassette radio . . .'

'Jesus, Lobo,' I protested, 'can't you ever stop, even for one moment?'

'Certainly not, much you are needing to learn. If you do not understand the first time, I am having to look for another example. Now. You are listening?'

Screwing my eyes shut, I nodded.

'That is good. Now you make the effort to understand.'

I could even hear Lobo smiling.

'After I get the Baby I am deciding I need music. Now, I am not like the other fellow, I do not go to any car and take the first one I see, no, I only want the best for my Baby. So I check with all the magazines and choose the model. Then my Voice it leads me to a car-park, it tells me the direction to walk, then it says: *Stop. This it is the car.* I look inside and there is the machine. My Voice it never lies.

'Now, for the peoples who are the thieves, they are ripping the machine out, and not caring for the damage to the car, but I am not like this, always I must to make a good job, and you know it takes time, to bend over each wire and tape it up. I am doing this when the owner, he returns.' Lobo laughed. 'You know, I think this man he is very surprising. He shakes, and he is more a mouse when he says, "You are taking my radio." Lobo mimicked the man's shrew-like face and whining pitch. 'I tell him, "You are exactly correct, I am taking your radio."'

'And what did he say?'

'He does not say anything at first. He is holding his head and moaning, the

71

way you do sometimes, then he is asking, "Please, why you are taking my radio?" I tell him, "I do not have one and this it is the model I choose."'

'What happened next?'

'Oh, I keep on working. You know how it is. So many wires to take off. After a time the man he sits beside me. Many problems he has. No one there is to listen to him. His wife she does not love him. I say, why bother? All of them they are the same, how is she any different? A hole is a hole. So many of them. I tell him he could have a life like mine, but he is too afraid. He then tells me he does not care I am taking the machine, he is insur-ed, he buys it cheap, and it is a profit he is making when he makes the claim. Such peoples, I tell you, is they that are the crooks, cheating the whole of their lives. It is they that are the devils, the sheeps for the slaughter. I am a neither. I am my own fellow. Does not the Jesus you are always complaining to say that the day he returns he is bringing a sword to clean the world from peoples such as these? Look down and ask yourself if you want to walk in their dirty shoes.'

As I looked again, suddenly all those weary shoppers passing in and out of the yawning mouth of the supermarket seemed so many de-oxygenated blood corpuscles. I saw myself then as an anaemic white cell, trudging every day to work, never asking questions I didn't know the answer to . . . As I saw this, a great bubble of anger burst on the surface of my brain, and I realised in my soul I would rather kill than be trapped in such a life again, I understood that this imprisonment had always been my greatest fear. This whole belief structure of mine was a rotten house of cards, but I couldn't play Samson on my own, I needed a conspirator to help bring it crashing down. Despite my inner disquiet this multitude with so many different ways to say no, I must try to listen and understand what Lobo was communicating . . .

And I knew then there was one Voice within that spoke true. And I had to make every effort to hear it, for this Voice never made any allowance for the hard of hearing.

'Now,' Lobo continued, 'the next lesson is, after you think it out, never do anything you do not believe is correct. Do you want to ask me a question?'

'Well, yes. I can't deny your logic, Lobo. But for the moment all I'm wondering is, when are you going to show me the practical sides of this philosophy. I mean, what happens if you get caught?'

Lobo laughed. 'Now I know your problem. You are afraid, and that is wise, for everything you take a-hold of in this life, it is a two-bladed sword, and when you play this game you have to always be preparing to pay the piper. But here, in Australia' – he cast his hand wide – 'I have no worries. These asleep peoples are the most stupids ever I am meeting. The only thing ever they notice is if you try to hide. This I know. If you feel there is nothing wrong in taking, then you will not act like a thief, and then they will not be seeing you. This it is the secret. Anything you can do as long as your mind it is clean. And now, to make my point, I dress up and give you a show.'

When Lobo finally stepped around the car he was resplendent as a cheeky pirate stepped straight off a film-set: Errol Flynn meets Nobody Dick in Dead Dog Town.

Every item of his outfit looked split new. Nike jogging shoes, red-and-white striped cotton socks pulled up tight – I wondered if he'd freshly shaved his legs, his burnished skin shone so. Trimmed in white cord, those red satin boxer shorts hugged his crotch, and I didn't think he was into cotton wool. His tie-dyed purple-and-blue string vest, the ultimate in bad taste, had a Mickey Mouse wind-me-up key printed on the back. And the topping to all this wrapping, still looking as if it was glued to his head, that ol' bandanna, a white rag dripping with red Chinese script.

The jaws of the supermarket gaped like the mouth of a whale. No, I'm not joshing you. These concrete and fibreglass monstrosities had been spawned in some developer's dreamtime – the dreams of the few are the nightmares of the many. I could just imagine the fat cats poring over the final plans, discussing every detail right down to the lurid, tonsil-style light fittings. Ugh. Incredible? Well, maybe. But we're talking about bush civilisation here, strictly for the cobbers. All those packed untidy aisles, teetering and tottering with canned foods. This was no well-oiled dream. The enticements and blandishments here were aimed squarely at grazing merino sheep. Baa bloody baa, Old Mother Australia, waving her dummy tit in my face.

Five minutes, that's how long I'd been waiting for Lobo on this side of the check-out tills. How did I know? Watches on the hands of the shoppers and security guards, and over in the handicraft section, a half-size Black-Forest plastic grandfather, a pupa emerging from its bubblewrap chrysalis, tocking furiously along with the rest. Where is one secure from the march of time, or even being reminded of it? Five minutes. What does such a measure mean to an expectant father fast-pacing the Brylcreem shine of a hospital corridor? What indeed.

Lobo's theatrical exit almost blew me over, the shock-wave was so great. The epicentre read mach five on my surprisemograph. That certain pirate's swagger had been replaced by a penguin's paddle, he was overloaded so. A pyramid of goodies balanced on his stiff little fingers, and only that cute little beak protruding.

I couldn't believe it, for as he waddled towards me, past the ten-deep queue of sheep at the check-out till, past the security man swinging his keys on a long chain, it was as if his self-assured, mocking air had rendered him invisible –

either that or orders issued by his terrifying inner Voice had commanded them all to look away. Humming a damnable little ditty – *Do-dlodle-do-dle-loo-dleee-llum* – in a repeating, looping ascending scale, which somehow managed to insert itself into my brain as *All the fish in the sea got nothing on me*, Lobo slipped a slippery glide slide to the outside, winking at me to follow.

I commended him on his haul, spread out for my inspection across the seats. You know, the usual sort of sundries to be found inside the belly of the supermarket whale. Sneering derisively, Lobo said triumphantly, 'You see, how it is with these Australians. All of them asleep. But now, to prove yourself, I think it is time you do the work for a change. Or perhaps you prefer to go hungry?' Reaching forwards, he patted my stomach. 'What does the master of this house think about that, huh?' Grinning hugely, he continued, 'Since it is your turn, could you not contribute something? I am leaving the choice of brand to you.'

'Well, I'm not too sure . . .'

Stroking his chin, apparently lost in thought, Lobo mused, 'Perhaps also something to make you smart? Sunglasses?' His nose crinkled. 'Or maybe after-shave lotion, to cover up the smell? You know, I do not like the book you write in, so crumpled at the edges it is.' He pushed his head close, peering into my eyes. 'So silent, not the usual talkative person. Afraid of sheep? Huh!'

I felt my face reddening. 'What, me?' I said hotly. 'I'll bloody show you.'

I tried to remember all he'd said about taking. This was a new trade to me. According to instructions, the first thing I had to ask myself was, did I believe what I was about to do was correct, ethical? But when had I ever been sure about the ethics of any of my actions? I could just imagine my obituary reading 'Born in Sin. Died in Sin. Nothing in between.' Such is life. Trouble with these descendants of yogis is, they all live on such a high moral plane. Us sheep are another matter. Of course I was afraid of sheep. After all, what sheep isn't? For instance, take that big, black-faced ram that sired me, my father. The tracklines of the conditioning he'd indoctrinated me with were about as undeviating as the trans-Canadian Railway.

After taking nightclasses in psychology – how my mother complained – and reading up on the Oedipus Complex, he'd decided no son of his was going to castrate him. If it came to the bite, he'd get there first. An army man, in his book authority was a pyramid of paternalism, occupied at the peak by the Ultimate Arbiter – and below that tyrant, judges, courts, police, schoolmasters, sergeant majors. And the bellowing black-faced ram had a tier all to himself, self-appointed of course.

It was my father's most oft-repeated statement that 'the law is the law' – to be obeyed without question first, and then later, if one abased oneself sufficiently, one might be permitted to voice one's opinion.

A bubble of marsh gas erupting from a sewer of memory; an incident from before the fall: sent by my Mother on a mission to the ironmongers . . . So small it was only by standing on tiptoe I could see over the counter. No one else in the main shop, but through an open door at the back loud male voices streaming. The subject on the table, my mother. One of them said: 'Ocht, that fuckin' Mrs Questing, aye, ye ken her wi' the knockers, I'd fuckin' like tae rape her, if ye really want tae know. She's a high-class, stuck-up snooty cunt, an' we all ken what they really want – a good shaggin . . .'

I didn't know what 'knockers', 'rape', 'cunt', or 'shaggin' were, but somehow I caught the man's drift. Enraged, I grabbed the nearest thing to hand and strode out the door. All through my childhood that luminous clock stood sentinel beside my bed.

Shopping. The centre of culture in Bathurst was the art-shop-cum-gallery – such nice people, such high prices. I mean, who'd pay twenty-seven dollars for a sketchbook, or twenty-five dollars for a biro. I was convinced the assistant's eyes were on me, but where was there to hide? This basement was so small, so bijou, so tasteful . . . I tucked the book under my arm, the pen behind my ear. Oh well, artists are absent-minded, everyone knows that.

Thrusting tendrils of clinging guilt away, I strolled to the door whistling softly . . . Had she seen me? Of course she had. The question was, how deep was her sleep? I pushed the glass doors open and shakily ascended the steps to the street, ready to turn at the first sound of that voice and 'discover' the book under my arm, the pen over my ear.

Suddenly I was brimming with exultation, kicking the air – as if by this act I'd claimed the world as mine, or at least as much mine as anyone else's. Did I not have a terrible need for a hat, nail-clippers, shades, chewing gum . . . Oh yeah, aftershave . . .

I found Lobo outside the optician's, nonchalantly lounging against a lamppost, a black holdall slung on his shoulder. Proud of my new shades and Sherlock Holmes deerstalker hat, I strolled past him as if on a catwalk.

Lobo nodded his head approvingly. 'Hmmm. The hat it is very distinguished. But shades with white rims are not for you. So pale they make your face look. Here, I help you.' In a lightning move he plucked the glasses from my nose.

'Hey!' I protested, snatching at empty space like snatching at an over-active fly.

Lobo stooped to peer at his reflection in a shop window, then clicked his heels with delight. 'What do you know? They are a perfect match for my skin. What is the word? They make compliments to me. And the colour perfectly matches the Baby? I am so pleasing. After all your moaning, it is so nice to receive a present.' He stepped forward. 'And what else do you have in your pockets, let me see.'

We spent the rest of that afternoon working as a team. Lobo chattered like a machine-gun to anyone who looked like an assistant. 'Oh, you have such a nice store here, and the air it is so clean. I feel so rested after the dusty outside. You know, I am travelling for holidays in Australia. I like your country very much.'

I would hear snatches of this mind-warping drivel as I drifted to the door, the goods secure in the black holdall slung from my shoulder. 'Yes! My father he was a dentist . . . Yes, of course, my father he was a doctor . . . And you know, you never met a man so very, very clean . . .'

11

We were taking another unscheduled reorganising stop in the 'cool' of a garage. I kid you not, for the thermometer affixed to the wall in the darkest shadow read a cool forty-two degrees centigrade. God knows what it was out of this shade. Vibrating at a speed that would have turned any *hausfrau* pink to the gills, stripped to the waist, and turning a darker hue by the second, the Tibetan dildo was in the process of dismantling and reordering the entire back section of the Baby – right down to the last razor and bar of soap, everything itemised in its own island of space on a large plastic sheet.

We'd just argued some. The reason for the contretemps? My need to get to wherever we were going and put some food in my belly.

'Yes, yes, Frankie, and then you will fart. I am getting to know you Scottismen. All of you have stomachs as deep as your famous Loch Ness, and you with a worm as big as the monster. Never I see a man who eats so much. How else it is you are not getting fat?'

I waited in an agony of impatience for the better part of the day. Eventually Lobo was ready to go. We climbed aboard the Baby – the Baby. Such a silly name for this prowling thing padding the soft asphalt of this suburban, heat-shimmering mirage. The asbestos bungalows all ablaze. Australia a-dreaming, and my eyes on a slide-glide as we nosed out of town.

Lobo's violent slap knocked a disc or two out of kilter. 'Hey-hey! Frankie! We get to Sydney, maybe three, four in the morning. No hurry, plenty time.'

I growled, 'Oh yeah? This trip is already stretching half-way to eternity. I thought it was just a long day's drive from Melbourne to Sydney.'

Lobo, making his face mock-sad, raised a crackle of static electricity from my back with his vigorous rubbings.

'Frankie, I promise, it is a good time we are having from the now on.'

Passing the small joint I had just rolled, I drawled, 'Listen Wolf Man, I've been meaning to ask: where and how did you acquire this car?'

'It was this easy.' Grinning amiably, Lobo paused to suck hard on the joint, the smoke hissing out in volcanic emissions.

'Well . . . Come on, tell us all about it. I can't imagine you'd ever pay cash for anything, and come to think of it, I don't see a road-tax sticker anywhere.'

Lobo waved, langorously dismissing such a ridiculous notion.

'What about the cops? I mean the cop-es, what happens when you get a pull? From the way you seem to know every place we've been, you must have driven all over Australia.' I pointed at the milometer. 'Twelve thousand miles. That's a lot of tooling around, mate, *if* you got this from new.'

Lobo laughed derisively. 'What do I care for cop-es. It is their job to catch peoples who are criminal-es in here.' Lobo tapped his forehead. 'If there is no guilt to see, they go looking elsewhere.' Lobo stared out the window, clearly bored by the subject.

I guffawed. 'Lobo, you can't expect me to believe that.'

Lobo whipped around, his eyes narrowing. 'Yes, I know you find it strange the way I live my life. And I know you study me, though you try not to show it. All the life you play the fat and lazy slob, so why now this surprise when you find the feet stuck in the mud. Frankie, do not you see, I hold the keys to the life that is possible. I offer them to you. I tell you the secrets, just as my master, he teaches me . . .'

I sat back, blinking, unnerved by his certainty, this extraordinary self-belief system that turned the whole of reality inside out.

He levelled a finger. 'Always do the best to keep clean. Everything. The body. The words. The actions. Then after a time, if you keep up the effort, your mind it will become clean. Always you must to be patient for the result. If you have possessions, look after them. Take nothing you have no need for. Do nothing you believe it is wrong. If you do, I warn you, it is the same as picking up the dirt. Only when you follow these instruction-es will you begin to hear your voice clear. It is a hard work. And even after you are clean, always you have to work to keep from falling into the same hole. It is not easy, but it is this simple. These are the secrets of life I tell you. There is no need for knowing anything else.'

Silence wreathed the cab, and I that puppy cogitating on his master's voice, looping around and around on black vinyl. Maybe it was a bigger ear trumpet I required. Even with the windows open, from the vantage of this cocoon the great outside seemed like so many flickering reels projected onto a backdrop. Yeah, I decided, this was an old movie. Hadn't I been here before? Dan Dare at my side, burning salt-dust roads, the corrosion of time.

Time . . . Time . . . A wheel rolling, the vast numinous, incandescent chariot ball of it, careening over the horizon, seeming to dip, drip, drop and roll before it finally slipped behind the melting hills, leaving a trail of burning embers, Hiawatha's sparks fading in the twilight.

Lobo stole the silence. Correction: the sneaky fellow snuck up and 'took' it.

'Frankie, reach under the dash. A bag you find in the pocket, and do not go spilling it.'

'Yes sir, no sir . . .'

Inside the bag were two home-made cookies, two apples and a small box of raisins. I didn't bother asking where he'd got them.

Lobo beamed. 'You see how it is? I tell you , I am always thinking of you. I am your patron saint in the sky above.' Lobo pointed to the cushioned roof of the cab.

Involuntarily, I shuddered at the thought. Pushing a cassette into the slot, I reached for the skins. 'Come on, Lobo you still haven't come clean about the Baby.'

Lobo smiled, 'Always so many questions.'

'Goes with my surname,' I mumbled into the slipstream.

'OK! You know, it is many years I am teaching the children of rich peoples to ski. In that time I find all the ways to make the other fellow feel he is the important one. But' – Lobo waggled his brows furiously – 'behind the eyes always I am watching.'

'Lob, can't you ever keep to the subject?'

Lobo tapped on the steering wheel, 'And when do you pass me the joint?'

'Hold on,' I said sucking until it became hot between my fingers.

Always graceful, even when balancing ash and tipping it out of the window. Snorting smoke, he exclaimed, 'Pah! Do not you know, if you are mixing tobacco with the joint, it is the mind it is clouding.'

'Gi'es a break, Jimmy,' I said, reverting to the diction of my forebears, 'it's three-quarters grass.'

Lobo paused, eyeing me with some disdain. 'I am already telling you I am working with a skiing agency all around the world, but the worst slop-es I ever find are on the Blue Pimpl-es – so stupid the Australians are, for calling them mountains, when the snow it is not lasting the whole year round, and the skiing only a few months . . .

'So when the season is ending my company has for me a new job, in a ski-shop in Sydney. The first time ever I am meeting with artificial slop-es. Soon, my the classes are full to the brim, and because I am always telling my pupils what to buy, the business of the shop, it goes up many times. I know this because at lunchtimes I check with the books. The owner he makes a killing, but for why should I care? I only do what I want to do.

'But then comes a heat-wave, all the pupils on the beach. The owner he is telling me I must paint the showroom. He is forgetting the contract he signs, I am employing only for the teaching of skiing, and he must pay me if there is work or no. But even for this I am not much caring. As you know, Frankie, always I like to make everything clean and fresh. And so I enjoy painting the walls, also fixing the doors, and many other things. But I am forgetting one thing about what I learn from before, the bosses always think the helpful fellow, he is the most stupid. Yes, maybe you do not believe it, but this man he thinks this of me. So one day he is making a sad face and telling me the business it goes down, no money there is for my wages. Then his sad face it goes. What do you know? He can do me a big favour. Even with half the money, I am a lucky fellow, also his house it is needing painting. I tell him if I search for a hundred years, never I find a boss as good.

'And so it is I am taking out all the windows, the doors, the carpets, everything. I explain this is to do a better job. Is the way my father teaches me. This man who never once in the whole life works with the hands, believes me. So stupid he is. Then one hour after I am making him buy all the paint, for the inside and outside, I go to the showroom, say so very sorry sir, but I have to leave Australia if you cannot lend me one thousand dollars this very day. I am making a girl pregnant, if I do not pay she tells her father.

'The owner he says, "Forget the bitch. Always they are trouble."'

'But I explain him, "I am not like you. I am Tibetan. I lose face, my honour it is the stake."'

'You know, always it is easy to know what such a man is thinking, he does not want to lend me the thousand dollars, but also he is not wanting to lose me. He knows never he is finding another worker as good as me, and yet he cheats me at every turn. This fool he is only giving me the money because he wants to steal the life from me. This it is a lesson, I learn much from it. I decide to myself, from that day, I am through working for bosses. It does not matter how good a job you make, always they try to steal from you.'

'With my thousand dollars, I get this car.' Lobo stroked the dashboard lovingly. 'You see the life it is always simple.'

'Come on, Lobo,' I said, exasperated. 'Cut the crap. This car is virtually brand new, and worth a great deal more than a thousand dollars.'

'It is. But I think my Baby is more than just a car.'

'Well? How did you get this Baby that is more than a car, for a thousand dollars?'

Lobo smiled. 'You are a good listener, Frankie. It is like this: I take all the things from his house — the paint, windows, doors, carpets, furniture, everything, and exchange for the gardening tools you see in the back. I make a good deal. I get what I want, and so does the other fellow. The next day I go to the bank, show the manager the thousand dollars, the garden tools. I tell him in Switzerland I am good friends with the banks, I instruct them to send money to his bank every month. I am rubbing my hands about so much business there is in Sydney for land escaping. I do not lie when I tell him, no one in my country works so good in the garden. We shake hands. I sign paper for business contract. The manager he gives me chequebook . . .' Lobo grinned hugely.

'And?' I said, snapping my fingers.

'You know how it is, Frankie!' Lobo chuckled. 'A new business, a new car, change the life. At the garage showroom the salesman is greedy for what is in my pocket. When is it not the same way? The world it does not change the direction. So it is not with difficulty I make him give me the car I already have my eye on. Then I tell him it is only a thousand dollars I have. He is all smiles then, you know, the stupid saying, "No wurries", I do not know how many times he is telling me this. Lobo grinned. 'Never there is a problem here in Australia. The man shows me the HP paper. I say I cannot understand to read English. He fills in the form, writes I have been working years in Australia, and many other lies. I sign my name. The bank manager on the phone says I am a good chap, he is having no problems with me.'

Lobo leaned back, stretching. 'Do you begin to understand how I get the car, it is through the greed of these two men. Both the bank manager, and the salesman want my money, and this is how I trick them. It is a lesson, no?'

'But Lobo. Don't you realise, it won't just be the HP company looking for you now. This car will be on the police wanted list.'

'Pah!' Lobo shot back. 'You think I worry for such things? I tell you once more and never again, always you have to pay the piper.'

12

Why did Lobo always take such obscure meandering night-time trails? An aversion to traffic? The watchers of the night? We hadn't seen another car in hours.

The sky bathed in an azure gloam — was it just before dawn or just after sunset? I didn't know. And that ivory reaping hook, stitching this swirling cerulean canopy to the wheeling frame of the celestial wigwam, was the moon. Distantly I made out a scattering of galactic dust, as if out there was the rest room at a mega-celebrities' convention and some asshole just sneezed.

On a more mundane level, below the curving rim of this terrestial toilet bowl, a couple of hills glowed like radioactive turds, the lights of a small town pricking up between them.

The petrol indicator, ever approaching and now touching the red, was a constant reminder of all the money I didn't have. And it was coming round for my turn. A few more tanks like that first one and I'd be skinned, wiped out.

Interjecting his commentary into my thoughts, getting the last word in as usual, Lobo tipped over the applecart of this silence. 'Yes, it is more petrol we are needing. But this time it is not only the Baby we are having to feed. We must also fill the cans to the brim, then when we hit Sydney we do not have the nuisance for thinking about it.'

He lifted a finger. 'And I will remind you, this time it is your turn. Not for worrying!' he smiled foxily. 'I am not minding for standing in for your shoes. For I know that you are still uncomfortable with taking, and in this you are most correct. You must never do anything if you are not believing it is right.'

Snapping out of my slouch and shaking my head to rid it of this grass torpor, I lashed out. 'Don't you go telling me what I feel. D'you really think I could sit in the car, knowing you were out there doing all the work for the two of us? I'm all for taking petrol, but . . . But you'll have to show me the way, because I don't know anything about skulduggery.'

'What is this skull . . . buggery?' Lobo pursed his lips, rolling the word round his tongue.

'Oh, you know,' I told him, 'it means living like a pirate, and being a pirate.'

Lobo's face took on new curves, slit-eyes lifting at the corners. 'I am so pleasing when you say this.'

A bobbing Russian doll. You know the type? Inside, another doll, and so on. Only with Lobo there's no end to the charade.

'And now,' he said, tap-tapping his temple, 'listen to everything I say with the whole in the mind. For I do not repeat myself. It is a serious business we do. Here it is not the city, with everywhere chickens rushing with no thought but for themselves. These country peoples always watch for their possessions. I respect this. Guns they keep under the bed. Here you can die for what we put in the tank. Mark my words. It is a dangerous thing we do.'

Cruising . . . Another small-town parade, and every bungalow a beached whale, speared by Ahab and left to rot, bloody gore rendering these tidal banks maroon . . . Doorways, windows, rents, tears, bloody leering mouths . . . And there, that black sprawl on patio-white, an ugly mastiff, his early-warning gear turning with the sound of our passing.

It seemed as if the *Bungalow interruptus* trees either side of the road were marching, nay striding with us, their branches interlinked filtering and softening the prismatic glare of the neon orange. And below the leaf corner — such a scattering of lazily parked cars.

Turning into another long street, apparently identical to the last, Lobo pulled up by a headless streetlamp, slotting into a tight space between two bumpers.

Taking his key out of the ignition, Lobo leaned over the steering wheel and, viewing me sideways, spoke in a cool monochrome.

'I will say this, and I use the same words as my master he is telling me. Everything that you fear it is beginning first in the mind. Now, I ask you this. You are walking the street carrying a big can, it is late, maybe three in the morning. Is there anything wrong in this? Do you worry? I think not. For walking with a can, you do not have to explain to anyone. But if you carry a hose as well as the can, and someone sees you, it is a different matter.'

Casting his eyes this way and that, Lobo snickered, 'I should not like to rescue you from these butch farmers. So many of them about, you know.'

Wiggling his hedgerows, he made like a temple fan-dancer, or maybe a

Tibetan aquatic bazaar urchin, waving long fronds at a passing saw-toothed shark.

'Frankie, not to go off dreaming again. Always you must make effort to concentrate.

'Yeah, yeah,' I replied absently.

'Look deep into my eyes. Now, think to yourself for a moment. Who it is the best animal at moving at night?'

I shrugged, spreading my palms. 'Who knows?' I almost added, 'Who cares?'

'OK, I answer for you, it is the cat. They stand so, then . . . Poof! You see them on the branch. The bird it is dead. And always cleaning with the paws. You ever watch?'

'Yeah, I've frequently cleaned up the shit they leave around the house.'

Lobo frowned. 'Always you are disappearing from the subject. For why you not stay in the same place? I am telling you, think of the cat as you move. The tip of the toes. It is easy to imagine you are one, and that is how you do it. And another thing' – his emphasising finger did a swinging tick-tock – 'if the car has a cap that is lock-ed, leave it. Never break anything when taking. So many fools there are who forget to use them. The best car is the one facing the hill. Then you can take to the last drop.'

The mirror blazed with lights. A big car lurched close. 'EEEEhaaaaaa!!!' Through the driver's window came the scream of a rodeo cowboy.

About a hundred yards distant the tail-lights flared as the car bumped into the driveway of a bungalow. Three rednecks began heaving crates of beer into the house.

Nodding in their direction, Lobo opened his door silently. 'Not for worrying. Come you. It is work we must do.'

Reaching under the tarp, Lobo soundlessly withdrew his two camouflaged army cans.

'Take this,' he said, passing over a short length of hose. 'It is small for rolling into the palm of the hand, and long for reaching the bottom of the tank. It is easy to use. You are paying the attention?'

'Uh, yes.'

'Good. The first thing is, push the tube in the hole and blow. When you hear bubbles, put the head down, three sucks – that is all. Then the petrol it will flow. And then you can whistle, put the hands in the pockets, look in the windows of the nice houses, until you hear the funny suckling noise of a sheep. Otherwise . .'

I stared at him blankly, wondering if he had a screw coming loose.

'Do you hear anything I say?'

'Yeah, yeah,' I said, 'everything.'

He frowned, then, watching me intently, continued: 'If peoples they are about, I leave the tube to do the work. And if they watch me, it is always good to make a pee.' Lobo sniggered. 'Always the nice peoples look away.'

Lobo pointed to the petrol cans twinned on the sidewalk. 'Pick, and choose your direction. And one more thing,' he growled. 'Always leave everything as you find it, the petrol cap must be screwing back tight. You are ready?'

I nodded, suddenly afraid.

It was probably because I was trying to think myself into a more feline form that I didn't notice the brick lying next to my container. Big Ben strikes one.

Lobo, can in hand, froze in mid-movement, hissing, the nape of his neck arching. 'Make no noise! Now, walk like the cat. Like this!' And with that he set off, a high-stepping Tibetan tom in the Antipodean night.

Walk on razor blades, walk on breakfast cereal – damned leaves and gravel all over. High-stepping like this was hard work. And every time I slackened my grip, this rubber hose wriggled like a determined serpent. Damned locking petrol caps on every car.

I began to wonder about the sexual symbolism of all this.

> You put the tube in the hole and blow,
> Then you watch the petrol flow,
> You fill up your can, you walk like a man,
> Hey ho, hey ho, hey ho . . .

> Lobo . . . Big bad Lobo . . .

This street was depressingly the same as the last. What time was it? I didn't even know the name of this town. So dazed was I by lack of sleep and endless joints that day and night had become the blades of my dreamtime blender, and I the egg-white. Shaddup! Shaddup!

I thought I'd found the source from which all good things flow, a cherry-red Datsun facing an incline, but I couldn't find any petrol cap, locking or otherwise. I could have screamed in frustration. (Years later, on a visit to Tokyo as an *aide de camp* to Prince Charles – Flatulence van der Post couldn't make it – I discovered the fiendish Japanese often conceal them behind number plates. But remember, here in Oz I am only an apprentice, and ignorance is the last testicle of my knowledge.)

My eyes fastened on the first non-locking petrol cap I'd seen. Squatting on my haunches, I forced my brain to concentrate on the task in hand.

Bubblings, vaporous treasure wafting from the bottom of the well. So far so good. Lowering my head, I sucked determinedly, three times. Nothing. Not a drop. On the fourth suck my mouth immediately filled with petrol, a steady flow. Spluttering and cursing at the foul taste, I rejoiced that I'd at last got a result . . .

Big lights sweeping the corner. Jeeesus . . .

It was only when I reached the concealment of the bushes at the side that I remembered Lobo's advice and spread my legs, adopting the posture of peeing. The sound of big tyres slowly rolling on gravel as the vigilante patrol crawled past . . . They didn't look away. Definitely not 'nice peoples' around here. Eyes like oil-burners.

As soon as I saw the pool of petrol welling out around the base, I realised in my panic I hadn't stuffed the springy hose deep enough into the can. And now in my haste to rescue the situation, I'd knocked it over.

A fusillade of barking, sound of something big dragging a heavy chain, and then the bushes at my back erupted. Lights started flicking on in the houses around. Grabbing can and hose, I ran, ducking low, keeping to the shadows, turning the corners, until I'd put a league between me and the barking.

Leaning into supportive foliage, my chest heaving after the oxygen, bile in my mouth . . . And petrol, and Lobo's words regurgitating on me, *We must also fill the cans to the brim . . . You must never do anything if you are not believing it is right . . .*

Perhaps Lobo perceived me as a domesticated cow, always looking over my shoulder, the ever-ready butt for his 'humour'. Probably the Tibetan dingo thought he had me tethered. Never in my whole life had I taken so much shit from anyone. And he'd said he was going to take the dirt out of my life. Jesus.

And then I remembered what he'd said about always putting the petrol cap back on. I'd left the last one lying in the dirt. Maybe he was right. The only security in any situation is to attend to every detail.

I imagined him now, seated behind the wheel, patiently fitting the barbs of his reproaches to his long fisherman's line. And out back, 'neath the buttoned-down tarp, strapped in, stowed away, his canister would be filled to the brim, and the Baby ready to roll.

How could I possibly face the tyrant if I returned empty-handed. Come to think of it, I didn't have any clue as to where precisely the Baby was. All these fucking streets were practically identical. Another harpoon of panic twisted in my vitals. I was lost in the dreamtime again, my mind as slippery as a bar of soap in the troubled waters of this murky bath.

And then it seemed I'd woken up. Across the road was a pair of black, scrolled gates, invitingly askew; and behind, with its cute nose tilted up the steep, short incline to the garage, was a small white hatchback.

Carefully, mindful to keep to my toes, I high-stepped across the tarmac, not pausing for breath till the gates were at my back. I reviewed the situation. Before me was a white bungalow. Behind the screen frame, the inner door of the house was half-open. From an open window just to the side of the car, net curtain fanned outwards on a light breeze, which also bore the sounds of a heavy breather. I imagine him curled up in white pyjamas a few feet away through that thin asbestos wall – a butch, red-faced farmer. And underneath him, a double-barrelled shotgun, primed and ready. Primed and ready.

The catch: the no-lock shiny petrol cap was sited on the window side of the car, the long net curtains occasionally brushing it.

Did I really have any choice?

I held the can tight to my chest, inching around the car, keeping my head well below the line of the windowsill. Fingers trembling as I gripped the shiny cap, for a moment I stared uncomprehendingly at my own reflection – a wild-eyed maniac reaching out to burgle my soul.

Blast and damn! The fucking thing was screwed on too tight. Metal ground on metal. Leaning hot cheeks against cold paintwork. Christ, something in my hair! I almost screamed. Just the diaphanous touch of the billowing net curtains.

The breathing at my back stopped. The swishing of starched sheets, a body turning on a hair mattress; and mixed in with this, the untimely roar of the blood coursing in my ears. The breathing became regular again.

I unfroze, knees cracking as I bent to the task again, a schoolboy waiting for the cane of Damocles to strike. Christ, I'd better get on with it. This had to be done like a military operation: insert tube, blow, pause, three firm sucks. Nothing. Suck again. Shit, another mouthful of petrol, but at least a good flow. Stuffing the hose in the mouth of the can. Petrol dribbling into the empty metal chamber. Christ, the sound! Even the cicadas momentarily stopped their rubbing.

Nothing to do but wait. Better stand in a shadow.

I was alerted by a curious noise, like a sheep snickering, since you ask. God Almighty, is that the way Australians snore? Imagine sleeping next to that. The snoring suddenly ceased. Silence, except for the busy cicadas and the plop-plopping of roaches falling from the trees. I was on my haunches again. Tilting the can. Bastards! It was only half full. The sound of gibbering sheep had been the signal that the petrol was about to cease syphoning, and I should move the hose to a new position. Cursing the drug-induced brevity of my attention span,

I coiled the hose around in my hand and carefully screwed on the petrol cap, as tight as I could.

I had to get away, and as quickly as possible. With the gates at my back, I hesitated. Which way had I come? I looked left and right and then up to the sky that was so unfamiliar. The moon had slipped from sight. Shite-bags! It seemed I'd been in this swamp of pus for hours. My head was swimming from inhaling and swallowing so much petrol. Damn roaches. I swatted one as it landed on my shoulder. Any other time it would have freaked me out.

I won't go into the pain that I experienced on my journey through the labyrinth. No dead ends – each street a-stretching to Babylon. I don't know how many corners I turned in my desperation. I wished I'd made chalk marks on the pavement.

Looking up, I suddenly noticed the familiarity of a dud streetlamp, broken glass seeming to scream 'X marks the spot'. I was actually standing where I had left Lobo and the Baby. That cheating son of a bitch was gone.

That should have been the end of this tale. I was abandoned. Somehow, I made my way out of Australia and returned to my blasted heath. But this is the stuff of dreamtime, and Lobo my Pied Piper through its never-ending landscape.

I caught Lobo's unmistakable, cheeky mien, framed in the white of his Baby's window, at the next intersection, I shouted, but it was too late. He was gone.

I reached the crossroads. No sign of the night thief. I spun around.

There, just crossing the intersection from whence I'd come, another freeze-framed glimpse. Nothing else to do but return to the broken streetlamp and wait. Two minutes passed, then the white bird swept the corner and big tyres crunched dry leaves at my side.

His voice came crisp as bacon crackling. 'Where have you been losing yourself? I have been so worried. I look everywhere. How you take so much time? My gosh, I fill my can more than one hour ago.' His voice turned rancid. 'I hope you have a can full of petrol.'

I shook my head, blurting out: 'It's almost three-quarters of a can. Well . . .' I smiled as disarmingly as I could. 'Maybe more than half.'

I feared for a conflagration, there was so much combustible material lying about. Suffering like a Christian in the Coliseum, I endured the inevitable tongue-lashing that cascaded from his lips – clipped Teutonic phrases, each one the hard side of Everest, granite blocks landing on my head. *Tête à tête* we continued into the night, Sydney bound.

13

In our shafting arrow, we hit Sydney at a hell of a pace. Wide, empty, streets, the glitter of fresh rain reflecting city lights and a sky that hung above us like the swollen underbelly of the Great White tinged with red – the legacy of Ahab's lunge.

'Exactly where are we going, Lobo?'

'Hey, do not you think it is nice just to cruise?' Lobo waved his hand indicating the panorama: Port Jackson Bay, big ships in the harbour, the *QE 2* ablaze with lights. Fucking shitheads, I thought ungenerously. All that luxury, all those beds.

Sydney had been my port of arrival in the Land of Oz, but I had never seen it like this: snatches, twats and august cameos flicker-framed in the night slot of the Falcon's windows. The water of the harbour was an unyielding wire-brushed Prussian blue. A couple of dragonflies skimmed the waves – two early morning windsurfers so fragile next to the great cake-slice sides of big ships lying at anchor. The arms of cranes like praying mantises, talking in clicks.

But what about my companion? Lustrous, bound-back black hair, the white scarf streaming out the window – seen from this angle he reminded me of nothing so much as Peter O'Coole, tooling along on his camel called Lawrence of Arabia, sandblasted until his eyes were slits, his face the cherry round of a baby's bum.

Of one thing I was sure, I was travelling with the messenger of the gods; either that or the arch imposter Dialobo himself, grinning like a tiger despite the world.

Without warning Lobo tugged the steering wheel – hard. The car surged, bouncing as tyres hit the curb, then the drive became a cushioned swish, as we cut a swathe across the soft verdure of a city park.

Curling his top lip derisively, Lobo thumbed something stubby at the non-existent traffic behind, 'You know, I am getting so mad at the cars always blocking, at traffic lights. Why not they just drive through?'

Why not indeed? I wondered if he was serious, despite the huge grin implying the huger joke.

'And always, you know, we must be remembering to save petrol. When you have to work this hard to take it, you soon find out the real cost. This is the why I do not let you drive the Baby. I know you put the foot down.'

Lobo flapped a hand, directing my attention to the park all around. 'And now you see, by taking this cut short, we save two, maybe three miles. Is good, no?'

Lobo doused the lights as we careered through the gloom of the thin morning mist, trees whipping past as if we'd been transported into an impressionist painting, the whole of reality turned by a painter's brush into microscopic dots. I felt as if I were tripping. I was so tired, yet so alive, the weights of the world seemed to have no claims on me. Here was a man with a purpose. He knew where he was going: Manley Ferry Terminal. At least that's what the sign over the entrance said.

All around us were rows of neatly parked cars. Lobo, the master surgeon, slotted the Falcon into a tight space, our wheels tipping the edge of a raised cinder track. Below us were just three feet of steeply-banked yellow sand, then sea. There was no one around, only the soft slappings of water soothing my flagellated brain.

'Hey,' I said, putting a measure of enthusiasm into my voice. 'This is perfect, huh? Just give me a few hours kip and I'll be ready for whatever you care to dream up.'

Lobo regarded me acutely, his eyes, his bearing, his muscle-tone – everything broadcasting 'Totally on the ball.'

'You think we come here to rest? My gosh, I never meet anyone so lazy. Does every person in Scottisland sleep so much? I look at me, and I look at you. I get the petrol. I drive the car and you know I make all the jokes. If I tell stories it is because I feel you are unhappy. Do not you think then it is you who should be full to the can with beans?'

'Lobo,' I said weakly. 'What time is it?'

'I do not waste my time thinking of clocks, but for this once I will tell you. It is five-thirty precisely on the dot of the button. One hour before the computers drag these cars to their stupid works.'

Shutting my eyes momentarily, I strained for an answer. 'Lobo, I'm not like you. You say it's five-thirty in the morning. I haven't had any sleep for twenty-four hours. Don't *you* ever get tired?'

Lobo glared. 'I do not believe the words I hear coming from your mouth. My Voice it has told me, you are not one of these stupid battery hens, every day doing the same things at the same times. I am the same as you, I get tir-ed the same, but the difference is I make an effort. I look at me and I look at you. You are dirty. Your hair it is untidy. Your fingernails unclean.' He screwed up his nose, an expression of disgust marring his features. 'And always you are stinking of petrol.'

'Can't you give me a break?' I clawed at my hair. 'I thought we were friends?'

'Yes, that is precisely and exactly correct. And it is because I am your friend it hurts me to see you so lazy and dirty. You must to understand, I want only the best for you. Why do you not see this?'

I shook my head, unable to speak.

He continued, 'Always I am doing the thinking for the both of us. Here you get a chance to make up for the mistak-es of the past. Look around you now. All these cars. So many choices. So while you are contributing to our journey, I reorganise the Baby.' Lobo smiled. 'You know, when you clean up the house, you are working on yourself, if you are clean you have more beans. It is this simple.'

Was there no end to the energy of the man? For the life of me, I couldn't recall witnessing even a yawn. Patently this Tibetan misfit had access to a spring that never stopped flowing. And never the slightest hesitation . . . The way he zeroed in on the target, even if the target initially only manifested itself as a need. For instance, gnawing hunger. How did he know that chicken supper was waiting for us in the middle of nowhere? But he did. The only conclusion I could draw was that this constant, harping assault about cleanliness, reorganisation and 'taking' was indeed correct, and these three things were in fact the Holy Trinity of the fountainhead of virtue. He was so full of energy precisely because he followed his philosophy to the letter, vigorously practising everything he preached.

I decided then: I will learn and apply this system to myself. I came to this continent because I could not handle my life. I needed a new direction. It was a matter of pride if nothing else. No one had ever bested me the way he had.

And so I replied with as much pzazz as I could muster. 'Yeah. Thank you so much for being so concerned for me. I'm serious, you know. I'll get the petrol. I think it's a very good idea. You reorganise the car.'

I found it surprisingly easy this second time. Oh, to be sure, I experienced the beginner's anxiety to get everything right, and consequently shoved my hose in a couple of more or less empty tanks, taking more than a few mouthfuls of the noxious stuff in the process. But when I eventually found the target, it was a dawdle whistling while I waited for those cans to fill. I even wondered what all the angst had been about. I even had plenty of time for rinsing, gargling, spitting, not to mention splashing my face with sea-water. And yet the sickly aroma of the pernicious substance clung to me. Oh well. Lobo's mountain of perfection was an Everest, and I but a poor pilgrim staring up from the foothills. How did that song go? *Climb every mountain* . . .

I found Lobo crouched at the water's edge, idly flicking pebbles to the same spot as concentric circles bubbled outwards. Flick, plop! Flick, plop!

Lobo raised his face, a strangely vacant look. The mask of a new manikin, I decided.

'Oh, there you are Frankie.'

Was he tired?

'And what is the time now?'

No, I decided, just bored.

Taking the weight off my leaden limbs, I squatted down beside him, venturing, 'Ten to six?'

'It is six-thirty precisely on the dot of the button.' Lobo enunciated the syllables with the precision of a mocking-bird.

Swivelling on his heels he stared out to sea. 'You see the boat over there? The first load of computers. Here in Australia it is the good life. A car for this side, a car for that side, all their children have cars, think how many tyres.' Flick, plop!

I was swaying with tiredness. Six-thirty, Jesus. Lucky 'computers' having beds to go to, it was a long time since I'd seen one.

Flick, plop!

This damned action was beginning to grate on my nerves. I demanded quickly. 'What are you doing? Don't you have reorganising to do?'

Lobo turned his head lazily, bounced lightly, springs obvious in his bended knees. 'I am not throwing ston-es. Look!' Lobo suddenly pointed.

Flick, plop! Sleight of hand. I didn't see the pebble. But it was there.

He continued. 'Do not you see the fish-es?'

'Whaaat?' I gulped.

Lobo nodded. 'Yes, the fish-es. They are liking the sound of my voice, you know. Sometimes they dance for me. When I sing, they are popping up from the sea. I tell you, when we go Queen-is-land we catch food in this way. It is nice to make a fire, cook with sticks. Never you need to get the fingers dirty. Life like this it is so good.' He beamed. 'The world it is our home.'

Leaning my eyes on the crutch of the distant horizon and speaking more to 'out there' than to Lobo, I said, 'Well, I want to know why it's you and me.'

Lobo brushed invisible specks from his shorts and bronze thighs, then planting hands on his hips, leaned over aggressively.

'Look a-here, fellow,' he snapped, 'I do not put up with your moanings for one minute longer. Now I am knowing the how you are cleaning the dirt from your soul. It is by work. My Voice it tells me. Already I see you make some effort, but this it is a start only. You are like the man who stands on the mole-hill shouting of his triumph.'

Lobo's tone softened. 'You know all the time I am playing with the fish-es, I have been thinking. I do not like the way the tyres are taking the kerb. In this country if the car it is not good in every respect you can die, the roads, they are so bad. We must get big fat ones for eating the road.'

Lobo pointed to the customised love-bug gently rocking at the end of the row of parked cars facing the sea. 'How would the bird look in shoes like those, huh?'

I laughed. 'You have a funny way of putting things. I'm sorry to disappoint you. I'm sure you'd like to take them, and the people screwing inside, but that car has a specially lengthened axle. Look' – I pointed – 'Do you see how they are set out from the body? Besides, you'd need larger wheels on the Falcon to fit those tyres.'

Lobo shook his head. 'I am so impressive when you talk like this. It is the voice of authority you speak with. You seem to know the whole busy-ness. Me, I always leave such things to mech-an-iacs. I am not liking to to get my hands dirty, but since yours are dirty the whole of the time, you will not mind to find your fat tyres for the Baby. So many cars there are.'

Beyond his shoulder a ferry was pulling in alongside the jetty. Beneath my feet I felt the throb of big engines vibrating.

'Jeez,' I said, 'you pick your times, don't you. What about all these people about to disembark? Just imagine, I'm ripping . . . ah, *taking* the tyres off a car, and the owner turns up. What do I say? Huh? I'm just taking your tyres? Have a good day?'

'That is exactly and precisely correct,' Lobo nodded. 'Now you begin to learn. It is good.'

I waited until the first lot of 'computers' had driven away. Lobo said another ferry was due in half an hour. Walking the serried rows and scanning the rubber on display, I guessed there'd be a few models with tyres that would fit the Ute. Wheels were another matter. Ours were five-studded. I found the likely candidates on a late-model two-litre white Holden saloon – fat, roadster wheels, big studs and chromium rims.

All the auxiliary implements necessary lay on the sea shore – a tree trunk and several large stones. Using these and our jack as supports, I removed the

Holden's front wheels, and not a moment too soon. The booming flatulence of a hooter echoed across the bay, announcing another imminent arrival.

I was sweating now as I scuttled between the rows, concentrating on keeping the wobbling tyre upright. Two fucking journeys. I left the first leaning against the car's side. When I returned, it wasn't Lobo I found, it was a scowling pixie perched on top of the black rubber.

'These they are not the right wheels, always you are mucking up the job! For why?'

Why indeed?

The new tyres did not fit, despite the similarity of the position of the five stud holes.

Lobo told me I should go back, but I refused, point blank. I'd had enough. We left the tyres on the beach. Lobo was not pleas-ed.

Again, Lobo knew exactly where we were going. I wondered how much time he had spent in this country? He seemed to know every road.

I did not need to open my eyes. Once more we were cutting grass back across the big city park, a jolting bump through our suspension at that same kerb; now the highway, a cacophony of horns and screeching wheels. Then I was thrown against the vinyl of my door, a rollicking, semi-comatose cloth dummy, my jaw clicking as it snapped against my shoulder.

Lobo laughed uproariously, thumping the steering wheel with delight. 'Ho-ho! Did you see that? The fools they think to stop us. Ho-ho! I tell you . . .'

I screwed my eyes shut, determined nothing would unprise them. Again the blaring of horns, then blessed peace, only the rumble of our soft tyres on a smooth road.

I squinted and blinked with the pain of the bright sunlight. I looked out, a city park with a strip of tarmac rolled over the verdant spread.

Approaching a crossroads, Lobo showed no hesitation as he took a left. On either side now, big trees marked even time. Lobo counted aloud as we raced along the avenue.

Slowing the Baby, Lobo took a sharp left. Now we were pelting through the leopard spots of a golden-leafed tunnel, the bright light of the risen sun a nimbus at the far end.

14

The sun was lifting over yellow sandstone cliffs as we entered the clearing. Ahead and around us was a U-shaped rock wall. I recognised what must once have been quarry offices and a weigh-bridge. The old clock had stopped at half past one. The corrugated roof had fallen in under the weight of vegetation, cliffs behind tumbling with green. This space reminded me of a created environment in a safari park, a shabby lions' den. The tawny rocks were reminiscent of the Kalahari. A long spume of white water descended the sandstone cliffs like a pipe-cleaner version of the Victoria Falls. This water, blessed be Allah, was the secret of all this life in this lonely wadi, so hemmed in by the encroaching sands.

I prayed to the god of all lonely wadis, to the god of all nomads. Give me a bed. Change me into a Bedouin. Take me one million miles from here . . .

There were traces of a hobo's fire. A rusting billycan lay on its side, shotgun holes in its base. The smoke-blackened jawbone of a huge moose was propped against a big stone, cracked by heat. In the drifting veil of the falls, barely visible, was Robert Redford, his arms wrapped protectively around Meryl . . .

A flurry of white rose up as a flock of seagulls took off from the cliff face, icing departing a cake, shrapnel pieces exploding outwards till they were specks on the blue of the cake-maker's face. His one good eye viewing the midgets in the canyon. Remember in this, the land of the blind, the one-eyed man is king . . . But he'll still need a damned good lawyer.

'Heh-heh-heh! How you think I find such a place?' Lobo tapped his head. 'You know, my Voice, it tells me. It sees everything. This it is the perfect hidey-hole.'

'Heidi-Heidi-ho-hole!' I leaned out of the cab window, yelling out my sudden uprush of exuberance. Whoosh! Marilyn Monroe stood over a subway grating. Whoosh! Wow! Hey!

Then the answering echo came from the cliff, 'Heidi-Heidi-ho-hole!'

'Hey, Lobo, do you have any secrets? Did you ever nibble on your little sister's door? Heh-heh-heh!'

Lobo's eyebrows collided, two express trains on the one line. 'You dare to talk of my sister in this way? I forbid you to speak her name, with your dirty mouth!' His down-turned lips looked like serrated bow-saws, both cutting through to the bone. I wondered when his chin would drop off.

He continued, each word a chip of glass puncturing the party balloon of my mood. 'My sister, I would not bring her to a place such as this.'

'Oh, come on Lobo,' I interrupted, 'it's a joke.' Feeling a sudden need for safety, I attempted to steer towards a familiar shore. Yawning, fingers to my mouth, I said, 'Suddenly I feel really tired . . . Aren't you?'

Lobo threw up his hands. 'I cannot believe how much of a fat lazy you are. I lose the count of the times you sleep.' He scowled. 'OK, you rest in the front while I change the back around. You know, it is because I am having to give the front to you, I have to make so many changes in the back, but never do you thank me.'

'But heh-heh,' he brightened, 'who else finds such a place so near to the city centre? Is better than any apartment, do not you think?'

'Yeah, yeah,' I muttered, 'much better.' I realised my sudden uplift of spirits was a product of exhaustion, nothing more. If I didn't get sleep, and soon, I would become hysterical.

Lobo, the mad Tibetan in pursuit of eternal fitness, kept appearing and disappearing at the cab window, hypnotically inhaling and exhaling. Knee-bends, I presumed.

I was almost dozing when he pushed his head into the cab. 'Frankie, remember always to be watching for bad fellows sneaking. I go to invest-gate. This it looks the unlikely place. These are the right words? Yes or no?'

'Yes,' I replied, no longer caring about anything.

He walked away, humming some awful ditty and leaving me to curse to myself.

Uncomfortably I attempted to stretch out across the seats. My back twisted and contorted, my head teetered on the narrow ledge of the armrest, my legs bent to avoid the steering wheel, calves cutting fat on the sharp edge of the open window, toes cooling in the light breeze . . .

These damned Aussie insects. As I pulled my feet back into the cab, my thoughts turned to Charles Laughton as the Hunchback of Notre Dame, ventriloquists' dummies stuffed into suitcases, Canadian logs breaking free from Canadian log jams, drifting ever closer to the blessed abyss of sleep . . .

Those damned marionette strings forever jerking me back . . . Bangs and thuds on the cab window behind as Lobo did his reorganisings.

If this was a suitcase, its interior was lined with elastoplast – the seats skinned my flesh every time I moved a freckle. My sweat was a deluge now, as the eye of the cake-maker rose to its zenith.

I don't know how long I struggled to get to sleep in this way, but finally, reluctantly, I gave up.

Angry and frustrated, it was my neck I cricked next as I craned to see what was happening outside. Somewhere nearby, Lobo was humming one of his excruciating ditties.

A short distance away Lobo sat cross-legged on a black, thumb-shaped rock projecting from the edge of a pool some three feet from the Victoria Falls. Hands resting on hips, he rocked slowly from side to side, bush naked, blue lightning flashes emanating from the cleft of his buttocks. A trick of the light, I should have said – the lightning flashes were stitched onto his red satin shorts. It'd be a mistake to ascribe to the chap the power of delivering thunderbolts from his buttocks. Another detail: sunshine glinting off a gold chain and crucifix I'd never noticed before. And finally, wrapping that hideous mug, a most unusually beatific smile.

'Doo-o-dol-oododolumbaloop! Balumdadoolaloop!' The sound bubbled from his lips like he was a Hottentot who'd been force-fed from a magnum tube of Alka-Seltzer.

He leapt to his feet, waving vigorously. 'Come, you lazy bone, look here, this water it is so clean.'

He almost split my ear drums then with his rendition of the Swiss national anthem, cupping his hands to his mouth, 'Yodellaayyyyydooolooooodoooooo!'

I was amazed when the echo was answered by an incongruous tinkling and clanking of bells and a soft rumble which shifted the earth beneath my feet. I was even more amazed when a loping herd of some twenty long-horned cattle crested a rise, a big Tyrolean cowbell swinging from the collar around each hefty black-and-white neck.

Adoringly the cows gathered in a half circle.

Lobo waved again . . . I felt like this was a Swiss Salvation Army camp. 'Come you, Frankie. You can learn much from the animals,' he called out.

Jesus, this is too much. First it's fish. Now it's cows. The birds will land next. Bloody St Lobo of Assisi.

Lobo clapped, then flapped his hands at the cows. 'Shoo, shoo, you must all leave me and Frankie in peace.'

Obediently but reluctantly the cattle began ambling back in the direction from which they had come, turning occasionally to reproach Lobo with their sad and mournful eyes, keeping this up until the last of them had trundled over the rise.

'And how are you feeling, Frankie?' enquired Lobo, rubbing his hands.

'Bloody exhausted, and PISS-ED off . . .'

'My gosh, do you never stop to moan? If you will tidy your possessions, you feel better. Always so much good advice I am giving. It is not to sleep you need. It is to get a grip on yourself. While you snore. I am reorganising the back of the Baby.'

'Don't start off again. I couldn't sleep because of the bloody noise you were making bloody reorganising!'

Lobo pursed his lips, imitating screwed up paper. 'I am wondering why you always tell such lies. I think it must be because the dirt has dug so deep into your soul it is now ingrain-ed.'

I sighed, truly exasperated. 'And I'll remind you we're in Sydney because we made a deal. Or have you forgotten? The grass, huh? But as soon as we arrive here you start talking about how this dump is better than any apartment, then you're communing with cows. Next you'll be bloody walking on water and raising the dead. What I want to know is, WHEN DO WE START SELLING THIS GRASS?'

'Oh my gosh, you are so impatient.' Lobo took his hands from his ears. 'Always you are shouting. We do not sell the grass today. Much there is to do first. The quality of a job depends on the preparation. This is the way with everything.'

Australia is a continent of paradoxes. It is possibly the country with the best damn climate in the world for growing weed. Fifteen million inhabit a land almost as big as the United States. Despite this, the standard price of second- or third-rate leaf is over one hundred and twenty dollars an ounce. In many European countries hash costs a lot less, and as any smoker worth his toke knows, an ounce of hash will last three times as long as an ounce of weed. Flowering heads? No, I'm talking about basic leaf. As if the high price wasn't enough, the police regularly mount national campaigns called 'Dob-a-Druggy Week', with a freephone hot-line for anonymous tip-offs. Cash rewards are offered for information leading to successful busts. It's a common sight in city suburbs to see helicopters methodically working the lines of bungalow squares.

If you're down and out and broke anywhere in this world and you want a quick, sure-fire method of setting yourself up – I'm talking about real money, a hundred grand minimum – get a bag of the finest seeds, go to Queensland, hike a few days into the bush, find a river creek, plant out the grass. Return in a few months and you'll have a crop worth a fortune. The Australian smoker is usually too busy contemplating his bong to even get to the beach.

'Queensland, fuckin' shuck mate, it's too bleedin' far.'

By now I'd had a shit, a shave and a shampoo, and felt one hundred and fifty per cent worse. The Blender of Anxiety was churning at 2,000 revs-per-second in my stomach. What was Lobo going to spring on me next? Over by the pool, the dingo was lounging on a large checked blanket. A bad sign. Idleness, in him, had the same menace as a tiger's stillness before the pounce.

Selecting a clean pair of trousers and yet another silk shirt from Rex's bag for bush-fire victims, I attempted to scrub him from my mind. Just one minute. Please?

'Hey, Frankie, get down to busy-ness.'

'Wait one minute,' I yelled, reaching under the seat for the bag of grass. 'Shit!' I exclaimed, struggling to keep the exclamation under my breath as I felt the bag's lightness. Ripping open the plastic, I muttered, 'Bloody stalks, hardly any leaf left.' We'd smoked most of it on the road from Sydney. 'Oh God,' I groaned, 'bang goes my plane ticket.

'Why the gloomy face?' Lobo demanded as I tottered towards the blanket square.

'Jesus, Lobo. It's a disaster. The dope's bloody gone.'

'Pass to me the bag,' he growled, 'and shut up with your dirty moaning. Always you worry so! What does it matter if we sell leaves from an old tree? All this grass we should keep it for ourselves, these stalk-es we can mix with anything. There is not a problem here.'

'Yeah, and bloody take the consequences, pay the Piper, huh? I've never done anything like that in my life.'

Looking up, Lobo smiled. 'Are you really serious?'

'Yes. Deadly serious.'

'OK.' Lobo shrugged. 'This it is your game. The cricket we play strictly by your rules.'

I noticed a roll of cooking foil and a folded newspaper at Lobo's side.

'I am waiting,' he said. 'What are you going to do now, huh? How much weight do you think you have?'

Involuntarily, I yawned. 'Oh, optimistically, I reckon three to four ounces. Stalks included.'

'Well?'

'Lobo, I don't know what I'm going to do.'

Lobo sneered. 'Always you are so full of bright ideas.' He leaned over, and before I could restrain him, dipped the mouth of the bag into the pool.

'Christ! Stop! You'll ruin it.'

'Do not talk such monkey rubbish to me. Do not you see it is heavier? Now, help me. Spread out the newspaper and let us see what we have here.' He slopped the sludge onto the centrefold, the pin-up girl at last modestly garbed.

'Oh, *fucking* . . . Shit, Lobo,' I wailed, 'You've ruined it!'

Lobo gritted his teeth, grimacing. 'Always you use the filthy language. It is too much. All this time I am hoping for an end to this dirt, but always it keeps coming. When will you learn?' He shook his head if to clear the dirty words from his ears.

'Now, please to be patient. Look, the sun already it makes steam. It is good, no? Look how the grass it fluffs up. Now, I have a way to make this smell strong.' He pointed. 'Go find a cow shitty that it is fresh, and you know I will be angry if it is a hard one.' And loudly now: 'Hurry, I do not want to be waiting all the day. What do you look like that for. Do not tell me you it is now you start minding the dirt.'

Ned Kelly in his iron mask, stumbling up the hillocks. This cursed helmet, all askew. It was only by squinting that could I see anything at all through this slit. Yes, these last three days of winding trails had narrowed my vision and spun me round and round till all I had to focus on was Lobo's penetrating nags. *Look about you now. Always you are moaning. You must to concentrate. Why do not you thank me?*

Through the slit I saw plastic packaging lying in the grass. Not caring about the dangers of salmonella in rancid chicken grease, I thrust my hands into its greasy interior and held it out like a Siamese surgeon's mitt, calling, 'Cow shitty-shitty, where are you?'

At the summit of a knoll, beside a sun-faded fertiliser bag, the mother of all turds lay steaming. Scooping it up with my makeshift glove, trying just to concentrate on the task in hand, I flipped it over onto the bag. Cautiously then, having disposed of the mitt, I lifted the fertiliser bag by the corners.

'Whoa! Steady now my beauties.' A trickle of shit, something sparkling. Damn it, a glint of gold. In my haste to grab at whatever it was, I dropped a corner of the plastic, loosing a further quantity of muck.

Bending down, I carefully wiped the . . . ring on the grass.

My heart dropped like I had magnets in my boots. Jesus, all that effort, and for what? I stretched up angrily, veeing my disgust at this foul trick to the leery cyclops in the sky.

Cheap trash. The green stone was far too big to be real, set presumptuously as it was in a square of paste diamonds. The thin, soft alloy of the shank was bent where mastoid teeth had scrunched it. Wiping it some more I slipped it into my pocket thinking, I'll save it for some dumbstruck Sheila, if I ever get away from that poisonous dago-dingo.

100

The eternal gofer returning, holding out his fertiliser bag like it was an apron and he'd just caught the soup. I found Lobo occupied making snaky patterns in the drying broth of grass.

He looked up, speaking in a Nazi falsetto. 'Ah, my friend Frankie, always I am so pleas-ed to see you. You have brought the shitty! Is it a good one?'

I grunted in affirmation, feeling somewhat menial.

'Put it down.' He pointed to the patch of mangy yellow earth to his left. 'And make sure to spread it, otherwise we are waiting the whole afternoon for it to dry.'

After I had washed off the visible dirt, Lobo motioned me in close as a scout master at a pow-wow. Dib-dib-dubbedy-dub, two men in a tub. 'Sit down, and make the effort please to concentrate. Stop the mind from wandering. I know you are tiring, but today it is not for holidays. Now I am showing you how we make sticks for computers.'

With a flourish, Lobo produced a shiny roll of silver foil. Then, taking the scissors from his manicure set, he speedily cut a bunch of long strips, each about two inches wide, snipping them off at four-and-a-half-inch lengths. Holding a strip between thumb and forefinger as one would a cigarette paper, Lobo took a largish pinch of grass from the dry mound on the centrefold.

'Watch closely,' he said, spreading a line of grass along the strip. 'Frankie, you must be careful when making these stick-es. This it is the same as any other busy-ness. If the product is dressed in a shiny package, you sell the double. This is how the world it works, Mark my words. And the stick-es they must look fat, no dents or dirty marks. You are concentrating?'

Lobo rolled the foil into a shining tube, neatly twisting both ends, 'Now,' he continued, 'this it is the important bit. I blow and twist like this so the air it is all trapp-ed inside. The stick it then feels more full, and it is only later when the fellow is around the corner he knows the whole story. Is good, no?'

Waggling it like a baton by the twisted end, Lobo emphasised his point as he passed the stick over.

Hastily I rubbed my hands on my shirt before accepting it, then tested its density, pressing it lightly between thumb and forefinger. Smiling lock-jawed, I offered the stick back to him.

Lobo cursed. 'Pah! I did not mean for you to bump it.' He sighed. 'Always you make so many problems. Now you must to make good with work. Mix the shitty in with the stalks and also a little dry grass. When you are finishing and cleaning up, we take some time off. Always to work makes the chap into a dry biscuit,' Smiling winningly, not to mention waggling his accurs-ed eyebrows, he surmised, 'I have the correct expressing, no?'

Of course I found it easy to make a lookalike mixture of cowshit, stalks, dried field grass and leaves, I'm not a clod. I even found some convincing-looking seeds on an honesty bush, enjoying the artistry involved and finding satisfaction in the task.

At turns Lobo came over to view my progress 'Hey! You know this it is good. I like the touch of the seed-es. But you should also make pee into it. The peoples then get ston-ed from what you smoke.'

Satisfied the mixture was convincing, I turned my attention to the silver foil, making a number of failed experiments before I mastered the knack. Even then, Lobo's eye for fine detail was a quality-control that was hard to pass. Finally, he was satisfied, but pointed out that even my best efforts didn't compare to his, and my sticks took twice as long to roll. He waited patiently while I caught up with his total. Thirty sticks each.

Then, of course, came the compulsory bathing. It was while occupied with this that I stepped on what I thought was an old conduit pipe. On examination it turned out to be a hollow aluminium walking stick, the rubber tip unperished. I suggested we might use it for concealing sticks. Lobo's packages proved a perfect fit; mine rattled somewhat. But no matter.

Lobo trumpeted, 'You see? My Voice it is right. You have a brain, and now, you make a contribution.' He swung the stick like Charlie C. 'You like my walk?' He hobbled a few steps. 'Now, you are watching?' Suddenly Lobo, pivoting on the walking stick, kicked empty space beside my head.

'Such a thing it is handy, no? All the peoples think I am cripple.' He lowered his voice confidentially. 'You know, always it is good to fool the opposition.'

Lobo, one hand over his brow, pretended to scan the bushes for concealed Indian scout-es. 'And now we make time for pleasure. We go to a movie? Since tonight you make good busy-ness, this time you pay.'

As Lobo busied himself with a 'necessary' reorganisation in the back of the Ute, I pulled out my money-belt from its hiding place. Quickly my fingers scuttled across the notes. Christ! I couldn't believe it. One hundred and eleven dollars? It wasn't possible. Last time I counted it had been one hundred and forty-seven. Had Lobo been at my stash? That wasn't possible either. Could I be losing my mind? I flashed back. I was sure that the first time I counted it I had two hundred and three dollars. Then it came to one hundred and eighty-odd when I recounted it. Now it was a hundred and eleven. I'd spent next to nothing – the occasional pack of cigarettes, a soft drink – ten dollars at the most. Apart from that, we'd heisted everything. Could it be this was the start of cracking up?

15

The other side of the antipodean coin is that thronging, throbbing lump of gristle, King's Cross. Things that go bump in the recesses of closets in any other part of Oz are out there for all to see in King's Cross: dispossessed Aborigines clutching raggedy bundles as if they were their own intestines, transvestites and hookers on parade, and everywhere businessmen, flushed, red-faced, drunk and leering. Here and there, desperate parents thrust photographs of lost ones into the turned-away faces of the crowd. Stiletto heels click in time to a Latin rumba played with dash by the Salvation Army Band from tonight's chosen bandstand – the steps of the subway station. There, stumbling backwards against this tidal flow of fevered humanity, stands an untouchable, unsanitary lavatory mop, clad in nothing else but a tightly-gathered plastic mac.

A plague of masks . . . And I haven't even mentioned the less visible but nonetheless apparent junkies, amyl nitrate salesmen, weekend weirdos, art students and tourists. And, of course, the ever-prevalent forty-one per centers, the gays, all possible variations and descriptions: crew-cut butch-boys all done out in Lederhosen; a surfeit of oil from the Levantines, fat and aromatic in silk suits; sailor-boys, diddy-men, romantic and poetic types holding hands, moustachioed newts splendid in worsted suits with coloured handkerchiefs flopping from breast pockets. I wondered if they belonged to some secret society – a gay lodge of freemasons perhaps?

It's a well-known fact that as recently as the 1930s, in this continent of paradoxes, males outnumbered females by three to one, thus causing a permanent warping of the national humour. Most jokes make a butt of poofters, which suggests to social anthropologists such as myself that homosexuality of the bully-boy type is rampant, though banged up and nailed into that closet. But not here in King's Cross.

There's a bar on the corner where King's Cross is joined by Darlinghurst Parade, a rough joint seen through the armoured-glass windows, a graffiti of bobbing silhouettes. Inside, the atmosphere is heady with smoke, beer and sweat. There is no space, except around the periphery. We found two seats beside the dripping windows, conveniently positioned for the pleasant cool draft from the door. Lobo rested the walking stick on his knee.

A tall, dark-skinned girl – Tahitian, I judged from the purple flower in her long brown hair – detached herself from the bustle of shadows ten deep at the bar. Wobbling uncertainly on four-inch stilettos, she took a perch on the windowsill and leaned forwards suggestively, a long, deniered leg brushing Lobo's white-trousered thigh.

Lobo looked up, a foxy smile licking around the corners of his lips.

The girl remarked loudly. 'I like you. You have eyes like mine. We two would make a pretty foursome.

Puzzled, I looked around for her friend. I decided she had problems counting.

Lobo leaned towards her, eyelashes fluttering, resting his chin on one hand. A slippery sliding and she'd moved in close, her voice a dream of cream floating with raspberry ripple, slooping over from a high glass. 'How would you like to spend the night with me, my daarling?'

Lobo's fruit-case was a sun-kissed melon. Reaching out he tweaked a suspender through the clinging lurex dress, then patted her rump condescendingly, pouting and smacking his lips. 'My darling, I cannot tonight . . . I am not thinking for myself, but for my friend, Peter.'

I looked around again, but he had gestured my way.

'What would he do to occupy himself?' Lobo continued, 'I would be so sad to think of him lonely.' He smiled wistfully. 'But if you can buy the next round of drinks, I will see if I can fix him up.'

Delighted to oblige, this Tahitian's elasticated ass shoved into the thick crowd around the bar, re-emerging with a jug of ale and three glasses. I noticed as she poured the drinks that her hand was shaking.

Taking his drink, Lobo played a frown as he looked her up. 'Tell me, is this a modest way to be dressing? You know, I am not liking girls who show too much of themselv-es. I have decided, my friend Peter is all the company I need.' Lobo slapped my knee, wrapped an arm around my shoulders, turned away and, sipping his beer, stared coldly out of the window. His was the unscalable silence of the north face of the Eiger.

A couple of times the girl made as if she was about to say something. She poked her teeth with a long red nail, then rolled a big circle in the air. The finger stopped, pointed towards the door. Muttering something in Tahitian, she slammed her glass on the table and tottered woodenly to the street.

Lobo nudged my shoulder, pointing through the window at the girl's departing rear-end. 'Look at the way he walks.'

'What do you mean, he?'

Lobo scanned my face for a moment. 'You are not fooling, surely?'

I gazed back evenly.

'Ha, I can see it in your eyes. You notice nothing. That girl is a man.'

'Oh, come on now, Lobo. Not everyone in this place is bent. Some people, you know, really are as they seem. I thought she was quite pretty. In fact I was about to get jealous, and I must say I think you treated her pretty shabbily.'

'Frankie' – Lobo leaned close – 'it is amazing. Only five minutes on the street, and you are wanting to throw yourself into the jaws of the first trap you are meeting. I tell you, it is impossible for a man to walk the same as a woman. These transvestidgees, they do not fool me, the only thing their bottoms are good for, it is spanking.'

It came back to me . . . The departing ass and its wooden, lumbar progress, not rolling as a woman's would.

'You're right,' I said glumly, staring into my empty glass.

Lobo stood up. 'You have had a good drink? You are finishing? Come, we go.' Lightly he clapped his hands.

It seemed I'd been in King's Cross many times before. A bit like Soho? Nah, that's a dump, unworthy of inclusion into the Sodom and Gomorrah guide. Maybe Montparnasse, only brassier. More people; more heat. Every car crawling, the crowd six-deep on the pavement, spilling out around parked cars. Blaring horns, angry, hurled remarks, earnest types rattling collection boxes, buskers in closed shop-entrances, all-night grocery stores, sex shops, arcades, slot-machine halls. Doorways with signs reading 'Nookie Bar' or 'Naked Bitch Service'. Billboards and posters of unclothed women smiling, with both mouths. Graffiti daubings, drunks out of it on corners. The fashionable and the partly-clothed. And the heat. The heat of the streets, and the eyes watching you with spermicide spectacles. King's Cross, Sydney, on Saturn's day night.

We walked some, Lobo's hobble imbuing him with an even greater elegance, as if his wound were a prize won on some far-off battlefield. He radiated presence, nodding and grinning at the crowd. At pavement cafés, Lobo occupied himself by displaying his cool – streetwise, a baron on his turf, snapping his fingers to order coffee. When we left he snitched five dollars from my pocket, leaving it on the table as a tip. The last of the big spenders. Ho ho ho ho.

I watched from the sidelines as he passed time with an ancient Aborigine moll, dressed up to flirt and captivate, a revealing cloth barely covering shrunken and shrivelled teats. Her grin was wide as the Australian outback, the blackened stumps of her teeth like mesomorphic rocks. Her laugh warbled like a kookaburra's dying breath. Lobo shared the drugs of some raw spirit from this crone's bottle. With a scraggy arm she pulled him close and sealed his lips with a drunken wet smack. Maybe she was on that as well. She whispered in his ear. He seemed to be listening intently, then gently pulled himself free.

Seated at another white plastic table at the opposite side of the square, I vented my frustration, demanding to know when we would kick the dope operation into gear.

Lobo shook his head reproachfully. 'Always you are so impatient. Did you not notice?'

'Notice what?'

'Really, Frankie, you are so dumb. You watch me with the lady. What you think I am doing?'

'Really, Lobo,' I yawned, looking away. 'I can't imagine.'

Lobo's voice was hard and remonstrative. 'I know this woman from before. She is the queen of the street. Everything that passes, she see.' Lobo chopped air, his hand a snap-happy guillotine. 'We are advertising. This is how you do any busy-ness. Mary the Aborigine woman, she tells her peoples. Even now they are spreading the word. We have to show ourselves. This brings some danger, but we can cover it. Relax, Frankie.'

Lobo laid a hand on my forearm, brown skin shading out my white. 'This it is the first day only, there is no difference from any military operation. First is coming the scouting. Since it is shitty-sticks we are selling we have to do the whole thing in one or two nights. Otherwise' – Lobo drew the flat of his hand across his throat – 'we lose our heads. This it is a certainty! Now, come you. Let us walk.' Lobo, leaning hard on his cane, hobbled on with redoubled vigour.

Approaching the corner, Lobo lurched into me, speaking in an undercover voice. 'See this man standing there?'

Trying not to move my head, I swivelled my eyes to their limits. A man was leaning in a shop doorway, picking at his nails with a long-handled metal comb.

Lobo rasped, 'Watch now! He will follow. My Voice, it tells me.'

The plastic protecting the large advertisement at the bus-stop afforded an excellent if distorted reflection of the street behind. Lazily, the man detached himself from the wall and strolled out not ten steps behind us.

'You see,' Lobo said, 'how it is? This man he is paid by the watchers to follow us. This I know. Already they are interesting. You see what he carries?' Lobo grabbed my arm. 'Do not look back on any account. The handle of his comb he files it to a point. These Maltese, they carry half of the blade in the palm, and if you are lucky they hit to mark not to kill. I hear of a person with a hundred wounds from these combs. But, as they say in this stupid country, no wurries. He is free to follow, no? It is because we are so strong on the street they watch us. It is good, no? Already our plan it is working.'

Lobo pulled me up in front of the window of a narrow shop selling red corsets, black bras, suspender belts, rubber hose. Lobo pointed at a bra with long tassles. 'You like to wear this pair, huh? Think how much sticks you can hide inside.'

'Shut up, Lobo,' I growled.

'Cannot you take a joke,' he laughed. 'What a mad kick-side you are. How ever I find you?'

Professor Lobo took me on an Open University tour of the streets. He pointed out a girl ahead, holding out her hand. As we passed, Lobo slapped the supplicating palm aside. Automatically it swung back, as if powered by a sprung hinge. The girl stared fixedly, pupils pointed pinheads, the whites of her eyes glazed and bloodshot. Behind us I heard the jingle of silver as some Samaritan dropped some small change into her palm.

'You see?' Every second or third person gives twenty cents. How much do you think that comes to in an hour?'

'Three bucks, maybe?'

'No. If you are using the brain, it come to twenty dollars. This place you know, it is very busy. Maybe she works four or six hours a night. More than a hundred dollars.' Lobo laughed. 'You see how the life it is? She has no mortgage to pay. She probably screws for the money too. Who is the more successful, I ask you, the man who works in the office, or her?'

'She more than likely spends everything she gets supporting her heroin habit.'

'That is exactly correct, Frankie, but why not? If that is what she wants to do.'

We walked and we walked and we walked. Gradually, under Lobo's tutelage, I began to feel the pulse of the street: a hand passing a package under a table; the language of nods and winks exchanged in busy places by too obviously distracted people; and the colour red. Red blood running down the nose of the girl. Justice, or otherwise, is brutal and swift in these parts. The pimp dealt the girl another wicked blow to the head. Mary, or Emma or whatever her name was, fell to her knees pleading for forgiveness. The pimp, for good measure, kicked her in the mouth. More blood. Everybody walked on by. Cruising cops turned their heads away.

On Saturn's day night, they get drunk in cars, they fight in bars.

Decent folk stay in, on Saturn's day night.

16

En route back to our hide-out in the Kalahari, Lobo droned ceaselessly about 'How it is in the street.' That's all the quote I'll give. When we retired to our separate quarters, the sounds of his reorganising lasted millennia. It occurred to me that intelligence agencies might gainfully employ his process for brainwashing.

Did I sleep? I don't know. I do know all my senses were used razor blades, sharp enough to cut me to the quick; but dulled by sleeplessness I didn't feel wounds. Lobo was slicing acres off my vast encompassing flesh, but as yet he was a long way from the bone. Bring on the chainsaws.

In the morning the imp from Tibet announced he'd slept surpassing well, but I suspected I was being fed a line. My hands trembled as I rolled the first joint of the day. Moodily, I stared into the surface of the pool. The day was as cloudy as my mind.

I listened woodenly as Lobo outlined the strategy for the coming night. It seemed his sentences were chiefly made up of 'key' words – sharp-edged petite icebergs, stumbling blocks for my paranoia. I'll explain, the way he did. 'You see, Frankie, this is it phase two. It is good we know the WATCHERS are out. Concentrate the mind now. Tonight we take all the sticks. I carry good sticks in the cane, a couple of bad ones at the end. But you do not mind to carry a few, huh? It is not DANGEROUS for you. Everybody they LOOK at me. YOU are like the shadow. TROUBLE, you slip away. Now we smarten up, always the image it must be good, NO?'

We set up operations in a concrete plaza dominated by an ugly piece of modern sculpture known as The Gazebo. If the wind gusts the smell of municipal chlorine permeates for blocks around. At the far end of the square stood a low ugly building, prominent because of its malfunctioning sign, which flickered out the name of this dislocated business: King's Cross Police Station. Busy traffic passed through its dirty plate-glass doors, jaded men in crumpled suits, many of them carrying trays of food from the nearby take-away.

We spotted our punter loitering suspiciously by the other side of the fountain. Garbed in the compulsory denim uniform of youth desperate to belong, he held his neck turkey stiff, eyes darting from side to side. Every now and then he would jerk around as if something was creeping up on him.

Lobo rasped, 'Pssst. Hey fellow, come here you.'

The youth gulped nervously, his Adam's apple more of a chin than his chin. Starting in Lobo's direction, he pointed at his chest, saying in universal sign lingo, 'Who, me?'

Lobo nodded prodigiously.

Chinless Punter, affecting a kind of spastic hopalong, ambled towards us, eyes twitching from side to side, both laces of his long, scuffed boots undone. Spots, plukes and pimples made a lunar landscape of his face. Hair? Well let's just say it was long and lank. Grinning like a hungry barracuda, Lobo seemed almost four-dimensional beside him.

It sounded more like a threat when Lobo demanded, 'You want to score?'

The punter tried to look cool. 'Uh, yeah man, maybe, ah, what have you got?'

Only the best, the finest. Have you been waiting for us long?'

Oh no, man. I'm here with ah . . . friends. They're coming back in a, er, minute.'

'I understand you purrfectly.' Lobo's teeth glittered. 'Nothing there is for wurrying. You want me show you?' Lobo snapped his fingers. 'Peter, pass to me one.'

'Oh no, man.' The punter's eyes shifted towards the flickering police sign.

Lobo held up a calming hand. 'No wurries man. I tell you, while you stay with us, not one of these fellows touch-es you. We have protection. Now, you want to see? If you prefer it that way, we go around the corner.'

As we strolled past the cop shop, entering a lane narrow and dark, Lobo, sticking like fly-paper to our mark, continued, 'How you find us? You very smart. So many bad fellows around. Now, what it is you want?'

'I don't know if I want anything, man. I just want to see the goods first,' the kid blurted defensively, suddenly stopping dead.

My sudden impact jolted him forward. The punter, alarmed, twirled around, hands raised.

Lobo's voice soothed, 'My friend. You do not have to buy. I like you. You have spirit. You hit lucky when you find us. Normally, you know, we are only selling to the other dealers.'

They started walking again, Lobo a rattlesnake smiling. The punter, was he hypnotised?

Lobo breathed, 'You were going to say what it is you look for.'

'Uh . . . Yeah,' the youth replied. 'Well . . . w-what do you have?'

'Everything.' Lobo winked, signalling me to . . .

Muscle in on the wongly dildo on the walkabout – his first night in King's Cross and he has to pick us. Then I remembered it wasn't grass we were selling, it was fucking mudsticks. Little shitty-sticks from the Kalahari, Godalmighty this was loathsome, and what's more we had to sell loads of these 'packages'.

I reminded myself then it was no different from any other busy-ness. Christ, I am already beginning to think like the Tibetan.

Mutating into an Argentinian used-car salesman of dubious repute, Lobo spread his hands wide. 'Tell me what you want. I cannot sell you the goodies until you tell me what you want.'

The kid gulped nervously, 'Uh, um . . .'

Lobo interjected harshly, 'You want pills? You want cocaine? You want hash?' The kid nodded negatively.

Lobo clutched the punter's arm. 'I know what it is you want, we have a beautiful grass. One hundred per cent flower heads. I tell you, my friend, it is a very special smoke. Have you a girlfriend?'

The kid nodded nervously.

'That it is good. She will go wild. It makes your cock as big as a mule, this grass.'

The punter stammered, 'H-h-how much is it?'

'Only thirty dollars my friend. Every deal, twice the normal size.'

He looked relieved. 'I don't have that much,' he said.

'How much you got?' Lobo demanded quickly.

The punter stuttered, 'Ohh . . . F-f-fifteen d-dollars.'

Lobo pulled him into the light of the only functioning street lamp. 'Let me see. You have loose change in your wallet. Count it.'

His cash float totalled eighteen dollars and fifty-seven cents. Lobo shook his head slowly. 'Oh dear. It is sad this. I say to myself, because I like this man, I give him it for twenty dollars, but at this price, I lose.' Lobo prodded me with a quick glance.

Dutifully, I chipped in. 'Come on Eldric, can't we afford this one, huh?'

Lobo's eyes turned inwards to consult an oracle. Punter looked around desperately searching for an avenue of escape.

Lobo gripped the punter's arm, 'Yeah, OK,' he drawled, 'for once we break our rule.'

A car crawled by. Lobo grabbed the money, 'Quick,' he shouted. 'This way!'

The youth protested. 'You said we were protected?'

Lobo hobbled convincingly, dragging the punter into the gloom of the alleyway. 'No,' he said emphatically, 'that is not the cop-es! It is the bad men who sell the smack. Pah! I would not touch the stuff. It is a evil. But no wurries. I do not run off with the money. You are OK. Peter protects you while I go to the stash.'

I was surprised. What was Lobo up to? We both knew a couple of shitty-sticks were concealed at the top of the cane. I supposed it was all in the name of doing a thorough job. Lobo was putting on a show as much for me as for the punter.

Our hapless victim gibbered with paranoia. 'W-w-when do you think he'll be back?'

'Don't worry about it, man. Don't you know? Never take anyone to the stash. It's a rule of the business. Now shaddup, will you, I thought I heard a sound.

Silence pealed off the dank walls, dripped from the Abyssinian harlot's soaking cheesecloth. I saw this in the soothsayer's dark glass I always carry concealed on my person. I did not see much else. The glass was so dirty. Where was Lobo? I peered and I peered and I still could not see . . I wet my finger and rubbed the glass, clearing a dark pane in the grime. Misty, inky, swirling, red-tinged turbulences. I rubbed some more. Surprised when the pane swung open under the pressure of my probing finger. Somehow I'd activated the mechanism of a secret panelled door. Without pausing to consider the consequences, I squeezed in through the small gap.

Somehow, sometime, I was back in my castle, standing in the dark and richly-brocaded timbered main hall, strangely insubstantial despite the gloom. That this was my castle was indisputable, yet I discerned vital differences. For one thing, through the lead-lined windows was a sky the likes of which I had never seen – red and black clouds billowing like the undergarments of a Spanish ballerina. Like my estranged wife's bloomers, when I thought about it. One of Beelzebub's favourite children she was, a genuine man-trap. In the scale of devils, I didn't even rate next to her colossal jack-booted bulk. It was too much to bear, the thought she might be nearby.

I became aware a typewriter was rattling nearby. But where was the source of the sound? I looked around in puzzlement. On the wall facing me was a convex mirror I'd never seen before. A very strange mirror, I came to realise as I regarded it, for it reflected some things not in the room and failed to reflect other things in the room . . . Me, for instance. I shivered. Perhaps I was a ghost and not here at all. There she was, Her Bitchy Omnipotence, by the massive stone fireplace, the flickering flames of the blazing logs gilding her normally cold and pellucid face with a strangely cheery glow. The Hag was rattling at a steam-driven typewriter, pouring out reams of manuscript by the minute, it seemed. Beside her feet, sprawled on a red Persian rug, lay her one-time favourite lover, turned in a fit of rage into a huge and dangerous black Neapolitan mastiff by the name of Shaun, chewing on the hindquarters of a bison . . .

It seemed I had been staring at the mirror for ages when a movement startled me, the high-backed executive armchair on the side of the fireplace swivelled round in a lazy half-circle. The figure lolling in it was more a straw doll than anything else, dangling feet barely touching the floor. For a good half-minute I failed to recognise the idiot savant face, then I realised with horror, it was my own. All of a sudden he looked up, and for a brief moment our eyes met. It was as if I − he sensed my presence on the other side of that mirror.

I regarded myself silently, my alter ego for the want of a better word, as he turned his attention back to the soothsayer's dark glass he held in his pale, thin and aristocratic hands, its curves reflecting the secret billows of my wife's undergarments, the dark castle room, and the panel I'd left ajar . . . That was a stupid mistake, for I failed to see the Boojum extending a long vacuum nozzle out from the secret door, and before I could grab a hold of anything, I was sucked bodily, with all the other wastes, out of the room, into a flesh-walled twisting tunnel which I knew to be the small intestine of a monstrous beast . . .

I found myself staring at my own reflection, as through a glass murkily. I was in a stinking back alleyway in Sydney. Beside me shivered a pimply-faced gangly youth.

It had been ten minutes. Lobo surprised us both by bouncing out of nowhere, a Charlie Chaplin lookalike nipping off the rubber stopper at the tip of the cane with his toe, then shouting. 'Catch!' and firing the shitty-stick with diabolical accuracy into the hands of the surprised punter.

I wondered if he'd been practising that trick these past ten minutes, and that was the reason he'd taken off.

As we left the punter tearing at his shitty-stick, I called over my shoulder, getting in the final parting shot, 'A-by-ssin-ia, Mos-cow, Cey-lon!'

Turning the corner, Lobo remarked, 'You say very strange words. Never am I understanding you, Frankie. I wonder if that it is the same for you?'

17

The municiple chlorine still drifted as a silken veil across the plaza. I welcomed the light spray, finding the sting on my skin moderately refreshing. Hey ho, the sights of King's Cross all blurry now.

I started with fright when Lobo grabbed my arm.

'Look,' he boomed, lips frighteningly brushing my ear-lobes, finger pointing at the crowd wall-lining the concourse one hundred yards distant. 'There, you see?'

'Where? What?'

'Not that-a-way dolt. Move the head. To that side. No, do you see him?'

'Uh, yeah,' I lied, spending the first coin to hand.

'The watcher who follows, the last night.' Lobo grinned. 'Now it is we who turn the table.'

Keeping a good twenty paces behind, or so I assumed, Lobo hobbled rapidly, pushing me along. 'Come you, we must not lose him. Walk fast now.'

Lobo growled, 'First you walk slow, and now you walk quick. Slow or we bump him.' Bending down, he rubbed his leg vigorously. 'Oh, my leg, it hurts so.' He looked up, grinning, 'You see, Frankie, I am learning your moaning ways. I think it is your wicked sense of humour you are always trying on me.'

Lobo stopped before a spreading flight of marble, dancing with pinks and blues rippling downwards from the strobing neon over the club's garishly-lit entrance. Such a gushing of paddy fields cascading to the street – no, they were steps, actually. I'm forced to make the excuse my eyeballs were exceedingly fatigued.

A stream of do-hickies ascended them like pilgrims to Mecca. The usual disappointment lurked on the other side . . . Is that all there is?

Finally literacy came to my rescue – I managed to read what the sign was flashing: 'Club de les Goils'. Goils? I wondered. Is that how they spell it here? The doorway was bedecked with photos of buxom half-men, typical Aussies, swirling with crinoline, lace-fringed nonsenses, rouged and powdered under pretzel-style bouffant hair-dos or turbans spouting ostrich feathers and studded with paste emeralds as big as pigeons' eggs. All of it was supposed to remind one of the court of Marie-Antoinette.

Lobo pointed. 'There, he goes, the watcher, you see.' He tapped his head significantly. 'I tell you, Frankie, this it is where the spider is making the web for the streets.' Lobo laid a hand on my arm. 'We have to be careful. You have the samples? Give to me a good one.'

Reaching into my breast pocket, I moved in close, shielding the transaction.

'What are you doing now?' Lobo demanded loudly. 'Stop this silly busy-ness at once. Pass it to me. No one sees.'

Angered, I thrust it into his hand.

'Oh, you have crumpled it.' Lobo's lips curled in disgust. 'Why always you are behaving so?' His talons, gripping my shoulders. 'Now, if you are ready, we go in. In the right spirit, huh?' Lobo hopped vigorously up the steps, somehow managing to limp convincingly despite his rapid progress.

Wearily trailing at his heels, I stumbled after him.

Lobo's progress was arrested by the bouncers, three orang-utans stepping out at the head of the stairs, blocking our progress with their heaving collective bulk.

One of them yelled to Lobo, 'Where do you think you're going, sonny boy?'

Lobo stood stock still, balancing on his toes. 'My friendz,' he said, his tongue a razor whittling the words, 'I hope it is not to me you speak in this way.'

Swivelling then, he passed the cane. 'Peter, hold this a minute. Maybe we get a-trouble here.'

The largest of the orang-utans, I'll call him Ginger on account of his flaming red hair, slapped his chest and bellowed, 'Fucking Jap-jerk. I am talking to you, slit-eyes. No one but no one gets in here without my permission. And you don't get in here until I see what you've got in you're pockets!'

A cliff of flesh about to fall on us – and then the ape on Lobo's left reached out to touch his shoulder. That one I'll call Fat Chance.

I didn't even see Lobo's hand slapping Fat Chance's arm away. Neither did the others. A couple of whips cracking, Lobo shot both fists out, his whole body snapping into a karate fighting stance.

It was too much – in a perverse reaction, I exploded with hysterical laughter. I won't dwell on my nether regions, how my legs turned into jellied eels.

Lobo's voice had somehow transmuted into a diamond-tipped drill – with hammer-action. 'Take back your dirty words,' he whined. 'Apologise this ink-stand,' he hammered, 'otherwise I kill the three of you.'

The next moment seems to me to be perpetually stitched up in the blink of a tiger. Somewhere on an alternative earth, this scene is replayed again and again: three large apes confronting a Tibetan and a Scotsman braying like a camel. A man with no values, just a collapsed hold-all containing one dirty sock, his very unclean and polluted soul. The one that Lobo's going to clean if they ever get out of here.

'Take back your filthy words, and apologise immediately, otherwise I chop you into pieces.'

The orang-utans grunted, jaws instantaneously dropping on account of the one brain held in common between them.

'Unless you apologise for your filthy language, you take the consequences. NOW!' To my utter amazement, the voice that issued from the fleshly lips of Ginger was sweet, apologetic, to the point of nausea. He rasped absurdly, 'Listen, matey, we were only doing our jobs. We didn't mean to be rude. That's how we talk to everyone. We have to check people who come in here for drugs and weapons. It's our job . . .'

Snibbing the safety catch back on, Lobo smiled wickedly. 'This time I accept your apology, and for your satisfaction, I tell you there is nothing but a handkerchief in my pockets. You can see it if you want. I do not care.'

As we passed along the corridor, Lobo remarked in a low voice, 'For once you did everything right. The way you laugh they think you are a maniac. It is good, this.'

I'd seen it all before. Laser lines wearily dissected thick smoke, the multi-coloured piano wire a little out of tune. This was the same worn old formula, disco-land, anywhere. Except for this twist: the glass-mirrored floor suspended the revellers on the soles of their reflections – all those sneak views afforded of throbbing gristle. Suspicious bulges, sanitary towels – a voyeur's delight. As they say in these parts, 'Chunder up yer Down Under, mate!'

Lobo jocularly slapped me hard on the back, broad teeth dancing with laser zits, 'Hey-hey! This it is the place, no? Now relax, Frankie, while I do the work for the both of us. He gestured like a majordomo who's just bought a majority stake in his club.

I did not seek out a partner. I was suspicious of everyone – gender differences were not a guideline here. It was enough just to whirl and lose myself in the fast-lane words of the New York 'street rap' blaring out from the massed banks of speakers around the console of the DJ in the jockey cap. The music was peppered with sounds of the street: car horns, screeching tyres, sirens, the babble and bubble of the crowd.

> Hey man, yo' walks a long way in de modern world.
> Keep yo' eyes to the left, eyes to the right . . .

> Junkies wid baseball bats in blacked out doorways.
> Hey man, it's a long way down dat elevator shaft.
> Keep yo' eyes to the left, eyes to the right . . .

The big diamante ball suspended from the centre of the ornate ceiling rose spun a zillion tinker bells, brilliant squares of diamond colours. And everywhere mirrors split infinities, the go-go revellers reflected as if we were so many microdots gathered on the facets of a fly's eye.

> Hey man, dis is the modern world.
> Hey yo', black girl in de red polka-dot dress,
> Keep yo' eyes to the left, eyes to the right . . .

> And the street hustler shouts, slappin' arms,
> 'Check it out, check it out, best crack around,
> Keep yo' eyes to the left, eyes to the right . . .

> Dem tall overcoats buttoned up tight.
> Checkin' him out, checkin' yo' out.
> Keep dem eyes to the left, eyes to the right . . .

I lost myself in the dance. Hey man, this is the modern world. Yeah!

Remembering my companion, I peered through the tunnelling crowd, spying him eventually, deep in conversation in the midst of a tightly-packed group around a table at the end of the hall.

I allowed myself to be swept along, out of myself, by Prince Ju-Ju Rapper. Simultaneously it was a release and a relief to fling myself out of the scrotum of confinement that was the cab of the Falcon and Lobo's nagging tongue. I hadn't felt such freedom since I couldn't remember. I became a spinning top, wobbling every now and then a little woodenly.

I was plucked out of my dervish trance by a hand. The hand dragging me towards the exit belonged to Lobo.

'Come! Not a moment to lose.' Something in his voice gave me the feeling of a door opening onto a huge steel mousetrap. No explanation required. We raced along the corridor, the orang-utans at the head of the stairs falling back as we burst past, taking the steps three at a time.

'What happened?' I demanded hoarsely reaching the street a half-leap behind him.

Lobo wrenched my arm, shouting, 'Come you! No time for talk. Walk fast. Move! Get away! My gosh Frankie, you screw the whole lousy thing up!'

Two blocks along the busy concourse, Lobo slowed his pace. 'Yes,' he declared, looking around, 'we are safe in this crowd. The watchers they cannot touch us here.'

Panting, I yelled, 'Lobo, for God's sake! Will you explain to me what the fuck is going on?'

'First you muck the whole thing up, and now you swear in my face. It is too much.' Planting his hands on my chest, Lobo pushed me stumbling backwards into the rotund bulk of a huge fat man.

'Sorry, mate,' I apologised as I helped pull him to his feet.

'Owf,' he heaved, 'Fuck, mate, don't ever do it again.' He raised his arm threateningly.

'All right, all right.' I felt myself cringe.

And when he snarled and waved his fist a second time, I found myself smiling ingratiatingly. 'I said . . . I'm sorry.'

With the stick Lobo was flicking dirt at his feet off the sidewalk and into the gutter. 'Frankie,' he said. 'you are like the fat pig you fall on. You swear the same. Both you cannot keep the feet, but the worst was to hear you say sorry.' He shook his head vehemently. 'You know, I am not believing my ears. My gosh, I am asham-ed for you!'

'Christ Jesus, suffering Mary, is there no end to your nagging!'

'Do not talk in this way!' Lobo exploded, raising his stick. 'Come, we return to the car. I tell you I am so disappointing in you, I could fill two tears with my buckets!'

It was unbelievable, no puppy had ever felt so dejected, rejected. Why didn't I just tell him to piss off? What did it matter what he thought anyway?

We passed the cop shop and into the network of narrow alleyways beyond.

'Look, Lobo, for God's . . .' I bit my tongue. 'For goodness sake, please will you tell me what happened in the club?'

He whirled around, looking me up and down. 'How is it, always you are spoiling everything. In the club, the peoples who run the street I have them eating from the fist of my hand. The trouble at the door with the bouncers it works to our credit. These they are greedy pigeons, when I tell them we have quantity they want to buy the lot. My gosh!' Lobo raised his hands. 'Paf! You almost pickle the both of us into stew.'

118

'Please, Lobo, please tell me what happened, I still don't understand.'

'Ha!' Lobo laughed derisively. 'Oh yes you do one thing right. It is a good job you make of the sticks. It fools the man when he rolls a joint. But the smell, when he lights it. MY GOD!' Lobo pressed his fingers to his lips. 'Do you see what you make me do! Soon my mouth it becomes as dirty as yours!' Pressing both sides of his head, he began to wail.

'Come on, Lobo,' I said weakly, 'don't start going on. Just tell me what happened.'

Lobo pinched his nose. 'Still I am smelling the sheet! I tell you, now we cannot sell on the street, the watchers they look for us everywhere.' Lobo glared. 'And you know they are working with the cop-es. My goodness, I am so . . . very . . . very angry.'

On we walked, on in silence.

At first as we walked through these alleyways the streets were alive . . . and kicking. The fun this time of night seemed to consist of drunken brawling around the steps leading into dive-in bars. But with this marching into silence had come a dimming; the only illumination now was the occasional flickering streetlight. Gone, the slapstick hooligans and those crazy, neon signs, dripping fantastic light.

We'd walked miles it seemed. Lobo's zigzag stitching of this haystack was painstakingly designed to mislead any 'watchers' hot on the trail.

Always my mind kept running off on tangents . . . All I could think about was a childhood tale of Brer Fox misleading Brer Rabbit through a bramble patch.

Finally we turned a corner and there she was, Lobo's Baby, sepulchrally radiant and pristine against the backcloth of this black-sack, trash-can alley.

On reaching the car, even though I knew it was locked, automatically I pressed the door-handle button, astonishment smiting me rigid as the door clicked open. My neck and face flushed with heat.

Christ! It just had to be my side . . .

Lobo, who'd been engaged checking the shadows for 'watchers', was at my back in a trice, thrusting me aside and pulling the door wide.

And bellowing, by Jesus . . .

'Always I am telling you, lock everything. I cannot believe you are leaving it open! And in such a place as this!'

'B-b-but Lobo, I'm more than positive I locked it . . . I . . couldn't've . . .'

Lobo snapped, 'What the heck are you waiting for? Get inside, see what it is gone.'

'For heaven's sake, Lobo.' I protested, following him around the back of the car, noticing with relief that the taut tarpaulin's smoothness was undisturbed, 'I know I left it locked.'

Lobo's reflection, upside down in the lustrous waxed paintwork of the cab, smiled beguilingly. Christ, and he was waving a fist at me! 'My goodness, what are you looking at?' he raved. 'Get to your side and start checking this ink-stand! My gosh, you are making me so mad I make the words wrong.'

I wasn't just saying it. I knew I'd snibbed that door before closing it . . .

My hand shuffled the shadows under the dash, feeling the familiar outlines of the sounds machine, and no cassettes missing from the case. Kneeling down beside the car now, I groped under the rubber mat. Thank God! I breathed again. The bag of sticks, shitty and otherwise, all present and correct.

Lobo, who'd been balancing one foot on the newspaper protecting his seat as he searched behind it, suddenly jerked out of the car. 'Oh my gosh!' he wailed, spinning on his heels, tearing at his hair. 'Such a terrible thing it happens. My camera, she is gone.'

'What camera?' I gawped, rising on cracking knees. 'I've never seen any camera.'

Lobo stopped spinning and glared over the nose of the Baby. 'Now you are doubting my word. It is too much. I am telling you, my beautiful motor-action Canon, she is gone. My sister Heidi, she gave it to me. My gosh, why are you looking like that? Check to see if anything else it is disappearing.'

I delved into the disorganised pile of my possessions, the clothes and bikinis all mixed in together. Everything as I'd left it . . . Well, at least it seemed that way.

Slumping dejectedly back on my seat, the adrenalin subsiding, I noticed for the first time that the thin cotton of my shirt was sodden with sweat. I shook my head, trying to blink away the spots of exhaustion dancing in front of my eyes . . . Maybe I had fucking hallucinated locking the door? Could I be sure of anything?

I turned. 'What can I say?' Lobo was seated staring dead ahead. The way his hands gripped the steering wheel spoke volumes of what he'd like to do with my throat.

'It's all very strange,' I said, 'Apart from the camera, nothing's gone. You've checked the back?'

A cursory nod from Lobo.

'Nothing missing?'

Another nod.

'Even weirder. Well,' I sighed, trying to suppress the yawn, 'it's lucky they didn't smash a window to get in. I'm sorry about the camera, but . . .' I shrugged again, trying to make myself sound more sure than I felt. 'I'm absolutely certain I didn't leave my side unlocked.'

I tensed, preparing myself for the tirade that never came.

Lobo was gazing at me from between open fingers. After a while he lowered his hands and began to laugh – softly at first, but soon he was shaking, vibrating all over, teeth chattering, pressing his hands to his sides . . .

I couldn't stand it. To be swept up like that, by that damnable laugh. It was an affront to my dignity, however shredded it might be.

Gradually his fit subsided. Eyes glittering with dark amusement, he intoned solemnly: 'Frankie, I am accepting the task my Voice it has given me, though I am not understanding the why, but I will say this, at the end of this journey, the both of us, we find the reason. And I tell you now, and mark my words, on that day you will be clean!'

Lobo began to stare upwards. Joining his hands at the fingertips and then raising them heavenwards, he announced, 'What do I care for this camera, even if my sister gave it to me?' Swivelling then, he pointed the wedge of prayer my way, smiling, flapping open his hinged palms like a book to read. 'Never it is worth to make cry baby after the milk it is spilling.'

Outside in the alleyway a yowl split the silence, then a blur of movement past Lobo's head as a mangy black cat jumped onto a trash can half keeled over against a pile of bulging and burst polythene bags.

Lobo suddenly ripped apart his hands, flinging them to the winds. 'Frankie, do not you realise, every moment in the life it is new, and never the same it is as the last? You too can make a fresh start here.'

Lobo turned and motioned towards the cat, now tottering on the rim of the trashcan, one paw reaching inside. 'Is this what you want to live, for that it is the life in the city.'

Suddenly, the can rolled, toppled, and the cat, howling, claws extended, leaped to the side.

Lobo laughed. 'I want to feel the sun on my skin, to bathe in it, to taste and smell the surf, not this stink of the dirty city all the time around. Look you at all the mess the peoples make, everywhere the dirt it is pil-ed. Even if you do not see, it is still there. In the north, I promise you, we sell all the grass and bikinis. You have money then. But I am not understanding for why you must have it, when we are living in this way, each day taking only what we need?'

Lobo leaned over and lightly tapped my shoulder. 'Ahey-hey! You know the old song? *Pack up your troubles in the old kit- bag, and smile, smile, smile.* I want to see you smile, Frankie. What do you say?'

It was my turn to tear at my hair, to yowl and howl in the alleyway. Would that I had. Instead I just sat woodenly. I was lost, damned to perdition. I could have withstood any tongue-lashing, but not this awful forgiveness . . .

After a moment of speechlessness, my brain adrift in clammy glue, I said, 'Yeah, all right Lobo. Sunbathing, surf . . . I'll go for any of that. Don't worry about the camera. Somehow I'll find a way to pay you back, or get another. But before we go, couldn't we try again, I mean to sell some sticks? We've only sold one, after all.'

Lobo frowned. 'Tell me how, my friend, when the streets they are past the brim with watchers.'

'I know,' I said, brightening. 'We'll sell from the car. Any trouble, we just move on.'

Lobo slapped my back. 'At last! You use the sausage in the noddle. You have a good idea.'

And so it was, some time later cruising the almost deserted Darlinghurst Parade, we spied a frumpy, buxom transvestite (I presumed) muscularly hauling a skidding example of the topiarist's art behind her, poor bastard struggling to sniff at every stiff shit it passed – about one every five feet this stretch of the street (I'm including the recumbent, splayed, dribbling drunks in this survey).

Lobo breathed, 'My Voice it tells me, she is a good buy. Remember' – a nudge from his elbow – 'what it is you must say?'

'Yeah, yeah, I'm ready Lobo, pull in now.' Leaning out of the car, and grinning, I called out, 'Hey-hey! Sinsemill-ya. Twenty dollars a stick. Come and git it.'

'Exactly correct,' Lobo whispered encouragingly.

Perhaps I should not have been surprised by the remarkable ease with which we sold that first stick. After all, didn't Lobo's Voice point out the mark? Twenty dollars. One shitty-stick. Trouble was, not too many people were walking the streets. At three in the morning with the neon lights guttering out, this was a dying trade.

Our next target was a leggy prostitute dressed in skimpy, skin-hugging leathers, selling his or her wares at the next street corner. In one hand a tasselled leather whip flicked idly to and fro. Leaning out of the window, I repeated the magic formula. 'Hey-hey . . .'

The little whip cracked and then again. The leather-gloved broad demanded roughly, 'Show me! I don't buy till I see.'

Lobo snapped over my shoulder, 'No, Peter, he steals it.' He shouted, 'It is the best. Take it or leave it. And do not argue for the price either.'

The painted mask of this dude was cracking as he/she snarled, 'Well, it better be, or I'll tie your balls around your necks!' Reaching under the waistband of his/her skirt, he/she pulled out a sticky wad of notes. He/she spat out, 'I'll fucking see you dead if it's bad grass.'

'No wurries,' Lobo called out as I snatched the notes and passed across the stick.

VRROOOM! Lobo hit the gas, laughing, waving one hand, the Lone Ranger whirling a lasso. He exulted, 'You see how easy it is? I tell you, my Voice it never lies.'

By the time the thin light of dawn began to stretch across the rooftops, we'd sold two more of the shitty-sticks. The street was all used up. Eighty bucks to the good. I split the take with Lobo, even though he looked away haughtily, saying he did not care.

We were cruising Sydney Harbour Bridge as the first glimmer of the sun broke over the sculptured brilliance of the city. Down by the water, at the end of its promontory, the Opera House, a staggered stack of nautilus shells, turned a lighter shade of pink.

The road it was a-beckoning.

But (yawn) before we could head on into the wind, we had to fill up our tank . . . from their tanks . . . and get all the shopping. We targeted a twenty-four-hour supermarket.

Working as a team we pulled a massive load. Lobo hypnotised the assistant, horrifying him with a story of a gigantic mouse on the shelves. The mouse was me, scuttling out the store pushing a trolley stowed with plunder. No 'watchers' in sight. Bound to be one in the bushes, though. Always they are watching. Every Tibetan knows that.

'Hey-hey!' Lobo shouted. 'Turn up the stereo. Roll a joint. Make it a pure one now. We need the smell to cover up the way you stink of petrol.' He thumped the steering wheel – Wak! Wak! – the ball of his hand marking the beat. 'Dooby-dooby-doo – Wak! 'Hey, did you see the face of the shopkeeper?' Wak! 'He-he-hey hey!'

No zombie albatross had every descended into a deeper realm of catatonia. As the sun rose, my only sensation from this migraine blade was a slow paring back of the peel round this soft orange, my head. At least, now, I was getting air into my poor addled brain. One day, I had been assured, it would be clean.

18

No doubt there are worse hells than a beach packed with Australians, but I've yet to meet one. I imagine I will in due course. I believe in the hereafter. (On the other hand . . . I've just checked through *Dante's Infernal Directory*, the best authority on what awaits us on the other side, and nothing described in the listings remotely approaches the horrors of Australians at the seaside.)

As a general rule, beaches are busiest during the evenings and at weekends. Families, Neighbourhood Watch Schemes, Methodist Lay Preacher Bible Associations, heavy-drinking clubs, you name it, they all set up concentration corrals, protecting territory with watchtowers, hidden mines, electric wire, and high-sided plastic windbreak screening, enclosing all the paraphernalia – pyramids of beer-crates, portable barbies, frilly airbeds, parasols, blaring cassette-players, portable giant-screen videos . . .

The great majority of adults are overweight, pink as tinned Australian salmon, and every child is worthy of a star role in 'The Omen'. It's no surprise that occasionally, hidden among the sand dunes, one stumbles over the charred traces of a satanic ritual, and a stake, still smouldering, plunged through a young but ancient heart.

The young, hip, up-front and gay display the latest refinements of beach technology. Fashion's frontier developments into the land of erogenous zones take the stage of a micro-g-string, so taut over that bronzed, muscled body you'd get a C-sharp if you twanged it. There is the Aussie version of the Emperor's New Clothes – skin-tight transparent briefs. Financial worth is displayed by the weight of gold chains.

Visiting one popular nudist beach just to the north of Sydney – a rare occasion – I was lightly dozing when I was awoken by the tropical drink seller. I'd spotted her earlier, plying her trade among the range of mostly male sunbathers. The first thing I noticed when I opened my eyes was the sun glinting off the collection of rings decorating her hairy pudding. She stood astride me, legs wide, gazing down, a high-pressure sales tactic if I ever saw one. But this is the beach, any beach, Australia, so if the sights are not to your taste, you're free to walk on. Get an eyeful of the joggers in profusion, pounding the sand, or muscle-bound Mr Universes grunting obscenely, jerking their weights to the sky . . .

And here come the good guys, the ones with their tootsies (at least) on the next rung to a better hell. Every-ready teams of life-savers mark out safe zones for swimming with flags, orange tape, plastic bollards. Splendid in one-piece striped bathing suits and conical rubber caps, they harangue the bathers through loud-hailers from atop mobile Toyota Jeeps.

The highest accolade of beach culture, however, I would award to surfers. For some genetic reason, I guess, this super-elite seems to be blue-eyed and blond to a man. Most left school early, and subsist on welfare, travelling the shores in search of the ultimate wave. It's a hard life-choice. By the time these guys are thirty, their brains are rinsed, wiped clean by the surf. Fifteen years spent within sound-range of big breakers would take its toll of anyone. Roll, crash! And back again . . . Roll, crash! I imagine after a time this monotonous thunder gets trapped within their skulls, like the sound always contained within a sea-shell, the whispering of sailors forever crying for release from Davy Jones's locker.

In a firm archive there is footage of a surfer somewhere off Hawaii, just a long shot of him balancing his plank on top of a seventy-footer, and then a huge wall of sea-foam, and he's gone, brains dashed out on the rocks. Thirty years old and nowhere left to go, so he took the biggest roller-coaster of them all, died a hero, translated for ever into the surfer's Valhalla.

If Lobo had travelled this route to the north before, either he had photo-graphic recall or his sense of place was uncanny.

Without warning he chose one of a myriad dirt tracks abutting the long Pacific Highway; and after a few miles of dodging dunes it delivered us to a perfect stretch of burning gold, no one to share it with save screaming seabirds and the drowned sailors calling to us from the surf.

Lobo had a clear image of the perfect life. In his book, everything was to be gained by scrupulous attention to hygiene and order. This was his straight track to personal power, and by God didn't I need it. Beside his brilliant image I hardly rated. Less than a week together and my self-esteem had crumbled, taken like a sandcastle by an encroaching sea.

Of all my afflictions, I suffered most from absent-mindedness. Smoking lousy dope didn't help. Take any activity, shaving for instance . . . I am awkwardly squinting at my reflection in a small hand-mirror. I stop to squeeze a pukey blackhead brought to a boil by the fierce rays of the blistering sun. I lay the razor down, and then cannot find it. It *was* before my knees in the sand. But as I look for it, I forget what I am looking for. It seems incredible, but I've lost a razor half-way through a shave. This incipient condition had become x times worse since I'd met Lobo, my self-image blurring in this constant exposure to the radiation of Lobo's fierce spirit.

Lobo stiffened my resolve to overcome my memory lapses with a starchy piece of advice. 'Frankie, instead of looking so hard for the thing you have lost, better stop. Do nothing. Calm the mind. Attempt to recall what it was you were doing when last it was in your hand. The way you rush so, it fills the mind with noise. Do nothing, relax. Then, when the memory plops back into mind, you will see it. It is this easy.'

Another pearl of wisdom laid before my pig's-trotter feet. Now, where is it?

So much work to clear the ingrain-ed dirt out of these stables, hardly ever did I get any rest. Oh, there'd be half-an-hour's compulsory meditation, splayed on my pale yellow towel (so drab next to Lobo's huge spread of alpine peaks), the giant bottle of Perrier water fizzing in the foreground.

Lobo was insistent I learn the yogic art of breathing. In his own words, 'My guru teaches me the most important thing in life is correct breathing. Even more important than keeping clean. You know, the natural life span has six hundred and forty-four million breaths.'

I did a quick calculation. About ten in and ten out a minute. Six hundred in an hour, times twenty-four, fourteen thousand four hundred, times three hundred and sixty-five, approximately five million breaths a year, divide six hundred and forty-four million by five million . . .

'Lobo, that comes to nearly a hundred and thirty years.'

Lobo frowned. 'It is not so unusual in my country to find peoples of this age, and older. They are living so long because they are so clean and they breathe correct. The trick is slow and even. Every one the same. Through the stomach, not the chest. The breath, it must travel in a circle, and not up and down the way you do it. Even more important it is when jogging to do this. In the nose for three steps, then out the mouth for three steps. You must to make a rhythm, listen for how the wav-es crash on the beach. Let the mind be carried by the sound. Dream on it. In my country the masters teach the breath is the life. In for life, out for death. We spend the whole life between the two.'

Lobo had become very strident, emphasising his points by jabbing at my midriff, at the same time hopping up and down. 'In my country' – jab-jab, hop-hop – 'there are men who are known as Lung-ump-as, chosen for their long legs. They are for carrying important messages between the camps of the monks.'

'Don't you mean monasteries,' I interjected.

'Do not interrupt, I am concentrating. Now, some of the distances between the camps are hundreds of miles, my country you know, it is mostly a desert of stone. All the water frozen. Only droppings of yaks for fuel. Lung-ump-as have a special system of breathing. It is as I tell you, in through the mouth, three steps, out again for another three. You must to follow the rhythm.' Lobo was now beating on my chest with his hand.

'Yeah, yeah, I've got it Lobo.'

'Lung-ump-as run more fast than any runner you ever see, each step is more than twenty feet. They look up to the sky, but never they fall in the hole or over a stone. They care nothing for ice and cold. Build a wall of a thousand miles, and they run around it. But if somehow you catch and wake him, he is dead, for his Voice it leaves him, if his trance it is breaking.' Lobo's voice had grown soft, even warm, as it often did when he talked of his homeland. 'Do you listen, Frankie?'

'Ah . . . Yeah,' I replied distantly. 'Please go on, I am absolutely fascinated by these Lun – what did you say they were called?'

'Lung-ump-as,' Lobo replied, a martinent sharpness edging his tone. Clasping his hands he continued, 'Clean the ears. And please to catch every word. If you listen close, and do as I say, you find you too can run in this way. The Lung-ump-as just go, and when they are arriving they have no memory of the in between. It is because their body does all the work while the mind is elsewhere. It is as simple as that.'

Despite my efforts to express it, I belched a laugh.

'Frankie, I see you do not believe me' – jab – jab – 'but I tell you, many of my peoples are having powers white peoples find strange, but for me it is more strange to find a peoples so without them.'

We ran the full length of the golden mile and then back, the sand burning underfoot.

If there's one thing in life I hate, it's running. Oh yeah, I'll stretch my legs to catch a bus, or to make an important appointment. It's a question of motivation. Running for the sake of it? No thank you. Besides, that afternoon I couldn't do a hundred yards without having to suck in a sharp breath through my mouth every second step. Lobo pushed me along, his hand on my buttocks. All the motivation I needed.

Now, if there's one thing I hate more than running, it's swimming. When I was five, I was rescued from the sea unconscious. I've been filled with fear of deep water ever since.

Lying on my back, splayed out on the sand, I was so puffed out I felt I was dying.

'God,' I protested to Lobo, standing menacingly over, eclipsing the sun. 'I can't move another step. Go away.'

'Frankie,' he demanded imperiously, 'you must wash away all the dirt the sweat is bringing up on the skin. Now, come you. Follow me.' And with that he sprinted into the surf, dived under the first big breaker and, rising up out of the boiling foam, flung up an arm. Veritably it was a cork-filled platypus which shouted, 'Come, join me Frankie! It is sooo clean!' His voice huge for a man of such small stature.

Wearily gathering all my powers, I ran full tilt at the sea, threw myself under the first breaker. And so I ducked, I swam, I bobbed. I even managed a passable crawl. But twenty minutes in that boiling surf and my limbs became so leaden – I know I'm moaning now, but they really ached. I had only just stumbled out of the sea and spread out on my towel, when the Lobo-tomy kid loomed over.

'Frankie,' he grinned, rubbing his hands, 'after the swimming, it is good for the muscles to do pressing-ups.'

This is Lobo's version of pressing-ups. Follow an outward arc, lowering the torso slowly to the ground, and with the up movement change the direction of the arc. Each pressing-up should take one full minute. As he'd predicted, I failed to reach ten; and when I collapsed in the sand, he cackled with derision.

That brings me to another subject: sand that gets everywhere. The perfidy of the stuff, or, rather more accurately, my own dirty ways. Now, you know how it is on a beach. Spread out the towel, run across the sand towards the sea (here's a point of interest, sand in Australia squeaks underfoot, a phenomenon I've not encountered anywhere else). Then after your dip, run back across the squeaking sand, smooth the towel out, lie down, and make sure your sand-encrusted feet are sticking over the edge of the towel.

Well, that's just what I did. And before returning to the car I shook the towel extra vigorously, making certain there wasn't a grain adhering to it. Next, sitting on the seat but with my sand-encrusted feet dangling outside the car, I carefully rubbed them clean, not forgetting between the toes. But despite all of my efforts, I always discovered a few grains of offending grit on my side of the floor. I'd be attempting to sweep them out when Lobo would return. He was always so impeccable in his timing.

'My gosh,' he would declare. 'How come you make so much mess. You do not even sweep out the Baby properly. Look,' he would point, 'I see sand there, and there, and there. Why do you miss so much?'

I'd repeat the whole process of sweeping out, but somehow, when I looked down, I'd always discover more grains of sand. How come his side was always spotless? I began to wonder if Lobo secretly sneaked back to the car, and dusted my side of the cab with sand.

I had also begun to wonder if he was human. How could he be so impossibly perfect? Surely Teutonic quartz hummed within this android-robot's fine-tuned digital perfection. His was an overwhelming personality, an extraordinary mixture of impishness, a Quixote-like willingness to tilt at any windmill, Baden-Powell, Charlie Chaplin . . . but come to think of it, he was unlike any of these jokers. Always he was unmistakably Lobo, as pure an archetype as I am ever likely to meet . . .

If you were with him it was for a very good reason. His reason. To have passed the gauntlet of his merciless perceptions and be invited to join him was a compliment indeed. If you spent time with this man you could not walk away 'unchang-ed'. He was so unbelievably fast, and always so watchful. If he had been a racing driver he could have given a description of the person who sneezed into a pink handkerchief, as he passed the grandstand at 200 mph. He could even tell you that your handkerchief was embroidered with the monogram M, and was not freshly laundered. Lobo would notice that.

All this beaching had begun to grate on him, and me. So that night we took to the road once more. Northward, ever northward, and hey-nonny-no, it's the petrol roadshow again. We found the precious stuff in a lover's lane somewhere in the backstreets of Port MacQuarry on the far north coast of New South Wales.

It was dark, I guessed about half past eleven, the lights in the bungalows beginning to dot off. The wide beams of our headlamps searched the interiors of several scattered cars as we swung into the lover's lane car-park, the couples playing statues under the beams.

Flicking a switch Lobo doused our lights. He leaned his body towards me. I jerked back involuntarily as he slung an arm around my neck. He pulled me back, his arm gripping my shoulder tightly.

'Frankie,' he rasped, 'we must appear as if we are kissing.'

I pushed him away. '*What?*'

Lobo hissed with annoyance. 'Not for wasting time! The petrol it is here, my Voice it tells me. We must act natural, otherwise they think we are detectives after their number plates.'

Reluctantly I complied, joining him in a silhouette of groping lovers. Gradually the occupants of the nearby cars resumed their former postures, satisfied now that Lobo and I were not the citizens of the local Neighbourhood Watch committee.

Our two heads close together, Lobo raised a finger to our collective mouths, stared intently into my eyes, then began whispering instructions in short, clipp-ed phrases.

'Stay here you. Now, listen. When I go out of the car, crawl over the seats. Put your back up, shake it about. You must to make the car rock and roll like these other ones. I go for the petrol.'

While I raised my bum in the air, Lobo engineered a smooth exit, slipping backwards out the blind side of the car, making not a sound. I felt ridiculous heaving about with no one underneath me. Outside Lobo was doing mysterious things. I almost collapsed with laughter. It seemed so ludicrous.

I froze as Lobo opened the Falcon's door.

'Do not stop,' he sniggered. 'So funny you are looking. Really, I love to make a movie of you at this minute,' he breathed. 'Frankie, it is working fantastically. I use the long hose, it is draining the petrol of the next car into our tank. Do not stop. Keep moving. Hey, I think it is a full tank. Maybe I do all the other cars as well. Then we get enough to drive all round Australia.'

'For God's sake,' I whispered. 'Aren't you ever satisfied?'

'No.' He reached over, patted my humping butt. He pouted, saying in a mock-mournful voice, 'Poor dear Frankie. So tiring you are. But all you must do is roll the joints while I drive. Is not too much to ask?'

19

Our night-time journey was painful in a way I'd prefer not to describe. One word covers the subject: haemorrhoids. Now you know. I had thought of entitling this section 'In search of the Quiescent Anus', but on reflection I decided it was too intellectual.

Our time together followed a rhythmic cycle, lulls followed by the peaks of Lobo's complaining, the lulls filled mostly by silence.

'I do all the driving. I make the jokes. I do all the tidying. I always find the way. I get most of the petrol and the food. What do you do, Frankie?'

I guess the answer should have been pointedly obvious. I rolled all the joints. And the more I was criticised the more I rolled, adding more tobacco as my stash diminished. This prompted more criticisms, so I rolled more joints. This activity added to my growing sense of being a rudderless spittoon adrift in a foggy basin of unknown size.

A thousand leagues, and a thousand leagues more, and still no bloody land in view . . .

We put ashore at Coff's Harbour, just in time to see another sun rising over the blue lagoon. Promoted in all the tourist brochures, Coff's is the Australian Mecca for newlyweds and the recently engaged. They come from all over, set up little tents in the woods, and make whoopee. There's not much else to do, except for painting rocks. To quote from the official brochure: *And it has become a charming custom amongst them to paint their sentiments for all eternity to see on the boulders piled high along the seashore. This delightful custom attracts many day-trippers and tourists to the sandy cove.*

I was reminded of the Bob Dylan song which goes, *Says Judas Priest to Frankie Lee, Eternitee! It's just a house down the road, some call it Paradise.*

Is 'Paradise' the sentiments of young lovers? *Two hearts forever one* – the paint withered, cracked and peeling. Forever is such a short time. More rocks and more fading inscriptions, slowly tumbling into the sea, hieroglyphics from the fifties to the eighties, and some from before: *My love is like a red red rose.*

Give me a bomb and I would blow Coff's Harbour to eternity and kingdom come. All those promises broken. Circles of gold and crowns of bloody thorns. The tree with the serpents winding around its base. Rotten apples and drunken worms. Nemesis contained in every lover's tiff . . .

I was glad to get back into the car with the joys of another night-time journey up ahead. Riding into the sunset, Frankie and Lobo, those two warped adventurers hitting the road again. All right, Jack, get back. Nail down those memories. Ashes to ashes, dust in my hair. Dustin Hoffman in my hair . . . Get back . . . Shit.

As we crossed the Queensland border I saw my first Australian snake, a liquid oscilloscope ripple of black, side-winding across the tarmac at unbelievable speed. I wondered if it was an omen.

Ever since arriving in Australia, I'd heard a rag-bag full of traveller's tales about Queensland: mysterious disappearances of hippies travelling the roads in the remote north, attributed to killer cops who stalk the wilds; people being jailed for possession of one single marijuana seed; rumours of Nazis biding out their time, in outback fastnesses. To my sleepless, deranged eyes, this was a hallucinogenic country, superficially a simulacrum of the Home Counties of England: spires and spikes of trim Tudor-style mansions competing with the trees; vivid green pastures spotted with black-and-white Hereford cattle. But here is the difference, hence the hallucinatory blend. The rolling green downs are bedecked on their northern flanks with orderly phalanxes of banana trees. Had Macbeth lived in one of these surrogate castellated mansions, his end would surely have come from a disciplined platoon of marching banana trees. Read on, Macduff, life's but a passing through shadow . . .

We crossed the borderline between fact and fiction when, in a clearing carved out of the wall-to-wall banana trees, we were confronted by a sixty-foot banana-shaped billboard, beneath it in large letters THE BIGGEST BANANA IN THE WORLD. Apparently we'd stumbled upon one of the main tourist attractions in the northern state. There was also a motel, gift shops, a car-park, and vendors sweating under corrugated affairs garlanded with bunches of the things.

That's the way of the world. The banal is always the biggest attraction. The Australian tourists were clustered around the crude representation like so many flies around a recumbent yellow painted turd. The thought occurred to me that maybe we'd stumbled on a weird religious cult.

Lobo bore that by now familiar expression of acquisitive attention. Before us were all those tourists' parked cars.

I needn't have worried. 'Look at all these bananas hanging from the trees, all of them green like your face. Maybe these bananas will get more ripe as we go more north? What do you think?'

'Your logic surpasses me, Lobo. With a mind like yours, you could conquer continents.'

'Ah!' He grinned. 'I see you are beginning to get the right idea. Come. I feel for driving. Are you OK?'

I winced, even managed a smile. 'Yeah, good idea Lobo. You drive and I'll roll the joints.'

'That it is the spirit. And what about some music. The one about the twin travellers. Hey-hey, I like that one.'

The words went something like this:

Twin travellers in the night,
Only stars to guide their way,
Travellers on the road to life.
Movin', they're always movin' on.

All roads lead men to Rome,
Life's a serpent's winding,
And all roads lead men to roam . . .

After it was finished, Lobo said, 'Put that on again, Frankie. And roll me a big joint, please. Make it a pure one this time, and the drive it will be the sweeter.'

The strobe of the setting sun was shafting through rushing foliage, hypnotically dancing in time to the beat. Golden light, deep red golden light, and the day turned to night, deep varicose-vein blue, wading ankle-deep in the vulva night. Stars were twinkling their seven-by-seven points at us. The scimitar of the moon rose, its curve reflecting a stray sunbeam from ninety-three million miles away. We crossed the galaxy that night, underneath the awful blanket of Australian night, punctured only by the cruel seven-pointed stars.

Without warning Lobo drew the car to a stop in a gravelled lay-by. Below us lay a lush, darkly mysterious green field, bordered at the far end by one of those orderly phalanxes.

Lobo flicked off the lights. 'Bananasss,' he said, wriggling his eyebrows.

'Sí,' I replied, switching effortlessly into Spanish. 'Este gringo está listo para joder y follar todo. ¡Vamos! ¡Rapido!'

I followed him across the field. Reaching a corner of the square of trees, I pointed. 'You take this side and I take the other.'

One minute I was bathed in cool moonlight, the next I had stepped through a curtain into another dimension I could sense but hardly see. It was the realm of bugs of every description, little squigglers glowing red, dumbstruck bloody worms aghast at my crashing progress, sticky threads slung across every space, suggesting something horrible hiding behind every leaf. The only light filtering through was faint patches of blue, mostly thrust away by the leaves of the banana trees. I felt like a Tom Thumb in a dark-nouveau wickerwork basket. On each tree stem hung a great testicle of unripe bananas.

I stood breathing heavily, hands on hips, peering into the gloom, biting down my twin *bêtes noires* – fear of entrapment in confined spaces, and the nastier things of the insect world. To encourage myself, I tried to think of the head-nipping that would welcome me if I returned without so much as one ripe banana. Going on past experience, the pigdog probably had a sack by now. In desperation I attacked one of the bunches, bringing the huge clump crashing on top of my head. I raised myself up on my knees, for a moment stunned by the blow.

Curse it! Every one was hard and green. I couldn't take much more of this. A spider with a mainframe bigger than my fist scuttled across my thigh.

'Jesus Mother of Mary, get me out of here – BUT WHICH WAY?'

Never run in a banana forest. My foot caught on a root. I fell, rolling head over heels, and burst out into space.

I lay for a moment, savouring the feel of cool grass on my face. I opened my eyes. Before me was a ten-foot-high chain-link fence topped with twisting razor wire. Inside the compound stood a white-washed, pan-tiled bungalow and beside it a block of efficient-looking stables. It reminded me of a house I saw once in the Black Forest near Wiesbaden in Lower Saxony, the birthplace of Heinrich Himmler.

A furious barking broke out. I froze, unable to breathe for the tightness across my chest. Three liquid shadows broke across the compound, conjoining into one single hound of hell, a slavering wedge of gnashing teeth launched at my throat. The impact bowed out the mesh till it almost touched my head.

Simultaneously floodlights mounted on poles high above the fence flicked on. Unbelievably, a loudspeaker crackled as a heavy voice boomed out orders. Doors slammed. I didn't want to find out any more. I plunged back into the banana forest, cursing and swearing, tripping and stumbling.

I crashed through the dark wall at the other end of the plantation, crossed the field in two bounds like a kangaroo, like a bloody Lung-ump-a, I took the cattle fence in one flying hurdle. My heels skidded on gravel, I fell heavily on my bum.

Twin beams of light suddenly pinioned me. I heard a whistling by my ear, followed by a popping noise somewhere behind. 'CHRIST!' I realised it was a gun. Some bastard trying to kill me, and for what?

The Baby's door flew open as it screeched close in to my side. I grabbed a hold onto the edge of the seat. Lobo hit the throttle hard, hauling me in by the shirt collar. The car spun on the gravel. The suspension bouncing as we hit the high ridge of the road.

Lobo roared with laughter. I lay back panting, almost bleeding with relief. I thought about my haemorrhoids. Lobo passed a freshly-lit joint. I took it with a shaking hand. 'JESUS MOTHER OF GOD, WHERE THE HELL WERE YOU?'

Still chortling, Lobo slapped his knees. 'Frankie, one minute in that wood and I know there are no bananas for eating. You are so enthusiastic, but always at the wrong time. When I am returning to the Baby, I hope you do not mind, I roll for me one joint, I am lighting the second when I hear barking and crashing and screaming. But funniest of all is when you come running out. You take the fence like a race-horse, Frankie, we should enter you for – what is it called, the Grand National? I sit on your back, hit you with a whip. I think you like that, huh?' He leaned over, grinning and nudging.

'Shit, Lobo,' I protested, hiding my head under my arms, 'give me a break. Please.'

Lobo thumped the steering wheel again and again. 'The way you jump the fence, the farmers shooting at you. Ho ho ho, completely unbelievable. He gets shot for taking a banana from a tree in a wood. Ho ho ha.'

I drew my knees up and slumped into the corner between the door and seat, my hot head cooling against the dark glass, the adrenalin flooding my veins subsiding as my heartbeat slowed. I viewed Lobo from a new and slightly altered angle. His laughing mien changing in appearance through my half-closed eyes.

'Ha ha ha, hee hee hee, ho ho ho . . .' The steady machine-gun snicker, as remorseless as a Hare Krishna chant. No, more. As remorseless as the steady beat of the sea.

A fleeting night-bird shadow swept across Lobo's face, hovered for a moment, then perched on his top lip, its dark wings brushing a cheek. A matrix was formed and out of the split image another face emerged.

I groaned aloud. The image shook me so much. It was such an exact portraiture. A chimera! I was travelling with a shape-changer. And his actions, too, his wak-wak, thump-thump on the steering wheel exactly mimicked the gestures of Der Fuhrer at one of his Nuremberg rallies. DEUTSCHLAND UBER ALLES. The crowd roared. My God, and here he is, I thought. Born yet again, suffering the indignities of yellow skin and zip-eyes. But no . . . I shook my head. This is no Camp Granada Adolph. He bears his pride like a staff, for at last he has joined the higher race, the peoples from the tableland of this world, the land above the snow-line from where the watcher sees all that mortal men do, do be do be do, do dum. Wak! Wak!

You've probably gathered that one of Lobo's chief attributes was his Voice. Whether intuition or in fact some entity, as a guide it was faultless. In the wee sma' hours the Voice instructed him to take a winding side road rising into some low hills. I know, because Lobo told me so. I cannot say that I was tired any more. I had passed far beyond that state. My eyes twitched from the army of flies encamped on my lids. I could go on about the aches and the migraine and the plukes I felt bursting up on my face. Not to mention the haemorrhoids.

How was it possible Lobo could be so fresh. Oh, maybe he yawned a couple of times, but I was convinced that it was theatrical, just a chumminess of the road, as if to say, 'I'm made of the same stuff as you, mate.' Patronising bastard.

It was almost too much to bear, the superiority he wore as a grinning jock-strap across his face. Obviously his genes were more alto than mine. He's inherited them, no doubt, from yogi ancestors who'd wandered naked for untold generations at oxygen-thin altitudes in the clean snow wastes. Not a speck of dirt anywhere.

We came to a slinking halt by a hut at the end of a funnel of night-dark trees. The thin crescent moon now hung low, dipping into a swirl of ink-blot numinescence. Lobo declared brightly, 'Time for beddy byes.' The words sounded quaint, even sinister, in his German accent. I was finally able to sleep. I believe he crashed out too, though for a time I was disturbed by the sounds of his reorganisings in the back.

20

When I finally awoke I guessed from the position of the sun in the sky it was about eleven. I was dripping with sweat. Painfully I raised myself. From outside came the drone of a swarm of flies. No, a grass-cutter.

Blinking into focus I saw Lobo had parked the Falcon next to the shed of a large necropolis. This cemetery was unlike any other I'd seen — wide-open space, an entire hillside, rambling with drunken headstones and mausoleums.

Lobo emerged from behind the wooden hut, crinkling his nose. 'Ah, Frankie. Are you sleeping well? Come out and see this.'

Wearily I stretched an aching leg, then another, before following him around the side of the cedar-wood shed to a small wire-glass window at the back. 'You see this?' He pointed.

The only light illuminating the hut's gloomy interior came through this dusty window and the crack in the door. The shelves were cluttered with tools and jars, all the things you would expect to find in a cemetery: specially shaped long-shafted spades; fine-pointed picks and sickles for trepanning the dead; big saws and axes. But we weren't interested in such things. A large, red-painted barrel struck out from underneath a bench. It was marked in big, important black letters: GIFTS FOR WISE MEN.

I turned to Lobo, saying, 'Do you think it could be petrol?'

'For sure it is petrol. Do not you smell it.' Switching into his disapproving mode, Lobo pressed his lips together, almost rolling the bottom lip over, curling his mouth down at each corner — a very idiosyncratic gesture.

'Do you think we should try and take it now?'

'No. Too many peoples there are around. The one who is cutting a circle in the grass through the trees, he swings back round every three minutes. He will see us. The can will make noise. We come back later. Not for worrying, enough petrol we have for today. While you are sleeping, I am busy. Already I am filling the tank from these people's cars.'

All that long afternoon we toured the local countryside, taking all the side roads in a fifty-mile radius from the cemetery. We took in the sights of OBX Creek, and climbed to the top of Shea's Nob. Then Lobo polished the windscreen at Tallowood Point, and I got out for a piss at Halfway Creek, and we visited the famed Guy Fawkes National Park, where we jogged between tall, thin eucalyptus trees. We took a wrong turning at Ward's Mistake, which was of course blamed on me for distracting him . . . We passed a lot of nobs on our way back to the cemetery: Fletcher's Nob, Rosy's Nob, Mac and Tandy's Nob – and it made me laugh when we passed through Willy-Willy, taking the road via Five Creek and Nulla Nulla, then crossing Paddy's Plains, Cascade, Timbertop, Scotsman, Towallum. We saw Nymboida Power House, but we weren't impressed, and then it was a short trek over the hill to Bucca Carumbi Bridge, over the humpback, and we were back at OBX Creek again.

It was night by the time we had located the obscure road through the tunnel of trees where Lobo doused the car lights, and then we parked by the stores of the necropolis again.

I declared brightly as he turned off the engine, 'Right then, I'll get the torch out of the back of the car.'

Lobo rasped. 'When will you learn to be quiet! Do you not see the house on the far away hill. Look! It is lighted. And you never can tell who is walking in a cemetery at night, so button the mouth.'

'OK, OK, Lobo, I will, but please, let's just get on with it. I'm sure nobody's around. Don't worry, I'll make short shrift of that door. Where's that steel bar?'

Lobo pulled me back before I could get out of the car. 'I have told you never to break anything, always there is another way. First we must take off the screws of the padlock clasp. Now get me the screwdriver, the big long one. And please do not make a sound. There is danger around. My Voice it tells me.'

Lobo hissed at my every noise. We worked together side by side, taking out each long screw of the clasp, our progress halting only for argumentative intermissions. By this stage in the trip, we'd become adept at burgling and arguing at the same time. Lobo finally removed the last long screw. The door swung easily on its hinges making barely a creak.

Lobo held me back with one hand as we stepped gingerly into the darkened interior of the hut.

'Sshhh,' he hissed. He pointed at the shelves. 'What it is that up there? You are tall, reach and get it.'

I pulled the metal object down by its handle. It was an old-fashioned pump with an apparatus for clamping it onto a drum.

Lobo was delighted. 'You see?' he whispered vehemently. 'Now you will not have to get your mouth full of petrol. Now, help me roll this big drum out. How do you take this cap off? Come on, Frankie. You say you know so much about these things and yet you stand here like a stupid sheeps.'

'Don't start, Lobo. It's no problem. You need a special key. We have to break it. Pass me that screwdriver and the hammer.'

'The hammer?' Lobo exclaimed in alarm. 'Frankie, you must not to make a noise. What the heck are you going to do?'

I growled, 'Just shut up. Come on, give it over and pass that oily rag from the bench.'

With obvious distaste Lobo followed my instructions. I wrapped the head of the screwdriver in the cloth, and struck the drum a glancing blow. The point of the screwdriver burst through the thin aluminium of the cap, puncturing it. But I'd overestimated the force needed, for the hammer continued and smashed into a belljar of chemicals, shattering the glass. Green liquid cascaded, broken shards fell to the ground. The vitriol-like substance started to froth and steam, and a pungent, eye-smarting odour filled the night air.

'My gosh! You are a maniac!' Lobo snapped in acid retort. 'I will not leave this place until you clear up the mess. It is disgusting.'

While I swept the pieces of glass into a corner under the bench, Lobo fitted the petrol pump to the now open drum. He demanded, 'What do you wait for? Hurry, get the cans from the car.'

'Yes sir, yes sir, three bags full sir, anything you blooming well say. At the double,' I grumbled as I left the hut. I returned with the two empty five-gallon cans.

Lobo frowned. 'More cans we are needing. You must to find more. We can take all of this petrol. No more sneaking about in the night, Frankie, I am sick in my teeth with it. Enough there is here for many days.'

'Yes, yes,' I said impatiently, 'fill these ones, then we can go looking for more.'

The clanking noise of the pump was enough to wake up a cockatoo on a branch three hundred miles away. If he'd continued. that is.

Lobo was horrified. He almost shouted. 'Why do you not tell me it makes so much noise? What it is wrong with the thing?'

'Don't worry, dear friend,' I said. 'If we roll the barrel out of here, we can find a safe place and hide it. If we fill these cans and the car's tank, we'll have enough for a couple of days, and then when we come back south, we can visit our store.'

Lobo was round-eyed with amazement at my suggestion. He announced it as if it was a marvel. 'Now your brain it is starting to work. That is the best idea ever you have. But first we finish tidying up this place. More broken glass there is on the ground. Then we screw the padlock back on the door. Always we must to make a good job.'

We moved the now two-thirds-full petrol barrel to its new-found home – a neo-Florentine mausoleum with thin, fluted pillars and a classical arch bearing a bust of a Neapolitan called Quignogg. That's what it said. We covered the barrel with a few fronds and left it as an offering.

21

I mused as we set off on the long, early-morning drive to Brisbane. Who was this skuldugger, this chance stray particle who had picked me up and taken me on this whirling, rollercoaster ride, without so much as a by my leave? Six days on the road now, and Renaldo's house in Melbourne seemed a lifetime away. It had all happened so damn-ed fast. Was this character with the venetian-blind eyes actually real? I imagined if I took a scalpel and stripped off the flesh I'd see wires, and LCD lights. Here was some perfect cybernetic onion of myriad layers grown out of the Australian dreamtime, every day a different mask covering the same button-blank face.

I examined his shadow, the other side of this superhuman vehicle for his master's Voice. It told me nothing. I wanted to put my side of the case. Damn it, I wanted to meet the director, this 'watcher' who had been for so long now playing honky-tonk boogie with the warp and weft of my life, setting up stumbling blocks and pitfalls so I would fall over them and into them. Each time I got out from an accursed pit, the landscape had changed. Gone were the landmarks I knew, the place names all different. Sometimes even my own reflection seemed that of a stranger.

I sighed. Maybe this was all a projection. Yeah, it was a projection. Was it? Could Lobo be the Arch-Fiend himself, a born-again Mephistopheles presenting me with a contract written on the recycled paper of my life, saying *Write down what I tell you, so all may know how to cleanse themselves of the dross of this world.*

One day, if you faithfully follow Lobo's dictums, you will emerge out of the anus of some great creation, take a look around and say, thank God that's over. What's next? One thing's certain, it won't be what you're expecting. Life's a never-ending bubbling of surprises, even if all the fun, when it pops, is just marsh gas.

Somehow, somewhere, we're back in Oz, flashing along the dreamtime parade. Gripped by the secret somnambulance of the sleeper, I'm desirous but not able to wake up. I flew over some edge back at the cemetery, fell into some pit of my own making when the belljar cracked and poured forth that green slurry. Some of it splashed onto my bare ankles, and I still carry the burns to this day, as a reminder.

Along with the manacle sores.

I was curiously affected by the atmosphere of Brisbane. A dumpling drabness seemed to resonate with the heat shimmer.

As a city it's pretty enough: mid-range high-rise buildings mushrooming in the centre, glass panels reflecting the claustrophobic hemming hills of the suburbs; at ground level, verdant, red-paved pedestrian precincts are cooled by gushing fountains; up above the sun shines on yet another boring, blue-sky day. Not much changes, one senses. The city runs like a clockwork machine. No anxiety strains the blotched pink pork-pie faces tidily lined up behind bus stops, or queuing at kerbsides, patiently waiting for the green man to flash his permission to cross.

As I stared at the automatons crossing I realised I had never seen such a profusion of the genes of the law-enforcer. Either that, or seventy per cent of the population were in plain clothes for some reason. Piggy little eyes followed Lobo's every move. Such interest wasn't surprising, for these past days of sand and surfing had wrought a dramatic change in his pigmentation; Lobo had turned a shade of charcoal. Apart from the darkest of Aborigines – not in any case to be seen hereabouts – he was quite the blackest man for hundreds of miles around.

In the back of the car, Lobo was occupied with rearranging his mix-and-match colour scheme. When he finally stepped around, jauntier than ever, he was kitted out in Pirelli-soled trainers, blue-banded white socks pulled up tight, blue-edged pink satin shorts and a steel-coloured string vest. With the designer dried-blood and Chinese lettering on his surprisingly loyal bandanna, his image suggested a tricky tennis star, prone to arguing with the umpire over the cost of replacement dentures.

It was depressing to be cast as the foil to reflect his startling glory, clad as I was in the dull armour of my usual blazer, light-grey flannel trousers and yet another cream silk shirt plundered from the bag set aside for the victims of bush fires. Frankie, Lobo's jockaroo, the Friar Tuck to his Robin Hood, grown lean and thin through complaining and not complaining. . .

This stage of the journey I felt out of sorts all of the time. My groans and whines represented but the tip of a soggy cornflake iceberg, melting in the sticky humid heat of Brizbayne, Coinslayand.

Lobo strode into the heavy traffic, a five-foot-two Moses parting this tide with one raised pinkie. I had to keep reminding myself of his actual size, as he seemed to have turned the tables on me in that department. Perhaps I was shrinking.

Lobo tugged my sleeve as we reached the corner. Chuckling, he pointed out the large windows of the 'Skiing and Winter Sports Emporium.'

'Tell me, for why are there so many of such shops in Australia? Here in Brisbane the sun it shines the whole year round. Never there is any snow.'

'If I lived in this shit hellhole, I'd do anything to get away from it. All this bloody endless sun, and the fucking humidity.'

'Frankie!' Lobo snapped. 'Stop this dirt coming out of the mouth at once. This it is why you are feeling not well most of the time.'

Indignant at this fresh round of criticism, I demanded angrily, 'How else do you propose I dispose of it then? Swearing is the same as having a shit. It cleans out the system. I think you're constipated.'

'Do not shout so.' A hear-no-evil monkey, Lobo clapped his hands to his ears.

Furious, I continued my tirade. 'Listen to me, you Tibetan ape! What am I supposed to do? Block up my mouth? Shut up all the dirt inside? Tell me, how am I to get rid of it? Answer me!' I jabbed his chest. 'Swearing is a meta-biological function, it's a way of relieving stress and pressure.'

Lobo's voice grated like a dragging manhole cover, lines emerging on his normally smooth forehead. 'Frankie, I am so very impress-ed. You talk like a lawyer who knows everything, so why do not you tell me the solution, instead of showing me you are helpless in this way? So good you are with words, you fool yourself, but not me. Ask yourself now: how come you to be carrying this dirt inside you?'

Unable to prise up the lid of my mollusc shell of handy replies, I stood mouthing sticky air, a beached, down-at-heel Scottish carp.

Lobo pointed towards the shop. 'New training shoes I am needing. My Voice it tells me this it is the place.'

'What? I've seen you wearing at least three different pairs.'

Lobo nodded, crazily reminding me of Black Sambo on a charity box, tipping his hat as a coin is placed in his hand.

'I am commending you, Frankie, for your sharp observation. I have four pairs in my Baby, and each is for a different purpose.'

'And what is the next pair going to be for then, huh?' I leaned over him, trying to gain some advantage from my height.

'Enough!' Lobo snapped. 'This is not work we do, talking like this. We have shopping to do.'

The card pinned to the lapel of the thin bespectacled blue suit informed me I was talking to Martin McGee, the manager of this enterprise. Obviously he was of Scottish descent, and by the looks of him his genes weren't doing so well in this tropical clime.

I sensed I was talking to a prospective punter as I outlined the nature of our travel company. The name, I announced in my best Scottish accent, was 'Rough Jock's Bloody Tours'. Our avowed purpose, to knock the lily-livered Australians into shape. Our premier tour of the season was to be an assault on one of the loftier Himalayan peaks – Katchen Junga. Getting into my stride, I told him every Rough Trekker had to sign a waiver renouncing the right to sue for broken bones. We thumbed our noses at climbing ropes, pitons, and oxygen masks. All we would allow in the way of equipment was toothpicks, storm-tents, biltong, ice-picks, girlie magazines, arctic sleeping bags, Dr Prickle's pocket warmers, socks, garlic capsules, goggles . . .

Without a diminution or let-up in the verbal, I sneaked a glimpse of Lobo. He'd lined up at least thirty pairs of training shoes in front of a full-length mirror and was marching up and down the row, a general inspecting troops on parade.

Still burbling like parakeet high on haggis . . . 'Ahm preepared tae offer yer store free publicity in oor sales brochure, eeef ye'll gie us a big discount on the order we're preparin' tae place wi' youse. So ah want youse tae assembull all yer catalogues an' all, an' wurk oot wi' yer pals whit ye can knowk off tha price.'

I found Lobo preening himself by the mirror. Lifting up a heel he murmured, 'You like them? I think these pair are the best. Good for climbing walls.'

'Very good, Lobo, but don't you realise everybody in this store knows you've been trying them on? What are you going to do? Just walk out?'

'Frankie,' Lobo shook his head sadly, 'always you worry so. I do not leave out the shop because we have other things to take.'

'Such as?' I demanded hotly.

Lobo thumbed over his shoulder towards a display of smart leather briefcases by the counter, making his idiosyncratic down-turned-mouth expression. 'I want a case from there. Now, why do not you go and talk to the manager. Look, he is smiling and calling to you. Such good friends you are making. You should introduce me. Tell him I no speak mucha English, ha-ha-ha-ha.'

'OK Lobo, provided you co-operate and do exactly what I tell you to.'

Lobo smiled, eyes glittering. 'Anything you say, boss.'

Holding Lobo by the shoulder, I propelled him towards the counter.

'Martin, I want tae introduce ye tae me pal, employee an' oor Sherpa, Dgordgi.' Lobo stiffened under my hands. I had spoken his secret name. But the manager wasn't to know, and Lobo was under my command. Wheeling him around, and staring him deep in the eyes, I delivered my instructions in staccato pidgin Scottish. Gae tae th'motor. Get photo's o' youse on th' mountains. This mon' – I waved my hand at Martin – 'He *pal*. Gie uz *guid deal*, ye ken? Now, cunt face, hurry, get case.'

Lobo saluted smartly, thunking his new trainers together. As he trotted out the door the day-glo tags on his soles seemed to be winking at me leerily.

Still wearing the same shoes, Lobo returned a moment later.

'Master,' he piped up, 'I no ken where you put case. Maybe you leave in hotel.'

Scrolling my eyes in mock and real desperation, I moved my body to cover Lobo's hand snaking towards the display of briefcases.

'Martin,' I said, shaking my head wearily, 'ye see whit I hae tae put up wi'? I'll hae tae gae back tae th'motor mesel', eef it's no' there we'll be back in hof an 'oor. This, ye ken, is the reason we cannae carry much equeepment on oor tours. This cunt's th' porter.' I thumbed towards Lobo. Then, with a sinking feeling, realised I'd done the wrong thing. Martin hadn't even looked at Lobo until I directed his attention that way. But . . . Oh no, Lobo was making it worse.

Holding the executive briefcase flat against his chest, he bowed low. 'So nice to meet you, sind kir,' he said.

The manager was asleep, like all the others.

We repaired to a nearby coffee house decorated in the style of Vienna just before the Nazi putsch with wrought ironwork tables topped by red-veined slabs of marble. I wondered if it was owned by a Nazi renegade. Perhaps, I conjectured, this state's run by them.

I returned with the coffee, paying for it out of my shrinking wad. Lobo was examining the open case. He remarked, 'So very disappointing I am. No card there is with the combination number. But hey Frankie, pay for me a cake. I do not feel like taking. Give me five dollars.'

Reluctantly reaching under my shirt and unzipping my sweaty money-belt, I took out a crumpled note. An expression of distaste marring his features, Lobo took it between thumb and forefinger and, holding it suspended, strode over to the counter.

I looked up as the café doorbell rang, a large man slamming the door behind him. The resultant air-shock caused the lid of the case to fall. It locked automatically. In my panic to wrest it open before Der Fuhrer returned, I only succeeded in displacing the tumblers in the combination.

Frowning, Lobo placed the platter of cakes on the table. 'Why you do that? Now we must to take it back and get another!'

I slammed my palms on the marble. 'Lobo, I am not going back to that shop. Ever!'

Pushing the tray of cakes aside, Lobo leaned over the table towards me. 'I only test you, Frankie. We do not need to return. I have the combination in here.' He tapped his forehead. 'My Voice it knows. Now tell me, how the heck do you manage to shut the case? It is only one minute I am leaving you for.'

I'm a fucking trout on a line, always the bastard's playing with me. I smiled. 'It was a gust of wind,' I said decisively. 'That fat man,' I indicated towards the corner table with a nod of my head, 'he slammed the door.'

'Always with the excuses ready. I thought Scottismen are made of stronger stuff. So disappointing I am.'

Godalmighty. I looked away. Best form of defence is attack. I thumped the marble angrily. 'If you know the combination, why don't you open it?'

Lobo smiled. 'No, I am the patient fellow, I wait till you work it out for yourself.'

'Tell me!' I yelled.

'OK. Frankie, how many cups of coffee do you have today?'

'Two, I think. What has that to do with it?'

Lobo's superior smile widened. 'You are finding out. Now, what is the time when we arrive in the centre this morning?'

'Oh, I remember that one,' I said grumpily. 'About nine.'

'Correct again.' Lobo's eyes narrowed to slit trenches. 'And now we are coming to the last part. Try to guess me a number between five and seven.'

'Six,' I answered blankly.

'Now,' Lobo continued. 'What are the numbers once more?'

I hesitated. 'Uh, two, nine, five, six, seven.'

Lobo tapped the case and passed it over. 'Now, you try that.'

I did, and the case clicked instantly open. 'You son of a pigdog,' I exclaimed. 'How in the heck did you do that?'

Lobo's lip curled up. 'Now do you believe what your Voice tells you through me? You must realise it is your Voice too. We are brothers in the spirit you and I.'

Lobo stood up.

146

I motioned towards the cakes. 'Aren't you going to have one?'

'No.' Lobo shook his head. 'Such things as these are only suitable for the fat pigs such as the peoples in this restaurant, like you for example.'

Lobo walked out of the shop and I had choice but to follow.

22

I had an address. Renaldo insisted if I was ever in Brisbane I should visit his oldest Australian friend, Nealga Riventrop, a very socially committed person, dedicated to fighting the sexual exploitation of women and a vigorous campaigner for Aborigine land rights. He also told me she was a lesbian, whatever that might mean in this topsy-turvy land. Knowing Lobo's negative feelings towards Renaldo and his friends, I broached the subject of a visit delicately.

I was baffled at his sudden burst of enthusiasm.

'Frankie! Such a good idea you have. It is about time we find new company. Hey hey!'

We discovered the house in a suburb called Redhill. I'd never seen anything to compare with the constructions in that street: band pavilion from an era long gone, a windmill from the Zuider Zee, a Victorian seaside amusement hall. All had one thing in common — each was raised on giant hardwood poles. I deduced the reason for this crazy style of architecture was to preserve the structures from the predations of termites. Brown tide-marks on the stilts suggested lashings of creosote, and underneath little notices written in Termitese read: 'Keep Out. No Entry. Electrified Poles.'

Number fifty-four was just a shack on sticks set at a crazy angle, one of the poles half-eaten through at the base. The steps bounced as we climbed the long flight. The shiny door-knocker was a big snake curling round a half-eaten pole. It was a pleasure, the way the brass thudded down on the plate. The entire shack shook with the impact.

'I do not like this place,' Lobo growled over my shoulder. 'Come, we go. No one is in.'

'Hold on a minute,' I said, thumping the knocker again. Something stirred inside. A door slammed, then big footsteps sounded.

I don't quite know what I'd expected, maybe a buxom thirty-five-year-old Miss Reese, my first gym teacher. My flesh winced at her memory. But I was taken aback by my first sight of this thin-wristed, spade-handed, six-foot-plus 'female' with short platinum-dyed hair, who threw back the door so violently. I say 'female' in inverted commas because although her tight T-shirt made pointedly obvious the large nipples of her smallish breasts, this person, this fella's granite chin was darkened by an after-eight shadow, even though it was freshly-shaved and smooth.

Putting together the pieces of the picture, I decided that this person had probably been a man who'd had a sex-change operation and then become a lesbian. It's a weird world this, the underbelly of Australia.

'Yeys? And wha' doo ewe want?' Nealga boomed, standing on the top step and leaning over threateningly.

Temporarily at a loss, I was only able to mumble, 'Um . . . uh.' Then, recovering, I shot forth my hand. 'Nealga, you don't know us.' I grinned as hard as I could and waved the tambourine that wasn't in my other hand. 'I'm Frankie, and this is Lobo. We're both good friends of Renaldo's.'

'Oww.' Nealga's black plucked eyebrows shot up. 'Bloody 'ell. Sow . . . Ewe're Frankie.' He gripped my hand between huge mitts, shaking it with extraordinary vigour.

What's all this about ewes I wondered as I massaged my hand back into existence. Is this a bloody sheep parlour, or what?

Nealga continued, 'Ay've 'eard abowt ewe.' As he thumbed towards Lobo a sneer lifted the corner of his mouth. 'And eys theis the Teebetayne mizfit? Renaldo was nowt sow enthyusiaystic wheyn 'e towld me abowt 'im.'

He seemed to be hesitating, perhaps coming to a decision, as he patted down an imaginary tutu. 'Ewe'd better bowth come own eein. It's a teyrribuel meyss ay must worn ewe. Oww, Frankie' – the door shut automatically behind us – 'ay've gowt a sorpriyse fer ewe.'

'What's that?' I ventured, as we trudged two steps behind him down the dark, narrow, wood-panelled hall, two dwarves beside his lofty height. A thin yellow light spilled through dirty lace curtains covering the fanlight above the entrance door.

Nealga shrugged mysteriously, kicking flat the ruckled, worn-out runner carpet as he opened the dark-stained timber door. Then he stepped smartly to the side and saluted like the doorman at a select club. Playfully he tried to smack me on the bottom as I jumped quickly into the room.

Nealga shouted after me, 'Down't wurry abowt the meyss, sling thowse paper sacks owff the settee and mayke ewerseylf at howme. Steck ewer feet own the tayble. Reylax, ewer in bluddy Owstraylya.' And then his tone darkened. 'After ewe, small blayck mayn.'

Hard laughter edging his voice, Lobo replied, 'No. You get it wrong. You go the first. I follow your behind. That it is the way. I think you are a naughty boy, and in need for a good smacking.'

I wondered if any of this was happening. Perhaps I was dreaming. Absent-mindedly, trying to be relevant and connected in this unhinging tropical station, I grabbed the heavy, recycled-paper refuse sack occupying most of the sofa by its neck. The bottom of the bag ripped open, spewing a screed of pamphlets onto the deck.

Nealga was beside me in a trice. 'Down't wurry abowt tha', Frankie. Ay was gowing to sort owll tha' stuff throo. Bloody Abows. Ewe'd think ay'd uv given up thayt cawse yeers agow. Ay'm jest a bloody bleedin' 'art, thayt's my trouble. Ay down't know why ay cayre. The bleedin' powliteyshins seyllin' the whowle stayte owff to the Jaypanese an' leyttle blayck pingwins frum TierraDull-Fwaygo liyke this wun.' Sternly he looked down at Lobo. 'And now my young pingwin chappee, geyt owt of my way. The gayme's owver. Ay'm gowing to geyt some beer frum the freedge.'

'Yes, certainly,' Lobo declared, but holding his ground. He raised a stiff finger. 'One minute, if you please. My friend Frankie, he asks me before we come to request to you, because he is too embarrassing to say. You see,' he shook his head sadly, 'he is a dope addict. If he has no grass to smoke for a few days the cracks appear in him. And I must warn you, when he is desperate like this, it is anything he is doing for a good blow!' Lobo grinned at me hugely.

I glowered back, kicking futilely at the papers; then changing my tack, I flounced onto the sofa, folded my arms behind my head, stretched out and propped my feet on the low table between the stacks of pamphlets.

Nealga marched in, awkwardly carrying a small green glass bong and a largish bag of grass, and under his other arm a frosty six-pack of stubbies. Gingerly he set the bong upright on the table, placing the bag of grass at its side. He ripped two stubbies from the plastic wrap and suddenly threw one at me and the other at Lobo, who was stood by the wall. He was reading aloud from the small print on a poster. The graffiti headline read: Land Rights for Aborigines Now! I took it to be an original piece of artwork by Nealga. Lobo was piping up in a cherubic-little-boy voice. 'What is this place call-ed Yellow Bum Tree? Is this where you all hang about?'

Lobo didn't even look round. He caught the can in a backhand snatch, ripped off the ring-pull and directed the can towards the poster. The shaken mixture sprayed the poster – three Aborigines, fists raised in a Black Power salute, behind a ring of barbed wire, their screaming, starved faces modelled on a Munch painting.

'Oh dear, what a mess.' A finger to his mouth, Little Jack Horner pulling out a plum. Idly now, a jackass or a dingo or a composite of both, he strolled insolently to the only unlittered seat at the other side of the low coffee table. Stooping to dust the seat off with short flicks, he sat down, crossed his legs and then with a glazed expression turned to gaze out of the window, making it pointedly obvious his only desire was to escape from this hellhole.

The small window obviously hadn't been cleaned since the first white settlers arrived in these parts. It was speckled with the one-cent-sized blown-fly turds that this particular area of Queensland is world-famous for. Yeah, that's what I said. Did you see the programme where David Attenborough featured the blown-flies of Queensland? One of the little buggers planted a shat or a shot dead-centre of his shiny forehead. He wore the caste mark like a dumbstruck Brahmin on an Irish walkabout with the Pope. I'll say this for our star David, he recovered magnificently. He licked one finger, wiped the blown-fly turd off his brain-filled forehead, licked his finger again. 'Delicious,' he announced to all those billions of viewers. 'This rich form of protein the Aborigines collect and then make into a very tasty dish called the Soup of the Yellow Bum Tree. And there is even a song, the literal translation of which is, "Tie a Golden Ribbon Round the Yellow Bum Tree."'

I was startled when another door opened – just a glimpse of pink walls, a big brass bed, a Japanese lampshade hung low over it, the bedspread silly and frilly. A plump, dark-tanned hairy knee peeked around the corner of the door, then the Grande Dame of Melbourne flashed into view.

Renaldo made a giant entrance as usual, throwing his arms wide like the mother of all churches, then just as rapidly lowering them because his chrysanthemum-patterned, almost see-through kimono flapped open exposing a surprisingly long prick. It had pink ring marks on it, and was painted baboon-blue at the tip. Of course my eyes had deceived me, it had to be bruising. I wondered if we had interrupted something. Renaldo's curly perm was dishevelled, eyes scooped with black shadows, skin strangely shiny. Yes, definitely, I decided, we had interrupted something.

I jumped up with delight at this unexpected pleasure. We met at the side of the coffee table, my knee colliding with one of the tottering piles, knocking it to the ground. The ensuing cloud of dust caused Renaldo to sneeze violently.

'Bless you,' I said, simultaneously with Nealga, who had taken the seat beside Lobo. Then, as Renaldo and I stooped to pick up the books, we clashed heads. 'Oh . . . Oh . . .' Renaldo staggered backwards in circles, clutching his curly ringlets.

He collapsed onto the sofa beside me. After a moment he took my hand in his and breathed 'Now that's over, you can tell me all your adventures since I saw you last.'

His question momentarily took all the wind out of my sails. Inadvertently I looked over at Lobo, who appeared to be oblivious of all the goings on and was picking at his clean fingernails with his Swiss Army knife. I hesitated, then recovered and said, 'Oh, you know. Holidays mostly, you know . . . the beach.'

Renaldo, leaning around me, spoke sharply to Lobo. 'I hope you have not been leading my dear friend Frankie astray?'

Lobo lifted his eyes from his manicu ing. 'Ashtray? What does this word mean? My friend Frankie is more clean than ever he is before. I teach him how to live.'

'Ahh,' Renaldo said with emotion. Turning back to me, he took my shoulders between his pudgy hands and shook me lightly, smiling benevolently, role modelling for a fairy godmother. 'You must be very careful in this town. It is not like Melbourne. The police are very very heavy. It's not just that they pick out the gays or the dope-smokers. They don't like anyone.' He took my hand again. 'Now, let me look at you properly. Ahh, you are so much better for a tan. And now tell me, dear, you haven't been doing anything naughty have you?'

'Oh no, definitely not,' I said in a voice that I knew would convey we had been doing lots of naughty things.

Nealga leaned over, in his hand an unlit freshly-filled bong. 'Frankie,' he said, 'ay 'ate to enterrupt ewe tewe lovebirds, but as ewe seem to be the 'onoured gueyst, whoy down't ewe tayke the ferst towke?'

Grateful for this interruption, I accepted the green smoked glass. Renaldo was beginning to get hot. God save me from bum boys. I was only just recovering from my last days at the Analvice Steam Lodge where I got the rash. I didn't tell you about that one, it was too embarrassing. I'll just have to leave it to your imagination.

I had taken three deep tokes before the steamroller hit me. No, it didn't come through the window, it raced up my pants and walloped me on the back of the head. Jeez, this was good grass. I turned to gaze lovingly at Nealga outside the window. He was climbing a small, solitary mango tree . . .

The lights went out all over Germany. And in a darkened room, the young *hausfrau* was surveying her last three matches as if they were wishes. Suddenly, seen through the rivulets flowing like tears down the small, thick-glassed window-panes framing the torn tree bowed down by the rucksack of the night-wind, the face of the blond Teutonic knight she'd seen in her dreams appeared.

His armour rattled as he shivered from the cold. The micro-circuitry in the heating systems of his twenty-third-century battle armour had ceased working long ago. The girl yearned for his touch. She yearned to hold and caress his throbbing lance, to use superglue to bind it there. Never would she let him go.

She saw a steaming rivulet join all the others on the glass, start its slow glide down the pane. Yet another tall dark stranger seeking entrance without paying the admission fee, and meanwhile, outside the window, in the winter's night gale, the knight shivered and shook and rattled, popping quick-fire rivulets like a Gatling gun in every direction.

23

I was jolted out of stoned dreamtime by the night watchman's rat-ta-tat-tat voice beating at my door. Unwisely I lifted the letter-box flap to see who it was, and Lobo's sharp-taloned voice plucked me through the slot. Somehow I managed to press myself into the void cold mould of my body, positioned where I'd left it – slumped back on the sagging couch, feet stretched out on the table.

I jerked upright, immediately forgetting where I'd been. Whip in hand, Lobo was stood over me.

'Come now, Frankie! Much work we must do this night.'

Oh God . . . Wearily raising myself from the couch . . . No sign of Nealga . . . At my side, a beaming, blissfully stoned Renaldo reminded me of a floppy curly-haired eunuch out of an insomniac's Arabian Nights.

'Where are you going?' Renaldo chirruped.

'Ohhhh,' I moaned, momentarily swaying from dizziness. 'I do-no. I've got to go. Sorry Renaldo.'

Renaldo was struggling to rise from his seat. Pulling him up by the hand and still holding it, I said, 'We'll say goodbye outside. I'd better not keep his Imperial Highness waiting.'

The elastic tying me to Renaldo stretched to half a step as I tripped down the freshly ruckled runner in the hall. Outside the door at the head of the steps, I hesitated, swaying under the influence of booze, and grass. Down below, across the street, Lobo had already taken pole position behind the wheel. Renaldo's breath steamed on my neck.

Turning, I spread my arms to receive the embrace. Renaldo kissed both of my cheeks, whispering as he pulled me close. 'Dear, dear Frankie, I worry so much.

I cannot sleep at night for thinking about you. I miss your company. I know you're in danger. You must not trust Lobo. Now tell me, what have you been doing?'

I hung my head low, suddenly struck by shame. Or was it nausea? Renaldo squeezed my waist, pressing his loins into mine. My stomach heaved. An oyster enveloped in a fish stew could not have felt more molested.

'I can't tell you. But I'm OK, really.'

'You know best, Frankie. You must do what you must do. But don't ever forget. There is always a bed for you in Melbourne. Rex and I both miss you so . . . so very much.' His voice choked. Dropping his hands he stroked my thighs, a brushing reminder of how it might have been.

I shook him by the shoulders. 'Look after yourself too, dearest,' my finger stiff and admonishing, 'and remember to be careful in saunas. Always sit on your towel and no one else's. You know how it it with all these infectious diseases. There's a new one brought out of the germ warfare research labs every week.'

We embraced for one last time. Descending the steps, I didn't look back. I was too busy concentrating on maintaining my balance.

Lobo leaned over to push open my door. 'Hurry! Do you think to keep me waiting all night?' Busy fingers beat a devil's tattoo as he revved the engine, looking me up and down, face as cold as a fishmonger's marble slab. We wheeled out onto the long, empty road.

'And tell me, what is "dear" Renaldo whispering in your ear?' Lobo demanded acidly.

Smiling as enigmatically as I knew how, and saying to myself, *The less that Nobo knows, the better*, my inner voice thick with drink and smoke. 'Oh, you know . . . Renaldo invited me to shtay with him in Melbourne. He thold me Rex was ashking – assking after us both.'

Lobo sneered. 'I think it is not the whole story you are telling me. I do not trust this Renaldo. And what about Rex, huh? Does Renaldo tells him about his little affair with Nealga? No, I do not think so.' Lobo shook his head. 'I tell you, such peoples always are so boringly predictable. Living like fleas sharing the dirty undersides of their bedsheets. Now!' Lobo thumped the steering wheel. 'Pull you together, and tell me, what it is Renaldo really says?'

Outside the cab, the streetlights were a blur. Unable to focus, I rubbed my jaw. 'What did you say?'

'What is wrong with you?' Lobo snapped. 'I say, what is it I see Renaldo whispering in your ear?'

Irritated by his persistent questioning, I snapped, 'Oh, he told me to take care, to watch out for the police, and he doesn't trust you. What the heck do you think?'

'Ha!' Lobo's laugh was triumphant. 'You see how it is with such peoples? Always they try to drive a wedge between two friends. They want you to be afraid and weak like them, Frankie. But not for worrying. I teach you how to become strong. Like me.' He clapped his chest.

'Thank you velly much, Nobo,' I stumbled, my tongue tripping over the words. 'But no more monkeying tonight, please. Let's just find a camping place and relax. And sleep. That's all I want.'

'This it is your idea of heaven? Huh? Sleeping in the front seat of the Baby? Legs stuck out the window? Do you know what it is like to lie under a rubber tarpaulin always waiting for you to wake, stuck between garden tools and skis? No. That it is not my idea of a good time.'

Curling his lip, flattening the pedal, the car accelerating, the neon of the streetlights stretching to ticker-tape . . .

'Heh!' Lobo reached behind his seat and pulled out Nealga's bag of grass, flipping in onto my lap. 'While you do the day-dreaming, I do the work for the both of us. This grass it is better than the sticks, huh? Now roll me a good joint. Make it a pure one.'

Ish there is no end to hish perfidititty, I slurred mentally. Lobo's nagging voice rolled about in my empty geranium – I mean cranium, nothing else below my decks. Like the ghost-ship *Pequod*, I was rudderless and out of control, and Lobo's words had broken loose in the storm.

One tiny capsule of speed injected into Brisbane's main arterial route, the Pacific Highway is a long, cruel knife, sectioning the dead heart of this city of cabbages. On the periphery of my vision, low factory buildings smouldered. Suddenly Lobo pulled hard on the steering wheel. Rubber screeched and stank as we bounced and bumped through the central reservation.

'My God! Why did you do that?' I spluttered, clutching at the makings.

Lobo pulled to a halt just in front of the big wire-mesh gates of a factory. Signs were fixed to both gates, the bigger of the two blaring: 'CUT PRICE CANOPIES - Buy Direct from Manufacturer - Prices Start from $750'. A cartoon showed a pick-up much like ours except for the camper canopy on the back and, like some damned Pegasus, wings sprouting from either side. Inside the cab, two stick-men grinned widely. I didn't want to look at the other one. One glimpse of the German shepherd dog was enough.

I lit the joint, noticing my hand was shaking as I passed it over. Smiling, Lobo pushed it back. 'Only one puff you are having. Are you not feeling well?'

'Christ,' I replied. 'It's enough to scare anyone, the way you drive.'

Nervously, I took another deep drag on the joint. As the song says, *One toke over the line*. My stomach heaved.

'Oh, take it Lobo,' I managed to choke out as I reached for the door handle. I darted across the gravel to the bushes at the edge of the compound. Bloooelllchhh-ulchhh . . . And then another retch, and then I couldn't bring any more up.

Still groggy, I staggered back to the car, opened the door. Lobo shook his finger.

'No further, please. You smell of the sick. Wait one minute, I get out too.' Shutting his door quietly he circled the car. 'You are feeling better? You get rid of all the dirt?'

'Yes,' I lied. 'I'm feeling much, much better.'

'Hmmm, that it is good,' Lobo said, striking a match and re-lighting the joint. He passed it. 'You see what a good friend I am? I save it for you. Now smoke it up, Frankie, it makes you feel even better.'

I leaned back against the car, toking and staring up at the triplicate dancing stars. Definitely not what the doctor ordered.

'Ohhhhh,' I groaned, holding my stomach, a cold pool, way, way, down. Steadying myself, I rubbed my hands on my flannels before I placed them on the immaculate paintwork of the Falcon.

'Please,' Lobo frowned, 'not the fingers there. Dirty marks you make.' As if from nowhere, he was flourishing a yellow duster, polishing away all evidence. 'And now, are you ready?'

'What?' I squawked. 'Ready for what?' My voice boomed in my ears.

Lobo shrugged. 'Unbelievable you are. Do not you understand why we are here? I tell you before we set off. We have a work to do tonight. Look,' he pointed at the sign of the car with wings, 'my Voice it tells me, *Cross the road, and there you are finding the answer to the accommodation problem*. I look up and what do I see? Canopies for cars such as ours.' Lobo tapped his head. 'My Voice you know, never it is wrong. And now it comes clear to me, no longer can we go on living as we do. Either we get an extra room, and now, one that gives enough space for the two of us, or we get a divorce.'

Panic-stricken by Lobo's statement, for a moment I was driven to speechlessness. Fuck, if he dumped me now . . . No money. And in this place. Even drunk as this, I knew Lobo was not joking.

'You know I'd help you with anything, but right now I'm so stoned and pished . . .'

'If you must say this, piss-ed,' Lobo's lips twisted around the word, 'please to make the effort to speak it properly. And now, are you coming or no? I am fed into my teeth with this hanging around.'

Pointing to the high compound fence, I said, 'Before I do, explain to me two things. How the heck do we get in? And once we're in, how do you p-p-prose to get an enormous canopy back over that?'

Lobo sneered. 'Always you moan so. How many times must I tell you, my Voice it says we find the way. We only have to make a start. Now, are you coming?'

'I don't believe you can be serious,' I protested. 'I'm not in any condition to take anything. Don't you see, I can hardly stand upright.'

Lobo screwed his eyes shut. 'Do not talk in this manner. Take a grip on yourself this second!'

Breathing deeply, I said, 'Lobo, listen to me' – waving towards the fence – 'even if I was straight, it would be almost impossible to get a canopy over that, and besides, I couldn't handle taking it at the moment. I get much too paranoid when I'm stoned.'

Lobo closed in on me aggressively, placing both hands on his hips. 'I do not listen any more to this rubbish. If smoking dopes makes you afraid, why then do you smoke? When is my Voice ever wrong? It says we can take the canopy if we do it now.'

What else could I do? I gave in. Besides, I knew if I didn't agree Lobo would attempt the job anyway, and then it was certain we'd both get busted. He wouldn't leave the place till he got the damn thing out. I was bound to this man by an umbilical cord, and at this moment it was looped in a noose around my neck.

Lobo to the fore, we skirted the perimeter wire-mesh fence, following a path through the shoulder-high weeds of the untended waste-ground. Lobo, my Indian guide, turned every now and then to hiss, one finger to his lips, the other hand dancing, not a rustle betraying his movements. Compared with his sleek beastie glide, I was a blundering minotaur, my tracks pursuing us everywhere.

Lobo hissed, 'You must to be quiet! It is important!'

He had led me to the corner of the compound furthest away from the road, where the fence abutted a high brick wall. To the right, down a steep slope, ran the slow-moving pool of a river, thirty feet across, a bumping procession of bottles and floating muck on its glassy surface.

'What you look at?' Lobo demanded harshly.

'An escape route.'

'Ah,' he breathed, 'that it is good. Now at last your brain it begins to work. Now, come!' Lobo snapped his fingers. And then his hand on my arm – 'Look a-here. I see something.'

'What? What? Where?' He pointed at an architectural aberration in the

158

wall's design. The corner bricks were laid herring-bone fashion, every second brick jutting out like so many sore thumbs . . . or steps.

'You see,' Lobo hissed delightedly, 'how dumb the stupid Australians are? They build a wall and leave a ladder, for night-time fellows to climb up. Now come you. No time we have for losing.'

A drunken baboon swinging; overhead hung the chunky soles of Lobo's trainers, one day-glo price tag yet winking leerily. Balancing, he crouched on the top, impatiently waiting. 'Here,' he said, thrusting his hand in my face, 'take a-hold.'

Swaying on the narrow ledge, I took stock. Immediately below on the inside corner of the wall was an assemblage of boxes, cartons and long planks of wood. I shook my head, wondering at the lengths the go-ahead Australian business-man will go to provide easy access for nocturnal callers. Following Lobo, I managed to negotiate the descent of this miniature mountain without causing an avalanche, and joined him on cool concrete.

Two midgets in the wine cellars of Castle Perilous, we eyed the moulded canopies, racked like crouched animals in coffin holds, their polished surfaces reflecting a latticework of quasars from the floodlights above.

'Stop this dreaming!' Lobo ordered, tugging at the first fibreglass canopy. He turned, the whites of his eyes showing luminous. 'What the heck do you wait for? I cannot move it on my own.'

'Wait a minute, Lobo. You're going too quick. Even I'm not too drunk to see each one's bloody different.'

'What do you mean with your dirty mouth?' Lobo snapped.

'Gosh almighty, are you trying it on or something? All the canopies are for different types of cars. Look at that sticker. It says Z-6. And this one is Z-25.'

'My goodness, for the once you are perfectly correct. Well, do not stand there. Hurry! Find the right one for our Baby.'

'Oh Lobo,' I groaned, scratching my head.

At that precise moment a white station wagon drove into the forecourt of the factory and parked alongside our Baby.

'Quick.' Lobo's hand tugged at my arm. 'Duck down!'

The driver shut the engine off, leaving only the noise of my heavy breathing and the busy cicadas. The car door clicked open. Through a small gap in the racks I saw, first the gleam of a highly-polished shoe, then a purple peaked cap as the security man stepped out onto the halogen stage. No German shepherd, thank God. Gravel scrunched as he walked slowly round the Baby, rounding the tail-lights, testing the taut tarpaulin with probing fingers. Then, dropping to his haunches, he diced the interior of the cab with his torchbeam.

God! Did I leave any cigarette papers on my seat? And what did I do with the grass?

The uniformed man tried the door. I thanked God, and Lobo, it was locked. I knew I'd left mine open.

Fingering his jaw thoughtfully, he stood up. Tension edging his stride, he stepped towards the compound. Holding his torch high, he pushed his face close to the mesh fence. I felt myself shrinking back as if he possessed X-ray eyes. The prod of the beam turned the shadows into scuttling things. Lobo's vice grip tightened on my shoulder as blood pounded in my ears. A thin sliver of flashlight penetrated our hide, sweeping our necks . . .

Purposefully now, the security man strode for his car and, reaching in through his window, pulled out the radio-mike and thumbed the switch. Whatever he said was lost in a surge of static.

Slamming his door, revving the engine, the car spewing gravel as it roared onto the main road.

'Fucking hell. Jesus, Lobo,' I gasped. 'We've got to split, now! He's seen the car. He knows we're here. What the fuck are you waiting for?'

Dusting his knees, Lobo slowly raised himself from his crouched position. He spat out, 'I do not excuse you for the dirty words I am hearing pouring from your mouth. This is no place for panic. I know we can get our canopy. My Voice it tells me so. You worry for security men? Pah! I tell you, all of them are lazy and spend the whole night having cups of tea. We have time. Wait here while I go to get my measuring tape. Do not move!'

Shock still transfixing me to the spot, I cursed the day I was born.

Lobo reappeared, momentarily silhouetted on the crest of the wall as he scuttled back down the pile of boxes like a surefooted gazelle. In a couple of light bounds he crossed the concrete, then thrust the tip of the tape-measure into my hand.

'Go to the end of this canopy.' He pointed imperiously. 'First we must to measure the long and then the wide.'

'Ach!' Lobo exploded. 'This it is not the right one. Come, climb up to the next, and take care, this rack is not so built well. Now, lean forward, take the tape end again.'

This was not the model we wanted. Nor was the next. We scaled to the topmost berth, a couple of derrick workers on a Martian rig under whirling stars, the wood of the stanchions groaning under our combined weight.

'Ha! I bet you this it is the one. So often the way . . . The most difficult . . .' Lobo whispered. 'As I figure it, the long it is correct. Now, let go of the tape while I measure the wide. We have to work fast . . . Ha! Yes!' Lobo announced triumphantly. 'Frankie, this it is the one. Come on, it is not so heavy. We must get it down quick.' We began easing the canopy out into space.

'Hurry!' Get two of those long planks at the corner of the wall. Smooth ones. We have to be careful not to scratch this canopy. All the effort it is going to be worth it.'

Descending on aching arms, almost tripping over a heap of bricks as I crossed to the pyramid of boxes, almost causing an avalanche as I removed a plank . . .

Lobo hissed harshly. 'Dolt! Always you make so much noise. Bring the planks and hurry. My Voice it says the police they come.'

I don't quite know how we lowered the canopy from the topmost berth, but we did. We struggled across to the assemblage of junk then, with several great heaves, bumped it up the pile to within a few feet of the top of the wall. That was the moment three police cars swept into the forecourt, pulling to a halt around the Baby. Twelve doors slammed; a bevvy of porkers sniffing night air. No urging needed, I was moving like a rocket as Lobo slapped my bum, hissing hoarsely in my ear, 'Go!'

I cleared the summit of boxes in one vaulting leap, scraping my arse on the top of the wall and murmuring an Icarus incantation as I hung in space for a moment, wheeling, free . . . I was saved from breakages as I hit the steeply-sloping bank only by the looseness of my still drunken body. I rolled, plunging backwards into water, surfacing through a raft of bobbing refuse. And then, with the great fear of capture welling up inside me, I crossed the bayou, heaving and spluttering, a great Scottish narwhal with butterfly wings.

Hauling myself dripping onto the opposite bank, my ears as they popped filled with the cacophony of stentorian voices, clanging metal, barking . . . Dogs! I didn't wait to find out more. Stooping low, I scuttled across the flat stretch of marshy ground towards the cover of a building site a hundred and fifty yards away.

A hut raised on stilts – not nearly as high as the pavilions in Redhill, but just enough to afford me space to wriggle under. Reflected in the river, flashes from by the compound wall. The police dogs had found my trail through the bushes. Then the shadows moved back around the compound wall – car doors slammed, chains rattled as the gate-locks were secured. One by one the cars drove out of the forecourt. I counted three, and then one more. Only three had come in. It was obvious they had taken Lobo's car, and him too. Je-sus!

What am I to do? Everything in the car is taken, I mean stolen. When they find my passport they'll come back looking for me. And . . . Oh God! The dope! One year in this state for a single fucking seed. Oh why didn't I listen to Renaldo? Where the hell was Pavilion Boulevard? I hadn't a clue. I'd better wait here. At least I'm well-hidden under this hut. Give it ten minutes.

Ten minutes passed, so I decided to give it another ten minutes. Half an hour had elapsed before I ventured out into the still night air, realising for the first time how coated in filth I was – green slime from the froth on the bayou, mud from sliding under the hut. My clothes were steaming, the sulphurous stench of the river wafting up my nostrils.

Climbing a low wall, slinking like a river rat into the dark space between two giant hangars, and then the wide Pacific Highway was before me, stretching like a bloody Rubicon in either direction, the whole length of it flooded with neon. No sign of prowl cars. No traffic at all. The emptiness made it so much more desolate. I had almost crossed to the central reservation when I was pinioned by the twin headlamps of a car. My heart skipped a beat, and then another, as I recognised the profile of my diabolical companion, not one hair out of place on his immaculately-groomed-salesman's head.

'Frankie! My gosh, you are a stupid, and a fool. You lous-ed the whole operation, I am so worrying and searching all over for you. And how am I finding you? Cover-ed from the toes-es to the head in the dirt.' Pinching his nose, Lobo screwed up his face. 'And you smell so . . . Completely disgusting I am! Now.' Lobo pointed. 'You see by the side of the road that big tree? Walk there. I pull in by it and wait while you change. I am furious, hopping mad.'

Murmuring expletives that had better remain deleted, I attended to my toilet, scraping off the caked mud as best I could. Above my head twinkled an illusion of Christmas past, created by the neon illumination of the motorway, and the ass-shaped gourds dangling from every little-bittie branch of the vast, spreading Yellow Bum tree.

I had reached the final dregs of the bush-fire victims' bag – one crumpled, ill-fitting denim suit. As I changed, Lobo watched me out of the sneaky corners of his eyes – relaxing, feet out of the car, apparently attending to his manicure with his favourite diamond file.

Then, dread of dreads, he lifted his head and, after the manner of a lovelorn but unrequited dog, began to serenade me with these awful words:

> Frankie and Lobo go sho-hopping one beautif-u-hul ni-yight,
> Then Frankie hears a noise that gives him a gre-eeat fri-yght,
> He jumps ho-hover a wall, full twenty feet in the air . . .
>
> Nnneeeoooowww, chwksssplawshhlsh . . .
> And he-he goes swimming in the mud-cover-ed pond.
> Tra-la-la . . . Like the platterpuss. Quack-quack, dumb-quack!

Thumping the steering wheel in time to the beat, Lobo's other hand, deep in his armpit, provided an accompanying solo, making the dreadful farting sound of a Dutch tuba.

> His good friend Lobo he is so-ho-ho upset,
> Oh does not he worry and does not he fre-het,
> He thinks poor silly Frankie is bre-a-king his ne-heck, . . .

> Yodelooo . . . Yodeleooo . . . Yodeleeaaa . . . Yodeleaeee . . .
> Bum bum, tra-la, nyeh dee daah
> Dum-de-doo, wak-wak, quack-quack . . .

There were more verses, in which he clung repetitively to the theme of dirt, viz:

> Cover-ed up to his ne-heck in mud, tra-la, tra-la . . .

Breaking into subsequent meaningful silence, which I suppose was intended as a meditation period to reflect on my engrain-ed dirt, I asked, 'Lobo, what happened after I jumped over the wall?'

He grimaced, shaking his head with the utmost gravity. 'It is a very lucky Scottisman you are, to be standing here without a neck that is broken. Such a stupid thing you do.'

'But Lobo, you're forgetting, it was you that pushed me, and told me to go!'

'That is not correct. I tell you to stay. I try to pull you back, to grab a-hold of your pants. For why always you are lying?'

'Don't start, Lobo, just tell me what happened when the cops came.'

Lobo shrugged. 'Not so much. They are checking around for some time. There is one close moment when they try to get into the Baby, many keys they have, but the lock it is too good for the stupids.' Lobo's voice darkened. 'Fortunate it is for you they do not think to try the door you leave unlock-ed!'

My cheeks flushed like a cistern of guilt had just been pulled on me. Got to keep him moving . . . 'What happened then?'

'They are leaving.' Lobo scowled, lifting his hand to puff the dust from his nails.

'Surely, something else?'

Yes, there is more, but so boring it is.' Lobo jabbed the file towards me. 'OK, this once I tell you. The cop-es they puzzle much over the canopy on the pile. They take the dogs outside, soon they find the place where you fall in the pond. The men they make jokes about crocodiles. Then the security man drives up. You should see what you are worrying so much for, the way he walks, soon he is needing a stick.'

Lobo slipped the nail-file back in to its correct holder and then, as if finally closing the casebook, flapped shut the small manicure valise, zipping it tight.

'What happened then? Come on, Lobo.'

Lobo frowned. 'OK,' if you must know. The security man he tells them he passes a car, with suspicious peoples in it. The whole lot leave. After a minute I peek out from my hiding place behind the plank-es. You see, I do not move when you jump over the wall. The police are in the front of me the whole time. For the rest, you know the story.' Lobo stretched. 'You are ready? You are clear-heading to go?'

'Uh-huh,' I nodded, stuffing the bag of dirty clothes behind my seat.

'And now,' Lobo squinted venomously, 'we go back and make a good job out of the mess you make.'

'Whaaat? You can't mean it?' I gasped.

Lobo growled. 'I am not like you, always I say what I mean. I tell you, we go back this minute and take the canopy. Otherwise I go mad.'

'Lobo' – I shook my head violently – 'I utterly and absolutely refuse. You can do anything you like, but I'll not go back into that bloody depot, not tonight, not ever.'

Lobo slumped, bumping onto the steering wheel, and then, as he brought up his hands to cradle his head, his elbow set off the horn. 'Why must I to clean him?' he wailed. 'For why?' Shaking his fists above him. 'For why are you not giving me the reason?'

Slowly he lifted upright, his wrath setting on his face like a jelly-pan of cold aspic. 'Very well. This is the way it you want? This is the way it you have. I tell you, for this, the both of us suffer, every day and every minute, until we find another canopy. Now it is too late because you argue so much. I am so tir-ed! I drive. I drive. You . . . Shut up! My gosh, so disappointing I am!'

Never had I seen my companion like this, discombobulated, driving like an automaton in the last stages of battery depletion. Passing a garage, he braked viciously, pulling as hard as he could on the wheel to slew the Baby broadside into the forecourt. Only when we finally stopped, with two bare inches between us and a petrol pump, was I able to breathe again.

Fifty feet away, through the glass wall of the fish-tank garage shop, amid a jangle of fronds, rubber ducks, Cap'n Hook's Toy Castles and similar play-things, a bevvy of hideous pork-carp were gathered, the diminutive of which – a liver-lipped porker of gigantic proportions – was silently mouthing as he glared in our direction. I saw he was mopping furiously at his uniform – presumably a spill from the steaming cup gripped in his other flipper.

Oh dear . . . my vision drifted sideways, drawn by a rumpus in the adjacent lot. Be-Jesus, some sort of armed hold-up going on. And then I realised it was more of the same – about fifteen equally pork-carp, German shepherds, Land Rovers, a black-windowed van, and a battery of lights trained on a couple of very terrified, ashen long-hairs, thrust up against the luminous backdrop of a silver figure surfing the side of their large and very psychedelic pick-up.

Taking care to keep my face a mask of propriety, intensely aware of the scrutinising stares from the fish-tank, yonder, I remarked, as if to no one in particular, 'We should drive out of here nice and slowly . . . Now.'

Lobo snapped, 'I am sick beyond my teeth with all your moanings. I stop here because we are needing cigarette papers. I am not caring,' he sneered, jerking his thumb to the side, 'for these stupids, and I tell you if any one of them gives me a trouble I deal with him accordingly. Tonight I am losing all my sense of humour. Stay here and be trembling while I take the shopping.'

'For God's sake man! Use some money. Look' – I rummaged under the seat, pulling out my money-belt – 'here's five dollars. We could do with some nice biscuits, huh?' I held the note out as a peace offering.

'No!' Lobo snapped. 'Tonight, I do not feel for paying.'

'OK,' I said briskly, stepping out of the Baby. 'You stay here. After all, why should you do all the work? I'll get the cigarette papers. Anything else you fancy?'

'A drink, make it a cold one.' Moodily, Lobo turned to gaze out onto the empty road. 'And hurry, so tiring I am.'

Gulping manfully, threading the eye of this needle with necessary abandoned cowardice, strolling into the shop, I tried to look undangerous, normal, as if I didn't have a care in the world.

The pork-carp dabbing at the stain on his uniform glared at me angrily. I pulled up beside him, drawling in my best Aussic accent. 'Sorry, cobber. Did my mayte give ewe a shock stawlling the caar loike that, as 'e drowve in?'

I glanced back through the glass. Jesus! Lobo, framed in the window and concentrating on his reflection, was applying a fresh line of eye make-up.

The angry porker demanded, 'Whaat's a bluddy Blackie droiving a caar loike thaet?'

'Ow nooow,' I grinned, 'he's no Abo, 'e jest goes blayck in the sun, thayt's awl. He'll get bluddy skin-cayncer wun day. It taykes awll tiypes. Ewe know the saying.'

Turning away, I found myself staring up the truncheon of the biggest carp I'd ever seen, head and shoulders over me. 'Ow' – I thumbed backwards – 'what's awll thaet commotion at the siyde of the gerrage with them bleedin' hippies?'

Cap'n Hook himself couldn't have worn a more slavering grin, gums black and rotten, a teeth septic seaweed green. 'Yep, craziest thing,' he bubbled, 'bluddy gay hippy pooftuhs. High on drugs. Ewe know what they weynt end tried t'dow?'

'What?' I could feel my eyes bulging round with fear.

'Browke in a playce jest up the highway. Yeh, we cawt theym tryin' to geyt away. Weirdest theyng. Nun of the bleedin' caynopies in thet playce would hev fit an owld truck loike theiyrs.'

I jumped with surprise. Not at what he'd just said, but at Lobo blasting the horn. The fucking half-wit ape was waving so madly he'd set the car rocking on its springs.

The angry porker blared, 'Es thaet mayte of yours' a fuckin' fairy, or whaat?'

'Naahh,' I drawled, 'Definitely not 'im, sport. Thaet Tiger Tim pulls awll the girls. Yeh, 'e's wun of theez rich baystards whooz always trying to cawll the shots. Ay thinks I'll mayke him wayt another minute or two. If ewe'll excuwez me, ay'd baetter gaet what ay come foer.'

My attention was drawn to the pimply assistant by virtue of an enormous lime-green pluke dead-centre of his forehead, which, growing rapidly to lighthouse proportions, had begun transmitting a ghastly sonar ray.

Perhaps unaware of this new development up top, rubbing his hands nervously, this periwinkle asked, 'Yeah, myte, and what will eet be?'

Such a relief to transfer my gaze to the sweety counter. 'Ay'll hev a bayr of thet choclet. Thaet pack of besquits be'oind yer, an' a coupla cayns frum the freedge of diet cowla. Ay'll geyt theym on my way out. Yeh, end en ownce of Three 'eads rollin' tobacco, and a pekket of paypers, please. Gimme the blue wuns. Will five dollahs cover it?'

'Yeh, mayte,' he whined, the pitch oscillating with the high frequency sonar from his brow.

My hand was reaching for the glass door, the great outdoors and blessed escape, when the angry porker called out, 'Wayte wun mow-ment.'

Slowly twisting around . . . 'Ye-eh,' I creaked, 'Ennythin' I cayn help ewe with?'

'Yeh, eets jest come to me.' He pointed. 'Ay'e ve seen yer bleedin' mug somewhere before. Reefresh me memory.'

'Nah,' I said, shaking my head. 'This is the first time ay've bin in Queyensland. Ewe must be confusin' me with somewun eylse.'

'What's yeur name?' the angry porker shot back.

Keeping my face blank as a check-stub I replied, 'Riddle. And ewe ayn't never heard thet nayme before, cawse ay ayn't evuh bin in trouble. Watch how ya go.' I pushed on the door.

'Yeh,' the angry porker called, 'an' ewe watch yer bayck with thet fuckin' fairy friend o' yours.'

Trying to keep the tremble out of my step, I strolled for the car. I'd been really close. Right there. A Damocles hair's breadth . . .

Tossing Lobo the can of 'cowla', I flopped back onto my seat.

A gleam of respect seemed to have entered Lobo's eyes. 'You do well there, Frankie. You know they check you out very close, and for the once, you pass the test. So pleasing I am for you. Perhaps now you learn how to trick them good. Hey-hey, Frankie, roll for me a big joint. And do not think to use the lousy sticks. I chuck them away back there . . .'

'Whaaat!'

Secretly I was relieved, but I wasn't letting on.

They get there kicks down on Route 666. Well, I guess that was the Australian version, Pacific Highway Blues, down by the bayou. I didn't throw one backward glance at the poor freaks. Someone's got to pay the piper. Someone's got to take the fall. Poor bastards. Suddenly I was so happy to be alive.

Like two knights, we resumed our search for the one and true Holy Grail . . . the road.

Quoth the one to the other, 'Prithee, good Sir Lobo, where to next?'

24

We hit Surfer's Paradise in the lemon light of dawn. The sun was rising over tower-blocks, and miles and miles of virtually empty beaches. Only early skinny-dippers were about, hard-core nipples kissing surf, wizened monkey-nuts scuttling into the shelter of coconut palms to escape the cold grasp of the sea. On the dream-strip again, back in the land of empty holidays, endless sun, and mindless fun.

We set up camp beside the ubiquitous chain-link fence at the conclusion to a dead-end beach road.

Bliss of oblivion, I stole my first real sleep since Bathurst. Expert now in the art of contortion as usual, I lay with the back of my head propped on the ledge of the arm-rest, legs hung out the window, calves cushioned against the sharp of the frame by the softness of my towel.

I was snatched back into the jaws of this insane Australian dreamtime when the towel was ripped from under my legs and flung into my face. Covering my eyes, I groaned with the vertigo of sudden waking.

Moving swiftly around the car, Lobo jerked the door open. Plunging to a new nadir, my head thumped the metal step.

'Open your eyes and look!' Lobo's finger pointed accusingly at my head-rest, the arm-rest, partially adrift from the door.

Pulling the thin sheet over my head I yelled, 'Leave me alone you pudding-faced bastard!'

'Almost it is midday. Never I meet anyone who sleeps so much. Pay attention. Look at the damage you do.' Lobo rapped the vinyl above my head. 'If we take the canopy the last night, this does not happen.' His eyes narrowed.

'I am furious hopping mad you muck up the operation. I tell you, this day you pay the double!'

'Jesus! OK. OK. I'll do anything for peace.' I jerked up, throwing off the sheet. 'Just give me a screwdriver and I'll fix it.'

Faster than any gunslinger in a spaghetti western, Lobo produced one from his back pocket, revolving the yellow handle under my nose. 'You see, I have it in my hand, even as you ask. Now, show me what it is you can do.'

Gathering all my energies, rubbing the sleep from my eyes . . . In a fury, Lobo grabbed my arm, pressing the screwdriver into my palm, closing my fingers firmly over it. 'Come, you! No time I have for waiting.'

All through the job Lobo stood over my shoulder, looking on. Hardly had I declared the repair completed to my satisfaction when he pushed me roughly aside, leaned his full weight on the arm-rest, and ripped it away from the door.

'Pah! You are calling this a good job!' Folding his arms tight to his chest, he turned to gaze out to the far horizon, his huff one big cloud of hornets swarming about him.

After a moment, Lobo whirled around, eyes transplanted from a berserk Samurai. 'YOU ARE A MONSTER. The last night you lousy up the whole operation. This morning you break the Baby. And you do this while I am out working for the both of us. Look.' Lobo patted the hernias bulging from each side of his shorts. There came the unmistakable jangle of coins.

Blinking, completely unable to focus, I felt suddenly almost as drunk-stoned as the night before. It was all coming back, and with the memories, a splitting headache . . .

Lobo continued unabated . . . 'Already I go investigating.' He pointed to a tall clump of greenness rising from the crest of the dunes. 'You see there, where the track it ends, I find a barbecue place. Two machin-es. You put the money in, and the gas grill it comes on. Never I see anything like this. The peoples in this country are so stupid. So much wood there is lying about. I count twenty-seven dollars in ten-cent pieces inside. It is amazing, for just before I find this I am thinking to myself, it costs twenty-five dollars, maybe more, for doing the laundry.' Lobo laughed. 'And what do you know? I find the washing place, right next to here in this caravan park.' Lobo nodded towards the frayed mesh fence. 'The machin-es they take ten-cent pieces the same.'

Determined to make amends, I volunteered to carry the washing. I didn't realise how many bags there were. Bent-backed like a camel humping more than his fair share, I was hard-pressed to keep up with Lobo's bouncy stride. My aerial view of the brittle, yellowing grass reminded me of the thick stubble grating my lip.

Rubbish was strewn all over the parched savanna, crisp bags, food containers, I even spied a dirty disposable nappy. And where were the tourists? Any caravans we'd passed had been boarded up. Vacant. The only sign of life was a thin trail of smoke rising from a beat-up encampment up ahead. As we approached a collage of sounds engulfed us like a concerto by Igor Stravinsky — kettle drums provided by big Berthas scrubbing clothes in fat vats, the timpani section by plates and cutlery rattling in galvanised zinc tubs, while a sharp voice ticking off a screaming bratlet made a duet between an off-key violin and whining flute.

A tiny Aborigine waif poked out from the underside of a caravan. Mournful mulligatawny soup-kitchen eyes silently regarded us. Then a hand must have grabbed her feet, for she was whipped back, knees scorching gravel, her tousled mop bumping up against the floor of the caravan.

Her wails didn't last for long. I guessed life was a hard lot for these people. Perhaps they subsisted on welfare, or they were itinerant workers employed on the high-rises so thickly clustered around this park, each one a waxen Babel, salivating glass. Balconies piled on balconies, dripping spaghetti and tropical fronds. All that luxury. All that plumbing. All that waste. The sludge of lives. The endless canals of sewage spewing out to sea.

Lobo pulled at my arm, redirecting my course toward the low concrete building planted like an island in a wash of jaded green. This manoeuvre almost resulted in a plunge, as I tripped on a low sign staked in the turf. The flaky white letters read 'Mind How You Go Campers - Have a Nice Day'.

The contrast between harsh daylight and this cool interioor shade momentarily blinded me. At the far end of a long central corridor, Lobo was opening a door onto darkness. Then his hand slapped a bank of switches. One by one a multitude of fluorescent lights flashed into existence acres of white tiles, rippling divisions of upright porcelain, wet-look chrome. This room, with its low, curving roof, had to be at least a hundred feet long. The harsh, unreal light and the glistening highlights created the illusion of the inside of a tube of brilliantine.

Everything ordered in the neatest of rows. Everything designed to allow hundreds of campers to pee at the same time, shower at the same time, shit at the same time. The space echoing and vibrating with the time of this park's heyday. It wasn't hard to imagine the hoards of phantom pee'ers. I guess they're still there to this day. Why not? After all, this is the accursed dreamtime, and it's questionable whether there's any escape at all.

Lobo sniffed the odorous carbolic appreciatively, his voice booming metallically. 'So clean, huh? Come, we shower. You scrub mine and I scrub yours.'

The voice of the policeman distantly echoing . . . *You watch yer back with that fuckin' fairy.*

170

I thought of venereal diseases. The bastard had herpes! Already he was a panorama of soap-bergs, knee-deep in foam, clouds of it scudding over his flesh. I had to admire his technique. I'd never seen anyone squeeze so much out of a sponge.

'Hey-hey, Frankie, so good it is to come clean.'

'Gosh, Lobo. Why don't you wash some of that soap off? You'll stink like a powder puff.'

'Oh no!' Lobo giggled. 'See how I do it?' Pulping the sponge between both hands, his shoulders disappeared in a quivering white blancmange. 'And now,' Lobo held up the brush, 'I scrub it, like so' – with the vigour of a boot-black boy in Rio getting his first shine of the day.

'Watch closely now.' Withdrawing a telescopic handle from the base, he reached over his back, working the brush in long even motions. The foam slipped away from his ass, candle-grease drifting on a Teflon surface. I didn't watch closely. Truth to tell, I wasn't much interested. I began feeling much better as I shaved. I considered the stubble on my top lip. Maybe a moustache would be an improvement. Lobo was annoying again, his reflection dancing before me as he jumped between the hot and cold showers.

He pranced out of the deluge and grabbed at his towel. Methodical in everything, he was, even down to drying out the eight spaces between his toes.

'Are you ready to do the washing now?'

'What do you mean? We're going to wash the clothes together. Aren't we?'

Lobo grinned. 'Just take the money from my trousers, read the instructions on the machin-es carefully. You must do everything correct.'

'Oh, come on Lobo, you're so much better at these things. After all, it was hard work carrying all the bags.'

Lobo snapped. 'You call this work? When I do all the driving. I take all . . .'

Pressing my hands to my ears, screwing my eyes tight – at that precise moment I would have given ninety-nine tenths of any kingdom just to shut out his voice.

'God – I mean gosh, Lobo, don't start that up again. I'll do it. I'll do anything . . .'

'That it is better. Now I go. In half and one hour I return. When you are doing the washing, think of this.' Lobo held up a finger. 'When the man he learns to do everything the woman does, and do it the better, then he can dispose of them.' Lobo bared his teeth. 'I tell you, never I meet a good one yet. Of course, I am not counting my mother, and my sister Heidi . . .'

Lobo seemed to ponder his words for a moment. 'But she I do not see her in my dreams any more. She is hiding. Maybe she is chang-ed.' Lobo tipped his head as if consigning her, along with all the others, to a rubbish basket.

He grinned brightly. 'Do you not see it is possible to enjoy tidying because when you do it, at the same time you are cleaning yourself? And if you sing a song, you can enjoy even more!'

Yes, yes, Lobo, three bags full of washing, sir. Bye bye . . . Thank the good gosh . . . Ha bloody ha!

Before I get down to it, just to put me in the mood, a nice relaxing joint of Nealga's fine grass. Thank you Nealga . . . And thank me – I had had the presence of mind to snitch a couple of heads from the bag stowed in the car. Now, where did I put the skins?

I became aware of eyes, Dalek faces of the washing-machines studying me with a frightening intensity. Guilty conscience, obviously. I'd better get on with the job. How long had I been dreamtiming? Dropping from my perch on the table, I welcomed the cool of the concrete on my bare feet as, bent double now, I tried to decipher the tiny print of the instructions in fifteen languages, riveted to the machine at knee level. Ooohha . . . A sudden wave of giddiness threatened total black-out. I steadied myself, for a moment, leaning against the machine.

I didn't need to read the fucking instructions. Any half-wit knows how Daleks operate: pour the soap into the slot, pump in the coins. Na fuckin' wurries. Lobo's gotten me so paranoid about getting anything wrong. Shithead!

My mind drifted as the eyes of the machines spun hypnotically. God, wasn't this such a different life to the one I'd left? I wondered what the wife was doing. Who was she screwing? Bastards!

The machines had ceased revolving, and probably long since. Christ, that pig-dog will return soon . . . Better speed things up. And how! Moving rapidly, I transferred the load into the tumble-dryers, pushing levers, turning dials as far as they would go. Heat began belting out.

Time for a bit of sunbathing. Aaahhh . . . That's better. Leaning against a porch pillar, viewing my surroundings through half-closed eyes. A short distance off a couple of mango trees, and slung between them a washing-line, one sun-bleached terylene sock hanging limply. The grass below was smudged yellow with rotten fruit. Pity that we must have missed the season by a month or so. I rose – too quickly. My vision shortened. Black spots danced before my eyes. Valves closed down somewhere in my geranium. Stella Nova exploded. And faded away. And exploded again. Staggering backwards, only just connecting with the pillar, Christ, now my legs were turning to jelly. A tourniquet tightened around my chest . . . Slowly the attack ceased. Once more I could breathe again.

Lobo must have sneaked up behind me. Letting out a roar that would have freed any cat from any bag, he slapped me heartily on the back.

'And how are you, Frankie? Is the washing finishing?'

All I could manage was a mumble. 'No, Lobo. Not quite.'

'Come then!' He clapped his hands, 'What are you leaning against the wall for?'

Hard-pressed to keep up with his athletic stride, I tagged him into the laundry. Uh-oh . . . Red lights were winking on the dryers. Lobo rushed to the machines, flinging open doors and releasing a mad genie of heat to belt around the room.

Lobo was shouting, 'My gosh, what have you done! All of my cloth-es are ruin-ed. RUINE-ED! Look!' He pulled out a jacket impeccably tailored for a circus midget. 'It is unbelievable. Why you put this in the machine? The label says dry clean only. My gosh, you are a horrible Scottis madman! Why do not you see the dry cleaning machine? Look dolt, it is there!' A piebald Lobo now, clumps of his hair in his hands. 'These are all my cloth-es. Oh dear . . . My shirt . . . WHERE IS THE SILK SHIRT MY SISTER HEIDI GIVES TO ME WITH MY INITIALS ON THE POCKET?' His voice cracked, 'Ohhhhh, this it is so bad.'

He stepped to the far tumble-dryer – no flashing red light. Relief flooding my bilge-tanks as I realised I'd forgotten to prime it with coins. Lobo pulled the door open. His voice swung for my head like a mighty hammer. 'So the wash you do not ruin is your own cloth-es . . . Wait a minute, the washings they are all mixed up. My gosh! Sometimes your mistak-es are saving you from worse problems. Thank goodness, my blue tracksuit and and white stripey socks, two pairs.' He threw up his arms. 'Why you turn the other machin-es full on? I tell you this' – he swivelled around, a gorgon's mask writhing over his face – 'before we leave this place, mark my words, you replace the whole lot that is ruin-ed. YOU . . . YOU FOOL YOU. I cannot understand why my Voice keeps telling me to clean you . . . It . . . is . . . impossible . . .' he choked.

For a split-moment I thought, as he lunged towards me, he was going to slap my face. Side-stepping, he crossed to the table, picked up his blue hold-all by the corners and shook it vigorously. By some extraordinary fluke – don't ask me how – I'd managed to miss out more of his clothes. The last thing that tumbled out was the shirt from Heidi. Another bonus point to Frankie.

'I do not know whether to curse you for missing this out, or what. This once it is as well you are half-blind. Now you will wash these in the correct way, and from now on I check everything you do.'

He indicated with a lazy sweep the cigarette papers and makings scattered on the far end of the table. 'Now, roll for me a special joint and then I am in a better mood while I watch. You silly boy you.'

I spluttered. 'I'm older than you.'

'The age it does not count. It is a question of maturing-ty.'

Lobo instructed me mercilessly in the art of cleaning, drying, hanging, folding and ironing cloth-es: how to arrange a pair of trousers on a hanger; how you pressed the nose of a hot iron into the creases of a shirt-cuff; the correct way to fold a tracksuit. I could go on interminably about my wrong-doings as he did. I suppose what chiefly astounded Lobo was my sheer horizon-to-horizon lack of knowledge when it came to laundry matters.

The eye of the stormy afternoon arrived when I dropped his favourite shirt, the gift of Heidi. It needn't have been so bad, but at the time I was pegging it to the line strung between the trees, and in my haste to catch it I managed to tread it in the putrid mass of a squashed mango. Lobo cast it into some convenient bushes, never to talk on the subject again.

I think this last mistake was the place I hit the ground at the end of a prolonged state of free-fall. I was a Stan Laurel, the weight of the past like an obscenely enlarged Oliver Hardy strapped to my back.

It was early evening when we reached the crowded centre of Surfer's Paradise, a thronging, sometimes subterranean labyrinth of shops, plazas, spiralling walkways and arcades.

Lobo steered me into an octagonal plaza, the centre occupied by a water garden staffed by concrete sculptures – ibexes, storks, an occasional hanging iguana and, my particular favourite, the hippo, up to its knees in plastic fronds and spouting a twisting chain of sausages. The poolside was strewn with an assortment of plastic furniture in the shape of giant bananas, pears, oranges and slices of kiwi fruit. An Italian-looking vendor of flaky pastries conducted a busy trade underneath a striped awning. Next to his stall was a municipal chess set, the pieces five feet high and covered in mock velvet. Euch!

'You see,' Lobo whispered conspiratorially, 'this it is the perfect place for selling bikinis. We save that for tomorrow, huh? But for now, we have much shopping to get. You are not forgetting you must replace all the ruin-ed clothes. Look' – he pointed to a gold and glass shop front – 'do you believe it? Over there is is another skiing shop. The quilting jackets they are good for the mountains, do you not think?'

'The Tibetans would think you were a weird form of plant-life, if you turned up in those padded Polo mints.'

'Such enthusiasm you spring from,' Lobo sneered over his shoulder, as he pushed the glass door wide.

Steps led down into an air-conditioned, designerworld, mirrored cavern, an Antipodean upperworld basement hell. Flickering orange light fanned the slowly-revolving dummies from below, the schmaltzy classical music seeming to trick them into flaming life.

Lobo whispered, 'Keep him busy.'

I scanned the grotto. 'Who?'

'Stupid dolt,' Lobo breathed into my ear. 'The one who does not move. Behind the cash till. Remember to smile and flatter, always say what good ideas he has. I let you off the hook. I do the taking, for I know what a muck you make of it.'

It is not easy to concentrate a dummy's attention, even if he is the manager, for one full half-hour. I was forced to plunder my entire stock of gags and one-liners. I don't know how many different ways I found to ask questions about his wonderful concept in retailing. 'What a good idea . . . I see . . . You explain very well . . . That's marvellous . . . Now, can I ask you about . . . Yes, please go on . . .' The manager gushed each time I pressed the right button on his designer-wear polka-dot suit.

Every now and then I caught a glimpse of Der Fuhrer bending to slip his feet into a pair of brightly-coloured trainers, or holding up a looped, bulbous tracksuit, a lurid number printed on the back. Everything Lobo fancied was neatly folded and placed in the bag. I couldn't believe how far he was prepared to push his avowed philosophy of 'taking'.

Stepping in close under the cover of the counter, Lobo pressed the bulky hold-all into my hand. 'Hey,' he said smiling. 'Please to introduce me? The both of you are becoming business colleagu-es?'

I pushed the bag back towards the slit-eyed daemon. He stepped away. I edged towards him. He made as if he was interested in a display. Giving up, I turned back towards the manager dummy, floating my free hand to keep his attention from the hold-all. Then I lifted the briefcase from the counter. 'Hey-hey,' I said, aping Lobo, my facial muscles freezing with the effort of maintaining this ghastly smile. 'Introduce yourself, mates. I have to go outside. I need some fresh air.'

Shielding the 'takings' with the briefcase, woodenly climbing the short flight to the glass doors. I've heard that customs officers are taught to look at the walk rather than the face – apparently there's an awkwardness that affects the gait of those who have something to hide, implying a conflict of directions.

All hell broke loose. Klaxons erupted above my head. I was rooted to the spot. Damn it, I would return the things, explain we'd make a mistake . . .

Lobo bounded up the steps to my side, shoving me fiercely out into the plaza.

He was pulling my arm, dragging at it, shouting to the half-clothed promenaders, 'Out of the way! This man is hurt! Make way! Get an ambulance!'

So many pigeons, the shoppers scattered. We ran, dodging the pieces of the huge chess set.

As we ducked into an arcade, I caught a glimpse of the deflated Michelin dummy stepping into the doorway of the shop, head turned in the wrong direction . . . We slowed our pace, Lobo bouncing on his heels, whistling, his smile swelling to a cheery melon slice.

'God almighty, Lobo! What the heck happened back there? Why did that alarm bell go off? I thought I would die.'

Taking the bag and lifting out a striped, down-filled jacket, Lobo grinned the harder. 'You see this?' He waggled the collar, by the rounded cube of grey plastic clamped onto it. 'This it is what is making the alarm go off.'

'Bastard!' I exclaimed. 'You set me up!'

Yes, for once you are correct, I want to see how you take it when everything it goes wrong. So funny you are.' Lobo rollicked, clutching his sides. 'I tell you, without me, by this time you are looking at the bars of a police van. Much there is for you to learn. Now,' he nodded sharply, 'it is time we find a nice place for eating. We need food, I am surprised you are not already moaning for your poor stomach.' I was forced to jump to the side as he reached out to pat it.

It was while passing along some glassy arcade that Lobo spied a familiar peak – a mural seen through the open window of a restaurant called 'The Natter Horn'. We were welcomed by the patroness, a buxom maiden, her ethnic smock cut low across the deep of her alpine valley. Lobo told her she reminded him of his adoptive mother. After that dubious compliment, she couldn't have been more attentive.

The food was excellent, the wines superb. Over coffee and kirsch, Lobo mused on the concept of 'Rough Jock's Bloody Tours'. Predictably he drew a red circle around the word bloody.

Lobo tapped his head. 'It is not a problem to get the company started. You place an advertisment, the peoples must send a deposit. The banks they double the money when we are showing them so many chequ-es. And when we get to Nepal we have no problems. There, with the Sherpas, I am a prince. Never we have any need for money.'

'How so?' I demanded.

'It is this simple.' Lobo the woodpecker rapped his head again. 'The problem in Nepal is to find anything worth the taking. You can have money and still not buy. A Sherpa will work one week for one pair of Japanes-e training shoes. They like them very much. With a thousand, we live as kings for one full year.' Lobo laughed. 'I am beginning to think your title for this company, it is not a mistake. We take the peoples to the mountain, leave them on the side of a precipice with no ropes. I tell you, then these stupid tourists they have an experience for writing home about. Maybe then they are discovering the meanings for their lives. In this way they get a good value. No?'

Lobo continued, 'We make our escape. There are secret tunnel-es under the mountains to my country. The Sherpas they show us the where. My guru will be waiting in the cave. If by the time you meet him you are not yet clean, I hand you over, and mark my words, he is the business!'

Slowly sipping my kirsch and savouring the padded softness of this vinyl chair, I saw a picture clearing through the dark speckling in my mind's eye – Lobo, bronzed and naked, skiing in hot pursuit of a terrified Abominable Snowman which is running for its very life. With one hand Lobo cracks a leather whip, and with his other he operates a video camera. 'Stop! I must clean you!' he is shouting.

Planting my elbows on the table, I laid out The Plan. 'We'll take the twelve Australians up to the snow, huh? With your influence it won't be difficult to rent a hut or a cave to put them in. No problem there. We spend a few days working them over – a strict regime of corrective therapy. No booze. Maybe we'll put datura in their billycans. We'll hire Tibetans to wander outside the cave all night and every night making strange, banshee noises. We'll deny we ever heard the noise. That will freak the Aussies out. By the third evening we'll have built up the drama nicely. At the right moment, two small Tibetans, one on top of the other, inside a manufactured costume of the Abominable Snowman will lumber into view of the quivering Aussies sheltering in the refuge of the cave. I'll then rush out with the camera, tape about fifteen seconds of shaky, hand-held shots. This will be the first video record of the Abominable Snowman. The deranged Australians will be our witnesses, and none of them will be in any condition to see through the disguise. This piece of video will prove conclusively the existence of our not-yeti.'

'Frankie!' Lobo hopped about on his red-hot stove of a seat. 'This it is the most amazing of ideas ever I am hearing. We must to do this. It is a fantastic!'

25

We returned to our camping place at the dead-end of the beach road. Entering into the spirit of the occasion, the streetlamp above took it into its cracked and tilted head to start flickering. We three luminosities shared a joint. Lobo scratched his nether regions. A fine veil of rain drifted from the sea. Unusually, Lobo expressed a desire for sleep, and after warning repeatedly of the dangers of snoring, retired to his space in the ship's hold, insisting I secure every toggle of the tarp and fix the studs at the end, because of the rain. I wondered if he could breathe in there. But such considerations are unimportant to yogis.

I fell into a deep sleep. The sleep of the just. The sleep of the dirty. The sleep of the uncleaned. Earned or unearned, I needed it. But before I fell tumbling, it seemed, the flickers from above had tuned in to the wavelengths of my brain, my eyelids jumping in time to the bip-bip beep-beep dot-dash hiccuping morse code.

I was jolted out of catatonia by yowlings and thunderous clashings from a nearby discordant guitar. Yawning and dragging my aching frame to a sitting position, I rolled down the window. No, the sun was not yet up.

Leaning over the guitar, seated on the bench not five feet away – Lobo.

'Oh, good, awake you are. You like my tune? You like to hear more? Oh Frankie, he is my friend, and I must clean him. Oh-ho-ho –'

'Shut up, Lobo! God, what a racket.' Opening the door, I pushed out warding palms. 'No more, please.'

'Frankie.' Lobo patted the bench. 'Sit down beside me, and please to be preparing for what I must to tell you.' His voice was suddenly deep and sonorous. I looked up at where the moon should have been, but the wolf of night had gulped the celestial orb from the sky. I shivered, cold despite this clammy tropical heat. Pulling my sheet about me, I took a pew beside him.

Lobo smiled grimly. 'Two remarkable things are happening tonight. I see your face it stays a blank. You do not see the two puzzl-es? For why do not you ask yourself, how come I to be sitting on this bench, when you are so firmly tying with the rubber over my head? And how come this guitar, huh?'

I looked over to the Baby. The tarpaulin was immaculate, glistening with undisturbed lozenges of rain. All the toggles were in place and each of the press-studs at the corners snapped down.

'After you strap me in, I fall to sleep. This night I am so tiring. My head a piece of lead. Despairing for you I lose much energy. Suddenly, I am most surprising to find myself on the beach, this guitar in my hand. Never I see it before. I look all around it, the label inside says it is a Japanes-e. My favourite. I strike a chord.' Lobo raised his arm —

'Wait a minute. Stop. Please'. Stricken by sudden fear, I felt I would die if he released the chord.

'How so? The drops of the rain they are all the same. Show the one that has mov-ed.'

'Christ, I don't know. You must have flown through it then. What am I supposed to believe?'

Lobo shook his head. 'It is strange. I hear of such things happening to yogis in my land. But why do you not listen? I strike a chord.'

'No, no, Lobo don't do it.' His arm swept down, the chord crashed. Despite the reverberations, I did not die.

Fingers clutching at my my brow, I gulped down the choke in my throat. 'Look, Lobo . . . I-I-I can't handle this. I've got this right, haven't I? First you teleport out of the Baby, then you find this bloody guitar in your hand.'

Lobo pushed his head in close. 'Look, how often must I tell you —'

As Lobo and I talked, it seemed that the flickering strobe of the streetlight above punctuated the conversation, marking with a black spot every dot, every dash, even the b-b-b-b's and f-f-f-f's when I stuttered. Once it threatened to go out altogether. And it only flashed on again when I concentrated with all my mind, willing it to. At that moment I believed if it shut down I would die. It was all so bizarre. My hands shook as I rolled the spliff. Lobo's voice chattered like a road-drill, breaking up the cement of my head. Once more he castigated, 'And rolling joints will not help you. It is only by cleaning the dirt from your mind and body you make yourself strong.'

After the compulsory pressing-ups and beach exercises, next item on the menu: bikini-selling. My last hope of securing an independent cash flow . . . And escape.

We set up our makeshift stall by the assorted fruit seats, a few feet from the hippo spouting sausages and in full view of the designerworld skiing shop. Lobo insisted it was the best spot, and spoke of the shame he felt as a friend at seeing me succumb to such unreasonable fears.

Preparations were complete, the glittery bikinis arrayed in glittery rows. Hand-painted signs posted in nearby streets proclaimed stunning beachwear bargains. To the accompaniment of Lobo's crashing chords on his unearthly guitar, I took up my refrain, yelling out my sales pitch like a barrowboy from Shoreditch.

'Get yoour glittery bikinis here. Latest styles, HOT FROM BAAALIII!'

By the time the sun had reached it's zenith our sales amounted to one big 0. My voice was cracking. At three o'clock, success knocked faintheartedly at my door. A Jewish matron of vast dimensions had taken a passing fancy to one of our flimsy offerings, and after a fearsome struggle, coughed up the appropriate shekels. I don't know how many times I assured her the postage stamps would fit her ample tubers.

As I'd anticipated, she returned five minutes later, one fat bejewelled pinkie dangling the bikini by its broken strap. When I turned to Lobo for support, to my astonishment he insisted I behave like a gentleman and return the money immediately. Too hoarse to argue. I squirmed on my green cucumber seat, then unzipped my sweat-stained money-belt and grudgingly withdrew the seven damp dollars.

Hunched up and defeated, I whined (so uncharacteristically!), 'What am I to do, Lobo? These bikinis are useless. I'd chuck them in the pond next to that hippo, only I know some carpetbagger would claim them. Bastards. I'll never sell one, and I've only got forty bucks to my name. Probably less since I haven't counted recently. I'm fed up with this taking, it's no way to live!'

Lobo grimaced, his voice marching on me like a chainsaw squad. 'Frankie, always you are so quick to throw up the towel. Do not you remember? We make a pact to sell the bikinis. Never do I break a promise! Now, listen. We have two options. The first is we go north. There the season it is longer, and the peoples still buy, but . . .' A grimace daubed his mouth, as he took in our surroundings with a sweep of his hand. 'This Queenies-peoples, you notice how rude they are, everywhere their eyes following us? So much better it is in Perth. The best city I find in Australia. There we have no problem to sell the bikinis. Besides, my Voice it tells me the effort of the journey is good to clean Frankie's brain.'

Flustered, I could only answer, 'Yes, yes, I'm more than sure it would be, but Perth is a whole continent away, over three thousand miles. Even I know that.'

Lobo frowned. 'You are correct, but I think if we drive most of the time it takes at the most . . . Three days, and I am not minding the effort of such a drive. So why should you when all you must to do is —'

'But Lobo, come on, think of the petrol, where will we find it in the middle of the desert. It'll take hundreds of gallons.'

Lobo's finger waggled sternly. 'Do you really think I enjoy this sneaking for Baby food. When I start, I only do it to learn you the ways of taking. I tell you, such games they are for children. From now on we use the chequebook. I have one in the car. I tell you, never there is a problem we cannot solve.'

I started. 'You've got a chequebook?'

'Yes, it is in my Swiss name, Peter Justice.'

'And a banker's card?'

'What are we needing stupid plas-teek for?'

'Don't you know?' I laughed. 'No garage will accept a cheque unless you've got a banker's card to back up your identity.'

'Is this what you think?' Lobo shook his head sadly. 'So little self-belief. The plas-teek it does not make the man. I tell you, from now on we use the chequebook. You learn a new way of taking. It is as simple as that. And you should be pleas-ed at this opportunity, instead of moaning so. And now, you are ready? We go.'

'Wait a minute. Don't I get a chance to think about it? You've only just sprung this on me.'

'Always I am waiting.'

Shell-shocked by this sudden turn of events, I lurched, stumbling to gather up the bikinis. Goddamnit! When would my accursed wanderings ever cease? Perth. Perth . . . Christ, the last bloody time I saw the wife she was receding into a dot of damnation on the platform at fucking Perth station, screaming some abuse I couldn't make out. I should never have looked back, it's always a mistake.

Perth, as every Scotsman worth his salt knows, is the ass-hole of Scotland. Now I was headed to its Australian namesake. I wondered if it was any different.

26

If Queensland was a dead dog, we'd licked it . . . I mean, kicked it. Every way and which way. Surfer's Hell was a black spot, a blight on Paradise, somewhere back over the horizon. Our car, a jabberwocky alley cat lapping up the miles. Lobo yattered endlessly, his plans growing more fantastic with every passing minute – how we'd sell the car in Perth, fly to Bangkok, spread the herpes spores to all and sundry, take to the elephant trails through Burma to the high country . . . There we'd rendezvous with our Rough Treckers, film the 'Abdominal Snowman' and, neat and tidy in everything, push the Aussies over the first available precipice at the conclusion of their tour.

Slumped on my seat I was squinting with the effort of visually connecting, my shaggy ping-pong nets were sagging so. Lobo's remarks bounced in from all sides.

It was the dead of night when we rounded a corner and just about ran slap up the tailgate of the biggest creepy-crawly I'd ever seen, a garishly customised cockroach bursting with CB antennae, monster wheels, arrays of spotlights. When Lobo pulled out to overtake, the giant road-bug weaved to bar our way.

Lobo jammed his fist on the horn, held it.

Up ahead, a smoked-glass window rolled down, a black leather gauntlet flopping out, raising the second finger to the sky.

Lobo grimaced. 'You see this cheeky fellow? Watch, I show him how we drive.'

Wrenching on the wheel, grit churning on the verge, we blazed past this nocturnal creation. Behind us, that bank of spotlights found a use at last, as ten times the wattage of the defences of London in the Blitz seared the cab with atomic brilliance.

Lobo laughing, bouncing on his seat, blew the road-torch a whopper of a kiss.

The chase began. This was no creeping crawly. By the roaring behind, I figured the brute was powered by a four-litre job at the very least. But whatever we lost on the straights, Lobo's Alpine driving technique made up for on bends.

Lobo flick-snapping his fingers, shouted over the din, 'A-hey-hey! Frankie! Why the gloomy face? This it is the life. Turn up the sounds, roll for me a big fat joint!'

'Have you gone fucking crazy?' I yelled hoarsely. 'It's all I can do to hang on to the fucking seat.'

Fortunately for his concentration, my dirty words escaped him. His face bore the ecstatic delight of a kamikaze pilot going to a better life.

Yes, I realised as I gazed up the slipstream. This was no ordinary dreaming.

This leather-helmeted and be-goggled, no-shit Tibetan lunatic was now grinning and waving and bouncing and pelvically-thrusting all at once, positively squirting all over his cockpit. 'Yeh-hey, Frankie, hold on . . .'

Pushing hard on his joystick he sent the nose-cone into a dive, centrifugal force taking over as we plummeted spinning into the void.

The warnings words of the first policeman came flooding back: *There's killers stalk the roads up there in the north, sometimes they hunt in packs . . .*

Mercy! Blue flashing lights. Up ahead a patrol car was blocking the road, with a cop wielding a torch like this was Star Wars. Barely enough time to stop. But the fucking madman was *accelerating*. Instinctively I pushed my hands out, shutting my eyes as the slapstick face of the policeman was framed in the windscreen, grotesquely large.

Lobo grunted with effort as he forced the wheel to obey him. Then everything went topsy-upsy. Incredibly we skedaddled on two wheels, shaving the narrow gap between the patrol car and the trees lining the steep bank to the side. A screaming of half-flayed rabbits as we bounced down, tyres gripping the road once again.

'Fantastic!' Lobo shrieked. 'How you like that? These stupids think to play chicken.'

I pointed at the fuel gauge, dead set in the red. 'Lobo, we're running out of petrol.'

'You forget yourself. It is you who suggests we leave the tank at the cemetery.'

Once more I was able to breathe . . . 'But where is the turn-off? I remember a track, but . . .'

'Do not worry,' he growled. 'It is ahead. Do not you see the turning?'

Before us, just the long straight sucking into darkness. 'I see nothing, Lobo.'

'We come to it in a second, round the next bend, and not a moment too soon. For look!' Lobo thumbed over his shoulder.

Behind us was the Blitz in all its glory, *and* that accursed siren with the blue strobe. And then, as I remembered the CB aerials on the road-roach, I realised the bastards were working as a team.

Shooting round the corner, braking fearsomely, the Baby slewed in a hundred-and-eighty-degree arc. We were pointing up a dirt track. Dousing the lights and cutting the engine, Lobo directed our glide into the shadow of the overhanging trees.

Conjoined leviathans of the night, trailing blazing colour, the hunters shot past.

The orange of the lighter illumined Lobo's face. He puffed on the joint slowly.

'That was well done,' I announced shakily.

'I do not know why so frightening you are. As a friend I am asham-ed to see you tremble so. If I did not know the better, never would I believe the Power is inside you.' Raising his eyebrows, 'Now, where is the turning to this cemetery?'

'But you said this track was the way.'

'I do the driving. I do the tidying. I organise. You are so lazy you do not even try for navigating. You seem to forget, we drive on a different road on the way north. But not for worrying. My Voice it tells me we find the place on the next hill. The petrol we have, it is enough to take us. Relax. But before we go, I want you to think on this, it is only by effort you learn to lose this fear.'

No respecter of dead Aussies, Lobo drove across the humpy green swathe, pulling in close to Quignogg's mausoleum. Praise be to the watcher (I know which side my bread's buttered on). The barrel marked 'Gifts For Wise Men' was as we'd left it, camouflaged by fronds of foliage.

Lobo delegated the task of syphoning the petrol to me. It was the least I could do. 'Thanks, Quignogg,' I said, as I patted the benevolent bust. Empty sockets stared back mournfully. It came to me that he understood what it is to suffer with fortitude. Dear old Quignogg, our St Christopher of the road. We took to the trail again, our collection of cans topped to the brim.

Somebody up there must have been dealing us lousy cards, for not five miles from the border the vigilante highway patrol was tucked up in ambush.

The second time around this chase seemed a more serious affair. Lobo was champing at the bit – another joint, actually. It's not easy to roll a joint doing a ton on a switchback road. I know I'm congratulating myself here, but false modesty's no virtue. In my old hippy days I'd never have been able to do it. I didn't even spill one jot. The task gave me something to concentrate on, calmed my mind, but one thought intruded: if we had a blow-out or crashed, these guys would blow us off the road. I knew it.

When we crossed the state border, the chase was over. It was one of those psychic things. Perhaps my inner master was waking at last. I didn't need to turn to know that the beasties had swung their monstrous tails for the north. But just to make sure, I did.

Gradually, like a bloody, hyperventilating tide, the tension in the cab receded. We pulled into a roadside motel called Truckers Stop Inn. It took me a few moments to get the name right. The first neon red letter fizzed, making it appear more like an F, and the second letter was totally kaput. Lobo appeared not to notice. Just as bloody well. Hungry Horace the Horse could not have been more sta-ha-ha-arving.

'Hey, Lobo' I said brightly, flapping with my hand to clear the thick steam hanging over our massive bowls of slops and stew, 'when we get to Sydney, what say we take in some exhibitions? The New South Wales Gallery, for instance.'

'It makes a change to hear you with a nice idea,' Lobo said, stabbing his fork in the direction of my head. 'You know, checking out beautiful things, it is another way to rid the mind of dirt.'

'Jesus H. Christ.' I groaned, 'Can't you ever forget about dirt? Just for once?'

'Pah!' Lobo grimaced, turning to carefully place his fork on the plate at his elbow. 'Always are you calling on that man. For why? He allow-ed his enemies to crucify him. I tell you, no one gets the chance to hammer nails into my hands.' His face darkened. 'My Voice it warns me if ever peoples make dirty plans for me.'

'Oh yeah,' I shot back, 'don't you think Jesus had a Voice too? Perhaps it told him to accept his eventual fate. After all, wasn't he supposed to die so that mankind could be cleansed of their dirt? Or didn't you know?'

'That it is not true.' Lobo leaned over the table. 'Always you try my patience. For your ed-i-u-ca-tion,' his razor tongue split the word into sunflower seeds, 'I tell you what I am learning from my master about this fellow, and please not to interrupt.'

His icy scowl froze to immobility the flighty remark poising on the springboard tip of my tongue.

'After this Jesus disappears from his cave, he travels secret paths to my

185

country, where many years before he is studying the knowledg-es. The lamas they heal his wounds. In the records of a monastery where I stay, it says he lives to almost a century. Do not you laugh, I see with my own eyes the place he is buri-ed. There is a tree, the same age as the tomb. To this day the sick in body and mind gather under the leav-es, and many miracl-es there are.

'And for the next, I am not needing my master to tell me, for I read it myself in your Bible. When Jesus he returns, for visit number two, he brings with him a sword, for disposing of all the dirty peoples of the world. For does not he not say, "I come sneaking in the night, and I bring with me a sword"? Lobo laughed. 'I tell you, after he does the work here, not many Australians there are left.'

'Yes, Lobo, and he will chop off their heads, hands, feet, toes-es, toss the lot into a bowl of slops, like they serve up here, and make a new batch of gingerbread men. None will be white and underdone, none burnt and black, and of course it goes without saying there will be no women, and all will be deliver-ed into a new world golden brown, baked to perfection, all of them clean, and every one of the little buggers call-ed Lobo.'

'Enough!' Lobo's head emerged from the upturned basket of his arms. 'Always you are talking. If you are not saying stupid things, you are moaning. You remind me of that fat horrible bending over the pot. How long you think it is since she wash-es her hair? Can not you see it touching the food? At this moment I like you even less than her.'

Lobo pushed his unfinished bowlful away, wiping his lips with his travelling serviette. 'I refuse to pay for the such muck.'

My jaw sagged. 'In heaven's name, why? The cheque is going to bounce even more than the steak.'

'It is the principally of the thing. I refuse to write chequ- es, good or bad, for rubbish such as this. Then perhaps in the future, the food it improv-es. But I do not think these peoples learn any lessons from us, so dirty they are. Come. Let us go. He stood up, snapping his fingers imperiously.

As usual no one looked up. I wondered, do lots of people walk out of cafés and restaurants without paying? Does it happen all over? Takes the meaning out of having to work for a living. Was it moral? Was it clean? I must admit, I was completely confused.

Sydney Harbour Bridge, a couple of hours after dawn (yes, we were moving fast now). A crush of snails lined up end to end, tight lanes separated by peculiar metal bollards daily inserted into the road at rush-hour. Weird? No! Australia, the mother of surprises.

We had plenty of time to admire the stupendous view. A few cars up, in a space thoughtfully provided between the bumpers – presumably by parents anxious for their offspring's education – a couple of kids were chalking hopscotch squares on the tarmac. Down below – such an embarrassment of pink blushing, those lovely fat ivory cheeks, the Grand Dame of Sydney, the Opera House, flaunting her cameo nakedness at the end of that silly little prick of a pier. And yonder, spiking the sky, what Sydneyites fondly called the 'Hypodermic' soaring above the war zone of the commercial city, the radio needle flashing gold and red over the early morning banded haze – Australia's memorial to all those junkies of progress who have died or are currently slaughtering each other in her service.

One itsy-bitsy problem – two missing left-luggage receipts. Not a sign of them in any of my bundled possessions. When I originally handed over the cases, I questioned the attendant about the eventuality of such a doomsday scenario. I had some difficulty putting together the pieces of his reply, as he was a recent immigrant to the land, so I'm forced to provide an approximate transcription. 'You must to get Justice of Peace to say OK to your face. If signature good wait six month. OK!' No doubt, in this manner the little Mafia in Sydney's main railway station manage to acquire a copious assortment of baggage every year from absent-minded travellers such as myself.

However, no mountain is too high for Lobo, no chasm too wide. He would cleave their clefts like a bloody Lung-ump-a.

We parked the Baby at a bus stop directly opposite the station entrance. 'Stay there,' Lobo twinkled, 'and not to get out of the seat. I get the bug of an idea.'

By this stage of the game, we were intuitional partners. I sensed the plan coalescing, and agreed. Nothing was said. It all happened in the merest flicker of my blood-shot eyes.

Minutes later, Lobo emerged underneath the arch of the station's entrance, waving fit to burst. The lady at his side waved too. I think I'll call her Florence, on account of the red cross emblazoned on her starched apron. Lobo signalled to Florence to stay where she was. Dodging the traffic he was at my door in a trice.

'You see, Frankie,' he murmured, lips brushing dangerously close to my ear as he bent over, 'what you can get if you ask the right person. Now I carry you across the road.'

With that, just like Rhett, with his true love Scarlet O'Hara in 'Come and Go with The Wind', he scooped up my vastly greater bulk and with never a totter carried me past the gawping faces, finally setting me gently into the wheelchair I'd forgotten to mention.

I played the part – biting my lip like a war-wounded hero, blinking back the tears, gazing into Florence's sweet, misting-over eyes. 'You poor dear,' she cooed, tucking the red tartan blanket around my legs. 'Don't worry, I am sure the baggage handlers will go out of their way to find your cases.'

I could only groan mutely . . . I was so busy scripting the story in my head, which ran something like this:

'I am the victim of a hit-and-run driver. I was left to lie for hours face down in the road. Then someone stole my wallet, containing all my money and my two left-luggage tickets' – and this is where I twisted and pushed the dagger of sympathy home – 'I'm booked on a flight to Britain tonight, and on arrival I'll be whisked into hospital for an operation. If I don't have it, I'll be paralysed for life.'

The cases were eventually located in the depths of Sydney station's luggage pyramid, and I was issued with a further ticket (fee twenty cents, waived by the understanding management) number 13636. Could it be that I was the 13636th wheelchair victim who had arrived to claim his possessions since that cloakroom's inception?

According to Lobo's diktats, you have to be clean to hear the Voice of your inner master. I was itching to get on that road to Perth. But Lobo's Voice had provided certain information. And so it was, cruising the wide streets of Manley at approximately nine p.m., that Lobo spotted the canopy of his dreams bolted to the back of an identical Baby.

Seemingly awed by his Voice's precognition, Lobo touched my arm. 'You see how it is?' he said. 'My Voice never it lies. Now do you believe?'

The other Falcon was parked opposite a six-storey block of flats. From the glass door opening onto a third-floor balcony came a lurid disco beat; banged up against the balcony railings, a couple of figures were urinating – a gauntlet through which a mob recently disgorged from two vans drunkenly parked below had to pass.

Lobo hissed. 'You see how Australians enjoy? Even in Switzerland such things never happen. It is a-perfect, no? The noise from the party it covers us.' He held up a cautioning finger. 'But now it is not the right time. We must wait till completely it is dark and all the dirty peoples are all inside. What is the shopping we need?'

'Cigarettes?' I ventured. At the thought of this next mission impossible, my stomach had slunk under the slabs of my gall bladder.

Lobo studied my face, trying to ascertain whether I had just made a joke. 'You are serious, huh! I am surprising your Scottis worm says nothing on the subject. We have a journey of three thousands of miles, and all you are caring about it is cigarettes. You know, my Voice it tells me you should stop this habit.' Would there ever be an end to his pestilential naggings?

Finding a crowded all-night supermarket, we worked as a team, arguing constantly, selecting two of everything, one into the trolley, the other into the blue hold-all slung on Lobo's shoulder. All the Sydneyites saw was just another quarrelling gay couple.

'Sixty-three dollars, fifty-three cents,' the check-out girl said drearily, her thoughts on a mountain far away.

After a moment's pause, I said, 'Well? Come on darling, you've got the wallet.'

'No, no, no,' Lobo countered, I remember distinctly, you drop it in your pocket as we leave the house, I know, you leave it on your car seat.' He shrugged, smiling at the girl. 'Always he so absent-minding . . .'

'Now look here,' I said in a remonstrating tone.

We lobbed the subject of who'd left what where for several spirited rallies until we reached set point. The lengthening queue of shoppers behind us occasionally broke into discordant, shuffling applause.

Smiling with a sweetness that was the purest distilled vitriol, Lobo shook his finger. 'Yes, it is as you say, Peter, except it is you who leave it behind, and on *your* seat. But not to worry, daharling, I run back to the car, and as fast as my two little feet will carry me, for I think you are falling in love with this beautiful girl here.' He winked slyly.

Blushing to the black roots of her long blonde hair, the check-out girl hung her head low, and so did not notice the bulgings of cans and packets.

After a minute he returned. No bag. A handful of reproachful fingers. 'It is as I said. The wallet it is in the car, but you forget the plas-teek. For why do not you bring it with you?'

'It's not my fault,' I whined. 'It was you who insisted on leaving the apartment in such a hurry, I never had time to water the plants, and the sheets need changing . . .'

Lobo spread his hands, bringing all the shoppers into this floor show. 'You see what I have too put up with? I think I trade him for a later model.' He smiled at the girl. 'Do not worry, I exchange him somewhere else.'

We pulled in some ten metres behind our target, the other Baby with 'our' canopy affixed to its back.

All Lobo's smaller tools, arrayed in their cloth wrap, he laid out on his knee – screwdrivers, adjustable spanners, dental picks, even a magnifying glass. With a surgeon's workmanlike precision, Lobo filed each instrument in its appropriate pocket inside his padded camouflaged jacket – no sound of metal clanking against metal.

In the severest tones, Lobo delivered his instructions. 'You stay here' – prodding the driver's seat – 'the hands on the wheel, ready to move. The eyes of the hawk as you watch the street. If there is a serious problem, whistle, like so.' Lobo imitated the warbling call of a bird. 'You can do this?' His penetrating gaze searched my face. I nodded. 'When I give the signal, drive very smooth, and mark my words, not too fast or slow, or the engine it is loud or stalls. OK? Fit the Baby tight close to the other car so we can take the canopy in one move. You have it all in the head? Yes?'

Apparently satisfied, Lobo silently closed the door.

As he cased the target from the shady pavement side, I noted with approbation how the lizard green of his jacket imbued him with a chameleon's invisibility. If I hadn't known where to look I would never have seen him.

Through the balcony window across the road, a neon strobe encapsulated the skyline of this suburban 'rage' – metronomic bobbing profiles, upraised glasses, erupting party poopers . . .

The headlights of a slow-moving car blazed in the mirror. No need to make a 'warbling call', Lobo had already assumed position Number One, hunching forwards into the grey-green foliage, mimicking a peeing phantom. The car glided by, Lobo's frame jiggling as he shook the drip off his non-apparent penis.

Returning to the real job in hand, a brief tussle and Lobo had breached the defences. Tadpole legs wriggled into the back.

An aeon of drab time passed, punctuated only by the strobe's flash and my rapid breathing. Then the canopy door lifted up and Lobo's black shape appeared, his thumb upraised. I brought the Baby to a halt a step away from the target. In one smooth movement, we had it. It didn't even need fixing, so exactly did it fit the back frame of our Baby.

This canopy was a 'real beaut'. Glass on three sides. Neat sliding windows protected by fine mosquito-netting, the back door fitted with tinted glass. An indelibly marked security number sat smugly on the fibreglass roof.

Cock-a-hoop with our evening's work, Lobo drove a few blocks to a municipal car-park, reaffirmed in his mastery over his environment.

But after we'd bolted it down, it seemed something had crumbled from his cheesey cake. 'Frankie, take a look. This is only a temporary job.' He tested the canopy, pushing it. 'The trouble we have is the bolt holes do not all line up. Only with the correct drill can we make holes in the right places.' Lobo tapped his head. 'Hey, but I know where we find the right equipment to do the job, wait you and see.'

Refusing all offers of assistance, Lobo instructed me to stay up front while he meticulously organised the new room at the back. Feeling more than ever a mere appendage, I gloomily skinned another one from the scrapings of Nealga's grass; then, after a moment's deliberation, tucked it behind my ear to share later.

I turned around to see Lobo's mug contorted against the glass, grinning insanely.

Everything was arranged so artfully – centre-stage, a double-bed raised on a wooden pallet, the space underneath providing ample storage; to each side of the bed, two extension speakers rigged up to the cassette players.

I shook my head in wonderment. 'I don't know where you got all this stuff, but I'm looking forward to resting on a bed at long last. The cover makes it look so homely.'

Plucking the joint from behind my ear, Lobo retorted venomously, 'If you did not spoil the last operation with your stupid fears, we could have been living in luxury all of this time. Instead, the arm-rest in the front it is broken, and still you do nothing to fix it, but for now –'

Lobo astonished me then with his theatrical production, a mighty yawn worthy of a giant mule.

'Oh my gosh, so tiring I am.'

'Lobo, I thought because of your system of inner cleanliness you don't suffer from such mortal afflictions.'

'The reason I am so tir-ed is because I have to carry the dirty load of you everywhere. My gosh! We both go to bed. The now! I take the right hand. You keep to your left!'

This was a new experience. For the remaining hours of the night I lay staring at the ceiling, trying not to look at my Brer Fox companion apparently sleeping so peacefully beside me. A couple of snores was all I could get out of him.

27

Situated about two hundred miles from bustling Sydney, Lemon is just another sleepy outback town. We'll put it this way: the main street is one long snore, and the shops yawn at each other.

Henry, the owner of the Motor Accessory Store, was to all appearances an unremarkable specimen of the typical Aussie middle-aged male. The equatorial spreading centrefold indicated a normal chap's appetite for home-grown chemical beers. And as for that belch of an interruption between his shoulder blades . . . Let's just say whatever brains he may have possessed were prevented from descending into his gullet only by his most protuberant feature, the stop-cock placed where his Adam's-apple should have been. Lips? Murderous maroon slugs writhing across the crushed wallflowers of his pale blotched skin. Hair? Try to imagine fusty low-budget horror movie cobwebs. Eyes? Surely not the proper appellation for those watery thyroidal bulgings looming so huge in the scratched lenses mounted precariously on the tip of his flaming bulbous. One of the arms of his spectacles had been repaired with fishing twine. Yes, I could just see our Henry slouched in a reverie by the riverside, one dangling hand straying absent-mindedly between the maggot tray, the sandwich basket and the crate of stubbies.

Acquainted as I was with so many of my companion's prejudices and so few of his preferences, I was much mystified when Henry and Lobo performed the 'Mad-March-Kangaroo-Mates Dance'. My astonishment ascended in a logarith-mic spiral as I became privy to the First Greeting Ritual of Canadian Freemasonry – the 'Grand Lumberjack Handshake', which as every initiate knows is performed cross-legged, facing your partner squarely, hooking fingers into his opposing left hand, and 'see-sawing'.

I was very relieved they didn't enact the gruesome second ritual, 'Blowing the Log Jam', which is also performed squatting, but is so much more intimate. I'll just have to leave that to your unlaundered imaginations.

Finally it dawned on me, with a growing sense of peering into a pail of the blackest molasses, that this scurvy, mud-crawling Croc was an intimate of Lobo's inner circle.

Having detailed his assistant, the swarthy and vastly silent Boris, to take charge, Henry announced he was taking the rest of the day off, 'to be with my friends'.

Pondering on what all this could possibly mean while keeping a safe distance, I followed the mates as they walked arm in arm, but counted up to ten before ducking through the verdigris-stained ribbons of the plastic curtain concealing darker recesses.

Rounding a bend in this small-town intestinal tract, I was surprised to find Lobo gazing with amusement into a tiny, cluttered, windowless room, as Henry rolled out the proverbial red carpet, covering up the litter of boxes of air-filters, spark plugs, cans of oil, styrofoam packing, and gosh alone knows what else.

The result of digging in a busted filing cabinet was three tumblers still in their dusty promotional wrappings. Cracking a chamois cloth from its cellophane, Henry's elbows worked overtime until the glasses fairly twinkled.

Reaching up then towards a nudie calendar, Henry commanded us in the sternest of tones to look away, adding, 'I've had a bottle of bubbly stashed away in the wall safe for this very occasion.'

I couldn't buy that, but middle-class roots have spread their tendrils deep into my foundations. I turned away.

Plonking the bottle of Kampuchean Spumante on the table, Henry the Host waved towards the chairs.

Despite loud toasts to future health and happiness, Henry couldn't relax, even after a few tumbler refills. His scrawny turtle-neck wrinkled as he strove to follow Lobo's every gesture.

Finally he summoned the courage to spill what was obviously on his mind, demanding of Lobo what the heck he'd been up to since . . . since . . . whenever they'd last performed these gross rituals. His use of 'heck' surprised me. Perhaps he too had once been indentured to the Alpine finishing school.

Leaning backwards to the limits of his chair and seeming to sniff this mustard-pot mustiness to the very dregs, Lobo drawled, 'Oh, not much. Recently I show my good friend Frankie around.' He shrugged diffidently. 'You know how it is for me, Henry, holidays mostly.'

Then, in a sudden diving lunge, Lobo placed both hands firmly on Henry's thighs. 'I am meaning to ask your advic-es about some problems I am having with my car. A Falcon Ute, only three month-es old.'

Concern, or was it excitement, foamed on Henry's face. 'Nothing serious, I hope.'

Lobo turned, blinking disingenuously. 'When it is I am buying the canopy, Frankie? Yesterday?'

'No, Lobo,' I said perversely, 'it was a week ago last Monday.'

Lobo beamed at Henry. 'Every day like the seagull flying, and so many of them. So easy to loose the count. One day for me is more than week for Frankie, so much he is sleeping. As I am saying, yesterday I am buying a canopy for the car. Is good for camping, no?'

Henry the Toady nodded vigorously.

'A second-hand, but I think as good as new. The small problem, the bolt-es we have do not fit our hol-es. And one question, Henry, do you think fifteen thousands of miles is enough before we make the first change of oil? Should I leave it for more?'

Eyes widening, Henry fingered the crab-apple O of his mouth. 'Did you say fifteen thousand?' He jumped to his feet in a manner I was to discover was characteristic. 'Lobo, it's far, far, too much. We'll give you a full service, you know, plugs, points, bolts, whatever you need. In fact I'll set Boris to work on it straight away. He may look a brute, but he's an ace with his spanner. And I won't accept any payment in return. For you, nothing is too much!'

I reflected silently. Isn't this unbelievable? Everywhere bursting zippers – Henry would sell his soul for just one hour of Lobo's time.

The lads failed to notice my slinking departure, so engrossed were they in each other. Always the diplomat, I did not look back.

As I dawdled off, window-shopping, marvelling over pyramid displays of sunbleached colonial brands, that long since, in every other place, had simply faded from existence, I suddenly realised this was the first time I'd slipped the leash since the minute before we'd met. I was free, at least for the time being, to resume my true profession, that of the perpetual tourist forever shambling through life.

My criss-cross journey of the main drag's dusty arcades finally delivered me to the pleasures of the municipal park. For a time I was content just to circle the ironwork of the ornate Victorian bandstand, imagining I could hear those convict brass bands rattling their balls and chains.

Sauntering to the bowling green, I leaned on the white trellis fence. Not a cloud to shame the puffy cheeks of the vaulting blue. Before me, three ruddy-faced, silver-haired gents, sharp and trim in white cotton suits and matching pork-pie hats, set out bowls on a shaved green.

At that moment I couldn't think of anything I'd rather be doing than leaning on this particular trellis fence . . .

'Frankieee!'

Damn it. I knew it was too good to last.

'Ah, Frankie, my Voice, you know it is telling me I find you here.' Snapping fingers behind him, he called excitedly, 'Hey! Henry! Frankie, he is here!'

Stooping over three dripping ice-cream cones, Henry tottered out from behind the foliage shading the corner of the bowling green. Spreading claws cat-wide and spinning on the balls of his pads, Lobo sprang upon his victim, shrieking mock delight. Recoiling, Henry jumped back, the three cones suspended in a line before him, and then, too late, snatched wildly . . . Fingers met in the cones' ice-cream centres.

Typically, Lobo turned this 'accident' to personal advantage.

'You know, Henry, I am not minding you drop my ice-cream. And I am sure I speak for Frankie as well. He too must pay attention to the figure. No good it is to let the looks go.'

Back to the tight-knit group, gathered by the neat trellis fence. Lobo shouted to the bowlers. 'Excusa me, excusa me, sirs, I vant to ask you, kind sirs, a qvestion, please, sirs.'

The taller of the gents, probably better of hearing than his fellows, shuffled on carpet slippers towards us.

The cats whiskers, creamily smiling, Lobo asked, 'Ahem, please, can you be telling me what this game you play? Never before I see it. So sorry, I no speak a-good English. Me tourist in your country. Love velly you much. Having vonderful time. Yes! Yes!'

If I had ever wanted to learn the finer points of bowling, this was my chance. Lobo elected himself first. His ball dead on line but, unusually, a little too tentative, rolled to a stop just five feet short of the white.

My shot was accurate, but just a shade too forceful, the ball just slipping past the white.

Henry's monster delivery smashed into Lobo's, sending both balls into the trough at the end.

The kind gentlemen judged me the winner.

I don't know if that was the reason Lobo looked peeved, or whether the cause was Henry's motiveless assault. But he recovered quickly, clapped his hands, and called in a sweet voice, 'Four chairs, four chairs, please for the gentlemen.' He bowed and clicked his heels, as well-mannered Tibetan gents always do.

In the first brief moment as Lobo held open the door to the courtyard, I failed to recognise the Baby, so plastered was it with every name brand under the sun. The windows were uniformly mirrorised, and across the back door two muscled surfers sped through tumbling waves.

Lobo grinned. 'It is good, no?'

'Fantastic! No one could recognise it from before. Just as well Lobo,' I winked, 'we've left quite a trail, haven't we?'

Frowning, Lobo flicked his eyes to his left and, just to make sure I understood, trod on my toe. Across the small courtyard, Henry was flapping his ears as he piled trash into a garbage can.

'You know,' Lobo said loudly, 'my good friend Henry is so helpful, look at these lovely stickers he is giving us, and he gets Boris to change the oil. Nice new wipers! Better sprinklers for the room at the back. And hey, look! A new petrol cap. Is not it shiny? The lock it is a good one. No more wurries!'

Grinning like an over-heated chocolate soldier, Henry appeared at Lobo's shoulder. 'Time for our visit to the squash club.' He rubbed his hands in anticipation, 'Nothing like a bit of exercise, huh? I've been in training for this match, Peter. You'll, uh, have to be in top form . . . ha ha . . . if you want to beat me.' More giggles.

'Oh yes,' Lobo said, deadpan, 'I want to beat you very, very much.'

Henry bobbed like a jockey on a dead-beet kangaroo. 'You both wait here while I close up the shop. I've yet to get the hang of the burglar alarm. The procedure's quite complicated so I'll be a few minutes.' He turned to walk away.

Lobo tugged on his sleeve. 'Hey, hold on. I help. Better to leave Frankie here. Such a bad mood he is. The why I do not know.'

It seemed we had the club all to ourselves. While the lads took up their squash rackets, I steamed and bathed; and later I watched the contest through the one-way glass window. As he had promised, Lobo was giving Henry a very sound drubbing.

As soon as Henry emerged from the shower-room, I sensed something was up. For one thing, his quick turn to study the noticeboard wasn't rapid enough to hide the colour blazing on the right side of his face – as if he'd had a brush with a furnace. Then the door swung wide, and Lobo bounced into the foyer. Swinging his legs from the arm of my chair, he asked, 'Hey, you watch the game?'

'No, Lobo,' I lied, too tired to gratify him with compliments. 'I've been having a very nice time on my own, thank you very much.

Lobo lit a cigarette. 'You know, it is not so easy to beat a champion.' Casually he let out a large smoke-ring, sending a tiny one scudding through it. 'Me, I do not play for one whole year now.'

'That's quite a lot of seagulls, Lobo,' I grinned.

Lobo frowned. 'Yes, so very funny you are. As I am saying, I beat him three games out of three. You could have a game, too. Always you miss out.'

Henry called from over by the entrance. 'Hey, you two. I've got a table booked at the Chinese restaurant. We're late as it is.'

Half-way up the stairs to the street, Lobo dropped behind Henry, bending to tie a shoelace that was not undone. Impatiently Henry strode on ahead. As I drew level, Lobo whispered, 'Frankie, Henry is a sheet! Everything it is finish-ed between us. You watch. I fix him good.'

The reason, for this sea-change in Lobo's affection? The incident had apparently occurred as the bosom buddies lathered up in the shower. Henry had stepped over a clearly demarcated line. Exactly how, I never found out. But the upshot was that Lobo had slapped Henry, very hard, which accounted for Henry's flushed right cheek.

As we pulled our seats up to the table, it seemed Lobo's foul mood had gone the way of the bubbles bursting in our glasses. I have to confess, I only half listened as he and Henry shared reminiscences of their Blue Mountain skiing days.

Henry had just passed round cheroots when the bill appeared. The waiter placed the folded paper in the no-man's-land between us. Since lighting up, Henry had developed an annoying habit of speaking Clint-Eastwood style, cigar clenched between his teeth. As he leaned over to pick up the paper, I noticed an inch of ash fall into his glass.

'It's my pleasure,' Henry announced in an absurd Texan drawl. Laying his cheroot down, he raised his glass high. 'Here's to you boy!' Smacking his maroon slugs, he reached for his wallet, muttering as he drunkenly counted the notes, 'Shit, I thought I'd brought more . . .' Guiltily smiling, nay wincing at Lobo – 'No problem, I've got a Platinum Amex card. Got it the same time I opened the store . . . Hell, where is it?' He rifled his pockets. 'I know it's here somewhere.'

Lobo leaned across the table, reassuringly stroking Henry's arm, his voice turning soft and even. 'Chinese people are very understanding. They know you come back.'

Jerking to his feet, Henry's knees almost keeled the table over.

Concealing a secret smirk, Lobo watched: Henry in a state bordering on panic; Henry forcing a way through, bumping into the backs of the thickly-packed diners; Henry beside the doors to the kitchen, wildly gesticulating in

Cantonese at the machete-wielding Chinese cook – in lieu of the manager, presumably.

Leaning close, waggling my eyebrows – 'Nothing to do with you, eh Lobo?'

'No.' Lobo shook his head curtly. 'If Henry cannot organise his life properly, do you think is it a fault of mine? I tell you, that man he is a sheet. And now,' his tone was final, 'I get itchy for going.'

'What? More herpes?' I said.

'How many times I must tell you, I get rid of the dirt completely.'

The goodbye scenes were nauseating. Seated in the car, I averted my eyes while Lobo and Henry went through the rituals of parting. Distantly I heard Lobo say, 'Henry, always you are my best pupil.' The cautioning finger wagged, no doubt. 'Make sure to do a little slimming. It is good for your health, Henry.'

Most of Henry's words seemed to choke at his stop-cock. As we drove off I watched him in the wing mirror, a shrinking midget, so alone in the centre of Lemon high street, pathetically waving and waving until he faded out altogether.

'Well, here we are,' I said, 'just the two of us again, and just about enough grass left for one little joint. When d'you think we'll get to Melbourne?'

Slowing the car, Lobo growled, 'We do not get to Melbourne tonight. Work there is to do.'

'What work? Always it's bloody work with you. Can't we have just one drive without any incidents, hassles, or missions bloody impossible?'

Jamming on the brakes, Lobo pulled the car to the side of the road. He switched off the ignition and leaned over me threateningly.

'Now listen a-here, Frankie. Sometimes I think you have no eyes in the head. Do you not see the combination of the safe?'

I had looked away. Just because Henry asked me to. I didn't know why, but I felt ashamed.

Lobo continued, 'Yes and I am most surprising you do not add your eyes to mine when he turns on the alarm.'

'But Lobo,' I protested, 'that was before whatever happened in the shower. I thought he was your friend.'

Lobo's eyes narrowed. 'Always you are interrupting. For why? I am talking about the stupid alarm. All the pads and wires he shows to me. The sheet. I tell you, we get even with him. Five hundred dollars in the safe. We take it all, tonight!'

'For fuck's safe, Lobo, just because the guy reached for your piddling cock is no reason to break into his shop. A couple of hours ago you were the best of friends. You told me. You can't wriggle out of it.'

I'll delete the rest. We didn't break into the shop, but Lobo made a meal of my head, all through the night. Da . . . Da . . . Da . . . Da!

28

Another zig-zag night trail. There is one thing about native Australians, virtually all of them are cocooned by the huge size of their continent. Touring the country you discover people who live in Sydney and have never been to Melbourne, or who live in Surfer's Paradise and have never been to Sydney. The distances are incredible. For instance, it's three thousand miles as the crow flies from Sydney to Perth. And quite apart from the places that roads give access to, there are vast intractable wastes. Place names are weird. Once, near the New South Wales–Queensland border, we travelled from Dundee to Bolivia in ten minutes. In some parts you can drive all night on major roads and never see another car. Through isolation, people become strange. Poverty of interest sucks at you from empty eyes. The man hunched over his drink looks up at you enter the bar. But to him you're not there. You're only a shadow on the flickering TV set of his life. And as the traveller, you pass on, leaving this bar-fly in his gelatine prison. No wonder he blows his mind out on booze. Most conversations I had with punters in Australian bars were about Australian beer. All I could taste were the chemicals. Nice chemicals.

Dawn breaking, and we were conserving fuel, just coasting past paddocks, eucalyptus trees, bungalows – a far-flung northern tentacle of Melbourne, all as yet wrapped in twilight's lonely blurring. Any neon that wasn't dead was rougeing empty and chained forecourts. All the garages on this stetch were closed. And then we saw it, the winking Kangaroo sign of the last independent operator this side of Alice Springs.

Delegated to me now, the Department of Conning. And so, brushed up for parade, even the buttons of my blazer polished, I presented myself before a surly ogre almost indistinguishable from the old-fashioned and grimy pumps of the filling station.

Even before I began my impromptu tale about the dirty hippy who'd run off with our credit cards, this ogre seemed to baulk at my confident, bouncing stride, the dental polish of my engaging smile, and the gleaming leather executive bloody briefcase.

'You city-dwellers're all the same,' he sneered. 'This used to be bush terr'try, but look at it now.' He waved his tubular appendage behind him at the cloned, gormless faces of identikit bungalows. 'A bluddy cancer. Keep to yer own patch, mate an' I'll keep to mine. Bluddy cash, tha's all I'll take from the likes o' you!'

And when, mindful of Lobo's stern judgemental eyes in the cab, I protested vigorously at this this outrageous treatment, pushing the cheque on him once more, the petrol ogre thrust an oily rag in my face. 'Jest thank yer lucky star this ain't no gun.' His lip twisted. Shootin' yew 'ud be no worse th'n killin' fuckin' vermin.'

As we glided in search of the next petrol station, it was a wall-to-wall, head-butting exercise attempting to explain to Lobo the realities of the last encounter, and how if I'd been just stepped out of a sheep-dip, dirt caked under my fingernails, my clothes covered in bitumen, I'd have been in with just a chance.

It was there that the patron saint of outback travellers, Quignogg, and his attendant petrol genie went AWOL.

Lobo took a sabbatical in the monastic seclusion of the back. Worried as to what his silence might portend, from time to time I checked him out in the cab's mirror, but not once did he so much as twitch, lying plank rigid, unblinkingly staring at the ceiling.

I must have dozed, for he was shaking my arm, hauling it out of the socket.

'I have it! Frankie, I know how we get the fill-up!'

'How?' I groaned, rubbing my shoulder.

'It is this simple. I have pens. I have many.'

'What pens for God's sake?'

'Come on you lazy. Get out of the car! We have work to do. Always you are sleeping on the job!' Lobo planted a cardboard shoe-box on the bonnet, removed the lid with a flourish: biros to the brim, dull reds and blues.

Frowning I picked one up and rolled it between my fingers – cheapo, of the type dispensed free to punters in betting shops. The legend printed on one side read: 'I Helped Put a Quadraplegic Together', and in tiny lettering alongside, 'Friends of the Quadraplegics Association'.

'What the fuck is this?' I exclaimed, the dirt escaping before I could swing the barn doors of my mouth shut.

For once Lobo chose to ignore this attack of expletives, though his eyes bulged somewhat with the effort. Gritting his teeth, he thrust the box into my hands. 'You are the cause for why we run out of petrol. I cannot trust you for hunting with a can. So nows you must make the money to pay. It is the way you learn to change for the better. 'Look . . .' with a sweep he indicated the swarming bungalows. 'There you find the peoples who buy. And one more thing I will say, I am waiting for you with a sting if you return with less than one dollar for each pen.'

'Now wait a minute,' I said, unsuccessfully trying to pass back the box. 'There are some limits even you can't push me over. Jesus . . . F–' I ran a hand through my hair. 'How the heck did you come by these in the first place?'

'I am pleas-ed you make effort stop up the dirt. I will explain, but make sure to listen with both the ears, for you will need to know all the details to do the job correctly.'

His smile of dark amusement, I know, was conjured by the look of pain that must have flitted across my features.

'Not for worrying, this story it is a good entertainment.'

Screwing my eyes tight shut, I leaned against the Baby, screaming inwardly at the prospect of more 'entertainment'.

'It is the first time I am in Sydney, I do not know the place like I do now, and so I am making much effort to meet peoples.'

'Cut the horse manure.'

'It is as I say, I am seeing a notice in a paper. Fifty dollar-es in four hours for helping a charity. It is good, no? Scratch two backs with the one hand. At the address, I am finding a fat man hiding behind so many boxes on the desk I can only see his face. He writ-es the name I give on the card he says I must to wear. One hundred pens for my pockets. I sign a paper. He gives to me a certificate. A van comes, so many volouteer-es in there. They smell.' Lobo wrinkled his nose in disgust.

'I sit in the front. The driver he is explaining, this area they never sell pens before, so no stupid worries. It is night. He says he is coming back in in four hour-es. The one who sells the most gets a prize.'

'What prize?' I yawned.

'Always you are interrupting,' Lobo snapped, then frowning resumed: 'I tell him then, "So sorry, I leave wallet in office." When I return the fat man he is on the phone in another room. So many boxes. They do not miss one. I take this one from the bottom of the pile. It is good, no?' Lobo smiled.

'Terrible.'

Lobo ignored this rebuke. 'You see, all the way back I am thinking how they are making this business. For each one hundred of pens, they get ninety dollars, and the stupid volounteer-es only ten. How many you think these pens cost?'

I shrugged, not in the slightest bit interested.

'I tell you then, since you are too lazy even to make the effort for thinking. They buy in Korea, one cent each. Maybe less if they buy enough. And how much of this money gets to the kwadding-pleegics?'

I shook my head. 'Twenty cents out of every dollar. Who knows?' I spread my hands. 'Who cares?'

Lobo's eyes blazed daggers.

'OK then,' I said. 'How much?'

'Nothing.'

'Oh come off it. Even in Australia, no one . . . not even you could get away with that.'

'Listen to me. You say they give twenty cents. I say maybe the half of the half of that. And only because the police they might watch. But who do they give it to?'

'The kwadding-pissing-pleegics!' I exploded. 'Who else?'

'Wrong. They give it to another fat man also hiding behind a desk, the man who is running the charity for the —'

'Don't say it.' I covered my head with my hands. 'The kwadding-pleegics.'

'That it is correct,' Lobo said grimly. 'Now, you are ready?'

'What?' I couldn't believe what I knew I was about to hear. 'Ready for what?' No, it could not be . . .

'You might to make an effort, brush the hair, look' — Lobo pointed at my hand — 'the fingernails is dirty.' Lobo tapped his wrist and the non-existent watch. 'It is one minute from the clock of nine. Come! I do not wait any more. One day my Voice it tells me, you change, and I have no need to do the thinking for you, but for now we start with the bank, for is not that place the best place to look for the money? And after you learn the how to sell the pens, you can do the work for yourself. Is not too much to ask, surely?'

I shook my head. 'No! No! It's much too much.' I said, grappling under my seat for my money-belt.' Right now I don't care if it takes all the filthy lucre I have stashed, I'm going to pay to fill the tank, and thereafter I'm having nothing to do with selling spastic pens, now or forever. Have you got that?'

Lobo turned away, folded his arms. Neatly, as always.

'I said, HAVE YOU GOT BLOODY GOT THAT?' I roared.

Still no reply from Lobo.

My fingers were snuffling like a pair of truffle-rooting hogs in my belt. I looked down. I could not believe what I was seeing. Neither could my fingers.

Seven sweat-soaked dollars. Christ Hairy Jesus, I was losing my mind. There had been thirty-seven there last time I'd counted it . . . Or had there? An abyss opened up. I knew then as I felt this dread lodestone tugging my gut from its unimaginable depths, that the nadirs I'd experienced in this journey so far had been astral highs compared with where I was plummeting.

The ANZ Bank has a branch within spearing distance of everyone's back yard, or so the blurb approximately goes. A photograph on the brochure shows a naked Aborigine about to cast his spear at the photographer's assistant, just off picture. You can tell he's there from his shadow.

A long queue of short-sighted, grumbling customers snaked outside the bank. It being a Monday, many of them were pensioners, clutching yellow plastic koala bears heavy with coins. None of them, apparently, had read the small notice pinned to the closed door: 'Due to restoration work, would customers please use the rear entrance. Signed, A.R. Arbuttnot (Temporary Manager).'

Lobo pointed a stiff little finger. 'You see how many stupids there are? So many always to choose from. Good for you prak-tiking on after.'

We had reached the back door. Lobo turned around. 'Give to me the pens. Now, remember, you must watch and listen for everything.' He grimaced. 'Pull the collar down, it stik-es up. Now, you are ready?'

My eyes rolled . . .

Lobo pushed the door wide.

Banks in Australia are not the same as in other places. There is an atmosphere of hands-in-each-other's-pockets familiarity that I've not experienced elsewhere. Cashiers are prone to calling the customers, old and young, 'mate'. In country banks, such as this had been before the building work started, it's a common if grizzly sight to see a bushwhacker – a dead kangaroo or wombat, paws tied up with it's dripping entrails, slung Aborigine-fashion over his shoulder – cashing in his monthly social security chitty, which you can guarantee that very day he'll blow on booze, thus swelling the coffers of the richest men in Australia, the brewery magnates, before crawling back to his slimy hole to lie in ambush for the postman's knock in a month's time. It's a hard, if diligent, life in the suburbs of the outback.

No harping Lobo to guide me about the dangers to my posterior of the light loam of building debris on the this black-buttoned vinyl chair. Heaving a sigh of relief for the temporary respite of his absence, I promptly slumped down, leaned back, yawned and, stretching out my feet, prepared for the coming entertainment.

204

Ignoring the buzzer provided, Lobo briskly dusted off the counter with a hankie and, on tiptoes, rapped a fusillade on the glass below the sandblasted letters reading 'Appointment'. It didn't matter that a girl was already facing him patiently waiting behind the old-fashioned woodwork.

'Ah, so quick you are,' Lobo beamed. 'Plis, it is OK to see' – he looked down at a piece of paper he wasn't holding in his hand – 'ah, Mr Ar-not-but. Is correct, no?'

The girl couldn't help a chuckle, 'You must be meaning our manager, Mr Arbuttnot. I'm sorry, sir, but he's out at the moment.'

Lobo feigned amazement. 'But head office is saying appointing-ment all fixing up.'

The girl replied, 'There must be some mistake, Mr . . .'

'Lee Bruce. Ah . . . Of the Friends of Bush Fire Kwadding-pleegics. One hundred you know, in a bus. Many injured beyond relief.' Lobo shook his head sadly. 'I am coming from Jah-pan when I hear about this tragidee, all I can do to help.' Lobo brightened. 'I explain you. For each pen I am selling to staff, banking head office are giving charitee one more dollar, they make all appointing-ments. Is very kind, no? And they even give me driver. Hard work for him, so many banks, so little a-time.' Lobo thumbed my way over his shoulder, then, motioning the girl close, muttered something, making her laugh.

The bastard was at it again, getting a rise out of me. Even though I didn't in the slightest care, I felt my face redden.

Lobo smiled mournfully. 'Oh well,' he said. 'Next time. If next time! When if visit make sure appointing-ment fixing. So nice been meeting you . . .'

It was at that point that, a short distance behind my head, one of the builders started on the concrete floor with a pneumatic drill, so I'm only able to give you a summary of the subsequent events.

Making frantic signs, the girl insisted that Lobo wait. She reappeared half a minute later with the under-manager, at a door to the left side of the counter. Much bobbing and pigeon grins from Lobo. A pen was passed over. Then, after a vigorous hand-shaking session, Lobo was ushered behind the scenes. Astonished at his easy progress, I watched him moving from desk to desk, checking over each clerk's paperwork, passing over pens, and receiving back dollars.

Fortunately I was saved from the necessity of 'prak-tiking' my budding salesman skills on the pensioners by the diligence of the under-manager, who accompanied us out onto the street. The queue had grown to the ugly proportions of a mob. Assessing the situation in a trice, the under-manager seized us both by the hands, shooing them manfully, attempted a thump at

Lobo's back (only nifty footwork saving Lobo from the hearty assault), then lost all consciousness of our existence, it seemed and – ignoring the threatening rattle of koala money-boxes – began shepherding the pensioners around the side of the building.

Seated in the Baby once more, Lobo spread out a sheaf of dollars, more than enough to fill up our tank. No rest for this wicked, however. While Lobo began yet another reorganising, glumly I set out with a clutch of pens, selecting at random a long avenue of bungalows indistinguishable from all the others.

What about my protestation that I wanted nothing to do with this sorry business of defrauding the 'stupids' of their hard-earned dollars in such an unworthy way? I might as well have saved my breath.

Back to the bungalows then, the corner of the block. I awoke one typical Aussie housewife too early from her beauty sleep – about 999 years too early to be exact. Over her shoulder, in the darkened room, a vast television blared out an American hospital soap.

I held up the pen like a miniature slimline prick, the legend turned her way. 'Ugh!' she grunted as she attempted to focus her eyes.

I launched into my spiel, an image of Lobo occupying four-fifths of my cerebral cortex. He was lashing his forked tail, and just in case I should register any failures, a trident lay warming in the nearest unholy pit.

'G'die, madam! I've come here today to ask you to help the multiple disabled. Give me one dollar and you'll not only get this pen, choice of two colours, but the ANZ Bank has also guaranteed to match your donation. It's not much to ask, is it, one dollar, when you think you'll be making someone's life a little brighter. Ah . . . Think how good you'll feel.'

It was hard to concentrate, with all this TV action going on over her shoulder – a handsome doctor snapping condom-coated fingers – 'Quick, before the anaesthetic wears off, the vice grips . . .'

One pen, one grimy dollar. Walk back down the short gravel path, unhinge gate, close it, repeat the exercise at the next gate. A different coloured door, but otherwise nothing visibly different about this house. The room over her shoulder looked the same, and even after I'd blinked twice I'd've sworn it was the same woman. 'Madam, care to make someone's life a little brighter?'

Over her shoulder on an equally large TV screen, the doctor was peering into a green, blood-stained sheet. With a surgeon's muscular precision, he carefully lowered a singularly long probe.

Shit, the commercial break, just when I was getting hooked into this thing.

One less pen and one more guilt-stained dollar.

And so I proceeded, up another garden path, the same identical blooms in each shrubbery. I never did find out what happened to the doctor.

The next house was unusual in that it had a brass name-plate on the door – D. Mullins – and, underneath, a sellotaped label – Dan O'Flaherty.

The same identikit woman was about to hand over her dollar when she was shouldered aside by a red-haired fellow who looked as though he was still on last week's bender. He grabbed the pen from my hand saying, 'Let me see that!' After studying it and then my face, 'Yep, I bleeding thought so.' He called behind him, sharply, 'Dora! Call the police.' He smiled wickedly. 'Thought we're all stupid 'round 'ere, did yer? Well some of us 'ave got televisions, y'know. Saw yer ugly mug on Police File last night. You've been rumbled, mate. Yer a bleedin' con-artist.'

I had to think quick. Reaching into my breast pocket, I said in an official voice, 'No, I'm not a con-artist, but I am a Department of Social Security Investigator. It is an offence to cohabit without declaring it. Mr O'Flaherty, you're nicked.'

The door slammed in my face.

Around the corner, I counted my takings: twenty-three dollars. Time to return to my mental sidekick, Dialobo. Yeah, I wasn't just fantasising. One day I would turn the tables on him.

Some time in the early evening we limped into our next port of call. Remember 'Big Licks', the Australian Attila the Hun? His wife Maybeline? The house, just a peeling shack surrounded by decaying sheds and dried-up fields?

So there we were, Lobo and I, banging for all we were worth on BL's big brass door-knocker, but no reply. Nothing stirred inside. The only answer was a bleat and a clank of chains from Horace, tethered to a gum-tree at the side of the shack.

'A good job your friend he is out, huh?' said Lobo.

'What do you mean?'

'Were not you saying he has a few plant-es of grass hiding away?'

I shook my head firmly. 'There is no way I'm going to allow you to rip anything off from here, and especially BL's private smokes.'

A chewing-gum grin slowly stretched Lobo's baby-bum-cheeks wide. 'A-hey-hey,' he chortled. 'Frankie. This it is not the attitude I like.'

It's no use, I realised. He'll find them anyway. Grimly I led Lobo around the side of the shack, stepping over the stretched chain. Horace seemed pleased to see me, bleating and wagging his tail, but backed head down away from Lobo, as if he perceived something about my companion I did not.

We climbed over the dilapidated fence at the back of the kitchen into a small paddock; in the centre were three small bushes of grass.

Lobo's first swoop decapitated the thickest branch of juicy heads.

'Take it easy, for God's sake!' I protested. 'That's quite enough.'

Lobo looked up, his left hand sneaking for the main stem.

'Hey. Do not you think we should take the whole of this plant?'

'Listen,' I warned. 'BL is the meanest, most dangerous crazy son-of-an-udder-swining bitch I've yet to meet. And I tell you, if he caught his parents snitching so much as a leaf from his little babies, it wouldn't just be his mother that would get shafted, if you get my meaning.'

At that precise moment the Hun chose to roar into the driveway on his large motorbike, followed by Maybeline, a blur of pink behind the wheel of the family car. The swirling cloud of dust would give us enough cover to sneak back around the shack, or so I prayed.

BL swung his leg lazily off the bike. Pausing to light a cigarette, he strolled towards me, pulling off the straps of his metallic helmet zigzagged with SS lightning flashes. Ice-blue eyes stared into mine. Had he seen us?

'Nice car ye got there, sport,' he drawled, looking me up and down. 'Yeah, ye've come up in the world.'

'I sure have, corn-cobber.' We shook hands. 'Hey, Lobo,' I called, 'come and meet BL.'

A dark hand flapped up the lid of the Baby's back door and my lupine chum stepped out, his turd-smooth face steaming smiles. Taking BL's hand in the Prussian manner, he shook it curtly, bowing and clicking his heels as usual. 'So pleas-ed I am to meet you. Yes, I am hearing so much of you from our good friend Frankie. Always he is talking about you.'

'Yeah, well, 'e's fair dinkum, isn'e?' BL winked my way.

Lobo smiled. 'You know, so much of the driving I spend wondering how you get your name? Never I hear one the same.'

BL's eyes shifted towards Maybeline, lifting boxes of groceries out the boot of the car.

She waved. 'Allo, Frankie. I'm jes gowing to make a cup o' tea.'

I raised my thumb, beaming my reply.

BL tilted his head, saying, 'You should ask 'er about that, sport. She gayve it me.'

I was relieved and pleased – not so much of a rat's tail of a sus flicking in BL's eyes. He kept smiling, which was completely uncharacteristic. I wondered if it was something he'd been doing with Maybeline out in the bush on the way back from getting the shopping. Nothing like a little nookie to raise the spirits.

Lobo was chattering ninety-nine to the dozen. I couldn't believe it when I heard him say. 'Hey, BL, you know, my good friend Frankie is telling me what a good grass you grow. You know, so much time I am spending in Aussieland and never I see a good plant yet.'

Holding my breath . . . Jesus, the fucking dickhead's shaving it right to the bone.

Round the back, Lobo stooped to sniff the flowering head. 'Oh, my goodness, what beautiful plants you have. But,' he pointed, 'I think this one it is the best of all.'

My God. I looked away. The plant was about half the size it had been before our arrival. 'BL,' he continued, 'I must ask you. Do not you worry that when you are out the bad fellows they come sneaking, take the plant-es? Always so many of them around.'

BL's reply baffled me. 'I wouldn't moind if they did, mytey. It grows y'know.'

In our honour, BL heaved out a crate of stubbies. We shared a few bongs and through all the fuzz of the 'rage' Lobo managed to elicit information from BL on selling a car that has never been paid for. On parting, sweet adieus were exchanged: in true Aussieland style, we threw grunts and punches at each other.

Again into the wild blue yonder, bound for Perth, three thousand leagues distant.

We had a problem: no cash, and only three cheques left in Lobo's cheque-book. But Lobo had an ace tucked up his sleeve. Correction, Henry's Platinum Amex card.

'Gosh almighty,' I grinned. 'I should have known it all the time. You're turning out to be quite the master thief, aren't you?'

'You say I am a thief!' Lobo snapped. 'I do not steal. I only pay back double those that insult me. You think to make a wisecrack?' Lobo pointed to his lips. 'Watch and notice. I do not laugh. Be very careful from now on. My temper it is on a string that is short and breaking. Now, make an effort to concentrate. Look at the signature and tell me. Can you make another like it? Prak-tik while I drive. Our lives they may depend on it.'

In Adelaide, Lobo threatened to leave me. I'd foolishly told him one of my old lesbian friends occasionally sold hash. He demanded to know her address. I refused to give it up.

Subsequently Lobo would often remind me of this 'crime'. In the short time since we'd met he'd built up a catalogue of nags that rivalled my wife's encyclopaedic entries, and I'd known her for years. Hadn't he told me he could do anything a woman could, and better? He was proving it. Repeatedly the

Tibetan dog would roll out this bogroll list, reminding me of my intolerable behaviours at each and every opportunity.

Our friendship was unravelling at the edges, and, to make matters doubly worse, we'd run out of grass. My fault, of course. For the first time we were without the saving balm of a smoke to soothe out the bumps.

A black night somewhere in the eastern suburbs of Adelaide. After the long drought that had brought the bush fires, now we had floods. In all this rain Lobo's sense of direction seemed to have given up. It was only by conscripting a co-pilot, one very drunk and unclean female hitch-hiker, that we managed to find one garage open.

Although I bungled my first attempt at signing the Platinum Amex, and despite, or because of, the young manager's nervousness, we managed to relieve the station of one full tank of petrol, two five-gallon cans filled to the brim, and a hamper bursting with provisions for the road.

Our night journey continued frenetically, picking up pace as we neared that eighteen-hundred-mile road with no turn-offs looming so menacingly up ahead.

But first we had to pass Port Augusta, Australia's centre of ship-building and the southern state's chief provincial city, where steel mills rock around the clock.

We spent a couple of hours in a lay-by, just gazing at the dawn reflected in a brine-encrusted salt lake. To our left rose Mount Remarkable, and across the bay the steelworks town sprawled. There, simply by waving the magic Platinum and signing on the dotted line, the Baby was fitted with a new radiator, more suitable for desert driving, and four chunky rollerball tyres.

After Port Augusta there was no turning back, and to add to our troubles we had discovered that not one of the petrol stations on the road between here and Perth accepted credit cards, platinum-coated or otherwise.

Two kamikazes blazing a trail, we were committing ourselves to a one-way street. I sensed behind us a snuffling and sniffing, dogs on our tracks. We'd left quite a trail on our plundered route through Australia.

Lobo had been in the saddle forty-eight hours continuously, save for the pit-stops I dreaded. So much for this eternal gofer to do. Lobo would sit astride his seat, heels scuffing sand, filing his nails, one eagle eye never straying as I refilled the tank, polished the windscreen, inspected the oil.

Always a hive of impatience, Lobo would then deliver a lecture on the subject of tardiness or my lackadaisical approach to work. And finally, when he'd filed his tools away, zipped up his manicure set and replaced it in the correct compartment of the executive case, he'd key the ignition, flatten the accelerator with his offensive foot, and I'd be thrown back against my seat, hardly able even to bring my lips together as the G-forces mounted excruciatingly.

Incredibly he seemed to be gaining energy as the journey progressed. A paranoid little dickie-bird warned he was syphoning the energy direct from my tanks. But I dismissed the notion as unworthy. Was not this man helping me change my life for the better, cleansing the dirt from my mind? These past years it seemed to have been but a rooming house for swine.

The borders between day and night had long since become meaningless. The only existence I knew was this road, this blinding salt plain, this burnished dreamtime, this blizzard of cirrus suns and a thousand different faces of my scattered self.

> Australian salt lake dream,
> Use speed to get there.
> Salt dust in your face,
> Cross the honky tonk plains.

The spiky plant upcrops of the Nullarbor Plain reminded me of . . . well, had I been to Mars I might have had something to compare it with.

'Look you. Up ahead. There . . . Do not you see the camel?'

'What? Where?' I said, displacing several vertebrae as I screwed my neck way beyond its limits.

'Really, Frankie.' Lobo's lips twisted around the iceberg tip of his contempt. 'Last night I see three camels, then later two wombats they run across the road, and not two feet from the Baby. As I watch, I am despairing for you, so blinding you are.'

I transferred my gaze to the horizon, wherever that was. Jesus, the camels were probably three miles away, clustered around a rock or a figment tree of Lobo's imagination. Anyway, whoever heard of camels in Australia?'

Fact: in the early years of this century a circus showman imported camels from the Sahara. Some escaped and to this day their descendants roam the Nullarbor Plain, for the benefit of travellers' imaginations . . . There are more camel facts, but for the sake of brevity we'll pass on. At least I can report back to the tourist office – there are trees. Though Nullarbor in Latin means 'no trees', occasionally these same figment trees can be seen striding the horizon, sprouting their demented heads . . .

Truth to tell, it can get so hot (fifty degrees Centigrade and more) on those damned fly-infested plains that the traveller can see almost anything . . . or so they say. For despite fearsome tales of melting steering wheels, weeping sunglasses and deathrays from the dictator on high, for our journey the Nullarbor assumed a protective mantle, the temperature a mere twenty degrees. Still, it's a strange, ominous landscape, darkened by a soup-plate of cloud, and possessed by a feeling of imminence, of closeness to presence. And the cruel monotony of this slashing road, only a couple of millenia in length.

Dangerous to have Samaritan tendencies on this road. Any man thumbing a lift might carry a gun.

A hypnotic whizzing progression of road signs standing sentry, spaced, it seemed every ten metres. Many of the triangles warned of that most Australian of hazards, flying kangaroos. Don't laugh. Two hundred and forty pounds of hurtling flesh hitting anyone you know at a hundred mph is no joke. Incredibly, all of these sentries were peppered with gunshots, some even rendered completely illegible by the dents, holes, and graffiti daubings of enraged kangaroos, wallabies and the like. I had visions of open lorries frothing over with drunken gung-ho bushwhackers, blasting off at everything in sight.

Great banners by the roadside advertised the lobo – whoops, I mean the *logos* of native beer companies. We passed through Iron Knob, stopped for a drink at Denial Bay, Salt Lake Yanni was a blur. At Penong the road gained a breath of relief as it cut close to the coast. I may give a false impression here, mentioning these watering-holes as if they were towns. Each was no more than a fly-infested motel stop – spaced at approximately two-hundred-kilometre intervals – filled with surly types and signs saying 'CASH ONLY'.

'Frankie, you are dreaming again.' Lobo's voice burred like a woodpecker in my ear. 'Look you, up ahead! See the dragon breathing fire!'

I tensed, determined not to miss out one more thing . . . Then I relaxed. That plume of smoke was a dust-trail, and the flashings the sun glinting on the chromium scaffolding of a trans-Australia land-train, a monster truck hauling three ginormous six-wheel trailers. In the last second before we were engulfed in the dust storm, I caught a glimpse of the pill-head driver, high in the cab: a sunbleached frizz of hair, mad popping eyes, shaking and jiving and fingerpopping to a heavy-metal beat. The words of a Grateful Dead song came flooding back:

High on cocaine, driving that train,
Casey Jones you better watch yo' speed . . .

When we emerged coughing from the dense cloud, it was simultaneously a shock and a relief to find I was gazing out over a vast expanse of . . . sea. To the left, khaki-coloured cliffs, somehow looking like they'd been ripped fresh off Baden-Powell's backside. Millions of diligent Boy Scouts had contributed to these anal repositories tumbling down to yellow-brick beaches. The latrine bays were empty but for screaming seagulls and marching legions of sea horses.

That was my unclean soul speaking. Ignore it.

Reading the historical footnotes on the tourist map laid across my knees, I discovered that thirty thousand years ago the Nullarbor was covered by sea. I imagined swimming this eternity with Lobo my Cro-Magnon guide. Jesus Hare-Krishna, what a thought!

Someone had loosed a tourniquet out there. The bloody tide came gushing as the ruby-red sun dropped into the slit between quilted cloud above and slumberous earth below.

Reclaiming its dark empire, night casting its mantle wide . . . And I, just a translucent fading square of magenta parchment framed against this fluorescent midnight blue, like Destry riding out yet again, this time atop this dungheap pile of a world. So alone. All that cramming out there . . . All that teeming outback, the vast jaws of a nutcracker, closing in.

We stopped – I to empty the two cans into the thirsty Baby, Lobo to pore over the map, the cab spilling an umbrella of yellow light. For the first few moments, after I returned to my post, Lobo studiously ignored me: then, pressing a stubby finger on the map, he looked up, saying, 'You see this place four hundred Ks up the road? Madura.'

I craned over.

Lobo's finger slowly traced the line of the road. 'I calculate we have just enough petrol. About five Ks after we reach Madura we run out. The speed we must to keep down to seventy. We must miss out the station at Eucla, because if we are cashing the last cheque there, we cannot carry enough to make it to the end of the road. Now . . .' Lobo's finger tracked back to deep desert, and stopped. Shifting in his seat to allow me a better view, he said, 'You see this place a-here?'

'Yeah,' I replied, somewhat mystified. 'What did you say it was called?'

'I did not say.' Lobo's voice was cold, 'Cannot you read?'

Feeling ridiculous, bending low over his knees, I focused on the small print.

'M-A-R-I-N-G-A-L-A . . . Maringala?' I repeated, rubbing my leaden lids. 'I'm sure I've heard that name before.'

'Probably you confuse it with a stupid she-devil.' Lobo sighed exasperatedly. 'My gosh, for the once will you try to concentrate on the subject. Make an effort to remember the name. Our lives they may depend on it. Now!' He snapped his fingers. 'Pass to me that pen. I mark it with a big circle. And now, you are ready for the driving?'

I groaned. More miles, more leagues, endlessly unceasing, like a migraine that won't go away, this road a runner carpet to forever.

Another lay-by, Lobo dousing our headlights. That red blurring on the horizon waxing into recognition – the far-off lights of the next petrol station. Madura, our last exit sign from hell bleeding across the big-top sky.

'Now,' Lobo said briskly, 'do I have to tell you one more time? You must shave. Water you find in the canteen.' With a backward jerk of his thumb he indicated the spare room.

I stared back, too exhausted even to twitch.

Outside the bars of my cage, the moustachioed ringmaster raised his whip. . .

CRACK. 'Frankie! Stop day-dreaming this ink-stand! We must to prepare. When you lift the chequebook from the briefcase, every thing inside has to be in the correct place. The fingers on the handle, perrrfectly manicur-ed.' Lobo's voice rose in a trill. 'The same it goes for the Baby. If the garage peoples look in the cab, they see everything organis-ed, clean . . .'

The mad *hausfrau* began to polish the dials with a duster. 'Pay the utmost attention. Already I tell you how the quality of the sock-es gives the clue to the pocket. The same it is true with the cloth-es. If the last detail of the appearance it is precisely correct, every stupid person believes in any story you tell.' Lobo waggled a finger. 'This it is how we make the world work for us. It is not money that makes it go around. It is believing fools.

A perverted Cupid aiming his hypodermic arrow directly at my heart. 'If you do not follow my instructions to the letter, I warn you, by this time tomorrow, you find yourself bones in the desert. The ants around here, they do the work quick. Not like you.'

I chuckled feebly.

His frown plumbed a new nadir. 'Do not laugh. I tell you. Dark things they hide all around.' Lobo's eyes paddled back and forth, busy little Indians in dug-out canoes.

More instruction from the Fuhrer. His nasal twang pumped home the antidote to the catatonia I longed for. Drone drone. The whine of my father's bagpipes skirling on, and on . . .

'You must remember to write on the cheque-stub the precise amount we spend, the date, and do not forget to bring forward the balance from the last page. Every last detail, huh? And one more thing. This next place, it is I who tells the story. I cannot afford to have you muck it up.'

God! Is this purgatory? Have I died? Maybe he's the devil. Jesus!

It was only with luck and persistence that we managed to convince the station commander who shimmered like a mirage before my eyes that we'd left our film-crew and all the trucks out in the desert, every tank squeezed dry of gas. If we could get enough petrol here to bring them back, we'd book the whole motel. We assured him that his beautiful establishment would take centre-stage in the next scene of the film. Marshall McLuhan would have been proud of us.

We filled both our cans and bought ten more, filled them too, and the Baby. Over two hundred dollars on a cheque without a card. That's travelling, boy!

29

After another of a stream of interminable stops to fill the Baby from our cans, Lobo stuck his head out from the canopy window, in his hand the evidence of my latest crime. Apparently I'd dumped my bikini case on the basket of shades and cracked a lens. The glasses in question were by rights of plunder mine, but Lobo had 'taken' them some thousands of miles back, claiming the white rims were a better 'compliment' to his dark skin.

I was in no condition to argue about it. My head was buzzing with petrol fumes, and I was swaying like a ship's lantern in a hurricane.

After I endured this, it seemed I was not yet free to step down from the dock. Intoning with the solemnity of a judge, Lobo demanded, 'And now, give to me my driving licence. It is not in the correct place.'

Melt-down in my waxen core. I stuttered, 'B-but Lobo, it's in the usual . . .p-pocket of the c-case. I r-r-remember, I p-put it back after I s-s-signed the cheque.'

Lobo spat a burning coal my way: 'Why always you lie so, when you know very well it is not there? I search the case, the inside and the out.' He shook his head violently. 'This it is the worst disaster every you make. The papers for the Baby are inside, folded in the cover.' Lobo tore at his hair, a vein pulsing ominously at his temple.

'But Lobo,' I whined, 'I'm sure, I'm p-positive I put it back.'

'I remind you, everything it hangs on this licence. Without papers we cannot sell the Baby in Perth. So where the heck is it?' he thundered.

Wilting, I wondered if he was about to strike me.

Then, unbelievably, he forgave me for the loss — just like that, with a simple shrug of his shoulders. I could have taken any tongue-lashing, but this humiliating mercy was more than I could bear. It was the last push.

The grey, two-lane bitumen highway, the slashing straight-ahead road, the dead kangaroos, the pancake sky so flat and hard-edged, supplanting my grey matter as a soup-plate upturned on a pea. Who was I? I was a nobody, a little two-inch nobody dick, and this grey swirling above was the underbelly of the Great Australian Whale, the Mother of us all. I was so tired I couldn't even summon the necessary energy to pray for my release.

The 1800-mile road across the Nullarbor ended in the inescapable geometry of a staggered T-junction.

Lobo was always saying, 'We all have to pay the piper one day. And there they were, the pipers, the dogs guarding the pass, convex mirror-shades glinting in the early morning sun. The patrol car angled across the road just before the junction – the left fork to Esperance, Archipelago of Recherche, Butty Head and the Great Southern Ocean, the right fork swinging north to Kalgourlie, and Perth, seven hundred kilometres beyond. A fat dog flagged lazily, directing us to a garage to the left.

A snuffling snout pushed in through the window, black beady eyes scuttling like rabid crabs all over the interior, our faces, our bodies . . . 'Whose car is this?' As the cavernous jowl opened, a gust of rancid kangaroo pies belted out to fill the cab.

For the first time, Lobo seemed lost for a reply. Merely nodding his answer, he sat staring glumly straight ahead.

I glanced in the mirror at the big arse examining our rear numberplate. Raising a thumb, he called out, 'Yep, this is the one all right! The reg checks out.'

The police station seemed to occupy half of the town. Like everything else in these parts, it was prefabricated on Mars, then dropped from helicopters. Hemmed in by our escorting walls of flesh, we were frog-marched in, one of his master's dogs carrying Lobo's briefcase as a trophy.

Lino surfaces everywhere, even to the ceiling – this is an Australian police station, remember? Scrubbed, drab blues, carbolic and pig-sweat.

My attention fixed on the biggest of the three residents of this animal farm. This one just had to be the chief. For one thing, on his breast pocket he wore a silver star. But it was the tall white pastry hat that really set him apart from the rest, somehow giving him the look of a baker from Dachau. Grinning, rubbing his hands with the pleasure of anticipation, he stepped forwards. We were to be his *petit déjeuner*.

Stopping dead in his tracks and suddenly throwing off his rigid torpor, Lobo shouted at this pastry chef in a voice calculated to insult. 'By what rights do your men detain us?'

PC's shrewd eyes flicked between both of us. 'Cut the crap, you can't deny you passed a bad cheque at Madura for a very large quantity of petrol. If you can't come up with a convincing explanation, you're done. I don't like your fucking face, boy, and round these parts that's the same as committing a felony.'

Lobo appeared to inspect the cuticles of his nails. Then, lifting his head and staring PC dead in the eye, he smiled. 'Yes, we did pass a cheque in Madura for a very large quantity of petrol, as your dirty voice says, but what of it?'

Goaded beyond the bristles of his limits, PC reached out to grab Lobo's collar, but his fingers clamped on empty space. Lobo had jumped to the side and was dancing on the tips of his toes, the cutting edges of his hands extended in the manner of the Hong Kong school. The way his lips rolled back reminded me oddly of an inflating Mr Universe. I felt disengaged, an observer of this surrealistic scene.

Suddenly Lobo's Voice leapt into the fray to stand at his side, a tangible, even physical ally. *THE FIRST ONE OF YOU THAT DARES TO TOUCH ME*, it boomed, *I CHOP HIM INTO TINY PIECES*.

The void around Lobo had widened appreciably, and seizing the opportunity I squeezed into the gap, pushing my body between Lobo and PC.

PC's forehead glistened with tiny beads of sweat, glands dripping adrenalin and bacon fat. Bobbing furiously, in order to get his attention, I said, 'I think there have been some misunderstandings. Maybe, er, it would be a help if I was to mediate.' I spread my palms. 'Well?'

PC grunted, his eyes shifting briefly from Lobo's face. 'Explain! And it'd better be good.'

Laying a hand flat on my chest, I told him, 'First of all, myself. I'm studying Australia in depth. The sort of film we're planning, you can't get the gen staying in big hotels, so I hitch around. My friend here', I nodded to Lobo, 'offered to help me search out suitable locations. I'm not often wrong about people, and though I've only known him for a short time, I think I can say with complete confidence he would never knowingly pass a bad cheque. There must be a perfectly logical answer to the problem.'

PC blinked, his ice blues like splinters chipped off Old Nick's favourite block. Ignoring me completely, he said, 'I want to see this chequebook. *If* you would be so kind.'

Lobo had stopped dancing. 'Thank you,' he said, bowing curtly and, yes, clicking his heels. 'Now you choose to address me in a polite manner, I see no reason for not co-operating. Now, if my briefcase can be return-ed, I show this book to you.'

Laying the case on the counter, Lobo set the combination, lifted the lid, withdrew the empty chequebook and handed it to PC without a word.

The fat thumb of the cop flicked through the stubs as he scanned the meticulous record of the ground we'd travelled since Brisbane, as well as Lobo's other trails – an accountant's dream, connecting us to mysterious disappear- ances, probably in every state, each notated with name, place and date. My pulse skipped a beat. Right in the middle of the book was one blank stub.

PC's eyes lit up like a wildcatter who's just tapped a Texan gusher. 'And why is this one left blank?' he accused.

Glancing ceilingward, Lobo scoffed, 'Oh, you know, probably I buy marijuana with it. What the heck you think?' Swivelling on oiled hips, Lobo glared at each of the cops in turn. 'Surely none of you expect me to write in marijuana? My gosh! What sort of fool you take me for?'

In preparation for that certain deluge of kicks from those black, crêpe-soled boots, I began to shrink inside.

But then, unbelievably, it was PC who broke rank, retreating to a new position behind the desk, his face turning purple and blotchy. Gripping the edge of the counter with one hand and his throat with the other, he only just managed to wheeze out, 'What . . . I want . . . to know . . . is, did you cash all these cheques?'

Lobo paused to examine his fingernails. 'What it is wrong with cashing cheques? You tell me.'

Regaining a measure of his power, PC fired back, 'Nothing, if you have sufficient funds to cover them.' Jabbing at the open chequebook again, he demanded, 'Is this your name? You are Peter Justice?'

Lobo nodded curtly.

PC continued: 'For your information, then, Mr Peter bloody Justice, we have already been in telephone communication with your bank, and they tell us they have been looking all over Australia for you these past months. They wish to contact you immediately concerning your unsecured overdraft, which I under- stand is rather large.'

Drawing himself to his full height as he continued, PC seemed to be reading from the station's procedures book. 'I must warn you, Mr Justice, if this in fact is your name, it is a criminal act to offer a cheque if you have no intention of paying. I would like to hear you explain yourself.' He banged the counter, the blotches multiplying. 'And right now, Mr Justice.'

Lobo looked at him sneeringly. 'I do not like the way I am treated by you. I do not like the way you talk. Nothing I do for which I should be asham-ed.

Merely I am coming to your country and spending my money, and every month the cheque it is coming from Switzerland, so the mistake it is not mine. Why should I be held accounting for the stupids in your banks. Where I come from such things never happen. Tell me!' He rounded on PC, stamping the lino. 'Let me hear your explanations for that! And now I wait.' Lobo folded his arms dramatically.

PC growled, 'You will be required to stay close at hand while we make further inquiries. We are investigating your case, Mr Justice. You got that?'

Lobo nodded, a film of bored ennui masking his face.

'You will be required to present yourself at the magistrates' court tomorrow morning at ten a.m. sharp. And let me warn you, if you are late or attempt to leave town, you will be arrested. You will camp in the municipal car-park and nowhere else. You will leave all your papers, passport and other documents with us.'

He turned to me. 'As for you, Mr film-writer or whoever you are, I won't be needing any more of your help, and you can count yourself lucky. You're free to go.'

It was then I remembered my passport in the briefcase. I asked Lobo for it. He reached into the case. It was the only time I ever saw him react nervously. My eyes were not deceived by his elegant sleight of hand. My brain definitely wasn't malfunctioning. He palmed the missing driver's licence out from where he had hidden it between the pages of my passport.

I kept my new-found knowledge concealed.

30

We limped out of the cop-shop, two weary Indians after the battle of Little Wounded Knee. Nothing to do but to kill time's buffalo again and again. Too weak from hunger for the joys of 'taking', I had one lousy, stinking, solitary, sweat-soaked, scummy dollar left when we walked out of the supermarket. But we had food.

Twilight in the municipal car-park, edge of town. A couple of white-trellised enclosures side by side, one for lorries and the other, supposedly, for cars. The only other vehicles in our compound were two crumpled, cannibalised wrecks, blocked up on bricks in a corner.

The ritual of sharing food was calming. We ate in silence, the still life of our supper between us – a couple of pints of milk, stale French bread, salami, celery sticks, framed by the red-and-white check tablecloth.

Lobo's game of hunt-the-thimble with his driving licence set me trawling back to that first night-time trail, the long road between Melbourne and Wagga. He'd just stopped the car, middle of bloody nowhere, supposedly for a pee. Half an hour later, he'd reappeared, carrying a basket and, under this same red-and-white check tablecloth, chicken and goodies. It was only after I'd repeatedly pressed him that he'd explained his 'Voice' directed him to a lonely house in the wilderness, where the door was unlatched and this feast lay waiting.

His bloody Voice. How many times had he suborned me to follow his dictates, invoking the higher authority of his resident gremlin? My mind flicked through the trip like a catalogue, probing like a large sticky thumb. The first meeting, that first joint, I'd selected only flower tips. Lobo must have

221

reckoned I was holding a pile of dynamite dope. Perhaps that was the real reason he'd offered to drive me to Sydney.

Yeah, King's Cross, bloody Sydney. What a wind-up that proved to be. That first walkabout, supposedly trailed by the 'watcher', as Lobo dubbed him, the spy on the streets for the big crime bosses. Second night, we'd tracked this will-o-the-wisp to his lair. But on both occasions I only had Lobo's word for it.

Neither had I seen Lobo's confrontation with the street hustlers in the club. He said I'd produced a shitty-stick when he'd asked for a sales sample. I was so sure I'd handed over grass. We tumbled out of that club so damned quick, I hadn't thought to turn around, I'd been so blinded by fear. So what about the pursuit? Maybe . . . And maybe not . . .

I almost flicked past the episode with the kid, his pimply face staring out of my memory banks with all the luminosity of a dead squid in a sludge pit. Reluctantly I turned back to the page. Lobo'd left us in that trash-can alleyway a full ten minutes, perhaps more. The reason given? Our stash was some distance off. What stash? The shitty-sticks were concealed in the walking-stick all the time. When he'd returned he'd popped one out of the cane into the punter's hand.

That ten minutes would have been amply sufficient to return to the car, unlock my door. There had never been any camera, nor any break-in. It was clear to me now.

And what about the 'dirt' in my ear-holes, the 'dirty' words gushing from my mouth, my 'dirty' ways? How many times had he suggested I was tir-ed, suggested I was clumsy? That was the key word, 'suggested'. I was not much different from most other human beings. I didn't wash fifteen times a day. Neither was I to be found perpetually reorganising my possessions. I swore occasionally, more so when I was under stress. I needed seven hours' sleep every night. If I was deprived of it over a sufficiently long period, was it not a certainty I would become disoriented, and might even suffer hallucinations?

This Tibetan misfit was so full of pep, zap and vim it was abrasive. I'd never encountered any one with so much go. There had to be something to his belief that cleanliness and precise ordering creates inner power.

How many times on those eternal night-time trails did we drive till the petrol gauge was slap-bang on the red and we were lost in the vastness of the continent, when Lobo's Voice would advise him to take such and such a road, and the petrol would be there. It might not be obvious immediately – like the time we camped out in the cemetery and found the forty-five-gallon drum next morning in the stores shed.

I imagined Lobo's Voice as sneaky Indian scout, always reporting back from the road up ahead.

Why had Lobo chosen me for his companion? Maybe he just wanted someone to nag and show off to.

But wait, going back to the first meeting, hadn't I felt some mystical sense of connection? Was Lobo my best friend or worst enemy? He might have been exaggerating about his Voice, but there had to be some truth to it. At the very least, his intuition was uncannily accurate . . .

And then I remembered with a jolt. God almighty . . . Something so unbelievable I'd blanked it at the time. When I woke up under the dot-dash of that morse streetlight, it was the sounds of Lobo strumming a guitar. Surely a bulky item to hide in the back of the Falcon! On how may reorganisations had I seen him laying all and sundry out on the sidewalk? He told me he'd fallen asleep, then simply woken up on the beach, the guitar in his hand. How had he gotten out from under the secured tarp without disturbing the fine raindrops? If he had so much as bumped the tarp, the evidence would have shown as runs on the fine-grain patterning. I couldn't think of any other explanation but the bloody miraculous.

My questing mind's eye returned to the contents of this Baby. The cassette player was 'taken', as had been this spare room – the canopy – the spare gas cans, the tyres, the radiator, the bags of clothes, the basket and the sunglasses, the pens for kwadding-pleegics . . . And when I thought about it, even the car itself, discounting the small deposit Lobo *said* he had paid. Quite a list of charges when I totted it up. The least the bastards would do is throw away the key. I could almost hear it clanging as it bounced down a long stone corridor.

And what about our failed heist in Brisbane? When the cops swooped, he pushed me off that high wall, though he'd denied it later. Could he have been using me as a decoy to draw off the police? And earlier, he had admitted knowing the security tabs on the clothes would set off the alarm at the door of the designerworld skiing shop I had written that one down to his impish sense of humour . . . But there again, maybe he was just rolling those dice, and looking to score either way.

But wasn't I missing something out? The way my cash had been so steadily syphoned out of my wad, ten, fifteen dollars at a time? I'd blamed my losses on careless habits, preferring to believe I was going out of my mind than suspect my 'friend'. Perhaps, in the end, all Lobo had wanted was a travelling companion, and taking my money was simply a stratagem to prevent my escape.

Somewhere east of Cracow, deep in a dripping crypt, a hooded ersatz Polish priest broke off another wedge of the black crust from the sourdough host in the silver-lined skull that once had housed a Tibetan monk and in his next life served for his begging bowl, and placed the bread in the mouth that opened wide to receive it. None of the long row of shrouded participants knew who was to be the Chosen One, the one appointed to join with their master in the flames of the sacrificial altar. But the priest knew . . .

Their dirge went like this: 'Our Putrid Father, unclean is thy very name . . .'

Hooded in darkness Lobo hefted an ice pick at the silence . . .

'I have it!'

Rolling awake, I couldn't help groaning, 'Whaaat?'

He sat up swiftly, tapped his head twice. 'I have a plan. For it to work, it is necessary you not know the story. That way you play your part the better. You are listening?'

'Yeah,' I grunted, watching his every movement. 'Just tell me what I have to know.'

Lobo raised a finger. 'Tomorrow, in the court, when they ask you about the cheques, you must answer, you sign every one.'

'Yeah,' I said slowly. 'Is that all?'

'Yes, you need not to know more. Nothing there is for worrying.' He grinned, teeth, whites of eyes, rents in a black curtain.

'In other words,' I drawled, 'na wuckin' furries.'

'You have it exactly. You know, Frankie,' he laid his hand flat on his chest, 'I would go through the fire for you.'

As I stared wide-eyed at the apparition he had become, it seemed I heard a click as another piece of the jigsaw slotted into place. Lobo was setting me up as the fall-guy, as he had been doing since we'd met. His Scottish Amicable insurance policy. Hadn't he insisted I sign every cheque? Now I understood. The ultimate survivor from the land of the high snows was about to impart his final wisdom.

I lay down, turning my back, and gazed at encompassing night. No stars visible through this porthole. Folded in a black wing, I'd never felt so alone.

I waited till I knew the emotion wouldn't choke my voice. 'Lobo. Our only sane choice is to flee.'

Lobo sneered. 'Look at you now. You shake inside. In the police station I was impress-ed. I think to myself, he is strong. But . . . Pah! I was wrong.'

I murmured, 'I thought you and your Voice were never wrong.'

Lobo's hand was a contemptuous shadow flicking away flies. 'Is it not as I tell you, always you must to pay the piper. Frankie, I do not know why you worry so, when you are knowing our plan it will work.'

Outside, big headlights glared briefly in the parking lot, then red tail-lights flared as the police car took the ramp onto the road. I realised exactly why the chief had instructed us to camp on the edge of town. He actually wanted us to make a run for it. The nearest town was three hundred Ks distant, and only one road.

By now I guessed they must have telexed across state lines. The information contained in the cheque-stubs would give all the places, dates and times they needed. It would be obvious by now we were partners in crime, and tomorrow in court Lobo would make out I had led him on. After all, wasn't I five years older? He was so good at acting dumb and speaking pidgin English.

My gosh, I mean, my God . . . I could just see him smiling at the judge, his asinine face a mask of cherubic innocence, pointing the diabolic finger. 'Your Honour, he trick-ed me. I am simple man, first time come to your fine country. We meet in the train station. He so nice. I give to him all my money. He say he mak-es film. I get big per cent . . . Oh, I am so exciting. But I very confusing when he makes me sign paper in the bank. He say no one must know the name of the dictator. All part of plot. He say we need car with a flat back, good for shooting on, that before he film me taking canopy out of factory. He carry box with film in, but never it runs out. I no see where he get the picture in. I no understanding western life. So complicating. I live in a cave, learn from my teacher three things in life the most important. He is looking like you, Sir Judge, 'cept he bald and is wearing no cloth-es . . .'

Fucking shut up. I tried to squash Lobo like a bug out of my mind. Sleep. Sleep. And hadn't I earned it? Three-thousand miles and not so much as a cat-nap.

I seemed to fall down a tube that went through the centre of the world. I fell for a long time, a glimmer of light beckoning, growing in size. With an effort I managed to wriggle through the tight, fleshy-walled opening.

I emerged through a spiky thornbush; before me, my castle's spires glinting in the harsh light of a new day. I gasped, as I realised my Gothic dream was no more than a paltry, crumbling nightmare inhabited by broken-down cars, gnawed bones, empty bottles, shattered glass. I wandered through the rooms, kicking ineffectually at the garbage strewn about. Passing down a corridor I heard sobs. Feeling ridiculous. I sauntered through a closed door. My poor wife was hunched over a table, leafing through a bulging sack of unpaid bills, lawyers' letters, final summonses. There were other sacks. I suddenly realised what I'd done. I'd fucked off leaving this poor woman to the mercy of my creditors, and all the parasitical hangers-on.

It was then I heard a Voice, just like Lobo's. It boomed so my eardrums rattled. *This it is the mess you left behind, there will be no escape until you return and clean your stables. This it is your path of freedom. The past will always seek you out wherever you go. It is hard, but an incorrigible fool must be punish-ed if he is to change his ways for the better.*

I protested, 'But, but . . . I'm not here at all. I'm stuck out in the lousy desert about to be arrested by some deranged cops who wear pastry-chef hats. I'm in a stolen fucking module on the back of a bloody car with a Tibetan weirdo called Lobo. It's unbelievable. What have I done to deserve this?'

My heart it bleeds, and for the both of us. The Voice was harsh, overbearing even. *Do not forget what I tell you, for I do not say the same thing twice. Make an effort, and you can escape out of this trap. This is the only space we have taken out of time. If you are resolving I will help you. Otherwise, you and me, we go in opposing directions. This it is a small house we share. I cannot abide this dirt you bring in every day. Now . . . I take you back to see your mother. The visit does you good. Remember everything I have told you, and all you have seen.*

'OK, OK,' I said reluctantly, 'I agree. I suppose you have gotten me into a corner, and no doubt you know what's for the best. I'm going to clean up my act, but I know it will take time. I'll also make a resolution. No more swearing when I get out of this convict colony . . . But, uhhrrrump, can I ask one little thing? Can I keep my dirty thoughts on Sunday afternoons?'

No, no, no, no. You must be consistent in everything. There is no Sabbath for swearing.

I was awakened when a claw of light reached into the cab, ripping the adhesive bandages of sleep from my eyes. The headlights of the 'just-checking' police car swept around the interior. At my side Lobo slept, the expression of an angel on his face. I knew better. I knew a whole lot better.

At first light, fully intent and resolved, I woke Lobo, telling him if he wanted to face the pipers in the court that was up to him, but I was striking out of this trap.

He blazed with anger. 'If you run out on me, I warn you, there will be no holds barr-ed. I make this promise, at the court the whole of the dirt will be pil-ed on your head.' He made the low growl of a dog about to attack. 'And mark my word, either today you will be caught by the cop-es, or tomorrow find-es you bon-es in the desert.'

I flinched, then realised the bastard was trying to rob me of my new-found strength. Resentment welled up, but that Voice at the periphery of hearing counselled, *Say nothing in reply.*

It took pains to salvage only what I considered truly mine: my favourite blazer and the last shirt and tie from the bush-fire victim's bag, my notebook, and of course the piggy-bag of bikinis.

Then it exploded on me with all the force of my wife's backhanders: any description the cops might circulate would not include a kilt. Under Lobo's sneering gaze, I changed into the tartan of my forefathers.

I said goodbye to Lobo, genuinely wishing him all the luck in the world.

His reply was a howled Tibetan curse which I translated to mean, 'Fuck off, asshole.' He wasn't so far wrong. I had just crawled out of one.

It was important not to look back. I knew that. Even my own credulity was strained by this guise of Scotsman on walkabout.

And then, climbing into the lorry-park, I almost skewered my unprotected balls on the sharp points of the trellis fence.

A steaming chromium-plated monster was revving its engines. Raising my voice over the cacophony of big cylinders, I yelled, 'Hey, mate, can you give me a lift to Perth?'

A visage as hard as the customised metal, eyes flint-chips reflecting the mineral blue of the cab. An animal thing passed between us. Somehow, I knew he recognised in me 'the hunted', and took delight in denying even the word 'no'. Yep, I'd made his day.

I started walking in the direction of Kalgourlie, all those leagues away. Then I realised the absurdity in that. I had no choice but to walk into town.

Lobo wheeled out from behind the parked lorries. The bastard had been watching my every move. With the cold sweep of a prowling shark he glided past, travelling on a couple of hundred yards.

His next pass hurt more than my pride. A stinging shower of dust and dirt scalded my naked shins as he disappeared in a burst of acceleration around a far bend.

I felt I had but brief minutes to make my escape. This last turning had pegged me back into the trap that the town represented. But aided by a confidence my Voice had given me the night before, I was questing for a signal, a sign.

Up ahead on the other side of the road was a garage, where an Ansett Stateliner bus, caked with desert dust, was spewing out its cargo of travel-limp bodies.

Then it seemed a crack in the heavens opened and a hand stretched forth, for through the milling crowd I heard the dulcet voice of a Scotsman, and calling me . . .

Crossing tarmac, I made a bee-line for the ginger-haired, grinning owner of the voice.

His hand was pummelling mine.

'I could'nae let ye pass by wi'oot congratulatin' ye. That's the first kilt I've seen since I left home. Ye've got some bottle wearin' it in front o' a' these patsy oot-backers.' Reaching into his pocket, he pulled out a hip-flask. 'Ye'll be hae'ing a dram wi' me, surely.'

Looking to either side and leaning forwards conspiratorially, I said, 'Just a quick swig.' Then, speaking rapidly, the whisky lighting the fire in me, 'I'm in a desperate situation an' there's nae time tae explain why. Can ye gi'e me enough money tae buy a ticket on tha' bus tae the next toon?'

My new-found brother of the blood didn't hesitate, 'Wha'ever ye need, ya cunt. Aye an' a'll get the driver tae gie ye a seat. The bus is packed, but nae worries, ye'll be weel in, he's Scottish an' a'.'

I stepped into the bus, and not a moment too soon. The Baby prowled into the forecourt, drawing up alongside the bus. Lobo at the door, Lobo on the step, sniffing for my scent.

Ducking down behind the seat and modestly tucking the kilt around my thighs, I prayed the whisky would cover my tracks.

Lobo gazed intently about, then, striding rapidly, disappeared through the glass doors of the café.

My Scottish mate returned with a three-quarter-pounder, introducing him as Big Mac.

I guessed the walrus-moustached driver's provenance immediately. In my country, only Aberdonians roll their R's like that.

'Strrructly speakin',' Big Mac said, 'it's agin' a' the regulations. Hoo-everr, that rrule doesnae apply tae Scotsmen.' He nodded to the side. 'Jimmy teels me yerr in trrouble. A'll no' be askin' ye why, orr ferr onny money ferr the ticket.' He winked, smiling broadly. 'Aye an' a'll see tae it ye get tae Perrth.'

Perth. From Perth the spiritual asshole of Scotland to Perth the state capital of West Australia, twenty thousand bleeding miles, as my broken wings had zagged it.

Thanks I sent to where thanks were due, the almichty ane on high. In the attic of the lofty heavens, the God of my ancestors was beaming down. Fuck Tibetans, and especially fuck their heathen gods. My brethren of the clans were jumping to my aid out of this bloody desert.

Lobo's sneaky mien peeked around the garage door at the trickle of passengers returning to the bus.

Big Mac revved the engines, then sounded the two-tone horn. The flow became a flood . . .

Lobo strolling round the corner, slit eyes squinting this way and that. Bending down to tie a shoelace – I knew his tricks. Turning his head to peer at the mirrored windows of the bus . . . Our eyes met, black glass between us. Did he realise? Did his Voice whisper the knowledge I was five feet distant? I held my breath, broadcasting Dean Martin's twenty greatest hits on my studio's FM.

He walked on, staring intently at the baggage holds.

With a pneumatic hissing, the doors slid shut. Big Mac shifting gears . . .

Was this the last I'd ever see of Lobo? He was stood centre of the road, hands on hips, framed by the back window of the bus, shrinking to a dot . . .

Head butting through layers of the dreamtime onion, smells of oil and old leather, a protruding spring snagging a vertabra, this sagging seat, dust-coated glass, steam blowing from the tied-down prow, red sand, the only upright features of this dread Martian landscape the shot-blasted triangular signs jumping with 'roos and one lone yucca tree marching on the horizon.

For a moment, unable to come to terms with this sudden AWOL shift of reality, I gripped my seat in panic. What the f . . . How the heck had I gotten here?

Oh yeah. I breathed relief as it came back to me. Big Mac had pulled in for a pee stop at a desert lay-by. Such a bounteous outpouring, for one lone tree — thirty grown men, their willies dangling.

My Voice whispered then, *This road's for freedom.*

I had worried for my sanity as I stared the Stateliner into a smudging on the far yonder. Jeesz, it might be days before I saw another vehicle. Bones in the desert . . . *My bones* in the desert for God's sake. Overhead, high, or was it deep in that zero blue, two black birds circling . . .

Blowing a smoke ring, I passed Furry Freak a fresh-rolled joint. 'That's just about it, man. Except for one thing.'

'And what was that?' He asked, his eyes red polka-dots in a wire-brush thatch.

'I had a lucky break on that bus.'

'Yeah?'

I stretched over, plucking the spliff out of his dirty fingernails, took a deep drag, then passed it back.

'An old geezer, up front with the driver, voice like backsliding treacle — know what I mean? — said he'd won a competition for three months' free travel on buses to anywhere in Australia. Three months . . . I get constipation just at the thought of a bus journey. Three months!

'He was only another Scotsman of the unbearable MacPester clan. My mother-in-law's one, so I've got them taped to a tee.

'I was seated in the third row from front, forced by proximity to listen to his diarrhoea of verbal. According to him, he'd been a metal prospector back in the good old days.

'I began flapping my ears when he started describing his methods for locating hidden gold.

'"Whit makes it an art an' no a hobby is ah look on the wa's and no' on the groond. The first trick is, find the auld prospectors' huts. A lot of bad men aboot in thae days, and ye ken, them old-timers would rather die than tell whar the gold was hid. Many of them were Scotsmen of course. The usual place was the wa's o' the huts."

'Taking the seat beside him, I winked as I said. "Ye ken a lot aboot metals, eh?"

'"Auye, an' gems," he answered fiercely. "I kens aboot a' things tha' lies under the groond." He banged his chest proudly. "Forty years a mineralogist, ye ken? I was trained in the Sirloin Hills afore ye were weaned."

'"Varry interesting," I smiled. "Ye must be a long horn then. Tell me, hoo do ye pan fer gold? I've allus wanted tae find oot."

'That set him off, rattling on about washing and damming up streams and all the work they used to do in the old days when there weren't such pansy things as mechanical diggers.

'And then I remembered the ring which I'd panned from the cowpat. I brought it forth as if it was an object of immense value, saying, "I'd like ye tae teel me what ye think o' this fine emerald."

'Old MacPester leaned back against the driver's partition, steadying himself against the bar. Out of his top pocket he drew a watchmaker's eyeglass, impressing me with his expert manner as he fitted it into the leathery housing of his eye-socket. He held up the ring into the light, and after a long pause rasped. "Aye, a'll tell ye fer one thing, it's no' an emerald. An' fer two, this is a professional appraisal yer gettin' fer nothin'. An' fer three, the centre stone is a Tourmaline, no' normally very valuable, but since this is large, an' o' a good colour an' only wi' a wee flaw in the richt corner, it's worth a bob or twa."

'"And what about the little white stones?" I asked.

'"MacPester turned the ring around in the light. "Aye, the sma' diamonds arny bad at a'. It's a weel tha' that's a good settin' because the ring's aw' knocked oot o' shape. It's eichteen-carat gold, ye ken."

'I breathed slowly, then asked. "What's its worth?"

'"Ach . . . About five-hundred dollars, gi'e or take fifty dollars," he said.

'"Jeez. That's almost enough for a plane ticket," I choked.

'"If ye like, I'll gi'e ye a card o' a friend o' mine in Perth, who deals in such things. If ye tell 'im I sent ye, nae doubt, he'll gie ye a bob or twa mair."'

I turned to my companion, Furry Freak Brother, and shrugged. 'I guess that's the end of the story . . . Well, so far, anyway. As soon as I get the ring away, I'm doing a runner on my responsibilities. It's next stop Brazil. Fuck the wife. Fuck nagging Voices wherever they come from.

FFB chucked the roach out the window. 'Man I've never heard nuthin' like that in my whole life.'

'Really?' I said, brightening. 'Really, truly?'

'Yep,' he nodded affirmatively, prodding a nicotine-stained finger in my direction. 'Listen, myte, if you wrote that in a book, I'd buy it.'

'You would?'

'Yep, sure I would.'

Circle of Gold. It dawned on me. I wouldn't find it in Brazil. It was here, within me. I had found my road to Rome.

Loose Ends

'You can guarantee if you buy a tapestry and there are no loose ends, something's been snipped off and you've been short-changed.' I read that somewhere. The same is true, but only more so, about books, novels. I always smell something funny when a story's bagged up neatly like a Big Mac in a takeaway bag.

Here are some loose ends then – thread-worms more like, extracted only after taking the most violent of purgatives.

I arrived in Perth armed with two items (I'm discounting all those glittery bikinis which I retain till this day). One was the ring, valued by MacPester, if you remember, at around five hundred dollars. And the other was a certain chain letter, slipped away in my diary, called the 'Circle of Gold', which you may recall my dear wife had sent me as a polite way of saying fuck off for ever.

First goddamn thing I did after Furry Freak dropped me off in Perth was to pick up that day's newspaper from the trashcan at the bus-stop. Banner headlines stalked the front page. POLICE HUNT BUSH FOR ESCAPEE. I heaved a sigh of relief as I studied the photofit. The picture didn't look in the slightest like me. There was also a story about a 'Miracle Baby', complete with a gurgling picture. And at the bottom of the page was an article headlined 'CHAIN LETTER MANIA SWEEPS STATE'.

I had one address – a sense of insecurity before I'd left home had bid me inscribe it in indelible ink on a label backside of my underpants – the name of the only person in Australia I'd known from before, one-time Scout troop-leader, Norrie Patterson, the shining, acned face I'd hero-worshipped – but only from a distance, as we'd all sat round the camp-fire. Dib dib. Dub dub.

Changed days. So much of life is a kind of fiction. This balding, fat, sad-eyed

Norrie was an apology for that former lithe self. All I recognised was the few loyal blisters of acne still hovering around the corners of his mouth. Some people never completely grow up.

Norrie was immensely generous, as old acquaintances in far-off places usually prove to be. Beside the phone in his asbestos bungalow-shack was a basket filled with copper coins, a few pieces of silver scattered amongst them. Norrie told me to help myself, as I liked. By this means I was able to do the usual small city things, like take a coffee at a pavement café, catch a bus without fear of imminent arrest. Occasionally I helped, stacking boxes and the like, at Norrie's imported furniture warehouse.

I couldn't believe it. I'd got a call. Norrie was holding the phone out to me, covering the mouthpiece with his hand. 'Wouldn't say who he was, sounded funny . . .'

It was with a sad, sinking kind of feeling that I took the receiver.

'Hello?'

'Frankieee!'

'What the f . . . Lobo?'

'My gosh, I am thinking never I see you again.'

'How did you find me? I mean, I never told you about this place. I mean . . . How could I? Didn't even know about it myself until after I arrived . . .'

'I have a dream, in the night I see your face peeking out from under the yellow sheetings of a wide bed. When I see this Yellow Pages, I know where to look. The first number I try, Scottis Pine Beds. You have many there? Is good for bouncing on, no?'

'Lobo, we've got to meet. Where?'

'Tomorrow. You know the pedestrian plaza. Is so funny, when I am arriving in Perth I drive up and down the whole of the night, looking for you. I am explaining to the police, I no know what the meaning of this pede –'

'Lobo –'

'I am telling you,' he snapped, all the fun unmasked from his voice. 'The small coffee shop beside the American Expressing. The plaza. George Street. Tomorrow. Eleven of the clock. Do not get late!'

At eleven on the dot of the clock – I know because I was watching the second hand of Mickey ticking round in the window of the American Expressing across the plaza – a very different Lobo, bullet-headed and dressed in heavy-metal leathers, popped out from behind a display of shrubs and roses. Pulling up a chair, he sat down facing me across the small circular table.

His appearance had been so sudden I wondered if he had been watching me this last quarter of an hour. We didn't shake hands. Even from the beginning, a stiff formality had edged between us.

'You know you are a foolish,' Lobo observed, rubbing his palm across the one-micron growth of his recently-shaved scalp, then adjusting his red neckerchief.

'What do you mean?'

'You are lucky, and a foolish. You might have die in the desert. How you get away?'

'The bus . . .'

'It is as I thought.'

'And what about you. The police? The court? What happened?'

'Nothing.' Lobo sat back, inspecting his latest manicure.

'Jesus fuck!' I exploded. 'Tell me what happened?'

Lobo frowned. 'I see you have not yet lost any of your dirty ways. It is as I say. I am explaining as far as I am concerning I have money, always it is coming from Switzerland. Any problem it is with the stupids at the bank.'

'But what about the cheque-stubs, didn't they go into that?'

'It is as I am always telling you. These Australian police are lazy, so much there is written on the stub-es, they do not know where to start.' Lobo chuckled. 'At the end, you know, even they are giving money to see the back of my face.'

'How come?' I said, incredulous now.

'The magistrating, he tells me I must leave the area, never to come back. I say how is this possible, when now I am having nothing to pay for the petrol with. They give me fifty dollar-es. It is funny, no? You should see the face of the big policeman when he has to hand it over. But what can he do?'

Lobo shrugged, then leaned forwards, his eyes riveting mine. 'I tell you, Frankie, you are a stupid for worrying so much about these peoples. Before you flee, you know I would go through the fire for you.' He paused, searching my face. 'But now, everything between us it is chang-ed. So many plans I was having for the both of us.' Lobo reached into his pocket, pulled out the Platinum Amex, flipping it onto the table between us. 'With this stupid plas-teek, we visit so many places. Thailand – the best tailors in the world. Nepal, Tibet. I tell you this, one week with my guru, and the dirt I cannot cleanse from you, he takes away. Then we are finding the Abdominal Snowman. I even am thinking to help with your castle in Scottisland. There is so much I like to do in the garden. And you lose all this for no reason better than you are afraid. I will say this, and it is my last gift. The fear it is not the key to open the door of life.'

Picking up the credit card, Lobo stood up. 'I am through with taking. Such games as I show you are for babies learning to take their first steps in the world. And now' – he gritted his teeth – 'I return this plas-teek to the owners, these stupids.' Grimly he nodded over his shoulder across the plaza.

'Render unto Caesar what is Caesar's,' I murmured.

'What it is that you say?' Lobo demanded.

'Oh nothing. Just what another joker said once about such matters. No doubt' – I almost choked – 'I'll see you sometime . . .' I stood up stiffly, holding my hand out.

'When that day it is coming,' Lobo smiled, like a fresh of sunlight, 'it is the day you are clean, the inside and out. I save any handshaking for then.'

I watched him then, dipping under the horizon, bouncing across the plaza, handing the credit card to the girl behind the counter of the American Expressing . . . And then a last glimmer, his head bobbing through the Saturday morning shopping sheeps, and he was gone.

A couple more things. The ring proved to be worthless, but at least the star of its value kept me in hope, and by the time I located the dealer MacPester had put me onto I had other irons in the fire.

The 'Circle of Gold' chain letter. Nothing to lose, so I made up twenty letters, photocopying the adapted original. A pair of scissors and I substituted my name and Norrie's address at the top of the list. I also included copies of the newspaper article about chain letter mania in the envelopes. Finally, on the back of each envelope I scrawled 'From a Friend'. Ten days later I got my first reply, a cheque for fifty dollars inside.

I travelled out of Australia under the pseudonym of Isaac Irons, the name of the Scottish Jew who sold me his return plane ticket, bought with my windfall from the Circle of Gold and my winnings from the fifty dollars I laid on a horse called Golden Promise, running in a race Isaac assured me was fixed by some pals of his – the local mob. He did not lie. The odds were ten to one.

I returned to my blasted fief, and to the dirt I'd left behind. The dirt I had not been able to escape from. The dirt I'd been carrying pent up inside me across all these deserts and plains. How I cleaned it all up and rid my stables of the squatting swine is, as they say, another story, and you'll just have to wait.